TALES OF BEDLAM

BEDLAM MOON SERIES BOOK 2

KATHY HAAN

ISBN 979-8-9855077-2-0 (eBook)

ISBN 979-8-9855077-3-7 (paperback)

ISBN 978-1-960256-10-2 (hardback)

First edition May 2022

Book cover design and map by Leo Burk and Kathy Haan

Edited by Fervent Ink

Published by Thousand Lives Press, LLC

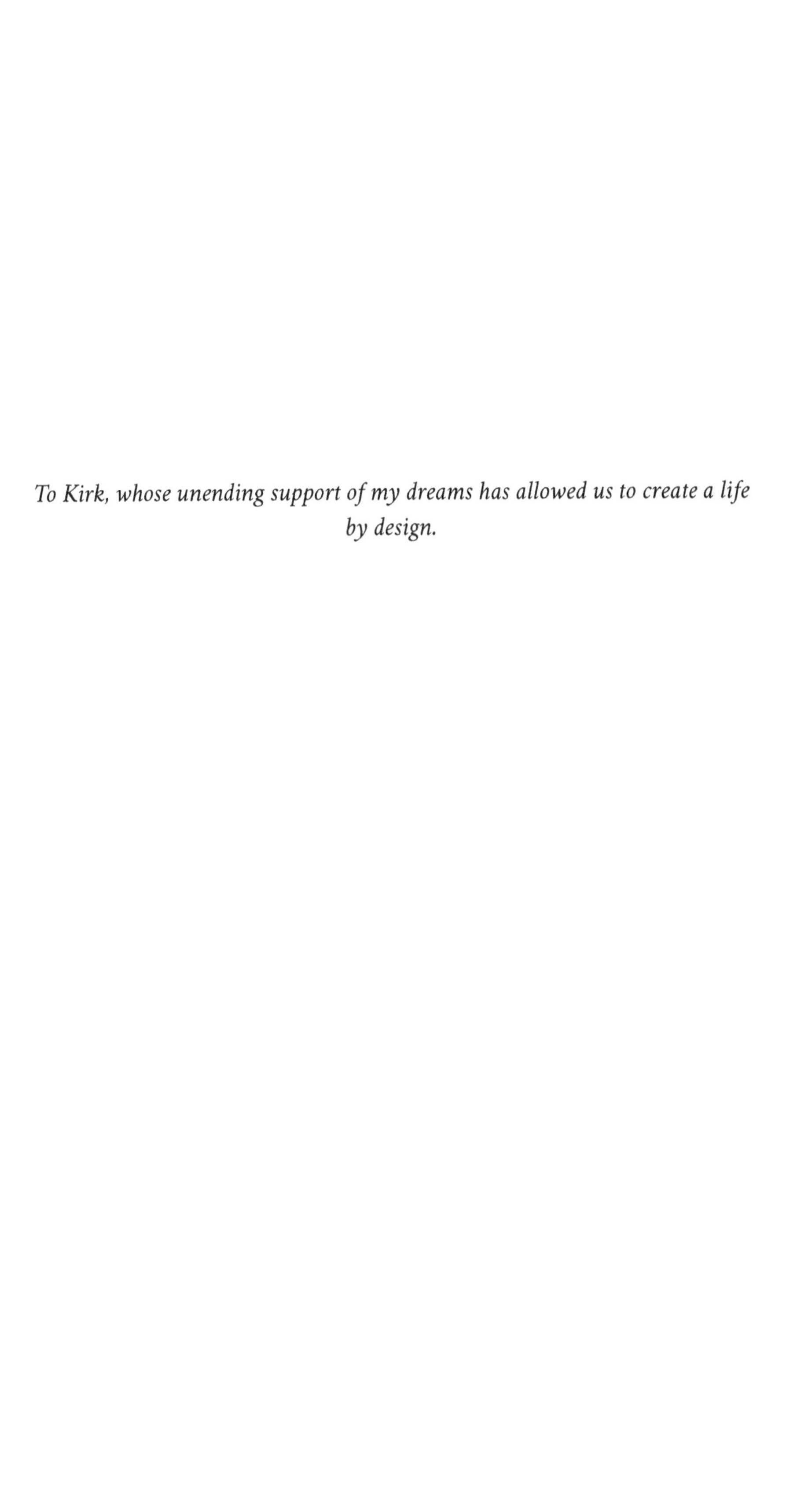
To Kirk, whose unending support of my dreams has allowed us to create a life by design.

ACADEMIA
BEDLAM PENITENTIARY
OCCASUS
DRACONU
REXUNA
CONV
SEA OF TRIUNE

LUPORIA
SUNDAHLIA
TRISTIQUE ISLANDS
PARALLEL ABYSS
VECTUS
N
W
E
S
BEDLAM

CHAPTER 1

LANA

Pain and I are intimately acquainted, like two scorned lovers passing in the night. Though I try, I can't forget the press of its claws against my womb, or the echoes of my soul ripping in two at the loss of my mate.

My body has writhed from the agony of labor. I've been beaten and on the brink of death after violent attacks by vampires. But nothing—nothing—cuts as deep as leaving my family for Bedlam. These emotional wounds are so severe, they will haunt me for the rest of my days.

The portal to the fae realm is a sea of black and biting cold. Gail-force winds take my shoes almost immediately—I'm lucky to still have a dress. The only light guiding me is a faint scarlet glow far in the distance. My eyes are mere slits to keep my contacts from drying, and the force of the squalls are so intense, I take hours to traverse the inky expanse.

When my bare feet touch the other side, I breathe a sigh of relief, and shake the dust and dirt out of my dress. The chasm between the portal and Bedlam is jarring; while still biting cold, there is no wind on the other side. I rub my hands together to create friction before tucking them under my armpits as I take in my surroundings.

The soft red glow of the moon overhead gives the forest I've landed in an eerie atmosphere. A gooey, glowing substance drips from the leaves of the trees, and frost covers the bark like a crystalline blanket. With tentative movement, I pad around the chilly forest floor, the sensation of mud squishing between my bare toes an unpleasant reminder of how much trouble I'm in without proper attire.

I take my time exploring the forest before I attempt to make shelter. Thanks to the color of the moon, my eyes have transitioned well from the dark portal to this red forest.

As I scout the area, the tree's twisted roots bulge from the soil beneath me, forcing me to step carefully. Their tangled branches form a canopy over my head. I've spent a lot of time in forests, but none like this one. Like something straight out of a fairytale, magic has warped and manipulated the trees into something *other*.

I couldn't bring anything to Bedlam with me, and this light dress I have on provides little protection from the elements. Before leaving Earth, my family taught me several skills and incantations to help me on my journey. The bulk of it I spent on spells, because both my dad and my husband, Oz, are witches. Granted, they're also vampires, but they still have magic.

Using the spell Oz taught me in our bedroom one night, I attempt to turn a seed I find on the ground into a hollow tree to shelter in. My body shakes from the effort and my nose runs while I struggle to will the kernel into something useful.

Not a single change happens. I rub my hands to warm them before trying again—perhaps my magic doesn't work well in the cold. Once they've warmed, I make the motions for the enchantment.

Casting is no use; the spell isn't working.

Do incantations work differently in Bedlam? The research my family and I did suggests otherwise, so why isn't this working? I reach into the oversized pocket of my dress for my grimoire, but the book is gone. My hands scramble to the other pocket, feeling for any holes. My Ebbswick key is gone, too. I need both in order to come back to the Earth realm. I hope they'll reappear when I need to go back through the portal.

I can't stay here forever.

Pausing my frantic movements, I crouch low to the ground and spot materials to reinforce my outfit. My fingers are so numb, I have difficulty keeping hold of the natural provisions while I work to weave vines into rope to bind branches. I rub them together frantically, breathing damp, warm air into my cupped hands. The reprieve from the cold is temporary, and near futile, but I manage to stave off the stiffness long enough to come up with something useful.

I fashion a makeshift belt to hold my dress up and tie goop-free leafy vines underneath for warmth. With sturdier branches, I craft a rudimentary bow and arrow. The vines don't hold high tensile strength, but they'll do for now.

I set out to find something to fill the pit in my stomach. Using my bow and arrow in the dim moonlight, I aim for a small animal resembling a squirrel, but miss. Archery wasn't high on our list of skills to practice before I left. Stumbling deeper through the woods, I come across a few berry bushes, though I don't dare eat them, given the circumstances. My stomach growls and aches from hunger, but I refuse to give in to the pain. Not until I can find something I know for sure is safe.

I spot a giant tree with a thick trunk that can serve as my shelter for the night, which is the most important thing. I'll work on finding water in the morning.

Exhaustion slows my movements.

Must.

Keep.

Going.

My dress is still too thin and papery to keep me warm, even with the additional greenery. I need a fire to stay alive, but the only flammable materials I can collect on the ground are damp from frost. If only my magic worked, then I could be warm right now.

Why isn't it working?

My body usually thrums with power, but there isn't even a trickle. I attempt to start a fire several times by rubbing a stick between my palms against a piece of wood before fatigue sets in and I give up. After some sleep, I'll have more energy and can try again.

I lug massive rocks to the base of the tree that's as wide as a sedan and build a retaining wall on each side to block the wind. When finished, I place evergreen boughs over the top before crawling into my makeshift shelter for sleep. The forest quiets, and I no longer hear the quiet hum of insects, nor the whistling of the wind through the trees. This should comfort me, but it lends an ominous pause to the night.

The cold seeps into my bones, but does little to numb the grief haunting my heart. It sits on my chest like a lead weight, making it hard to breathe, and buries me in despair. Thoughts of my life on Earth sneak up on me and roll down my cheek.

I'd planned to come to Bedlam to gain immortality and find out what happened to my mom, who disappeared somewhere in time when I was eight years old. What I hadn't planned on was Dolphina Darling, the evil cult leader obsessed with my husband, speeding up my timeline so I had to leave my two-day-old twins and family behind. I can see their faces in my mind. The twins: Rose and Bennett, and my mates: Oz, Gideon, and Auguste. If I concentrate hard enough, I can even feel the press of their fingers against mine. The soft stirring of the twins' breath on my chest while they sleep. All I can do is cry until I'm too tired to do so anymore.

THE SNAP of a branch startles me from sleep. I peer through the triangular opening in my sanctuary, eyes wide when I spot two red glowing circles straight from nightmares. The umber figure morphs into a hunched silhouette of evil. My heart races and my stomach plummets as the vile woman gets closer.

My options race through my head. If I flee, she'll catch up with me in no time. If I fight, I'll lose; this fae must be over seven feet tall and nearly as wide. Either way, with no magic, my fate will be the same.

Death.

Maybe she's harmless. Before the errant thought can take hold, a shout barrels from my lungs as her five-inch-long claws dig into my ankles and yank me from my shelter. Using the combat moves Auguste taught me, I work to get loose, to no avail. Her enormous weight makes my attempts to get away futile.

"Mm ... it has been a long time since I've fed on a witch. Your kind doesn't come here much, but I'll enjoy you, anyway." The deep timbre of her voice reverberates through the woods before cutting off in a cackle.

I thrash and kick, making small gouges in her thick skin and screaming until my voice gives out. She grips both of my wrists in one hand above my head while using the other to tear at my dress, exposing me to the frigid air.

"Please ... don't. I'm a mother." My hoarse voice cuts through the space between us.

My entire body trembles while she laughs. She's the size of an ox, and almost as heavy as one. The bones in my wrist threaten to snap under the weight.

"You think I give a fuck about your family? I know exactly who you are. You're the Queen of Vampires. They are filthy, fucking vermin. *Abominations.*" Spittle from her fang-toothed mouth lands on my cheek. "I'll take what I want from you. It's your womb I'm after. Behave and you might live."

I buck my hips up in another attempt to lift her off of me, and she chuckles. "Keep that up — I love when they put up a fight."

"Stop!" My raw voice warbles through the space between us. "You won't find—"

Her clawed hand clamps around my mouth, cutting me off, but also leaving me an opening. Despite the slice of her nails against my cheek, I use this opportunity to pull my leg free and sideswipe her face with my muddy foot, but she just laughs and pins me back down.

I sob and cry out while this monster slices my abdomen open with one of her talons. All thoughts leave my head, save for the excruciating pain. She lays a heavy arm to pin my hips down, and shame invades my psyche far more than fear does.

She shrieks when she finds me barren. "I'll rip her from limb to limb! She said I could have your womb before I killed you!"

With every move, her clawed grip carves into my flesh, wrenching sobs from my throat. I don't know how long she violates me, but I feel the weight of every single moment. By the time her anger retreats, I am but a husk.

Broken.

Bloodied.

So many lacerations, even slight movement is torture.

The cruel monster towers over me with menace in her eyes. "Don't think I'm done with you." She grips my leg hard enough to pierce through the skin and down to the bone.

Her next words aren't any I recognize, but the force behind them echoes through me. Searing heat races up my thigh, across my chest, and to the base of my skull. The pain is so immediate and intense; I shriek with renewed misery. "We'll see how your mates feel about that," she smirks and releases me. "If you survive it."

Rivulets of blood pour from my wounds, and my limbs fail me when I try to scramble away.

I curl into a fetal position while sobs rack my body. The heavy steps of her departure match the slow cadence of my heartbeat; the loss of blood is significant. Visions of my family play in my mind, and the passing of time means nothing. I'm numb.

My mom chasing me through the house with a hairbrush before tackling me to the ground to brush my wild curls.

Oz's sure and steady presence while I learn to fly.

Gideon's easy smile while we lay in the grass nestled in the Dolomites.

Auguste's grin when he realizes I bested him on the field where he gave me combat lessons.

The twinkle in Dad's eye when he pats his belly after a good meal.

My best friend, Hannah, and her giddy excitement at teaching her son, CJ, how to ride a bike.

Maeve's welcoming arms in her lab in Salem where she helped me figure out who sent me my mother's Ebbswick key.

Pippa's calming aura during the birth of the twins.

I don't feel the bite of the cold on my extremities, though my body is like ice. Sticky blood coats my eyelashes. When I close them, frost gathers like glue, and I don't open my eyes again.

I consider never getting up.

Just let the woods take me.

CHAPTER 2

FINN

Help me.
Please.

My eyes pop open and I dart my gaze around my cramped tent for the source of the noise. I'm a deep sleeper, but the sound of a woman's pleas has woken me. I've warded almost the entire mountain so no one can come close to my campsite. Neither fae nor witch nor any other magical creature can be here; I must've dreamed someone is nearby.

Before bed I left the canvas roof unzipped so I can see the sky, despite the chill in the air, and I do a double-take when finding a blue glow instead of stars. The beams of the red moon dull compared to the cerulean shimmer taking over the area. I check my watch. *Two o'clock.*

Fluffing my pillow and adjusting the body pillow between my legs, I settle into the covers again. I'll figure out whatever is going on after a little more sleep. My body needs it after expelling so much energy to reinforce the wards after the ripple I felt in them earlier tonight.

No sooner do I shut my eyes; I hear the voice again—here, but not. There's an ethereal quality to the sound.

Please.

Help!

Fuck. I throw the covers off and spring up in bed before unzipping the tent and slipping on my boots. Thick frost coats the ground, blanketing everything in tinsel. My foot catches on the tent opening as I try to climb out, and I stumble, but manage not to fall.

I'm dying!

I whip my head to the sound. The voice is definitely feminine and much more urgent than before. In the call's direction, a blue tendril of magic dances through the forest, like a string leading through the woods. The light pulses with each whispered plea, as though it were a sentient being. I've seen nothing like this before, so I take off running down the mountain towards the large beam of light about thirty miles into the valley. That must be where the injured woman is.

Every few miles I run, the pulsing thread of light weakens, so I pick up my speed. If I can make it on time, I should be able to heal whoever she is. Most fae have some healing capabilities, but my Luna order is the most powerful because we're the only fae who get magic from the moon, and supply it to the rest of Bedlam.

My feet carry me over twisted roots poking through the soft detritus. Thorns catch on my clothes, and branches snap in my face.

A dull ache in my chest grows more acute the closer I get to my destination. Even with my preternatural speed and my command of this peak, I take hours. The female is much farther away than I thought. Dread takes root in my gut and creeps along my bones when I realize where she might be.

The fucking *portal*.

No one should be in this area of the forest. Most witches and fae pass through in any of the capital cities—not in the most remote woodland you can find in this entire realm.

The mountainous terrain isn't what you have to worry about here; wild animals and dangerous fugitives make up the bulk of what stalks around in Noble Wilds. Combine those threats with the fact that a witches' magic won't work in these woods, and you're asking for a painful death. Never mind I've warded the entire mountain from sifting in or out—like teleportation—it's my best defense from surprise attacks. With the tightly packed trees, winged fae can't fly here, either.

As I near the beacon of light, the magic gossamer is but a tiny flicker, and my nose fills with the scent of blood so strong, I fear I'm too late. I don't slow down until I reach a small, handmade shelter several hours from where I camp. Deep gouges mar the soil, and in the center of an alarming pool of blood, I see her.

The beacon above the human flares—like a last stand—before blinking out. Adrenaline surges through me, riding parallel to a grief so deep it steals the breath from my lungs. *Do I know her?* I've seen hundreds of thousands of deaths. Maybe millions: such is war. Never has one given me such a visceral reaction.

Shit.

BEFORE MY LEGS can crumple from the shock and pain, I dart to where she lies and scoop her limp, ichor-covered body into my arms. *She's a witch.* I settle on the ground with her in my lap and place my palm over her most grievous injuries. Her clothing lies in tatters, and she's so caked in blood it's difficult to tell where the wounds originate, so I focus on those over her chest—doing what I can to kick-start her heart.

C'mon. Come back to me.

Nothing. Still no heartbeat.

Fuck.

Later, I'll address why this woman's death causes tears to fall from my eyes like she's the very breath in my lungs. I need to resuscitate her first. My fangs descend and I rip open my wrist, slide my thumb into her mouth to open it, and drip my life force onto her tongue. Fae blood works internally to heal, and I may be able to revive her with that and my Luna magic.

Several long, excruciating minutes go by with no progress.

This woman is a stranger to me, but I'm compelled to save her. She might have a family, and I've no way to know how to get in contact with them in the Earth realm; witches come with nothing to identify themselves with.

I drag my canine across my forearm to create a longer incision, and thick blood flows faster into her mouth. If this doesn't work, I can use a feather.

Shit. Did I really consider using a feather—one of the most coveted pieces of me—to save a stranger?

I catch a flicker of a heartbeat and hold my breath.

Another glimmer of life.

And again.

The air rents from my lungs in relief. I feed the witch my blood until I grow faint and her pulse strengthens. Once I'm certain she's on the incline, I rise to my feet and race towards the Sanaquam—a river with healing properties about fifteen minutes from where I found this outsider.

My blood loss affects my gait, and I pause against a tree, fighting the brain fog as it tries to close in. Healing fuels Luna magic, but giving my blood drains me.

Lana

"I've got you. Stay with me."

I smile into the warm chest that's carting me through the woods. Like every night in my dreams, he glows, but now he seems so real. No more sadness. No more pain.

Safe.

You came for me.

CHAPTER 3

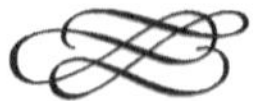

LANA

I gasp and flail my arms at the freezing water flowing against me like a raging bull. My resistance meets with the powerful body cradling me, and I tilt my head towards him. His pointy ears tell me he's fae, although the blue glow coming from his skin makes me do a double take. The male's ruffled, ashy-blond hair and icy blue eyes are familiar to me, but I can't place where I might know him from. He's easily the most attractive man I've ever seen in my life.

I know you.

I pause my thought process and dismiss the notion—I've only met one fae before and she was cruel. She's also the reason I'm in this male's arms right now.

"Who are you?" Despite my hesitation, I curl in closer to his warmth, trying to ease the chill in my bones. I let out a groan at the agony moving causes.

"Finian Drake of the Luna order, but call me Finn. Who did this to you?"

Luna. If I recall correctly, fae under the Luna Court are less ruthless than the other courts. Or was that the Terra order? I furrow my brows and survey our surroundings before responding.

"I'm Lana, the Queen of Vampires. Why do you have me in a river?"

"This is the Sanaquam—a river with healing properties. Do you remember what happened to you?"

I flinch, but relay through chattering teeth what the fae did to me. Finn stiffens his hold and I glance up at him to see a clenched jaw and flared nostrils.

"This has berserker fae written all over it." He's quiet, and after several minutes he explains he's going to help me clean my skin and hair so he can heal my injuries without blood impeding their location.

"Why isn't my magic working?" There is no way the overgrown monster of a fae would've been able to attack me — or get anywhere near me — not after all the training my mates put me through.

"Only fae magic works in these woods. Near portals, we protect our realm from any initial threats in case a witch with ill intent comes through. That's why we've got to move you out of here as soon as we're done getting you cleaned up."

Finn springs to the riverbank and I follow his gaze to see a creature the size of a small mountain lion with sharp fangs, razor-like claws, bioluminescent hair, and a tail. With a flick of his hand, Finn disintegrates the beast, and I freeze before panic sets in.

"What the fuck was that?!" I squeak, in a voice far more hysterical than I'd been aiming for. Never had I thought I'd be in so much danger in Bedlam.

"That," he tosses a few rocks into the water, "is a Harpis Siren. She's a distant relative to a siren; only this is more animal than sentient being." He pierces me with his stare. "I'm going to set you down now. I'll turn around so you can remove your clothes. Toss them my way when you're ready, and I'll bury them."

Wait, bury my clothes? Why does he want to bury my clothes? What am I going to wear?

"Lana, your dress is in tatters, and it isn't leaving a lot to the imagination. How else will the ground gnomes mend them?" He pinches the bridge of his nose.

I stiffen.

Another fucking mind reader. Crap.

Sorry, comes the silent response in my head.

My mind is wide fucking open, and I can't use magic or anything else to close myself off.

"My gift is incredibly rare. Some royals have it, otherwise, I don't know anyone else with the ability."

"You mentioned ground gnomes? What the hell are those?"

"Did no one prepare you for Bedlam?"

I use the back of my hand to brush away an errant tear. I'm thinking I'm more than unprepared for this realm. Did Bonnie Driscoll, our witch friend who spent twenty years in Bedlam, lie to us about what it was like? It sure seems like it.

"She likely didn't lie, but could only speak to certain parts of Bedlam. Few witches decide to go back to the Earth realm once they catch the hang of Bedlam; you just came through the worst possible portal to get here."

He makes sense, although it would've been nice to know about the better portals to come through before I got to the fae realm. With a curt nod, I instruct him to turn around before peeling myself out of my dress. I find it difficult to stand, but I manage. I toss the dress and what's left of my underwear at Finn's feet, and he kneels and starts digging.

I hurry into the river and gasp at the frigid water biting at my skin. My nipples form tight peaks, and goosebumps cover my skin while I wash away the blood. Thankfully, most of these are minor cuts, but I have several deep lacerations and punctures that need tending. I look for algae to help staunch the bleeding, but there is none. I spin around to the riverbank and a ripping noise cuts through the tranquil sound of water sluicing over rocks.

Finn has torn the sleeve off his shirt. With another rip, he tears off the other. He shields his eyes while shuffling his feet in my direction so he can hand me the scraps of fabric. I meet him halfway since he's walking blind, and as soon as I have the sleeves, he turns back around.

I sling both scraps of fabric over the back of my neck like a scarf so I can continue cleaning up. My mind wanders to the trauma I just experienced as I gingerly clean away the blood. My fingers tremble —

whether from the pain, the cold, or the emotional wounds, I can't be sure. I've been in precarious positions before, but I've never been so violated.

I don't realize I'm crying again until Finn consoles me inside my head.

I can't understand the depth of your trauma, but I can help you forget.

That perks me up a bit. *Can you?*

It's the least I can do for you, he answers me.

I take one sleeve and tightly wrap it around my abdomen, where the worst laceration is. Another secures around my ass, effectively flattening it and helping to take care of the laceration there. I also have deep bruising across my chest and arms, but there isn't much I can do for that without my magic.

"How far is the walk out of the woods?" I rinse more blood from my shoulders.

"Three, maybe four months, give or take. This is the largest forest in the entire realm and warded from sifting."

"Four months?!" I shriek. "I can't be here for four months. I have so many things I need to do before I get back home."

There are no vehicles in Bedlam, thanks to strict anti-pollution laws. Fae who can fly, fly. Everyone else walks or bikes where they need to go. Shifters can sift through space, and other fae hire them for transport, but many can't afford the cost. If I had my magic, I could be out of these woods in the time I take to build my destination in my mind and slip through the crack to wherever my heart desires.

But no, I'm here with just the dress on my back, or, well, in the ground, and not a dime to my name. I don't even know where my Ebbswick key and Grimoire went when I crossed through.

"You don't need either of those in Bedlam, so they sit between realms until you go back to Earth," Finn explains. "I know you want out of the woods, but where to after that?"

"I don't know where I'm supposed to go." I hesitate. "You don't know Dolphina Darling, do you?"

"Can't say I do. She a friend of yours?"

A hysterical laugh bubbles out of me. "She's the whole reason I'm in Bedlam completely unprepared. She wanted to be with my husband, Oz. She's spent millennia trying to win his affection with the help of her cult, the Lapis Templar. They've cursed me, poisoned me, and hurt my family."

Finn's spine stiffens and he whips his head towards me. "Why isn't she dead yet?"

I sink until the water laps against my chin. "We've tried, but she's strong, and has an entire army of worshippers. She'll get what's coming to her; my mates are working on that now." My eyes catch on his clenched fists. "It's another reason I'm here. I want to gain immortality since they're vampires. I also need to find out where in time my mom went. She disappeared when I was eight."

I wince as I dunk my hair in water to scrub the mud out.

Finn sighs. "I was afraid of that. You'll have to meet with the kings from all three royal houses. If they deem you worthy, they'll grant you immortality, but I must warn you," he surveys the spot where he buried my clothes, "the kings can be tricky. You need to be sure you want their help, because they'll ask something of you in return. They've got the resources to figure out where your mom is, and I can help you with the magic you'll need to defeat Dolphina."

"I'm one hundred percent positive I need them. And if you're willing to help me get there, my mates and I will reward you handsomely."

He stills. "I don't need a reward to help somebody who has come all this way and nearly died, all for someone they love. I, too, have made incredible sacrifices for the one I love, even though the outcome isn't guaranteed."

My hand pauses its ministrations across my skin, and unease settles in my gut. I file this information away for later. It's none of my business who he loves, even though the maelstrom in my gut at the thought of it is a visceral reaction hard to ignore.

"Thank you." I wring the water out of my hair, checking for any mud I might've missed. "How long do the ground gnomes take? I'm just about finished up."

Finn pats the ground a few times. The striations in his muscles flex in rapid succession before the dirt under his hand shifts. With fae speed, he reaches into the soil and pulls out my dress and underwear. Both look perfect. Finn shakes them out to dust the dirt off, and I call out my thanks to the gnomes — whatever they are, I'm grateful.

Finn reaches into his pocket, pulls out a couple of coins, and tosses them into the hole before kicking dirt over it. Chittering echoes from the ground before the gnomes scamper away.

"Good as new." He inspects the clothing. I'm so shocked I'm not even embarrassed that this attractive male, who is not my mate, is holding my panties.

Finn clears his throat and tosses his hair out of his eyes before covering them and walking my clothes to the water's edge. I meet him at the shore, but I'm not sure what to dry myself with. My hair is sopping wet even after wringing it, and at this temperature, I'll be sick before sundown if I put on clothes while soaked.

"Hang on." He hesitates before deciding. With one hand covering his eyes, he pats and rubs his body vigorously. My blood disappears from his clothes, and not a single trace of dirt covers him. My mouth gapes in shock, and when he reaches behind his head to grab at his shirt and slip it over his head, he reveals a smooth, tanned chest and washboard abs. Just above his belt line peeks the top of a tattoo, but I can't make out what it is. He holds out his shirt for me to dry off with, and I do so quickly before taking my clothes from him and putting them on.

Once I'm fully dressed, I hand him his shirt back. With a few pats of his hand, his top is dry again, and he slips it over his head.

Neat trick.

While climbing up the small embankment, the trauma plays like a reel in my mind but is stuck on repeat. Each pull of my wounds is another reminder of the pain I carry.

"I'm ready to forget now." I glance at Finn. He gives a shallow tilt of his head in acknowledgment and stands just inches in front of me.

When he speaks, his voice is soft. "I need to put my hand on your head, okay?" he asks, and I permit him.

He reaches his hand towards me, and I flinch involuntarily, so he retreats for a moment before approaching again. Finn cups my temple, and it soothes me — heat radiates off his palm and energy surges through his touch. The power reminds me of the tingling I felt in my hands when Oz unbound my magic.

You met a very dangerous fae who wanted to hurt you and take from you. She injured you severely, but you were so brave and strong, and you fought her off before she could hurt you too badly. You're going to take some herbs to heal you completely, and you'll look back at this day as one that only strengthened you. Finn speaks into my mind before letting go of my head and stepping back.

CHAPTER 4

LANA

"The herbs you need aren't far from here. We'll gather them and make a tea at our next stop." Finn's kind eyes bore into mine.

I shake my head to clear the fog from my mind — I don't remember what we were just talking about. Maybe the blood loss is getting to me.

I don't know how long we walk for, but I know we don't travel far because I limp more than I hike. I stumble a few times, but Finn catches me.

"I think you're bleeding again. Let's have a rest, and we can eat something while we clean you up."

I sit on a large, moss-covered rock and lean against a tree while I tend to my wounds. Meanwhile, Finn searches the area for something we can eat. He says his campsite isn't but a few more hours, provided we run. I laughed when he told me this. Even if I were uninjured, you wouldn't see me running unless we were chased. I might be able to run a mile without stopping, but definitely not without huffing and puffing the entire way.

So now, we won't reach his camp until late in the evening, and we'll sleep there. He wards the area from danger, so we won't need to sleep in shifts.

My thoughts slow. I can only focus on one thing: agony. The pain is so intense my body shakes. The fabric strips that wrap around my wounds cut off any form of blood flow and leave them open to infection; they're chafed raw from being pulled taut for hours on end as we walked through the forest together. My thighs ache with the pressure building under each tender surface, inch by inch.

He comes back into view with the bottom of his shirt pulled up and out to create a basket. His abs are on display, so I shutter my eyes before focusing on what he's collected.

"Nuts from the cruah bush and starseed apples." He kneels in front of me. Handing me a turquoise apple, he bites into one himself while nodding at me to eat mine.

I take a bite and an explosion of flavor coats my tongue. The taste is bright and watery — sort of like a sweet cucumber, but crisp to bite into. I moan while taking another bite.

"This is so good," I mumble with the apple in my mouth, and Finn chuckles.

"Those are my favorites. The nuts aren't all that good, but they'll help you heal." He takes a copper mug and a canteen of water out of his bag to make my tea. Using a little burner, he heats the herbs in the mug until the water is just hot. The flavor is pungent, so I down it like a shot once it cools down enough. Finn smirks, amused by my scrunched-up face.

"How are your wounds holding up?" He surveys me. Before I respond, he sighs. "You're looking a little pale, and I think you may have lost too much blood."

Before agreeing, I take a deep breath. "I'm slowing us way down. I think I'd prefer you just to heal me with your magic."

He'd spent the day casting worried glances my way, and I declined his repeated offers to heal me. Especially after I found out how he does it.

Finn gives a curt nod and uses his feet to shuffle sticks and rocks out of the way for me to lie down. He enchanted my feet earlier to protect them from the elements, so I'm surprised at how cold the ground is.

"Such a cruel thing to do," Finn murmurs to himself as his hands glide up my inner thigh. My skin hums under his touch, far different from my own healing magic. He cups the skin with tender care, kneading with skill while smoothing out any discomfort in slow circular motions of his fingers, just at the junction where my thigh meets my groin. I swear his skin gives off a glow as he tends to my wounds.

The wind whips through the tree canopy, its beautiful song reminding me to take deep breaths and think healing thoughts. I can tell Finn is trying to keep this as clinical as possible, but every so often, his hand brushes against the fabric of my underwear while he massages. The acupressure is about as appropriate as it can be, but the contact is enough that warmth spreads across our connection like wildfire through dry grass.

I close my eyes and shift my thoughts to Oz, to Auguste, to Gideon … to anything but the guilt at the way it feels when Finn's thumb strokes circles on the stretch of skin between my thigh and pelvic bone. I concentrate on what my mates might be doing right now. Are they feeding our twins, Rose and Bennett? Maybe they're chasing down a lead on the Lapis Templar. Or maybe Dad is teaching them how to make his famous pork chops in the Crock Pot.

A silent tear rolls down my cheek, reminding me of who I need to get home to.

Finn gives one last long stroke against my thigh before instructing me to turn over. Our gaze meets, and his pupils are blown out. Small fangs rest against the lip he's tugged between his teeth. I avert my eyes but spot his erection through the strain in his pants. I pretend I don't notice while I flip onto my stomach. The movement is jarring — I still have a ton of bruising across my front.

Finn removes the bandage from my ass and moves my underwear to the side. He kneads and massages my butt, and I try to think of anything else but the sensation of his large hands on me.

"I'm almost finished." His hoarse voice does little to tamper the heavy anticipation between us.

Once he's done, I lay on my back so he can heal my front. He can't cure some of the bruising without essentially groping me, so I just have him take care of the worst of it. I can deal with a little bruising.

Despite the chill in the air, heat radiates between us. I focus on watching the rise and fall of Finn's chest as he works on the muscle just above my breasts. A pass towards my armpit causes me to burst out in a giggle, and I squirm, effectively cutting the tension in the air.

"I ... I think I'm good." My voice tinkles with laughter. "Sorry, I'm just really ticklish."

"That I gathered." He smirks. His eyes are near black; the pupils so huge when he helps me up, and I dust off the dirt and grass from my dress. I hop up and down a few times and kick out my legs.

"Still quite sore in some places but loads better. Thank you."

"It was my pleasure." He coughs and corrects himself. "I mean, uh. You're welcome. Sorry." He runs a hand through his hair before pivoting around.

Yeah, buddy, I bet it was.

I help him gather the food he'd collected for us earlier, and we set out for his campsite. I enjoy his company because he's easy to talk to, and I learn much about Bedlam.

"So, what's your story? Why are you in the woods?" I glance at him.

"I like to spend moon season here — it's when I'm at my strongest. This part of Bedlam is closest to the moon, and my campsite is at the highest peak. Because I'm of the Luna order, I have to top off my magic regularly. The easiest way to do this is to hang out under the moon. When I'm fully charged after spending the season here, I head home to Rift Pass on Rexuna." He gestures to the West.

"How long does moon season last?" I pop a couple of nuts in my mouth, shuddering from the acrid flavor.

"Moon season happens every six months and lasts for thirty days. It just started two nights ago."

Hm, that must be the Bedlam Moon. He nods at the thought in my head.

We continue our trek, and Finn tells me about life in Bedlam. "What do you do for work?"

His steps falter. "I don't."

My face scrunches, and I sweep my hand to grab a good hiking stick. "You don't work?"

He gives me a small smile. "No, I don't."

"How do you live, then?" Is he purposely being evasive?

"Work is such an Earth thing. Magic is the basis of everything here. What we can't create on our own through magic, we buy ... from fae who sell what makes them happy to produce. Those who love to bake, do so, and sell to those who love to eat. Some families are traditional, though, and go by our old system of equity. Mining families tend to stay mining families. Same goes with military families, who are paid handsomely by the kingdoms they serve."

"Who takes care of the roads? Utilities?"

"The kings of each respective continent care for their own using magic. Neutral territories receive funding through the collective effort of each king."

"So, taxes cover it." I glance at him when he stops to dig up some kind of root.

He meets my eyes. "Not in the way you think." He shrugs, tucking the root in his pocket. "Magic is our main currency, although we have plenty of coin and jewels. Some types of fae have specific magic, such as the ability to glamour or heal. Naturally, those who have multiple gifts tend to be wealthier or in positions of power. They can offer their services to others in exchange for what they need."

I file that information away as we come to the edge of steep terrain.

During the last hour, we hike up a large hill, but when we reach the campsite after an exhausting day of walking, I'm longing for something luxurious. The site is primitive, with nothing more than a canvas tent set on a flat surface surrounded by trees — not exactly what I had envisioned during our climb up the mountain — but I am thankful. I'm so exhausted I could pass out before we even start the fire.

"Have you ever done any camping on the Earth realm?" Finn glances my way while he unpacks his canvas bag.

"I did a lot of it not too long ago. Oz and I spent our honeymoon hiking Patagonia before heading to Antarctica." A familiar pang in my chest at the thought that I am worlds apart from my family has me almost buckling to my knees. One day at a time. I take a deep breath and begin rounding up wood to keep my mind occupied.

My mates instilled in me that I just have to keep taking the next step — I shouldn't focus solely on how much further I have to go. I can get stuck in my head and tailspin into a full-blown panic attack.

The temperature has dropped dramatically during our trek, and the cold seeps into my bones. Finn lights a fire and drags a felled tree close to the heat for us to sit on. He has a small chest made of ice to keep food cold and now he cooks some sort of game meat over the flames.

With the sky getting dark, I can definitely see a faint glow on Finn's skin. It reminds me of the bioluminescent beaches I visited in Mexico.

"That's my Luna order charging up its batteries." He raises a smug eyebrow at me.

"Can I touch it?" I immediately regret asking because I don't know him. What a weird fucking question.

He chuckles. "Please do. I won't bite unless you say please."

Ignoring his obvious innuendo, I tentatively put three fingers against his exposed bicep, and the area surrounding my hand brightens even more. A pleasant, warm sensation races up my limbs. The strongest desire to pull him closer to me takes over. I'm afraid I'm about to do it, but I shake my head instead.

"Wow." I yank my hands back and tuck them into my lap while I stare at the fire, entranced as it spits and dances. "I wasn't expecting that."

I stifle a yawn. "I'm getting pretty tired."

He follows my eyes to the tent and tilts his head towards it. "You take the tent. I can sleep out here. Would you prefer the regular pillow or a body pillow?"

"You have a body pillow? While camping?"

"I sleep better with one." He cups the back of his neck, unzips the opening to the tent, and grabs the regular-sized pillow and a blanket for himself. "I'll sleep right out here. Don't be afraid to wake me if you need anything."

"There is one thing." I bite my lip. "Do you happen to have any paper and something to write with? I thought it'd be nice to write home, even if I can't give them anything. Writing will make it seem as though they're not so far away."

"Sure. Front pocket of my bag in the tent."

I nod before heading just outside of camp to relieve myself. I'm grateful for the soapberries Finn and I found on our way through the woods; they're little blue berries you just squeeze between your hands to clean your skin. I'm glad I didn't try to eat these near the portal.

"Goodnight, Finn." I crawl into the tent.

He fluffs the pillow under his head. "Goodnight, Lana."

Am I imagining things, or did he sound wistful? I hesitate for a moment before zipping the tent closed.

I locate Finn's brown leather satchel, well-worn and soft. In the front pocket are a pencil and a black notebook similar to those I used for college.

Flipping through its pages, I see he's sketched a familiar mark in the margins of each sheet. Where have I seen this before? Several small circles of varying sizes, and one is more of a blur. I'll have to ask him about the symbol in the morning.

I jot down my updated mission:

STEP 1: Get out of these woods with the help of Finn, all while learning magic I can't yet practice because it doesn't work in this forest.

STEP 2: Petition the kings for an audience and somehow convince them I'm worthy of immortality and to use their resources to locate my mom.

. . .

STEP 3: Make it back to Earth in one piece, hopefully sooner, rather than later.

I SCRIBBLE a quick letter to the family, describing the various trees and animals I've come across. I keep my note clinical, a way of disassociating from the difficulty of this journey. Rearranging the body pillow to use it both under my head and between my legs, I settle in.

Sure, I have to sleep in a fetal position to make it work, but I'm comfortable.

All that's left now is firelight shining through the cracks between the fabric walls, making me feel somehow less alone, even though I'm in another world.

CHAPTER 5

OZ

The twins stir between us, drawing our attention away from our own sorrow for a moment. I pick up Bennett, feeling my heart twist at the way he smells like Lana already. He grasps my finger with his tiny hand, and I can't help but smile, even though it doesn't reach my eyes.

I know I need to be strong for Rose and Bennett. They're our everything now. But it's so hard when I'm barely hanging on myself.

I miss Lana—my darling Sahira—so much it physically hurts. The cavern in my chest at her absence is a constant ache. The not knowing is what's eating me alive. If we knew when she'd be back, we'd occupy ourselves with the day-to-day; still missing her, but at least we'd have a countdown.

Instead, it's as though someone has cut out a piece of my heart, leaving an ever-bleeding wound in its place. Help is on the way, but when that help will come, no one knows. Will I bleed out before aid arrives? Will I go mad, waiting for any semblance of activity? Proof that she's okay?

I know she's only been gone a few days, but it feels like an eternity.

Gideon pulls me out of my dark thoughts, handing me a cup of blood. I know he's only trying to help, but right now, even the thought of drinking turns my stomach.

I force myself to take a few sips, though, knowing I need to keep up my strength. For Rose and Bennett. For Lana.

I'll do whatever it takes to get her back. Even if it kills me.

CHAPTER 6

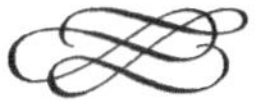

LANA

On my third night, I wake to the sound of pitter-patter on the tent, and my eyes take a little time to adjust to the dark. For a moment, I think I'm in Patagonia with Oz, but then I remember — I'm in Bedlam. I don't know how long I've been sleeping, but the moon still sits high in the sky. Wind whips through the trees, and the next thing I know, a torrential downpour pounds against the canvas.

"Get in here!" I shout over the rain.

Finn rushes to unzip the tent and crawls in, sopping wet. Through the light glow reflecting off his skin, I try to ignore his damp shirt clinging to his abs, to no avail. Why does he only glow sometimes? I haven't figured out the pattern yet. He smirks and begins patting his clothes until they're dry. I can't help but notice he left the shirt for last.

"Do you know what time it is?" Sleep coats my words, and I rub my eyes before sitting up. Lightning flashes across the sky, illuminating the entire tent for a moment. A crack of thunder chases it, and it startles me. Finn chuckles at my expense; a deep, purr-like rumble tumbling its way through a wall I'd carefully erected between us.

"We've got about seven more hours until daylight. It hasn't been long since we went to sleep." He situates his pillow next to mine. There's a certain gravel to his tired voice, cutting quick to my core.

"Oh, good." I plop my head back down on the pillow. I refuse to make him sleep in the rain, and there's no reason he has to be out there in the cold when we can sleep side-by-side.

Once he lies down, we are shoulder to shoulder in these tight quarters. While his body heat is a welcome relief from the frigid temperatures, the cold still burrows into my bones, and my teeth chatter. The soft plop of rain turns sharper; there's sleet now the temperature has dipped.

Finn situates the blankets to cover both of us, and my bare feet brush him while I tuck the blanket under me. He swears. "Your toes are like ice!"

"That's because I'm freezing, and I only have a dress on." I curl further into a ball for warmth.

He leans over me and rummages through a canvas backpack. The weight of his chest presses against mine, but it doesn't take him long to locate wool socks, gray sweatpants, and a matching hoodie.

"Sorry, I don't know why I didn't think of this. Put these on; you'll be warmer."

I snag them from him, and he turns away while I strip out of my dress. While the fashion is Earth-like, the fabric is much softer and made of a material I've never seen before. Goosebumps line my body in the frigid temperatures, and I can't dress fast enough. The clothes hang off my 5'10" frame — fae are far bigger than humans. I tuck my face into the neck opening of the hoodie and pull the drawstring tight, so just my eyes are visible.

"Thank you, this is so much better." I have a beaming smile on my face.

At least now I won't die of hypothermia. When Finn turns over and gets his first look at me, pure glee radiates on his face. I imagine I look like a child wearing her father's clothes, and he agrees with the nod of his head.

I crawl under the covers and curl onto my side, facing Finn. My thoughts wander to my family. What are they doing right now? How much have the twins grown in the short time I've been away? It isn't long before I'm asleep again. I wake several times in the night, curling up even further from the cold.

When I wake in the morning, my back is cold, but my front is toasty. In my sleep, I've navigated closer to Finn and am now nestled against his body for heat. His arm wraps around my shoulder and extends down my back. I'm sore from sleeping on the ground, but don't move away. Instead, I roll over, so my chilly back faces him, and I tuck his arm in closer.

He stirs, and I sense his breath hitch in recognition of the position we're in. Rather than pulling away, he wrenches me towards him even more and tucks the blankets under my front.

"Thank you," I murmur.

"You're welcome." He rests his chin on top of my head.

It isn't long before his erection grows against my back, and I freeze. I reassure myself it's just morning wood. This happens to every man, no matter their realm or species ... I think.

What I wouldn't give for this to be one of my mates. I still myself, exhaling a stream of fog. If it were Gideon, he'd just slip these sweats down and have his way with me. Oz would flip me over and have me ride him with my sweater off so he could watch my breasts sway above him. Auguste, on the other hand, would secure my wrists over my head before plowing into me.

Or, if they were all here, they'd fill every hole and —

"Gods, would you stop? I'm a weak man right now, Lana. This will never go away with you thinking about that," he scolds. "It's hard enough with you pressed against me like this."

Never mind the double entendre. "Sorry. I miss them." My voice is barely a whisper.

He sighs. "I imagine you do. What's it like, having three mates? They don't get jealous?"

I smile at the memory. "Oz was really jealous when our bond was still brand new. Initially, we tried for a primary relationship and having Auguste and Gideon as secondary, but we quickly learned equal footing is best for everyone. They're mere extensions of me now, and vice-versa. My vampire family—and the twins—are the best parts of me."

He rises to his elbow and props his head up. "I couldn't share you."

I scrunch my brows. "It's a good thing you're not my mate then, isn't it?"

I make to leave the tent to find a place to relieve myself. Leaning over to unzip the tent, I groan when I open the flap. Several inches of glittering snow coat everything.

"What is it?" Finn sits up on his elbows, and I move aside so he can see outside.

"The snow will slow us down. I'm going to see what I can find to fashion you some shoes."

I nod and trudge through the snow until I'm far enough away and go to the bathroom. I've slipped on Finn's enormous boots that are a little challenging to walk in. On my way back, I collect frozen berries and put them in the hoodie's kangaroo pocket.

"What are you making?"

Finn has long, thin sticks and several cords of vine. He's sitting cross-legged at the opening of the tent and has a determined look on his face.

"Snowshoes." He puffs up his chest in pride.

"Thanks. I'm going to get us a fire started."

Finding suitable wood for the fire takes a while — most of everything is wet, but Finn can use his magic to dry it. I gather a small bundle so we can get breakfast started.

After I get the fire lit, we eat, and pack up camp. Finn motions to my feet. I place a hand on his shoulder to steady myself while I rest my ankle on his thigh, so he can strap a makeshift snowshoe to my foot. His gaze stays on me while he taps my foot, indicating he needs my other one now. He glances at me, pausing on my face before a grin spreads across his, showing off his canines.

"What?"

The corners of his eyes crinkle. "Nothin.'"

I narrow my eyes and return his stare. The feel of his hand on my leg is like a flint to tinder, so I ask if he's done yet.

His grin widens. "I can't say I hate this position, either."

I glance down to see he's done with my shoe, and I scowl. He chuckles while I hop around in the snowshoes, testing them out. While it takes a little getting used to, these are far better than walking in wool socks or barefooted.

~

Gideon

MY LITTLE STRIGA,

YOU'VE BEEN in Bedlam for 926 hours now. I intended to make it seem like we're doing okay, but the truth is, we're not. When I promised I'd storm the gates of hell to be with you, I meant it. I'm in contact with fae on Earth to see about bypassing the portal to be with you, but so far, we're meeting dead ends. This is ancient, powerful fae magic. But if you can bend space and time to be with me, I can move mountains (portals? Doors to portals?) to prove my love to you, too.

I think the strain on the mating bond has us all exhausted, or maybe it's the round-the-clock feedings and diaper changes. More realistically, it's the bagged blood we have to drink. I hate the stuff. Even though we stocked B+, it's like drinking ash after I've tasted yours. It's adequate, but barely.

I've heard from other mates who have had to separate for a time, and I agree with them; it's actual torture. Wherever you're at in the fae realm, I hope you're not hurting like we are. They imbue the entire realm with magic, so it should dull the ache on your end ... hopefully.

We all thought we should write to you as often as we can, so you have an enormous stack of letters to come home to.

After the twins, I know you miss me the most, and it's okay to admit that. The others won't hold it against you (maybe I will, wink wink).

It's weird, not having you in this gigantic bed. We congregate here for naps and bedtime, but it's not the same. The babies are eating well and growing faster than human infants, but we're not sure if they're vampires or witches or both yet. Time will tell.

I know you're there, doing everything you can to come back to us. Tomorrow, we'll have our troops round up Lapis Templar members to await sentencing. I'll never forget how you stood there like a champ when we had to dispatch the last group. You're a true queen.

We haven't seen Dolphina since the day she attacked you in the woods. Mark my words, she will meet my wrath.

On our end, we haven't stopped trying to find information about your mom. We're moving to our place in Sydney next week for the base of our operations. Don't worry, I ordered a big enough bed for all of us.

We're going to get you out of there, my little Striga.

I love you.

Forever storming hell's gates,

Gideon

P.S. I will make those miscreants suffer if they've hurt a hair on your head.

CHAPTER 7

LANA

"What was the goop hanging off the trees near the portal?" I ask Finn.

It's nearly night, and I have seen nothing other than trees and undergrowth for six entire weeks. I'm sitting on a fallen log near the campfire, watching Finn cook dinner over smoldering embers. He says the smoke will help mask the taste of the small rodent he caught. He is shirtless, wearing only a pair of black, form-fitting sweatpants. How he can stand the cold is beyond me.

Being a witch makes me better at tolerating it than most humans, but I still can't tolerate the harsh sting of high mountain climates.

"The slime is excrement from sustai birds. They nest near portals." Finn licks his fingers and flips the small game he's cooking. He pulls off a strip of meat. "Go ahead, try it."

He holds the stick out to me. I take a piece and nibble at it. The game is warm, but the smoke does little to mask the flavor. I can't imagine what it tastes like without it. The creature looked similar to a guinea pig, but it had sharp pointy teeth and tiny wings on its back, although it can't fly.

I chew slowly, politely.

"How much longer will it take us to get through the forest with all this snow?"

Finn sits down next to me. "A couple of months at least." He tilts his head to the sky. "We're going to get more, and that'll slow us down."

"Is it normal to get a lot of snow up here?" I ask, afraid.

He bites the inside of his lip. "Not like this."

The wind picks up and howls through the trees. I'm thankful for the fire, but it's still cold.

"Shouldn't you have a shirt on?"

"Nah," he says with a wave of his hand. "My magic charges faster in direct contact with the moon's beams. They'll be out soon."

"But it's cold!" I protest.

He chuckles, which makes his eyes dance with mischief. He leans in closer to me. "I'm a fae," he whispers, his warm breath brushing over my face. His skin turns from golden tan to a luminescent blue, almost like a faint glowstick.

A shiver snakes its way through my body, and I hug my arms to my chest. He stands and walks to the edge of the campsite, staring up at the sky.

I continue eating my meat, but keep an eye on him. When the moon finally emerges from behind the clouds, his skin brightens even more with the iridescent blue glow. So much, it reflects on me, and brightens the campsite. The sight is stunning.

I stare at his silhouette, entranced by the brilliance. It's so beautiful, I forget how cold it is, even though plumes of my breath fog the air in front of me.

He turns back to me, eyes alight with roguery. Something moves in the underbrush. It's close. My eyes dart around the forest, but Finn doesn't seem concerned. He sinks into a crouch.

Something pokes out from the darkness in front of him, but I can't make it out yet. The trees shake and a dark, shaggy shape steps out to the left, meandering toward us without hurry.

"What is it?" I try to see what the creature is.

He swivels, moving in front of me. "Go back to the fire. Now."

"But ..."

"Go!" He snaps.

I stand and run to the campfire, grabbing his bag on the way. It has all our supplies in it, and I might need to patch him up if this goes bad.

The animal steps into the light, revealing its full size. He's taller than Finn and at least seven feet wide. The shaggy fur is the color of ash, and it has glowing blue eyes that meet mine.

It sniffs the air, then turns its predatory gaze toward Finn.

Its eyes narrow, gleaming with pure malice. It opens its jaw wide and flashes its jagged teeth at him before dropping to the ground on all fours. I'm too terrified to scream, but a squeak escapes my throat.

Finn takes a step back and kneels low to the ground. His eyes lock on the creature, his body tense and ready to spring. It bares its teeth again and a low growl rumbles from its throat. Heavy paws press into frozen mud, pacing toward Finn, but he doesn't move.

The creature lunges forward to attack. Finn rolls out of the way at the last second and grabs its neck in his hands, grappling with the animal.

The two roll into our campsite and the fire blazes higher as they tumble into the logs. Skin sizzles on contact, and fur shrivels to a crisp.

Fuck. I take a step back, trying to keep my distance.

The bear's head whips around and sinks its jaws into Finn's shoulder. He lets out a yell of pain and grips the creature's head with his hand.

I can't stand here and let him get killed. I run to Finn, grabbing the hot end of a broken branch from the fire. When I smack it into the creature's side, it only lets out a low snarl in response.

Finn's eyes meet mine and widen in surprise, but the animal rips the skin from his shoulder, and he drops to the ground. I swing hard and the wood cracks across the beast's face. A howl erupts from the creature's jaws, and it turns to me, but Finn grabs it by the neck and forces it to the ground.

He roars as he squeezes his hand tighter and tighter around the animal's neck. Its legs thrash, but it doesn't have enough leverage to buck him off. When its neck goes limp, Finn stands and stumbles back from the corpse.

Fear seizes my throat. I can't scream or utter a sound. I drop the branch and rush to Finn, but he collapses into the dirt before I can reach him. Blood pools on the ground where his shoulder once was. In its place is a raw, ragged mess of flesh.

I rip off several strips of fabric from my clothes to use as gauze. "Finn!" I shake his good shoulder, but he doesn't move.

"Finn!" I shake him harder, and his head lolls to one side. "Oh, gods."

I have to stop the bleeding. Pressing the cloth against his shoulder, wishing desperately my magic worked here, I hold my breath.

His chest rises and falls, but he doesn't wake. I press harder on the wound. "Come on, Finn. Stay with me."

Think Lana, think. What did Finn do to heal me? I bite my lip, fighting the tears swelling in my eyes. Every time he healed me, he had to touch me, and he glowed while doing it.

My gaze darts to the sky, but trees block the moon overhead. I hook my hands under his heels, wincing at the pain I'll have to cause him by dragging him closer to the fire under an overhead clearing.

Tears fall freely down my cheeks as I tug him across the forest floor. I grunt and groan through clenched teeth; he weighs far more than anything or anyone I've ever had to drag before. In his wake is a trail of glowing blue blood.

My stomach turns, but I have to keep going.

I reach the fire and drop his feet. His head lolls forward, and I lift it into my lap. "Come on, Finn."

I grab his hand and press it against the patchwork gauze, then reach up and place my other hand on his cheek. "I've got you. Stay with me." A glow emits from under my palm, spreading like ink in watercolor over his face and down his neck. Soon, his entire body glows.

What the ...?

His eyelids flutter open, and he gazes up at me. "You saved me." A sleepy lilt coats his voice, and an affectionate smile tugs the corners of his lips. He lifts his hand and places it over mine as it rests on his face.

I don't care what this is between us. I'll do whatever it takes to not lose him. "Of course I did." A sob breaks free, and I press my forehead into his.

When the magic ends, I'm left with his warm hand in mine. I try to pull it away, but he holds tight, and I meet his eyes.

"Don't let go yet. I like the way it feels when you touch me."

Finn's fingers squeeze mine, and his lips brush against my forehead in a chaste kiss.

My heart flutters in my chest, and I pull away, afraid of getting too close. "We need to get you cleaned up."

There aren't any rivers around for miles, and despite what we've been through together tonight, and the night he saved me, I'm not giving him a sponge bath. I grab the canteen of water we purified earlier. We're running a little low, but if we've got fresh snow coming, I can melt some.

He holds his arm out, allowing me to pour the cool liquid over the angry wound, already much better from his healing magic. He sucks in a breath, and his hand flexes around mine.

"I'm sorry." I wince, heat rushing to my cheeks. "I know it hurts."

He shakes his head. "It isn't that." He squeezes my fingers again, and I swear it's as though he's touching more than just the back of my hand.

"What is it, then?"

He holds my gaze. "It's good to feel something."

While I don't know how I feel about what he said, my heart leaps at his words. "I'm glad you're better." I smile, hoping it will reassure him.

"I have a confession to make." He licks his lips and averts his gaze.

My heart seizes. Oh, gods. He's mated or has a girlfriend back home. Or he's telling me I have to find my way to town myself. The way he's licking his lips, it must be something bad. "What is it?"

He grips my hand. "I'm the hi-"

A howl pierces the night, and Finn releases me. His head snaps to the trees and he whispers. "More ilab … the beast's family."

"What?" Fear paralyzes me. Ilab are what attacked us?

He bolts upright, but the movement sends him to his knees with a groan. "Stay here." He sucks in a breath, leaps to his feet, and sprints into the forest.

My heart plummets. "Wait!"

The howls come from all over, surrounding us. I jump to my feet, wrapping my arms around myself.

Please let him be okay.

Another howl cuts through the crisp air, this time close enough to send a chill down my back. I grab the knife from Finn's pack and wrap my fingers around the hilt. An ilab emerges from the trees, although half its comrade's size, its eyes aglow, saliva dripping from its fangs.

I know I need to run, but my muscles don't budge.

The beast's head swivels to the side, and it turns and runs deeper into the forest. I watch it go, my heart pounding in my ears. The howls continue, but they're more distant now, and I think the creature is gone.

I take a shaky breath and collapse into a seated position. What was that? Were there more? Were they after Finn?

My heart squeezes.

I won't lose him, too. Pushing up onto shaky legs, I grab his pack. I open it and rifle through the contents, looking for anything useful. Inside is the canteen we usually keep filled with purified water, which I snag before running deeper into the woods. It's empty. Might as well bring this with me in case I stumble across any water.

The wind picks up, causing the trees to sway overhead. Leaves and twigs fall to the ground, and howls still echo through the forest, but they're fainter. I scrutinize the direction Finn ran in, grit my teeth, and take off.

Chasing through the woods, I lose track of time and space. I'm aware of my body, but everything outside it is a blur. Eventually, I slow down, needing to catch my breath.

The moon casts enough light through the canopy to light my way, and the stars twinkle above me, mocking my inability to track my way through them. I don't know where I am, but hopefully, I'm not too far away from where Finn was. I lean forward to rest my hands on my thighs and take deep breaths.

A twig snaps behind me, and I whirl around. Are the ilab back? I press my palm against the hilt of the knife; the end worn smooth from use.

A dark figure stands twenty feet away, cloaked in shadows, and unnervingly still. My heart stutters as I take a tentative step forward, squinting at the form. I can't make out any distinguishable features. It could be fae, but it has a wild presence to its stance that tells me it's feral.

"I'm sorry." My voice quivers. "I'm not sure where I am." Maybe if I use friendly language, the creature or fae will help.

It takes a step forward, and I raise the blade, my hand trembling under my false bravado. Skin illuminates when it steps into the moonlight. I swallow, my throat dry as a desert.

"F-Finn?" I squint.

He captures me in an embrace, and I gasp. "What happened to your clothes?" Heat creeps into my cheeks—he doesn't have a scrap of clothing on.

Finn gives me a predator's grin, his eyes crinkling at the corners. He nuzzles my neck, his breath warm on my skin, and I tense with anticipation. My eyes trail down his naked length, catching on the tattooed symbol below where his pants should sit. *This is the same mark as the one in his journal.* It's similar to the birthmark I bare on my forearm, although it's faded so much over the years, it's difficult to tell.

He allows me a brief glimpse before pulling me flush to him again. A possessive growl rumbles deep from his throat, matching the grip he has on the nape of my hair. His lips press against my jaw before his tongue flicks the pulse at the base of my throat.

He walks us backward until I'm pressed against a tree. My breath comes in pants, my mind warring between stopping him and begging him to continue. Has he changed his mind about sharing me? He hooks his arm under my leg, pressing his erection against the heat of my core. Two thin pieces of fabric separate us.

His free hand comes between us, middle finger brushing against my pearl, and his hungry mouth presses against mine. Desire pools low in my belly. After weeks of holding back, our tongues duel, eager to sate their demands. He slips under my waistband, a deep rumble in his chest as his fingers find me soaked, and he slides my bottoms down.

"Finn," I moan.

My nails dig into his back while he slides his cock through my folds. I arch my pelvis forward, urging him on. Just another half inch is all it'd take before we're joined as one.

"*Mine*." His voice is more of a growl than anything.

"Wait." I pull back, my hand on his chest, the warmth of his skin seeping into me. "My mates will understand if I fall in love with you and bring you home, but I won't choose you over them. You said you won't share me."

He pauses at my entrance and meets my eyes, his pupils taking up most of his irises. He stills, chest still heaving, and his features soften. "I'm sorry. I got away from myself." A smile curves his lips. He lowers my leg, and he takes my hand in his before kissing the back of it, lingering for a moment before meeting my gaze again. "Fae can shift to more ... dangerous versions of ourselves. When I need to kill a group of creatures, or fae, my body can change into its primal form."

"Primal form?"

"I can shift back and forth, but when I'm feral, my mind has two goals in mind: either hunt or fight. This is the first time I've sought more carnal urges. I'm not untamed very often."

I wince. "And ... your clothes?"

"Shredded by the beasts." He smirks. "They're all dead."

I let out a long breath, my muscles relaxing. I'm not sure if I should feel relieved or pissed off because he could've got himself killed. At least his wound is gone.

Taking a step back, I thread my hands through his soft hair, twining the knife-shorn tresses between my fingers. "You should've let me help. Don't scare me like that." My voice shakes.

He nods, his eyes sincere. "I'm sorry." He rubs his thumb along my cheekbone. "I couldn't risk you getting hurt by them, so I led them away."

I blink, unsure of what to say. Finn turns his head and presses his lips to the inside of my wrist before regarding me with hunger in his eyes.

I swallow. "You need to eat after all that fighting and healing." I tug him towards camp. Finn whirls around, halting my steps. His brows furrow, and he sucks in a deep breath.

"What's wrong?"

He tilts his head, a preternatural stillness to him. "Do you hear that?"

I listen hard, but all I can hear are the sounds of the surrounding forest. I shake my head.

Finn takes off, jogging deeper into the woods, with me following close behind. He comes to a stop, his muscles tensing as he pushes through some bushes. I come up behind him and peer over his shoulder.

"What is it?"

He holds up a hand. "Shhh." His eyes stay on the dark shrubs ahead of us, his body rigid. He grabs my hand and tugs me back the way we came.

My heart pounds, and I'm not sure who's more frightened—me or him. He takes me back to camp and pulls out his dagger.

"What's going on?" I ask, my voice shaking. "You're scaring me."

"One of the ilab isn't dead." Finn watches the direction ahead of us with a tight jaw.

"How do you know?" I keep my voice low.

"The creatures have a magical signature." He glances at me, his expression serious. "And the bushes are moving in a way the wind shouldn't be moving them."

I swallow hard and nod.

Finn eyes me with a look that sends shivers down my spine. "You stay at camp and don't make a sound. Do you understand?"

"Where are you going?" I grip his arm.

"To kill the beast." He squeezes my hand, his face softening. "I'll be okay."

Tears spring to my eyes and I shake my head. "Let me help you, please."

He grabs both sides of my face, kneeling until he meets my eyes, and stilling my racing heart. "The thing these beasts crave more than fae blood is that of a witch. I'm going to cut off the trail before he can make it back to camp, which means I need you to stay here." He reaches into my pocket to grab the knife and presses the hilt into my palm. "You won't need this, but just in case, you know what to do. I'll be back in a few minutes."

I nod.

He strides off, his movements silent as he goes, and I sit by the fire, my heart threatening to beat out of my chest. Images of Finn being mauled by the animal plague me. My hand tightens its grip on the handle, ready to defend camp if the need arises.

A rustle sounds nearby, and I whirl to face it, but a small rodent scurries past. I let out a breath and remind myself Finn is strong and can take care of himself. Something crashes through the bushes, and I cower, my pulse beating erratically. A few seconds later, Finn emerges from the forest.

"The beast is dead." He nods at me before going to his pack and ruminating over something I can't see.

I release a breath of relief, my muscles relaxing.

"Are you okay?" His brows furrow with worry.

I nod and approach him, touching his arm. He turns to face me and wraps me in a tight hug. I melt into him, forgetting the fact he's still completely naked.

"You scared me to death." I curve my fingers over his broad shoulders. His muscles tense, and he exhales hard.

"I'm sorry." He holds me firm against him, his hands stroking my back. "I couldn't risk it getting to you."

"I know, and ... I'm glad you're okay." My cheek rests on his chest.

He tightens his hold on me. "I'll always protect you, Lana." His voice is soft and sincere, sending a wave of warmth through me.

I pull back and look up at him, gazing into his eyes as he studies my face. He leans down and kisses my forehead before drawing back.

"Let's eat." He turns away from me, making my heart ache with longing.

Finn whirls back around as if he can sense my emotions. He takes a step towards me and cups my cheek before returning to dig into the tent for clothes. I edge away from him, not trusting myself to be so close to him—and his naked body. He finds some clothes and gets dressed before heading after me, his face scrunched in a scowl.

"Lana ..." He trails off and shakes his head. "Are you still hungry?"

I nod, my mouth dry. His muscles flex, and he holds out a hand to me, leading me to my seat near the fire, and we eat in silence. I keep my attention on my food, too aware of how close he is.

After we eat, Finn turns to me. "Let's go to sleep."

I nod, keeping my eyes averted.

He climbs into the tent and waits for me to join him, like a captive audience, before closing the opening. Darkness consumes us both, but his warm presence beside me lends comfort in the night.

"Lana ..." He trails off again before he reaches out and tilts my chin up. "I'm sorry I scared you."

"It's okay," I whisper.

He releases a breath and leans in, brushing his lips against my temple before pulling back. His eyes search mine before he runs a hand over my cheek.

"Goodnight, Lana." He lies back.

I stare at him for a few seconds before I return to my pillow. There's something he needs to tell me, and I won't push him, not until he's ready.

Memory after memory of Finn looking out for me plays through my head. I trust him to keep us safe, and warmth spreads through me as I fall asleep.

CHAPTER 8

LANA

"What's this, Lana?" Finn leans back and brushes my hair to the side.

"What's what?" I look over my shoulder at him. My satisfied smile falls when I see the anger on his face.

"You have a fucking defixio mark on you?" He unzips the tent and storms out, pacing in front of the fire. "Fuck!"

"A what? I don't even know what that is. Where is it?" I turn over and clutch the sheets to my chest. His voice is angry, but the look on his face is one of absolute devastation.

"It's a curse! Should've known it's the only reason you'd entertain being with me." He picks up the log we'd used to sit on and chucks it against the tree so hard, it splinters into pieces.

I don't understand. Finn and I were just fine a few minutes ago and had been all night. I scramble out of the blankets and hurry into the first thing I could find — one of Finn's soft gray t-shirts.

"Don't shut me out." I sniffle, and race to where he's taken off to in the woods. He stops when I reach him, allowing me to turn him around. Desolation mars his features. There's despair in his eyes and his brows furrow in defeat.

"I'm not mad at you." I lean into the palm he places against my cheek, and he sighs. "You're... perfect. I'm just upset with the situation."

I take his hand and drag him back to the campsite. We reach camp, and I pull him into the tent. I use the back of my hand to wipe away the tears on my cheeks, and that's when Finn meets my eyes. He pulls me in and continues to hold me close to him while he explains.

"You said the fae who hurt you on your first night in Bedlam dug her claws into you?"

I nod. "Pierced me to the bone."

"She must've put this curse on you. At the base of your skull is the symbol—a skull with a heart between its teeth. It's called the defixio mark because it *binds* you to me. That's why you love me." There is no question in his statement, a pure and simple fact I can't seem to deny or explain away. His face holds only pain when I turn my head.

I pull away from him and start breathing fast, shallow breaths. *Oh, gods.* The tiny tent feels like it's spinning, so I rest my elbows on my thighs and try to calm my breathing. I pull at the hair against my scalp. The mark *made me* fall in love?

What have I done?

Gods. What have I done?!

Air. I need *air.*

I crawl to the window and unzip the panel as far as it will go. The cold air does nothing to the flashes of panic racing through me. It's as though I have a boulder sitting on my chest, whether from guilt or shame, I don't know which. Both, probably.

They'll never forgive me.

I'll never forgive me.

Doubling over, the walls close in, the roar in my head drowning out the sound of my rapid breathing. I flinch when Finn's large hand rests on my shoulder.

"Can you remove it?" I whip around to face him.

He nods. "I'm sorry, Lana. I didn't know it was there — it's right inside your hairline, and I wouldn't have even noticed it had I not been right behind you in the light. Please know I would've never taken advantage of you like that."

"But how did that fae know it would be *you?*" I accuse, and his shoulders drop. "Were you colluding with that monster?" I scream as I back away from him. Betrayal slices through me.

"On everything I am and ever will be, know I would never, ever do something like that." He reaches his hand for me, and I back out of his range until I'm pressed against the fabric walls. "The mark works on whomever or whatever you come into contact with next — be it man, beast, or creature."

I bury my head in my hands while I tremble and sob. My limbs weaken, and Finn offers me his hand, but I ignore it.

"What am I going to do?" I bellow. "They'll never, ever forgive this. I've destroyed my family." This mark must've fooled me into believing my mates would accept him if I loved him.

Finn wraps me in his arms and rocks with me. "This isn't your fault," he whispers. "So there's nothing to forgive. That berserker stole your freedom and choice from you." He brushes my hair out of my face and tilts my chin up to look at him. "Do you understand? Your mates will never hold something like this against you. If they need to be mad at someone, let them be mad at her or me. I tried to walk away from you, but I'm a weak man, Lana."

I hope I'll have the chance to explain to them what happened. I'd much rather they hear it directly from me rather than through someone else.

"How do you remove the curse?" I sit back but am still in his embrace.

"I massage it away while reciting a spell."

Finn

I DON'T KNOW how I can move on without her. Every fiber of my soul tells me we belong together. I'd move mountains for this woman, lay my life at her feet, give her all of me. Raze entire realms, if she asked. I suck in a breath, an iron fist on the pillow I hold against my chest where I watch droplets of rain slide down the tent walls. Appropriate, given the circumstances. She'll never know how much I love her. Gods, she can barely look at me. She's so ashamed of herself. If only she saw what I see: Lana is utterly perfect.

This curse is cruel, causing her to fixate on someone she doesn't love.

I'd thought maybe ...

I shake my head.

She's not my mate.

For a while, I suspected she was my soul bond—the one I gave up everything for—but it's the defixio mark. When Lana told me she wanted me, all felt right in my life, like the final piece clicking into place. A ship coming home after millennia lost at sea.

The sad part? I'm just as obsessed with her as she is with me, but *I'm not cursed*. And now, I'll undo her bind to me. The pain I have to cause will nearly match the agony I'll feel over having to let her go.

I cast a silencing bubble around camp; we'll need it, and we don't need creatures thinking there's wounded prey to eat. I crawl over to where she has her head buried in her hands. "Come on over to the blanket." Her red-rimmed eyes and cheeks stained with tears slay me, and I help her to where I need her. "I'm sorry, this is going to hurt. Probably the most pain you'll ever experience. I'll do my best to soothe the hurt as much as I can." I crawl behind her and ask her to tie her hair up with the thin rope around her wrist.

Tracing the curse mark with my fingers, I lean in and inhale deeply. Gods, she even smells like mine. There's no other way to describe her scent ... and I'll miss it when this is gone.

I massage the mark, concentrating on undoing the magic.

"Wicked curse,

This wound, I nurse.

Remove the mark,

Of love so dark.

Restore free will,

True love, fulfill.

For better or worse,

I remove this curse."

Lana's scream drills through the air and etches itself right into my soul. I pull her into my arms while she wails and sobs.

Kill me.

Kill me.

Kill me.

I can't take this. Please, please, please. End me now.

Gods. Kill me!

She's buried in pain so deep; she can do nothing but cry for me in her head. It's torture watching her. I can actually feel her suffering, as though I were going through it myself, and I clench my teeth against the onslaught. I'll do what I can to lend her the strength she needs to get through this.

I lift her into my lap and rock with her, whispering soothing words into her ear, despite my own torment. Hours later, our suffering subsides, but the echo of torture remains. We're both covered in sweat, our faces marred with tears. I lay us down on the pallet of blankets, and vow to myself I'll take care of her as long as she needs me.

As long as she'll allow.

CHAPTER 9

LANA

"**W**hy do I still love you?" I cry a choked whisper in the dark.

Tears dampen Finn's chest where I lay my head. He breathes in deep before releasing his breath — whether from relief or uncertainty; I don't know. How long have we laid here? The entire time, my mind's been playing reels of my mates, my children, the rest of the family. *Finn was in each one.*

"I think we're soul bonded." His voice cracks, and he runs his hand back and forth across my back.

"Soul bonded?"

"When I found you that day in the woods, I told you I smelled your blood, and I did. But long before I ever caught your scent, I heard you calling for me. It's how I ended up so many hours from my camp. I thought I imagined it when I was stirred from my sleep by a desperate plea for help. It was your soul calling for mine."

I don't know how, but I feel in the very depths of me that our souls are the same. Is this why, being in his presence, in his arms, I feel at peace? The entire time, I thought this was because of his Luna order.

A memory tugs at me.

Safe.

Safe.

Safe.

He is safe.

I am safe.

A chill snakes its way through my body and I shake it off. The mark didn't make me fall in love. It didn't make me think my mates would accept him, nor did it make me seek his comfort all this time.

The guilt I felt in my chest disappears as I gain clarity of the situation.

It was but our souls intertwining, a recognition of something so deep and so wide, no distance, nor time, could stop it. Of course my vampire mates would understand. They'd accept him, just as I would, provided he'd share.

Hurt sluices through me, like a cascading waterfall pummeling me against rock.

"Most people aren't lucky enough to know their soul bond. In your darkest moment of despair — when death was bearing down on you — your soul lit up like a beacon to guide me to you. I would have said something before now if I'd have recognized it for what it was. But now, I know."

CHAPTER 10

LANA

$\mathcal{W}$e spend the next couple of weeks with the same routine — putting many miles on foot, and camping at night. Finn teaches me what magic he can each evening. Without the ability to do it myself, there isn't a lot I can learn yet. We have no trouble with anyone we run into in the woods. With Finn next to me and our faces glamoured, they steer clear of us.

Finn and I spent last night in the forest eating up most of the food we smoked after several weeks of trapping success. In a few days, we should be in the first town and can sleep in a proper bed, and my muscles yearn for the press of a soft mattress. I don't have a dime to my name while in Bedlam, but Finn has offered to care for the bill. He's gone way out of his way to help me, and I owe him big for it.

"You know, you don't have to come with me. I know how important it is for you to top up your magic in these woods," I say between bites of food. The very words send a jolt of panic through me. Is this my abandonment issues manifesting again? I've grown to enjoy his company, and while I don't want to part, soul bonded mate or not ... I also don't want to be a burden.

He quiets, and I catch a brief flash of pain on his face before he schools his features. "My magic is at capacity now," he says, after a moment of pause. He furrows his brows before glancing my way. "Would you rather be alone?"

"No, but I don't want you to put yourself out any more than you already have. I've monopolized so much of your time."

He shakes his head and brushes the hair out of face. "I'd never leave you to fend for yourself. Not here, not anywhere."

"You expended so much magic while healing. How are you full now?" I grab a stick and poke the embers in the fire, causing them to spin and pop in the air.

"Normally I do, but Luna orders can charge in other ways." He stuffs a bite of smoked fish in his mouth. A mischievous glint twinkles in his gaze.

"Like?"

He takes a bit to respond because he's busy chewing, and he appears deep in thought. "Lots of ways. Healing someone, taking a life." He shrugs. "Arousal."

"Arousal!?" I spit out the swig of water I had in my mouth.

Is that why I sometimes see him give off a glow? He's recharging?

His cheeks flush, and he looks away. "Can you blame a guy? I rescue you and spent the last few months sharing a sleeping bag with you pressed against me."

No, I suppose I can't.

"Why have you never settled down then? It seems like that might be a lot easier than chasing to the woods every six months." A possessive flare of panic rushes through me again.

"Fae mate for life. I'd never settle down with just anyone. I've thought about going back to the Earth realm, but I'm afraid my stature—and intermittent glow—might allude to me not being human. Staying in glamour all the time isn't fun."

He is relatively large. "Maybe you could come with me when I make it home. My mates aren't as big as you, but if you hung out ... you wouldn't stand out too much?"

"Yeah, maybe." He stands. "I'm going to bed."

"Oh, okay." I'm a little deflated at his sudden departure. Did I say something to offend him?

I dig the small cord Finn made me out of the pocket of the sweats I'm wearing so I can braid my hair out of the way for bed. I don't have a brush here, but he uses magic to detangle my hair after I bathe, which happens in any moving body of water we can find.

What I would've given for that kind of magic as a kid. Mom used to have to chase me around the house, then tackle me to brush my hair. She probably would've loved this magic, too … but I'd give anything to have her chase me with a hairbrush one more time. I'd do things so much differently now. More 'I love you's and less running out the back door, staying out until the streetlights came on.

After squatting behind a tree, I use soapberries to wash my hands, face, and brush my teeth. Finn had an extra toothbrush in his bag, thankfully, and it's enchanted to clean far better than any I'd find on Earth. On my way back, I pick up logs, so we'll have wood in the morning.

I unzip the tent and my knee catches on the lip, so I topple onto Finn's massive form. A faint glow comes from him. He has a pained look on his face, and his pupils are blown out.

"Oh shit, did I hurt you?" I scramble to help him, my hand resting on his bare chest, and his skin flares brighter.

"Help me or get out," he growls.

I flinch at his abrasive words and take a moment to realize I just stumbled in on him, *pleasuring himself.*

"Oh gods, I am so sorry." I slap a hand over my eyes and flee from the tent before zipping it up and retreating far from camp. I'm mortified to have walked in on him. Yes, his order demands it, but knowing it and seeing it are two different things. I didn't see his junk or anything, but I saw his expression and his hand down his sweatpants. Had I been single, I probably would've joined him. I feel drawn to him, like a moth to a flame, knowing the danger but not caring. I break into a jog, desperate for some space between us.

When far enough away, I pace the woods. What the hell am I going to say when I go back in there? *'Hey, sorry for interrupting your self-love session, no need to feel embarrassed, we all do it?'* I cringe.

After another good twenty minutes, I decide to face the music. We're adults, right? I can have uncomfortable conversations. I tug the hood over my head and pad my way to the tent. This time, I announce myself before even touching the tent zipper.

"You can come in." His voice usually sounds like silk, but now it has a more gravelly depth to it.

When I enter the tent, I avoid looking at him while I situate my side of the bed. What do I say? *Say something. Say something. Say something!* I war with myself.

"I'm sorry. I didn't mean to sound cross with you. You just caught me off guard."

I finally meet his eyes. "You have nothing to apologize for, Finn. I'm the one who's sorry. I should've asked if it was okay to come in."

"No, you don't have to ask; I didn't hear you. I thought you'd be out around the fire longer, and I thought I had more time. Your mind was quiet." He adjusts my pillow just how I like it and peels the sleeping bag back.

I crawl in next to Finn and face him. "Should we maybe ... I don't know. Schedule some self-love time every day? You could have time in the evenings before bed when the moon is high, and I can have time in the morning?"

His skin pulses bright. "I didn't take you for that kind of woman." The hoarseness in his voice increases. "But yeah, I'm going to need it once we're out of these woods."

"It's a great stress reliever," I whisper to no one.

I can't decipher the look on his face or gauge what might run through his head. His chest rises in a deep and measured inhale before he answers. "Yeah, I suppose it is." The faint fog of his breath swirls on his exhale, and he tucks a stray curl behind my ear.

I give him a shy smile before turning away from him. Finn puts his arm around my waist and pulls me tight against his body, and heat surges through me — from both his warmth and the contact. I slide my fingers through his and bring them up to near my chin in contentment.

I'm about to doze off when I hear a faint whisper. "Maybe in another life, you would've been just mine ..."

I could've sworn he kissed the back of my head.

CHAPTER 11

FINN

I catch Lana's elbow, helping her keep balance as she stumbles on a tree root. She's quiet, eyes downcast like she's half-asleep already. I'm both pleased and concerned by this. Pleased because she's tired; it means we can make camp and spend more time together, but I'm concerned because I've seen how the traveling wears her out, weakens her.

"Snow, Finn," she mumbles, with a sleepy lilt to her voice.

I love hearing my name on her lips.

"Where's the snow?" I smile as I catch her again and lead her to a fallen log by the side of the clearing. She sits, and I ask, "Are you hungry?"

"No," she garbles in reply as she crawls up the log, finding a dry spot and curling up into a ball.

I sigh and sit beside her, not quite touching her, but close enough to lend warmth. We sit at the top of a small valley nestled against the edge of Loier Mountain.

"Do you want to talk?" I ask, wanting to keep her alert if she's not hungry. I want to gauge her health to see how long she needs rest.

She shakes her head, not even opening her eyes.

I sigh again, shrugging out of my jacket and draping it over the top half of her body. She's still shivering, and if we're going to stay out here all night, it will at least make her more comfortable while I make camp.

As she naps, I pitch the tent, gather firewood, and find some nearby roots to cook for dinner. If I can hunt, I may even get to make a stew to help warm her. Months of traveling with no real reprieve from the cold doesn't bode well for Earth-dwellers.

I worry about her. She's not eating enough; she seems colder despite the coat I lent her, and now she's falling asleep before I've even set up camp. I look for smooth round rocks and gather them near the fire. I can heat these up and place them between the blankets to help keep her warm inside the tent.

Stripping out of my shirt and pants, it leaves me in a short-sleeved shirt and thin cotton boxers. I walk to the river, washing off in the cold water, and think about how I can convince Lana to come to Rift Pass while we wait for an answer to her petition for an audience with the kings.

A small fish swims upstream, and I cloak myself to catch it. Its soft belly rests in my hands and is none the wiser when I raise them out of the water. I gut the animal on the shore and clean it, preparing to cook it for dinner.

Snow slushes under my feet as I walk, and my breath puffs out in front of me as it freezes. Once I reach the campfire, I place the fish into the pot of roots and gather the stones inside the tent.

"Lana," I say softly, shaking her shoulder to wake her. She stirs, grumbles a little and sits up. Several curls fall into her face.

"We're going to eat," I motion to the fire, "and then we'll go to sleep." I glance at the sky. We still have hours until dusk, but it doesn't matter. She needs restorative sleep.

Lana putters around camp, trying to help with dinner, but she's so slow and clumsy I have to stop her from hurting herself. How long have we been at this? Witches aren't built like fae.

I hand her a bowl of warmed soup and get her to eat it, even though she's not hungry. She drinks some water, too, and scoots closer to my side when I offer to help warm her. The fish and roots are good, and she eats everything.

"Tomorrow we're taking a rest day. You need some time to recuperate, and then we'll continue."

When she doesn't object, I lead her into the tent. Goosebumps line her body when I help peel her out of her clothes, right down to her underwear and bra. Skin-on-skin with a Luna fae is what she needs. She sighs as she slips inside the blankets, pulling them up to cover her face. I build up as much of a fire as I can manage, dress down, and go to lie beside her.

The stones provide some warmth, but the temps are still freezing. Lana whimpers softly in her sleep, curling up on her side like an infant. I roll closer, keeping as much of my skin against hers as possible. She doesn't wake up, but she relaxes again with me next to her. I pull her back against my chest and wrap my arm around her waist, bringing her flush to me, and she sighs in contentment.

Her heart rate slows, her breathing deepens, and my warmth seeps into her. I think she's finally sleeping soundly. Even her mind has been quiet all day, preserving its energy.

I tug the blankets up higher and close my eyes. My skin gives off a bright glow, not from arousal, but from healing. I've pushed her too hard for too long, and if it means we have to stay in bed, plastered to each other for weeks, I'll do it. Although it's important she reaches Convectus Castle to meet with the kings, she needs the rest—however long it takes.

How has this creature burrowed so deep into my heart? Is this what a soul bond does? Causes me to throw all reason out the window, and allow her to put herself in front of the kings with no guarantee of getting what she wants?

I want to hide her, protect her from prying eyes, and claim her to myself. Forget her vampire mates. The kings. Hard truths.

CHAPTER 12

FINN

Three days I lie here, only getting up to refuel the fire and relieve myself. Exhaustion weighs heavy on both of us, and I should sleep even more, but her bare skin against mine is distracting. I'm not sure I'll get any more rest, but I can give her this.

"Psst."

I open my eyes and glance down to find her looking up at me, a smirk on her face. "I'm awake," I say, and she giggles softly.

Lana gets into a silly mood when she's bone-tired. It seems to make her bolder. "I'm sorry I fell asleep on you." She sits up. "But I really needed to rest."

"I know." I pluck at a loose string in the sleeping bag. "You still do. Maybe we should stay a few more days." I hesitate a moment before continuing. "You need a break."

"I think you might need a break, too." Eight words say so much.

I smooth my hand over her wild hair, tucking it behind her ear before kissing the top of her head. I don't want her to see how much she affects me. "Let's sleep now."

"If you insist," Lana says with a giggle, pushing my arm aside and shifting onto her side so she can face away from me. I'm not sure what tempted her to tease me like this, but it's cute. Maybe she doesn't know how adorable she is when she's playful? She shimmies against me until our hips line up, then wiggles until we're twined together perfectly.

She's warming up, and the curve of her back fits perfectly against my torso. I wrap an arm around her waist and pull her in tight, my hand resting on her stomach, just under the swell of her breasts.

Her thoughts give her away. If I were willing to share her, there'd be no question. I pretend she's mine as I drift off to sleep.

I WAKE WITH A START, my head fuzzy and thick with sleep. I've been drooling on Lana's hair. Hope she doesn't notice.

We're nestled together side by side, our heads touching, and our bodies twined together. My arm still wraps around her waist and her hand cups my face, stroking my cheekbone with her thumb as I let myself wake fully.

I shift my hips ever so slightly, and Lana inhales sharply. Her heart rate speeds up, and a flush spreads across her cheeks as I adjust against her. My free hand rests on her stomach while the other slides into the nape of her hair, using my magic to help detangle it.

"Good morning," I whisper against her cheek, then kiss it softly.

Lana's eyes close and she shivers in my arms. "Morning." Her voice is soft with sleep and something else laced underneath it. Desire? Interest? Anticipation?

She presses back against me, shifting until our bodies align from the tips of our toes to the tops of our heads. My breath catches in my chest, my skin is suddenly too warm and my heart pounding.

Lana's hand slides around to cup the back of my head, her fingers threading through my hair until they rest at the nape of my neck. Birds chirp in the trees overhead, oblivious to the battle waging inside me. I'm not sure if she's encouraging me or asking me to hold back. I decide to take her actions for what they are and move forward slowly, giving her time to pull away.

She doesn't. I continue looking into her deep blue eyes until our lips meet.

It starts out slow—a soft sigh in the wind—but heat quickly builds between us. My mouth opens under hers and our tongues tangle together sweetly the way you'd think two lovers would kiss.

One thump.

Two.

Our hearts keeping time with each other's, galloping towards a finish line we have no business being near.

My hand on her stomach slides around to grip her hip, and she lets out a breathless moan as my thumb brushes the underside of one breast. I tilt my chin so I can move to kiss along her jawline, then down the long line of her neck. As my lips brush over the tendon above where her pulse is pounding, Lana gasps and grips me tighter. Her hips shift forward against me, pressing into my thigh that's wedged between hers. She wants more.

I groan. "Gods, do I want you." I pull us apart before we make any poor decisions about how far we can go without crossing a line neither of us is prepared for yet.

"Yeah," Lana says with a hint of embarrassment in her voice. "I'm sorry."

"Don't apologize," I whisper against her mouth. "I'm glad you feel this, too."

We stay pressed together but unmoving, lips barely touching as we breathe each other in.

"Lana ..." I start, not sure what I'm trying to say.

"I know," she interrupts. She takes my hand in hers and squeezes. "I know."

A grin sneaks its way across my face. "I didn't say anything. But I want to be clear; there's no pressure. I'm not trying to make you do anything you don't want to."

She nods and quirks up the side of her mouth in a hint of a smile. "I know."

"If you ever want this, I'm not going to say no."

"Finn." Lana looks at me seriously. "I want you. But things are complicated, and you won't share me, so I … can't."

"I'm not here to make your life more complicated."

Lana laughs. An honest, amused sound that makes my own lips twitch.

"I appreciate that." Her face is stoic, but I can hear the smile in her words. "I need to settle some things before this goes any further."

Lana's body language is easy to read: she wants me and wants to be with me. Her mind tells me she hesitates, and I know it has everything to do with what she left behind.

CHAPTER 13

LANA

My body overheats, and I can't move. The heavy weight on me makes me groan. I've turned onto my stomach, and Finn has me completely pinned beneath him — his leg swung over my ass and his heavy arm across my back. I grunt and groan, trying to get his tree-trunk-sized limbs off of me, but his erection against my back causes me to pause.

His hips thrust against me several times — his cock seeking my heat, so I arch my ass into him. I let out a soft moan when his hand snakes under my hoodie and tightens around my chest. He kneads my breast, and I guide his hand down the front of my sweats and into my panties. The glow of his Luna order illuminates the tent and I watch as his other hand grips the pillow.

His expert fingers slide against my core before plunging them into me and grinding his palm against my clit, all while moving his hips against me like the steady roll of the ocean. I reach behind me and free his erection from his sweatpants. My fingers barely fit around the soft velvet of his circumference, and I pump it while I ride his palm. His hot breath on my neck drives me wild, making a beeline straight to between my thighs, and I shimmy my sweats down.

I poise his thick length at my entrance and I'm about to beg him to fuck me when I startle out of my daze.

"Jesus Christ!" I curse.

Finn freezes, and we jump apart from each other. He immediately takes in the situation and swears.

"Fuck, Lana. Fuck!" He pants while tucking himself away and I scramble to pull my bottoms up. "I was dreaming, and when I woke, we're ... fuck! I am *so sorry*." He's talking a mile a minute now. "Gods, I thought I was *dreaming*!"

"No, it isn't just your fault. I'm to blame, too. I should've recognized we were dreaming."

"Luna magic has dominion over our dreams, although I'm impressed you could snap out of it at all. Must be because we're near the edge of the forest; your magic feels your pull."

I try to ignore the erection tenting his sweats, but my eyes keep finding it. My skin heats at the memory of it pressed so close to me and the feel of my hands wrapped around him. I clear my throat and shake my head.

Taking measure of his flushed cheeks and the bright glow from his skin, I know his thoughts aren't far off from mine. "I think I'll be taking my quiet time now, Finn."

He gives me a hooded smile and inclines his head before exiting the tent. No sooner does the zipper close do I throw myself to the pallet of blankets and hike the front of the hoodie up to ease the ache in my breasts. My hand is down the front of my pants just as fast. I place the body pillow between my legs and grip it with my thighs while I stroke my fingers up and down my slit. I am so wet and can still feel Finn's thick fingers pleasing me. When I straddle the pillow and start grinding against it, I try to keep my moans quiet.

I take my pleasure from Finn's pillow. It turns me on knowing I'm leaving my scent all over his things. Does he think of me while fucking his fist? Would he have spent his seed in me if I didn't stop us just now?

Does he fuck?

Or would he take his time with me?

With his fae strength, I imagine he fucks well and thoroughly. My orgasm builds, and I remember the feel of Finn's palm rubbing against my clit while his fingers impale me. All I'd have to do is ask, and I know he'd be in here wringing my desire from me while he drives into me with his massive cock. Maybe I should ask him. I can see it now — his icy blue eyes pinning me just as much as his body does as he sinks into me for the first time.

Guilt doesn't consume me when I think of Finn when I come, nor when I quietly call his name into the pillow as wave after wave wracks my body. My attraction to him doesn't diminish what I feel for my other mates.

I collapse on top of the cushion and just lay there, chest heaving and yet still so unsatisfied. While this was one of my best self-orgasms, it doesn't beat the real thing.

After several minutes, I emerge from the tent and spot him sitting in front of the fire. The temps are below freezing, but his shirt is off, and his skin is bright with his cerulean glow. His chest heaves.

Did he ...? No. Maybe he went for a run.

"It was hard not to when I was the subject of your fantasy while you thoroughly fucked my pillow."

Okay ... so I guess we're going there.

"I'm not even sorry. What else am I supposed to think of immediately after you buried your fingers in me and nearly your cock?"

"Then I'm not sorry, either. It took everything I had in me not to accept the invitation you laid at my feet." He stands. "I about lost my will to resist when I heard my name on your lips while you fucked yourself. And to answer your question, I'd make love to you *before* thoroughly fucking you."

Holy shit. I squeeze my thighs together at the thought. Finn sends a brief image of him taking me in my mind.

"This is what you do to me every time you picture us together, and it sends images and clips of what's going on in your head, and you're driving me crazy."

"Sorry, I don't mean to make you uncomfortable."

"You're not making me uncomfortable." He picks up a pebble and tosses it before turning towards me again. "It's just a reminder of what I can't have." His hands run through his hair. "Look, Lana ... I have to tell you something. I—"

Finn angles his head to the side and freezes. In one swift move, he is behind me with a hand wrapped around my mouth and crushes my back to his chest. He puts up a finger to his lips and tells me in my mind a group of males are nearby. I nod at him, and he cloaks us. The campsite is spelled from detection, but they can still hear us talking or making noise. I take a long while to listen to what Finn heard minutes ago — loud men discussing the cession of someone important and the imbalance it's causing the realm.

Fear of another fae encounter like my first one, I stand frozen, eyes wide. Finn and I remain plastered together like this for another good twenty minutes after we stop hearing the group, just in case.

Only now does it feel safe to pack up so we can be on our way. It's only a few days' walk to town, and I'm so relieved and excited, but terrified. Relieved because we'll be back to civilization, with an actual bed and technology. Terrified because three kings, known for their cunning, hold the key to my entire future. Will the rest of my time on Earth be but a blip on the infinite timeline my mates live? Or will I spend the rest of eternity basking in the love of my parents, my mates, and my children?

I see my mom, hovering over the stove while dad looks adoringly at her from where he's propped on the counter. I see the twins attending prom, their dads staring down their dates in the foyer, doing their best to intimidate them. I see us uniting Earth and Bedlam, creating a harmonious existence free of fear or persecution.

And when I see Finn, he's there, too, having become an integral part of our lives. He's learned to share and get along with my other mates.

One can hope.

CHAPTER 14

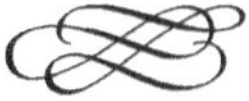

LANA

It's nightfall when we reach the forest's edge. The pleasant hum of energy races through my body, and I know without a doubt, my magic is back in full force. I squeal in delight and begin doing every single spell I can think of, much to Finn's amusement. He follows me around, laughing as I create tiny sparks in my hands, turn small seeds into towering trees, and make the wind howl at my command. It feels amazing to be able to use my magic again, and I can tell Finn is enjoying himself too.

Eventually, we collapse onto the forest floor, exhausted but happy. I lean my head against Finn's chest and listen to the steady thumping of his heartbeat as we watch the stars twinkle overhead. He pats my thigh.

"We had better get into town before everything closes." I grumble but reluctantly get to my feet. I dust myself off and take Finn's hand, feeling contentment fill me as we walk into town.

A breeze blows a curl free from behind my ear, and I whip my head towards him. I face him and clutch the front of his shirt while burying my head in his chest. Closing my eyes, I inhale.

When I open them, Finn has a bemused eyebrow cocked up, and the soft glow of his order is like a warm blanket on a cool night.

"My gods, have you always smelled like that?!"

"Like what?" he asks, a little self-consciously.

I close my eyes and inhale again. It's been too many long months of not being able to use my witches' nose. I envision running through an apple orchard, tapping maple trees, and finishing the day with a glass of smooth bourbon on the rocks.

"Your scent ... I could eat you. Caramelized apples, maple, bourbon. Maybe even a little cinnamon and vanilla."

He quirks his eyebrow further. "And this is a good thing? For me to smell like Earth food?"

"Oh, very." I take another huge inhale through my nose. Finn has an endearing smile on his face when I look up, and I step back to put some space between us.

"Sorry." I hop back more and adjust my clothes.

"I don't mind." There's definitely a gleam of something in his eye.

The first town we come to is a small village called Gala, with cobbled stones and mostly deserted streets. What little I spy from our vantage point in the shadows is already so different from Earth. The buildings are made of many materials, from stone to metal to woven tree branches. The few people on the streets are even more diverse than the structures they live in: some with wings, others without; some who can turn into animals and back again, while others have skin that changes color with their emotions. My eyes can't catalog fast enough. I make a private vow to myself: when this is all said and done, I'll bring my twins back here so we can experience this together.

Before we leave the shadows, Finn glamours us. He said it's best the kings don't hear about my being in Bedlam before I send the message myself.

Gone is Finn's silvery blond hair, and in its place, his hair is black as coal. His eyes are no longer light and instead are a chocolate brown. The clothes he's wearing are simple, nondescript garments a traveler would wear. I have on a simple dress with my cloak. It's not what I'd usually wear, but it will do.

We enter the village, and it's like stepping into a different world: the scent of food cooking, the chatter of its people, tinkle of laughter, and the smooth feel of the cobblestones under my feet. I'm giddy with it all.

Finn takes my hand, and we stop in front of a bakery. I inhale the sweet, decadent scents of chocolate and sugar. He buys two pastries, and we find a spot to sit on the steps of the town hall.

He hands me a baked good and I take a bite, cupping my hand under my chin to catch the crumbs. It's delicious. The chocolate is rich, and the sugar perfectly balanced. I close my eyes and moan.

"You like?" Finn smiles.

"Mmm-hmmm." I take another bite and this time I savor the flavor, rolling it around on my tongue. My hand stills while I take in the peculiarity of the fae spanning the streets. "Where are the elders? And the children?"

Finn hands me his pastry. "When fae are born, we reach maturity within eighteen months and stop growing soon after. Physiologically, our bodies don't really age past a human's twenty-five years."

"You're really old, aren't you?" I think of my mates, who are each thousands of years old. Auguste is younger than Oz and Gideon, but is still far older than I am.

He chuckles and grabs my hand to bring the pastry to his mouth. Before taking a bite, he grins. I stare, transfixed while he chews, watching his mouth, and waiting on bated breath for an answer. "Older than many of the fae, but younger than some. Age is less a thing in Bedlam compared to humans with their finite lives. I've watched Earth civilizations come and go; seen the rise and fall of empires."

"What was it like? To see all that?"

He shrugs. "It was interesting, at times exhilarating, other times heartbreaking. I'm glad I can't remember all of it, though."

"Why?"

Finn takes my hand in his and rubs his thumb over my knuckles. "Some memories are best left in the past."

I close my eyes at the onslaught of memories assaulting me. Of my mom's disappearance, of my adoptive parents, of the car accident that took their lives. Of the pain and loneliness that followed.

Maybe Finn is right. Maybe some memories are best left alone.

An ache forms in my chest, and I lean into him for comfort. He wraps his arm around me and rests his chin on the top of my head.

A fae with blue skin and orange hair walks by, and I try not to gawk. Finn chuckles softly. "You'll get used to it."

I hope so, because right now I feel like a fish out of water. But there's something about this place that feels like home. It's a bizarre sense of harmony I can't explain. While my reasons for being here aren't all good, I'm happy I got to see Bedlam.

Someday, I want to bring the twins here. They would love it.

"Do you know they have colleges in Bedlam?" Finn asks, interrupting my reverie. "Some humans attend. Maybe Rose and Bennett will do a semester here, especially since they're likely to be witches."

I blink. "I hadn't thought of that."

It's true, they would be able to learn so much more here than they ever could on Earth.

"We get sent to a special academy to learn everything we need to know. It's a lot like a traditional Earth university, only we're learning a lifetime of what we need to know in four years." He tilts his head towards the confectionary in my hand. "I got the lunch lady to always save me some of these at breakfast every day."

"Do you have the mind of children at maturity? Or how does that work?" I break the pastry in half and give some back to him.

"Fae inherit their parents' intelligence at birth. Academies focus on honing their magic, building alliances with other orders, and teaching life skills." He takes a bite of the pastry and his eyes light up. "My graduating class had to do a semester undercover on Earth, and I missed the food the most. Earth food is so bland."

"Where on Earth did you go?"

He shakes his head. "It's not there anymore. This was thousands of years ago."

We finish our pastries and Finn stands, holding his hand out to me. I take it and he pulls me up. "Let's find a place to stay before it gets too late."

As soon as we get to the hotel, Finn will help me submit a request for a formal audience with the royal houses. We're unsure when we will receive a response, so we plan to sift to Rift Pass after the hotel while we wait for word from the kings.

We walk down the street, our steps in sync, and butterflies swirl in my stomach as I take in my surroundings.

CHAPTER 15

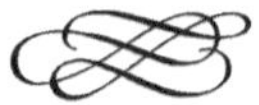

LANA

"Are you sure there are no other beds?"

"Deary, we only have five rooms in this inn." She places the key in my hand. "You'll have to take this bedroom."

I try not to stare at her. Her words are those of an old lady, but she appears younger than me.

I give Finn a defeated look and puff my cheeks on a sigh. We've been sleeping next to each other for months now — I suppose another night won't kill me. The receptionist doesn't make any remarks about my lack of a suitcase.

We'll get you some proper-fitting clothes.

I don't know what I would've done if I hadn't run into Finn. I'd probably be dead by now, or worse.

We climb the wooden stairs and locate the door to room five at the very end of the hallway in its own alcove. I'm surprised it's not like a modern inn you'd find on Earth. Instead, it has an old-world boutique hotel feel to it. The door sticks a bit, but as soon as Finn opens it, I smell mahogany. He walks in and inspects the place before nodding his head for me to come in.

"You know, I have my magic back now. I could already tell no one was in the room, thanks to my third eye."

"I could, too, but there's far more to worry about than just a person or fae."

"Like what?" I scoot in closer to him and dart my eyes around the room.

"Traps, explosives, that kind of thing."

Oh. He'll have to show me how to detect those, too. The room is cozy and comprises a twin-sized bed, a large, curtained window, a winged-back chair, and a bathroom half the size of the bedroom. Why such a small bed when there's so much room? My eyes immediately find the large bath in the bathroom, and I groan. Thank the gods. They sacrificed a big bed for a soaking tub.

Finn stands behind me while I'm in the bathroom's door to follow my gaze.

"You want a bath?"

"Yes, just about more than anything right now."

He chuckles. "Alright, I'm going to see about finding you some proper clothes while you bathe. There should be a shop a few minutes' walk from here."

I close the heavy wooden door before stripping out of Finn's clothes and darting to the tub. This bath is several feet deep and perfect for soaking my weary muscles. I look underneath the stone basin when I don't see the faucet or handles for turning it on. The wall shows nothing, either.

"Finn?"

He answers me from the bedroom, so I grab a towel from the bar and wrap it around me. I peek my head out the door and ask how I turn this thing on. He laughs, giving a shake of his head before heading towards me. I open the door and step aside. It's impossible to miss the slow once-over he gives me in the towel, but he doesn't comment on it, and neither do I.

I watch as Finn presses his hand against the ceiling over the tub and a shower head extends down. It's on a gooseneck of sorts, and he pulls it closer to the tub. He gives me a tilt of his head to beckon me closer and shows the buttons on the side of the showerhead.

"Press this one to turn on the water, and this one to adjust the temperature. Once the bath is halfway filled, you can press this button to turn on the massagers. Press the first one again to shut everything off, and this one to drain."

I study the ceiling. "What do short people do? Have tall people start their baths for them?"

He gives me a proud grin. "No one is short here."

Oh, right? I suppose any witches from Earth would just use their magic to get the showerhead down, too. At 5'10", I'm pretty tall for a female Earth dweller, but I'm dwarfed by Finn and any other fae we've come across. Seven-ish feet tall appears to be the norm.

He shows me how to access the panel with soapberries and leaves the room. Shortly after, I hear him enchant the room so no one — fae or otherwise — can get in while he's gone.

I fill the tub and make quick work of washing my body and hair before sitting back and doing my best to relax. I'm a bundle of nerves over finally getting to send my petition. Finn mentioned it's relatively easy for the kings to make me immortal, and with my being the Queen of Vampires, they might say yes on that basis alone. Allyship and all that.

With their combined power, they should also be able to investigate where my mom is. An insidious thought niggles at my consciousness.

Or what happened to her.

A sense of panic races through me at the thought she might be dead.

I press the button for the massagers, and trim panels open along the inside of the tub like jets. Sinking below the water, I hold my breath, trying to force my distress to ebb. I still my breathing, just as I sense Finn disabling the wards.

"Still bathing?" He's on the other side of the door.

"Just finished." I push the button to drain the water from the tub. Finn says they recycle the water of any pollutants and treatment facilities purify it to be used as drinking water.

I wrap my hair in a towel, only because I don't have a t-shirt to scrunch it, and throw another towel around my body before exiting the bathroom. Finn is taking many clothes and accessories out of the several bags on the bed.

"Oh, this is too much." I stare at the small hoard he bought.

"You have nothing to your name. While I love seeing you in my clothes," he grins, "and out of them, I'm sure you'd appreciate some of your own size. I'm happy to do it," He tosses me pajamas and underwear.

"Thank you." I tuck my clothes under my arm. I've never been very comfortable with people spending their money on me. "How did you know what size to get me?"

He makes a point of looking at me from my head to my toes before responding. "I just know." He gives no further explanation.

Okay then.

I unwrap the towel around my head, and Finn comes to run his fingers through my hair to dry it with his magic — per our routine. Unfortunately, this is magic inherent to his order and not something he can teach me. I don't mind, though. It's soothing to have him do it. It's a little different now that I can smell him ... it does all kinds of things to me with him this close. I don't realize I've closed my eyes until his hands still and he steps back. When I open them, his skin gives off a faint glow, and he cups the back of his neck before turning towards the bed.

My weary feet carry me to the bathroom so I can slip into my new pajamas. The bottoms are shorts, and the top is a camisole. The silk glides across my skin, and it's like being wrapped in a warm hug. After months of camping and hiking in the woods, the luxury fabric is a welcome reprieve.

When I emerge from the bathroom, Finn's skin pulses bright when he sees me. He gets a good, long fill before waving me over to where he sits in the worn leather chair near the window, a lamp illuminating the near-white waves of his hair. In his lap is a tiny silver device. I settle on the arm of the chair, curious about what he's up to.

"What's this?"

He pushes a small blue button on the contraption, which shoots a beam of light in front of us. It's enchanted, if the buzzing sensation coming from it tells me anything. "It's a hologram recorder. This is how you'll petition for an audience with the royals. Introduce yourself, and request to meet with them. Do *not* tell them why."

There's an edge of tight-laced fear in his voice. Although, the grip he has on the small piece of metal, and his sudden preternatural stillness might signal something else entirely.

"Why?" I jump up to change out of pajamas. If I'm going to be on video, I need to look presentable. "I'll be right back; I've got to change." My legs are like jelly from the nerves.

"You're fine in these pajamas." He tugs me back down and chooses his words carefully. "Fae are curious creatures, and they will want to know why the Queen of Vampires requests an audience. They won't refuse to slake their curiosity, especially when you're going to be cavalier about it."

I bite my lip. "You're sure this will work?" My trembling hands run through my hair, trying to flatten the wild mess of curls.

"I know it will." Though he tries to put on an unaffected air, melancholy clings to his voice and unease lines his features.

Okay ...

Finn sucks a deep breath into his lungs before he crosses the room to reach into his backpack. He pulls out a thick paperback and tosses it to me. "You should look as though you're reading this while I pan the camera to you."

I inspect the cover. "*Power Dynamics Between the Realms?*"

He grins. "Trust me. I picked it up when I got you clothes. The kings will think you're ready to ally."

Alright, here goes nothing. I lower myself into the chair and swing my legs so they hang over the arm, and open the book to the middle. With a deep breath, I close my eyes briefly and nod towards Finn. He rotates the camera towards me.

"Hey boys," I set the book on my lap, making sure the cover is visible. Finn gives me a Cheshire grin while I amp up my bravado as much as possible. "I'm sure you know the Queen of the Vampires when you see her. I'd like a word. Have your people get in touch with my people." I wink and return to reading my book.

Finn slumps onto the bed with his mouth agape. I shrug and pick at my cuticles. "What? You told me to be cavalier. Do you want me to re-shoot?"

He shakes his head. "You are exceptional."

A nervous chuckle bubbles from my throat and I swing my legs back to the front of the chair to stand. "I was the lead in a lot of plays in high school. What now? Do you think it'll work?" I seat myself next to him on the bed, breathing in his scent. It calms me.

"They'll grant it, but first the message will pass through the proper channels before making its way to the kings. We'll likely hear back in the next three weeks, and the royals will leave their castles to meet at Convectus Castle to give you your audience."

I lay my head on his shoulder. "That easy?"

"That easy."

I stretch and rub my hands down my thighs. "Thank you. Seriously, if it weren't for you ..."

"Hey." His hand comes up to tilt my chin towards him. "I won't let you face any of this alone, alright?" I nod and he lets go.

The rumble of my stomach interrupts our conversation, and Finn laughs before taking my hand. "Let me show you how the fae order in food."

CHAPTER 16

LANA

$\mathcal{I}$ let out a moan as I sink into the soft mattress. Have I ever felt a bed so heavenly? No. Never in my life. With a quirked eyebrow, Finn rounds the corner from where he was washing up.

"Despite hearing what's in your head, I still expected to walk into a completely different scenario just now." He ducks when I toss a pillow at him. He scoops it up and throws it back, but I catch it. Finn turns the light off before he peels the covers back and slides in. "Mm, you're right. This bed is great."

I flop on my side to face him. "Right?!" It makes me curious why there's a twin-sized bed in Bedlam at all. All fae are huge.

Every night for the last several months, I've slept in this man's arms for warmth. Now, we're in a toasty hotel room in a bed that also gives next to no room.

"Thanks again," I whisper into the dark.

Finn reaches to cup my cheek. Like a moth to a flame, I close my eyes against the feel of his warm palm.

"I don't think I'll ever tire of this." I meet his icy blue stare, now visible, thanks to the glow coming off his skin.

"So don't." His words shoot straight into me and settle in my chest.

"Come with me to Earth," I blurt out.

His eyes widen before I slam mine shut. I recoil and face away from him, cringing while I internally shake my head. How would I explain this to my family? Never mind that Finn already told me he'd never share me.

The longer the silence stretches between us, the more I regret what I said. I shrink into the bed and pull the covers over my head. Foolish.

"Lana—" he begins but I interrupt him.

"Never mind. Goodnight, Finn."

He huffs a frustrated sigh. "Turn over, please."

Holding my breath, I turn over again to face him. He raises his arm so I can nestle in the crook. I slide my hand across his chest and swing my bent knee, so it rests against the front of him.

"I'll come with you." Finn kisses the top of my head.

"Wait. What?" My eyes fly open to meet his.

"For as long as you'll have me, I can set aside my jealousy if it means I can be with you."

My heart beats wildly, threatening to gallop right out of me. "As long as I'll have you?"

He rolls his eyes before grinning. "You can try to get rid of me."

I smile into his chest and bite my lip. When I meet his eyes again, deep affection covers his features.

"Earth food, though, remember? It's bland."

He raises a brow. "I'd feast with the Caspari—the beasts who eat Bedlam's garbage—if it'd make you happy."

A smile teases my lips before it settles into a mask of neutrality. "And what about what will make *you* happy?"

He tugs me closer to him. "You do." the deep rumble of his voice has a hint of amusement. "It's always you."

My breathing shallows. "And what if my mates say no?" I've thought a lot about this. They won't say no—not if it makes me happy —but I need to know what Finn would do on the off-chance they did.

"How can someone look at what we have, and say no?" He twines his fingers through mine, taking them with him as he gestures wildly. "How can they look at a bird, and not see a bird? How can they hear the gallop of a horse's hooves, and not think of a horse? I'd spend the rest of my immortal life convincing them of what's right in front of them if I had to."

"What are you saying, Finn?"

"Love, Lana. How can any man, creature, monster, or beast not see that I would bleed for you? Protect you with all that I have, and all that I am? Give up everyone and everything, follow you to the ends of any realm and any time?"

Tears spring to my eyes. "Finn—"

He shakes his head. "They'd be fools to deny you the love I lay at your feet with no expectation of any in return. Take it. It's yours. *It's always been yours.*"

My eyes dart around the shadowed room while I let his words sink in. "You love me?" Why his words shock me, I don't know. As the months have passed, denying it has become impossible.

An amused chuckle rumbles his chest. "Isn't it obvious?"

Soft, rhythmic strokes of his fingers across my arm pebbles my skin with goosebumps and a smile splits my face. "You know, we all share a bed at home, right?"

"Is there room for me? I'm a good carpenter, even without magic, if we need a bigger one."

My tongue wets my lips, and a giggle boils out of me. "Yeah, there's a ton of room."

I adjust my position, causing my knee to knock into his erection. Finn clasps a firm hand over my leg to prevent it from moving.

I crack a grin, and he loosens the grip on my leg and runs his fingers along the length of my thigh back and forth. The glow from his skin intensifies. It's easy to guess where his mind might be.

He flashes images in my mind: him devouring me, tangled sheets, making love.

My skin flushes, and when the images stop, I make eye contact with him and sense something much deeper than desire. He leans down and places the lightest of kisses on my lips. That's all it takes for my walls to come down, and I pull his face back to mine. Our mouths crash together, and Finn slides his hand down my back and rests on my ass before gripping it and pressing me firmly against him.

I roll on top to straddle him, pausing to marvel at the glow of his skin, the solid hold of his grip on my hips. A smile crosses my face as the heat builds, the passion between us white hot.

His luminescence is just bright enough to highlight my soft curves while I peel off my camisole, revealing nothing but skin underneath. The hunger in his icy blue eyes weakens me. Finn's hands find my breasts, thumbs stroking in tandem across my nipples. He sits up to place a stiff peak in his mouth while he wraps an arm around my waist to hold me close. His tongue brushes against the small nub before nibbling with his teeth.

A quiet moan escapes me. Finn flips us over so he's on top, resting his knees on either side of my hips. He rises to slide my shorts off, keeping his gaze pinned to the swells of my bosom. I bite my lip and arch my back while his lips press a trail down the length of my torso, pausing at the apex of my thighs, parting my legs to take in my heat.

He sinks to his elbows, resting each of my thighs on his shoulders. "You have no idea how long I've been wanting this." He glides his finger along my slit. "So wet for me already?" He doesn't break eye contact while he licks the evidence of my arousal off his finger.

His hands clasp onto my thighs and open them further before running his tongue along my center. I slide my fingers through his near-white hair, like unspoken praise for such a pleasurable gift. My breath comes out in shallow pants, whimpers and soft moans. Finn works with expert precision, giving most attention to my clit. The pleasure building at my core races towards the edge for release. He sucks the little nub between his lips, sending me spiraling with sensations I've never felt before. My muscles contract and breath hitches, while he slows his pace, riding out the last of my orgasm.

"I love those little noises you make." Finn wipes his mouth with the back of his hand. His voice is muffled.

"I think ... I think my ears are ringing." I'd heard of people who experience temporary hearing loss or ringing in the ears after orgasming, but this is my first time.

Finn raises an eyebrow. "Makes sense." He grins before I pull him to me.

"Oh, look who's a proud peacock." I purr and nibble at his bottom lip.

"Did you just say I have a proud cock?" He bucks his hips against me.

I giggle and reach my hand into his pajama bottoms, eyes widening at how I can't wrap my hand around his girth. "This isn't going to fit." I shake my head.

He slides his pants off and I get a good long look at what I have to work with. Gods, even his penis glows.

"It's ... huge!"

His abs contract as he laughs, causing his *kickstand* to bounce. "I heal when I glow. You'll feel no pain ... I think."

I pull him to me and roll on top. If we're doing this, I'm going to control entry until I know he can't impale me. I let my hair down and run my tongue along the length of my hand. His attention flicks to my tongue before dropping to where my grip works in tandem with my mouth to give extra lubrication to his length. Finn curses and gathers my hair to one side so he can have an unobstructed view.

I bring him close before backing off. He helps move me to a sitting position on his thighs before I hover over him. Gripping his shaft in my hand, I place him at my entrance and lower myself inch-by-inch. There's no pain, only unimaginable pleasure as I sink to the hilt, both of us moaning on an exhale. He fits perfectly, riding the line between bliss and ache. Finn grasps my waist, and together we lower me up and down in long, languid movements.

"Is this okay?"

I nod. "Perfect." I lean down and press my mouth to his, tasting the remnants of my release on his tongue.

He flips us so fast; I barely register he's on top now. His pace quickens, pushing into me faster now that I'm adjusted to him. My nails score down his back, legs tightening to keep him close. Everything about this moment is exquisite, each sensation heightened by the way we fit as though made for one another.

My body constricts around him, pleasure building inside of me until it spills over in bright flashes of light behind my eyelids. Finn groans against my neck as his hips stutter against mine before stilling completely. His eyes search mine, for what, I don't know. He looks as though he's about to say something before deciding against it. Instead, he plants his mouth on mine in a slow, sensual kiss.

Everything about this moment feels right, and all the moments that come next. Our days, we spend in bed, making love as though our very lives depend on it, only leaving for food and hygiene. We wrap around each other, always touching, hearts racing every time our hands brush against one another, and our eyes never stop finding reasons to meet. We fit together like matching puzzle pieces, and I love this feeling almost as much as I love him.

CHAPTER 17

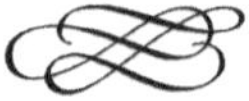

OZ

Rose and Bennett lay in the living room, bodies trembling. Their skin is a pale blue color, eyes half-lidded, barely able to muster any sense of alertness. Rose's mouth hangs open as she tries to breathe. Bennett isn't in any better shape, though he keeps looking at his sister to make sure she's okay. I cling to their frail life forms, trying to heal them with magic while Gideon feeds them his blood.

I'm at a complete loss. None of my magic seems to work. I've seen nothing like this before, where they're fine one minute, and the next, barely clinging to life. Shivers wrack their small bodies, and I fear they'll die without my help. I can't lose them, too.

My gaze flicks to Gideon's.

"We have to do something—"

In a whirlwind of speed, Pippa and Auguste rush into the room with medical equipment. I help set up vitals, and Gideon refuses to let Auguste take his place giving the twins blood.

"I can't heal them." My voice comes out as a choked whisper. I'm the only one with healing magic here, and I can't heal my own children. Not even blood helps. In my 5,500 years, this has never happened.

My chin trembles despite the clenching of my jaw, but no tears fall.

Pippa takes my hand, squeezing once in acknowledgment. The gesture doesn't stop the shaking in my body, nor does it soothe away my anxiety, but I appreciate it all the same.

"It's only been a few hours," Pippa reminds me. "We need to give them more time."

I nod, unable to get my mouth to work. We haven't left their side since they fell ill. How can I stand by, watching, waiting? I can't fail them, too.

When Pippa draws their blood, neither of them flinches. The twins should struggle, trying to escape the vile needle, but it's as if they don't even notice. Vitals register on the screen, but otherwise no change occurs.

"They're just children." Gideon's voice cracks, his face betraying the pain he feels. I grip his hand, and we wait in silence. "We promised her. Promised we'd keep them safe."

Tears pour from his red eyes, and I clutch at the fabric of his shirt, leaning into him. A cavern opens in my chest, pulling me in, drowning me in pain. The world fades, and I choke back the sobs that want to escape my throat.

I fall to my knees, clutching one of each of their hands. Praying to any god or deity who will listen for them to take me and not my children.

"No." Gideon's voice jolts me back into my body. I look up to find him with his head down, staring at the twins. "I won't let them die." Another tear falls from bloodshot eyes and drips on the floor, his head still hung low.

He slouches down next to me, hand trembling as it pushes through his messy hair. "I can feel them slipping away."

Tears continue to fall, my throat closing in pain. How can I lose them? My hand covers my mouth to muffle my cries, but they come out like fits of coughing. I don't know what to do. Pippa and Auguste look at each other, fear in their eyes, but neither has a solution. The room turns cold as my magic swirls around us, half full of fury at being helpless, and the other, agony.

One of Pippa's medical staff runs into the room with their labs, and she pours over them, eyes darting across the text.

Gideon stands, pacing back and forth. "What is it?"

Pippa doesn't look up from the paper she's reading, her face taking on a haunting pallor. Her hand goes to her mouth, and I jump up. "What is it?"

She doesn't answer, hands shaking as she hands the paper to Auguste. He reads it, clearing his throat before he turns to look at us. "Their cells are changing?"

"Into what?" I bite out, not sure if the hot anger I feel is from fear or fury.

Pippa shakes her head and points to some numbers. "I've never seen this before. Look at how fast these cells duplicate."

I yank the labs out of Auguste's hands and scan them, looking for any anomaly that might explain what's happening. The kids were fine one minute and the next, deathly ill.

When I find nothing, my body collapses. "I don't know what these cells are, either." My knees hit the floor with a thud. I drape my arms over the children. "I can't lose them."

Auguste kneels beside me, placing a hand on my shoulder.

"We'll figure this out. Together." His hand squeezes my shoulder, and I lean into his touch.

Oz

"DADDY?"

My eyes slide open, and I shoot up at the sight before me. Rose and Bennett are fine: a healthy glow, smooth skin, and rosy cheeks. I crush them in my arms just as the others rouse from their positions across the room. Sweet relief sinks into my chest and I smile, tears threatening to fall. "You're okay!"

I pull back from their embrace, looking them over. They're fine. Nothing but two little ankle-biters in pajamas. I stand with them still in my arms, and I can't hold back my tears. The weight being lifted off my shoulders relaxes my entire body. Their sickness is gone, along with most of that horrible ache in my chest at imagining life without them.

Gideon scoops them out of my arms, burying his head between them. They pass between Auguste, Pippa, and Dad before attempting to push away so they can toddle around the floor.

After checking their vitals and ensuring their health, Pippa leaves to let the rest of the family know the twins are okay.

"Bennett, Rose." Gideon approaches, his tone heartbroken.

The kids look between us before they frown and burst into tears. "Daddy sad?"

He swallows and closes the distance to run his hands through their hair. Rose and Bennett cry harder, clinging to his shirt. "Daddy's just happy now."

"No sad?" Rose shakes her head, pulling back to look him in the eyes.

He pulls her and Bennett in again, holding them tight. "I'm so happy you two are okay. "

I join in the hug, tears streaming down my cheeks. Relief is a powerful thing. And for the first time since Lana left for Bedlam, I can breathe easier.

Bennett rubs his eyes, looking up at me. "Boo-boo, Dada?"

I shake my head, smiling at the concern in his face. "No. I'm fine now that you two are okay."

Rose scrunches up her face, arms tight around Gideon's neck. She nods and looks at me with a furrowed brow. "Sad, Dada?"

I glance at Bennett and rub my sternum. "Nope." I sit on the floor and pull them in again, kissing their foreheads. "All better."

Their little chests rise and fall as they giggle. When I pull their faces to mine, Rose makes a kissy face. I give her one back, and she giggles again before pulling at my lip with her pudgy little fingers.

"Dada, you funny."

I smile widely and pull them into another hug.

CHAPTER 18

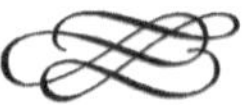

LANA

While we wait to hear if the kings will grant an audience for me to plead my case, Finn suggests going to his home in Rift Pass. We're like two thru-hikers, complete with large backpacks holding our stuff on our backs. I've never tried to teleport so many things through to another destination before, but I'll never know if we don't try. He can sift us, but I need the practice after not having done it for months. I think back to all the times I've teleported before; I simply envision the finest of details in my mind of a place, and the ground opens for me to slip through space or time.

Finn embraces me in his arms and whispers in my ear. "Nestled between two Rift Pass peaks, you'll find a house whose interior we carved of alabaster stone. A river runs underneath the house and spills over the side of the mountain to create the most beautiful waterfall you'll ever see. Clear floors mean you see can the water beneath your feet, and sections of the floor even allow you to reach your hand in to touch it. No matter which window you face on the south side of the house, you have a view of the Sea of Triune."

With my eyes squeezed tight, I build his home in my head and pull Finn through the opening I've created in the floor below us. A few minutes later, we step onto the clear glass floors.

Finn kisses my forehead. "Welcome home."

We slide the backpacks off our shoulders, and he takes me through the house. I trail my free hand against the smooth, bone-white walls. The sound of running water resonates throughout his home. Everything in this place is made of natural elements—less like a hunting lodge and more like a relaxing spa. On the back side of the house is a snow-covered valley far below, and on the other: the sea.

Walking towards the front of the house, my eye catches on a large silver fish under our feet. I marvel at the translucent fins resting like wings on its back, and follow its movement below. The current starts taking it faster, right towards the massive waterfall. I run out the patio doors and onto deck above the falls.

"It's going to go over!"

I clutch onto Finn when he comes to my side. He whispers in my ear. "Watch."

The fish spills over the ledge, and I watch the poor creature fall. The drop has to be thousands of feet; it won't survive. No sooner does the thought pass my mind do I see something rise through the mist. Those weren't fins on the back of the fish.

They're wings.

The beautiful creature dips and swoops through the spray before soaring into the air and out of sight.

"We call those spirit fish. No one has ever caught one because they're magic-resistant."

"What I wouldn't give for wings of my own." I turn towards Finn. "My flying is far less graceful without them. Can you imagine, feeling the wind gliding over your feathers as though you weigh nothing more than a paper plane?"

He winces. "This is probably where I should tell you about mine."

I laugh and tug him by the hand to go back inside, but pause when he stays put. "Finn?"

"Only certain fae have wings. One feather can fetch a fortune that would last generations because they can restore the dead. The amount of time the dead can come back to life for depends on the power of the fae. Sometimes it's only a few minutes, other times it's days, years, millennia. Forever, even." He leans against the railing before taking me into his arms. "They're so prized in our realm, most never show their wings, except to their mate."

I stare at him for a moment. Two. "You're serious?"

"No one has seen my wings. Not even my parents. Fae aren't born with them; they acquire them during puberty." He kisses the top of my head.

Lana

A WHOOSH of air blows my hair back and something blots out the sun. My eyes dart up and witness a sight so majestic, I weep. Finn flinches when my fingers trail over his golden downy feathers, marveling at the buttery soft feel of silk against my skin. He lets out a shudder and I spy cerulean feathers along the tips. These are the largest feathers, giving off a pulsating glow, matching the rest of his skin when he's healing.

"These are the most beautiful wings I've ever seen." I choke on a whisper. These can't be real. Finn cups his hands to my face and wipes away my tears, but more just fall in their place. He kisses each damp cheek before scooping me into his arms and bringing me inside. My mate carries me up a flight of stairs to a bedroom taking up an entire floor.

He peels out of his clothes, but I can't take my eyes off the plume of feathers dusting the floor. Finn chuckles. "I'm glad you like them."

I shake my head. "I love them." My eyes meet his. "Gods ... I love *you*. Thank you for trusting me with this gift."

He kisses my fingers. "I love you more than I could ever put into words."

Finn lays me down on the bed before stretching out next to me. "I don't know how many millennia I dreamt of finding you." His fingers twine through my hair, stroking my curls. "Dreamt of bringing my soul bonded mate to this mountain house, where I spent so many years perfecting it for her. No one else knows this place exists. Just you, and now it's a home."

His words fill my chest until it's flooded, the gratitude flowing down my cheeks in a steady stream. He lowers his body on top of mine, his wings fluttering over my skin. Finn softly kisses me, teasing my mouth open for his tongue. His lips work down my jawline, stopping to nip between my neck and shoulder before suckling the skin.

My fingers caress the arch of his wings just over his shoulder. He lets out a satisfied groan.

"You have no idea what this does to me."

I trace my fingers around the base of his wings. His muscles twitch under my touch. I smile and move closer to him, placing my hands under his wings, pulling them down.

"What are you doing?"

I kiss the base of his neck, then let his wings go. They snap back up to their original position, and Finn lets out a pleased little moan as they settle above us.

"These might be my new favorite thing."

He gives me a satiated smile. "I wasn't sure how you'd take it."

I smile and press my body into his, letting him know just how much I mean what I say. Finn wraps his arms around me and holds on tight, his feathers flexing above us. His muscles tighten under my touch. I explore every curve of his body, and he tenses with anticipation of my next move.

Slowly, I crush my lips to him again, starting from the base of his neck and working my way down his chest. I let my hands caress the inside of his thighs, and he squirms under my touch.

"Is the big bad fae ticklish?"

He scowls. "No."

I press light kisses where his hip joins his leg, keeping my eyes fixed to his jaw, which he keeps clenched tight.

"I think you're lying."

He lets out a frustrated growl. Suddenly, he grabs me by the waist and flips me onto my back without warning. I let out a surprised little gasp at the sudden move, and laugh.

Kissing me deeply, he pushes his knee between my thighs.

I raise a brow. "Not ticklish?"

He shakes his head and kisses me again, even deeper this time, his tongue exploring my mouth. I feel his hardness against me, and I grin at the feeling of it.

"Let's find out."

CHAPTER 19

LANA

"We have our soul bond, which is an internal representation of what we are to each other. If you'll let me, I'd like to mark our bond in the fae way."

"I'd love that. Are we giving each other tattoos?"

Finn reaches across his stomach to grasp a feather from the wing pinned beneath us. He winces and sucks in a breath before yanking it out.

I gasp at the glowing blue liquid coagulating at the wound. "What are you doing?" I sit up and inspect the damage with my fingers, and use a bit of my magic to heal him faster. This is the first time I've had a good look at his blue blood in the light.

"This is what I'll use to give us the mark. The process isn't painful, and each couple's signature is unique. I don't know what this'll give us. I'll go first." He hands me the long golden feather. Finn turns over his wrist and motions me to his forearm.

"What do I do?"

"Pierce my wrist here." He points to the spot just to the right of his tendon. "Then, the same spot on the other wrist."

I position the quill end of the feather above his skin and close my eyes. With my eyes closed, I clench my teeth and bring the sharp end down with a wince. It's like penetrating a cushion with a needle. On the removal, the point sticks but releases.

"You can open your eyes now." He chuckles.

I crack a peek and see two little dots of blood, but no tattoo. "You're not hurt, are you? Is something supposed to be there?"

"They show after both of us have pierced our wrists and say a few words."

"I'll do your other one, and then you can do mine." I place my palm against his warm skin and stab the spot with the feather again. This time, I keep my eyes open.

I lean in to inspect. There are more rivulets of blue blood, but the wound has almost sealed already. With my thumb, I wipe the blood away. My eyes find Finn's and the look of complete adoration on his face as I lean in to kiss the wound.

He reaches over and pushes my hair behind my ear. "Now, it's your turn. Hold out your wrist."

I hand him the feather and stretch my arm out across his lap. The soft glow of his skin on mine makes me feel safe and wanted at the same time. He takes his time, carefully aligning the quill and pushing it into my flesh. I feel nothing.

"One more."

Lifting my other wrist, I place it into position. Finn takes it and pricks my skin.

"Now, repeat after me:

No force in this realm or the next,
Can undo this ancient text.
Lovers bound,
Let thy be crowned:
Soul bond, mate, lover, friend,
Our union will never end.
Give us our sign,
Let everyone know you're mine."

I repeat the words as he speaks them. We clasp our hands together and lean in for a kiss. Energy races from our hands up to my shoulders before ricocheting through the rest of my body. There is no pain, only pleasure so intense, I have to rest my head on Finn's shoulder.

When the euphoria ebbs, I pull back to inspect our marks. A crescent moon sits where we placed the feather, and extending up our arms are swirls of blue, silver, and black. They continue over the shoulder and brush against the neck.

"Gods." Our marks match, like magic shimmering under the skin. "These are so beautiful."

Finn places the feather back in my hand and pins me with his gaze before closing his hand over mine. "I want you to keep this on you at all times. You never know when you might need it. Should something happen to you, this feather will bring you back in time for me to save you. You cannot take it off you, otherwise it won't work. Do you understand?"

I nod. "Where should I keep it?"

"You mustn't let anyone else see it—they could hurt you to take it from you. I can embed this on your ribcage."

"That's what you do to witches who become vampires, isn't it? With their Ebbswick key?" I think about the key embedded into Oz's ribcage. He was a witch before becoming a vampire. It's why neither he, nor my dad, can get into Bedlam. Thankfully, this also keeps Dolphina out.

"Yes, fae can't risk vampires infecting our kind."

"Will it hurt?"

He grimaces. "Probably. Unlike the vampires, where their key doesn't work once in the skin, this will. I've never used one of my feathers before, but I'm a powerful fae. This *will* save your life when you need it." He grips my hands. "You are the most precious person to me. Please do this."

"I was going to say yes, anyway. I just wanted to know if it'll hurt."

Finn cracks a smirk and moves further up the bed. We're both still stark naked, but I don't have any desire to cover up.

"This won't hurt as much as when I removed the defixio curse, but it'll be close. I'm going to hold you while I do this so I can heal you as it happens."

I get into position with my back against his chest. My head rests where his shoulder meets his neck, and his hot breath stirs my hair against my skin.

"Keep your eyes closed; it'll be easier. Are you ready?"

I nod against his shoulder and tense in anticipation of pain. "Your chest is so warm." I don't even have to open my eyes to know his normally tanned skin glows blue right now.

Finn chants in an ancient fae language, and I feel the press of his palm against the feather placed on my ribcage.

My skin tingles under his touch before turning into a searing pain. Tears prick my eyes and my jaw strains from clenching my teeth. I can feel the feather burrowing into my skin, and I just want to claw it out.

"It's nearly done," Finn coos into my ear.

A piercing scream crawls up my throat and echoes in the vaulted bedroom. My nails dig into his forearms holding me against him.

"Shh, it's okay. I've got you." He kisses my exposed collarbone, and the pain dissolves until nothing but warmth remains.

I let out a deep breath and relax against him. His chest rises and falls rapidly against my back, but he's completely still. "Did it work?"

"Yes, and I'm taking you with me." His voice is ragged and strained.

"Wh-what does that mean?"

"Shh, baby. I promise everything will be fine." Finn's arms form a steel cage around me, and he lays me flat on the mattress.

I stare up at him with wide eyes while he chants again. The slant of moonlight in the room changes to a glowing light, and it envelops us, sending me spiraling away.

When I open my eyes, I'm weightless, and staring up at moonlight. Only moonlight.

"Lana?" His voice is no louder than a whisper, but I can hear it clearly.

When I tilt my head up to look behind him, I shake my head of the fog and tighten my grip around him when I realize where we are. Thousands of feet above his home in the mountains rests a daybed, suspended in the night sky as though it were a stationary object.

"What is this place?"

"This is where I sleep when I'm low on magic outside of moon season. It's my favorite place in the entire realm. Like my home, nobody else knows about it."

The sky is clear, and for the first time, I realize there's more than one moon here. There are four, plus one that appears as though it's racing through the sky. I can tell it's not a shooting star—the look of the moon is very clear.

I sit up. "This is what you drew in your notebook?"

His gaze swings to the sky and he ponders for a moment. "You're right. I've seen this symbol in my dreams my entire life and never realized that's what it was."

"It's beautiful," I marvel. "Is this a bad time to tell you I'm afraid of heights?"

"But you can fly?"

"I didn't say I was any good at it."

He pulls me in closer to him and spreads his wings so they envelop us. "I'll save you. Always."

Finn

LANA'S EYES GLAZE OVER, and she trails a hand down one of the feathers. I bite back a groan when she whispers, *Finn*," her voice catching on my name like I'm the most precious thing in her world.

When my lips trace a path over her collarbone, she gasps, and the sound sends a current down my spine. I lower my body against hers, reveling in the feel of her skin on mine. "I love you."

Her fingers tangle in my hair, anchoring me against her as I leave a trail of kisses down her chest. She bucks against my hips, her core rubbing against my erection, but I don't give in. Not yet.

"I've waited millennia for you, Lana."

Her eyes gloss over, and she pulls me in for a kiss. "I'm glad you found me, Finn. I feel whole."

My hands grip the soft flesh of her hip, but pause when I hear the insidious thoughts in her head about her body.

"What is it?"

I shake my head and continue to caress her, trying to ignore the way she thinks others are superior to her. Shame over the white marks lining her skin from baring children.

She pulls back, observing my face. "I don't think I'm as beautiful as other women you've known." Her voice is quiet. "The human world differs from Bedlam in more ways than one." Her fingernails dig into my arm, creating indentions in the skin.

I cup her face, bring it within inches of mine, and shake my head. "Don't you see, Lana? You're my *soul bonded mate*. Our souls made us to the exact specifications of our ideal mates. Not a single fae, witch, vampire, or any other creature can even compare." I clench my teeth. "Gods, Lana. How can anyone look at you and not see absolute perfection? Who made you feel this way about yourself? Was it your vampire mates?"

"No, no. They're wonderful and treat me ... amazing. I'm a lucky woman."

I keep my ire to myself. It's going to take a lot to get used to her having mates other than *me*. "Then who made you feel like this?"

She sighs. "He doesn't matter anymore."

I raise my eyebrow at her.

"Early in my twenties, I was engaged to an asshole for less than forty-eight hours before I found out he was cheating. We'd been together for most of college, and he wasn't ... kind to me. It really fucked me up for a long time."

Her memories flash in her head. She's way out of his league, and he has the nerve to embarrass her in front of their friends? Saying, "haven't you had enough?" when she reaches for a bread roll, even though she was waif-thin then. Smacking her around when he's drunk?

I commit his face to memory. Mark my words, I will end this poor excuse for a man.

"Oh, Lana." I pull her to me and press my lips to the top of her head. "He was an idiot. If he couldn't see how beautiful you are, he wasn't worthy of your love. And I would never be so unkind to you."

I look at her with the hope she believes me.

Her brows furrow together, and she glances at my lips, then back at my eyes.

"I know you wouldn't. But it's hard to get rid of that feeling." She kisses my chest and snuggles into me. "You know, I've never done this before."

"What? You mean flown?" I chuckle.

"Made love above the clouds."

~

Oz

My Dearest Sahira,

They say time heals all wounds. I disagree. I've heard widows and widowers say you start measuring time as before and after an event. "Before Lana left..." or "After Lana left..." The wound is still there, raw and festering. You learn to walk around with a piece of you, severed, silently suffering, while the rest of the world acts as though my entire life hasn't fallen to pieces.

I want to scream and tear things apart at the injustice of it. I've only just found you, after spending millennia knowing my mate is out there somewhere in space and time. You've been gone several months. I keep your blog updated, although I'm still trying to figure out how to explain to your audience why the twins have grown so fast in such a short period of time. The twins are talking and toddling around already. Every night, the three of us share stories about you so they know how much their mommy loves them and is fighting to come home.

In my wallet, I keep the picture you took of us on the floor of the Mont Tremblant home. Your hair is wild, skin glistening, and your eyes? Satisfied. It's my favorite look on you.

Cherished.

That's how I'd describe your expression, and I hope you know it's true. You are so cherished.

I'll try to make my next letter less macabre because, by the time you read these, it'll be a joyous occasion; you'll be home.

Eternally yours,

Oz

CHAPTER 20

LANA

The sun disappears behind the mountain, and I still haven't heard from the kings. I'm trying to remain calm, but it's hard when I'm constantly thinking about my mom and what could have happened to her, and whether she's even alive.

My trauma of losing her at just eight years old replays in my mind like a broken record, and the not knowing is torture. I spent twenty-six years wondering why she abandoned me, only to later find out I was the reason she left. I screwed up when I tried to stop her from birthing me, and instead of aborting, she disappeared in time. To do what, I don't know.

My eyes shutter at the memory of seeing her when I traveled back in time, right before she left me forever.

"I don't know how to make this right, Mom. This stupid prophecy has caused so much irreparable harm." I drop to my knees and bury my face in my hands. She kneels next to me and wraps her arm around my shoulders, holding tight, and I'm flooded with a sense of calm. I put my head up to look at my mom and see her eyes are closed. The feeling of peace quickly turns to dread as I watch her vanish right before me.

Finn's warm hand settles on my shoulder before he pulls me into a hug. "We'll get answers." He whispers into my hair, and I cling to him like he's my lifeline.

"I hope so," I mutter, not truly believing I'll get what I came here for. The longer I'm here, the more I realize how hopeless this situation feels. If the kings won't help me, then I go home mortal, and with no answers.

Finn does his best to distract me, but even his magic lessons can't take away the anxiety churning in the pit of my stomach. I know finding someone who disappeared in time is difficult, but I can't help but feel like we're running out of time. The kings are the only ones who have the power to grant my petition and I'm praying that they will see me as worthy. I don't know what I'll do if they say no.

We spend the day in a hot spring a short hike from home. He teaches me how to draw on nature around me to fuel my magic. I was getting the hang of it, but as night fell, my anxiety returned. I tried to push it away and enjoy the time with Finn, but it was always there, lurking in the back of my mind.

As we lay in bed together, he verses me on the different royal courts with the help of a creased map he had tucked in a book.

"Penn is the king of Draconum, a mostly volcanic continent with hoards of treasure." Finn points to a reddish mass of land North of Convectus.

I lean in to examine the print. "Is this … coin?" I place my finger on the Southern section near a castle. Not a single speck of red pops through—it's all golden.

"He's a dragon shifter who restores magic from precious metals, jewels, and gemstones. It's said the original Luna fae to grant dragon shifters with magic tied theirs to shiny objects because the one he knew was greedy."

My eyes widen. "Which one is he in this photo?" I reach for the small photo of the three together. One edge of the photograph is torn.

"Can't you tell?" He smirks. "Blond hair to his shoulders, tan. Has a golden aura to him."

"I don't see auras." Although now that he's pointed it out, Penn does have a sun-kissed golden boy look to him.

My eyes dart to Finn when he chuckles. "What?"

"He's thousands of years old. I'd hardly call him a boy." Amusement warms his voice.

"What of the others?"

"Grimm's hair is black as night. Turquoise eyes. He's the King of Occasus, and a fae I'd rather you not spend too much time with." A continent with dark soil, vast forests, and mountains makes up most of Grimm's land.

"Why?"

Finn clenches his jaw and flexes his hand. His voice takes a possessive edge. "His incubus order takes even the tiniest shred of attraction, drops your inhibitions, and amps up your arousal with only a thought."

I scoff. "I'd never." Four mates are enough.

He gives me a side glance. "I know you wouldn't, but not many can resist the pull."

"I assume Casimir is the lighter-skinned fae? What's his order?"

"Yes, he's a wolf shifter and King of Luporia."

I find the large, fertile continent with a small mountain range and lots of green space.

"He's the most considerate of the three, but don't mistake him for being gentle. His beast is enormous and will rip the throat out of any foe."

Finn takes notice of my concern and sets the map down before turning towards me and placing a hand on my cheek. "I'll keep you safe. I swear it." There's an unreadable expression on his face I can't quite figure out.

The weight of his hand and the sincerity in his voice make my anxiety start to fade. I nod and Finn kisses me, his lips soft and gentle at first before turning more insistent. I forget my worries for a little while and get lost in him.

A quiet chirp and a flash cut through the darkness, pulling me from my sleep. I jolt up, searching the room for the source of light, and I find it across the room.

Finn grumbles and rubs his eyes. "What is it?"

I swing my legs over the edge of the bed and just as quickly tuck them back under me.

"Your pants chirped and they're glowing!" I scramble towards him on the bed. "Oh, my gods, do you think a ground gnome somehow got stuck in them?"

Finn's face pinches, and he clasps his chest before doubling over. "That's the—" he gasps for breath through choked laughter, "response from the kings. It's the device in my pocket."

I gasp and throw myself off the bed and clutch at his pants to extract the small black mechanism. Embarrassed laughter flutters out of me while I turn the device over in my hand. "I thought it was a ground gnome!"

Finn's face is red, and tears stream down his cheeks as he tries to catch his breath.

Adrenaline pumps through my veins, and I bite my lip as I carry it to the bed. "This is it." My heart thumps in my chest, a prestissimo to match the surge of anxiety coursing through me. I cradle the small piece of metal in my hand, eyes glued to it for several minutes while I cling to this monumental moment, afraid to step outside my carefully constructed lines of safety. This is it. "Can you do it?"

"Sorry." He takes the hologram device from me. "Of course." His words and actions make to reassure me, but a hint of stress underlines his tone. He's as worried about this as I am, but I appreciate the strength he lends me.

I wait on bated breath as he presses a few buttons.

The pre-recorded hologram flickers to life, and the kings' images appear. I barely register the trembling hand Finn places on my shoulder.

Three handsome fae, all shirtless and barefooted, sit on some kind of ledge with a view of the ocean. There's a casual air about them. One rests his arm on the knee tucked against his chest, his thick forearm muscles rippling with every tap of his hand against his outstretched leg. Another, leaning back with his palms supporting his weight behind him. The last leans forward while he talks, his piercing eyes somehow finding mine despite this being a video.

"We've received your request for an audience." The dark-haired one I recognize as Grimm speaks. A smirk teases his lips and unease settles in my gut. Is he grinning because he'll deny me?

"Shock doesn't begin to describe how we felt about your presence in our realm. Inter-realm relations don't permit us to refuse a witch of your standing, so we have agreed. Please sift to Convectus at your earliest convenience, where we have a room waiting for you. Your audience is at first light."

I release the breath I was holding and turn to Finn when the device flickers off. "First light?" I glance towards the window in a panic. "That's mere hours from now."

Finn shakes his head. "We can sift. I'll glamour us while in the city, and once we're safely in our room, I'll remove the disguise. This way, anyone who knows who the Queen of Vampires is, won't delay us."

"Okay," I say, still not entirely convinced this will go well. "What if they say no?"

He shifts his feet. "No matter what they decide, we'll figure this out. You'll have your answers, if it's the last thing I do, we'll see this through." His eyes take on a haunted look.

"What if my mom is just lost?" Excitement ratchets up inside me. "Trying to find her way home to me?"

"It takes three royals to complete the spell to locate her. While it takes days to complete, there should be no problem finding where in time she went, provided they agree to help." Finn wraps his arms around me. "I don't see them turning you away. Not for something so important. Immortality may require more convincing, though. They'll ask something of you in return."

"Like what?"

"Something big. Maybe a covenant between vampires and Bedlam. Or help with eradicating a species."

I shake my head. "If they won't make me immortal, I can try to get Gideon to turn me into a vampire, and deal with the consequences after. The only reason I haven't insisted on it is because I know how opposed Oz is."

Finn recoils. "I won't let it come to that."

We head to the bedroom to change our clothes. Convectus has a milder climate than Rexuna, although it has cold regions, like Noble Wilds, where I first came to Bedlam. With my trembling hands, I pull on a pair of light pants and a tunic before lacing up my boots.

"Ready?" Finn leans against the window frame.

"I never thought this day would come." I nod, and he takes my hand.

He sifts us this time, and we land back in Convectus, but in its Northern parts. Even in the middle of the night, the air is thick and humid, and I can feel the heat seeping through my clothes.

"Bedlam believes in air conditioning, right?" I clutch his elbow while I practically run to keep up with his stride. Our chatter rises and falls as nerves and excitement take turns to show up in our voices. We're about to have answers after all this time.

Finn chuckles. "You'll get used to it."

He leads me through the streets, and I can feel eyes on us. We must look strange to the natives: a fae and a witch. Although we're glamoured, I don't give off a fae aura, which all fae can see, I guess. I've yet to come across any other witches here; Finn says most congregate on Sundahlia, a tropical continent to the East of here.

We arrive at the enormous building and stand at the foot of the castle, looking up at its imposing facade. The walls are made of a glossy grey stone that seems to shimmer in the moonlight. Silver vines twist their way up the towers, and delicate flowers bloom in every nook and cranny. Panels of gold and red adorn the castle, like bolts of silk to decorate a formal affair. The windows are huge, and the stained glass depicts different scenes from Fae history. The door is equally grand, made of heavy wood with silver handles in the shape of dragons. I can feel the magic emanating from the castle, making my skin tingle with anticipation. I'm not sure what I was expecting, but this wasn't it.

It's beautiful in a way that makes me uncomfortable. Too perfect.

"Here we are." Finn pauses in front of a retinue of guards standing next to a door that must be at least twenty feet tall.

"State your business." A guard barks.

"Queen Lana Finlandian of the Earth Realm and her guard here to see the kings."

Finn steps in front of me and shows him some kind of badge.

The guard nods, speaks into a device on his shoulder, and steps aside to heave open the entrance.

The second we step through the entry; I'm assaulted by the most incredible sights and smells. There are flowers everywhere, blooming in every color of the rainbow. Their sweet fragrance fills the air, making me feel lightheaded, wishing for reprieve. The walls are made of some kind of white stone that seems to glow from within. And the ceiling ... it's so high that I can't even see it. It looks like the sky.

"This way." A guard meets us.

He leads us through a maze of hallways and stairs until we reach a nondescript door, places a key in Finn's hand, and steps back.

I take a deep breath and enter; Finn's right behind me. It's just past midnight, and I'm relieved to find a spread of light fair in our bedroom for the night. We share a long, drawn-out snack, not speaking much. We're both too on edge for small talk.

I'm exhausted by the time we finish eating, and Finn doesn't protest when I climb into bed.

"It's creepy."

"What is?" He furrows his brows.

"Your glamour."

He chuckles and drops the façade from both of us. I pat the mattress, and he climbs in next to me, wrapping his arms around me. "Not into role playing?" His voice a whisper against my ear.

"Sure I am, provided you look like you."

"Fair enough."

He kisses me then, and I let myself forget, for a moment, the gravity of the situation.

CHAPTER 21

LANA

"Finian. What a pleasant surprise. We wondered how the queen made it all this way without help."

The man's voice is unsettling, but we remain on our knees and keep our heads down. My heart beats fast, although I keep my breathing slow and even by counting the marble tiles in my field of vision.

"You may rise," comes another voice so deep and full of power it settles heavily in my chest.

Finn takes my hand and helps me off my knees, but he doesn't let go of it. He'd told me we shouldn't look the kings in their eyes, so I keep my focus on their feet instead. All three sets rest in front of their thrones, and none wear shoes. These are well-manicured, tanned, and appear very soft.

They are barefoot in case they need to fight; fae are more agile while barefoot.

"Approach the dais," a distinct voice instructs me. His is deep, but more sensual than the others.

We make to near the platform, but a booming voice stops us dead in our tracks. "Not you, Finn. Only her."

It's okay, Finn reassures me in my head and lets go of my now

110

trembling hand. This all sounded so much easier in my head when I didn't have to face them in real life. My chest heaves and I take step after step until I'm told to stop.

All three males stand, and I watch their feet advance towards me. My lips tingle from the rate at which I breathe. *Don't pass out, don't pass out, don't pass out.* I unlock my knees and pray they don't see that as a sign of aggression; I'm trying not to faint.

The kings circle me, and I feel each one of their stares take measure of me—a witch from the Earth realm and Queen of Vampires.

One of the fae pauses in front of me and unclasps his hands from behind his back. There's a very distinctive oak-like scent to him. His garments are black, with gold stitching, and an emblem of hearts rests on the top left corner of his chest.

This royal leans in and nuzzles his nose in my neck. I hitch my breath, afraid to let go, while he inhales deeply. He takes a small step back and tilts my chin up with one claw, but I keep my eyes on his mouth: his full, *sensual* mouth. Waves of arousal pour off him and wrap around me like a silk scarf. The intensity increases and heat pools low in my belly. What's ... happening?

"Look at me."

There's a collective gasp from the throne room when I meet his eyes. It's Grimm, the king from Occasus, and the one I was warned about. His pupils dilate and I release the breath I've held. This fae is attractive; thick eyelashes frame eyes the color of Tahitian waters, and strong eyebrows perform perfect arches. Silky jet-black hair rests on his forehead, and gods, that mouth—

He's grinning at me. In his mouth are delicate, pointy canines amongst the whitest and shiniest teeth I've ever seen. His soft, husky chuckle interrupts my thoughts, and I blink out of my daze when the lust retreats.

This fae darts his eyes behind me and narrows them.

"Does your mate know you're a royal?"

Who is he talking to?

Another soft laugh, but this time his chuckle isn't a kind one. His attention comes back to me, and he tsks and takes my hands in his. "Lana, darling. Your mate abdicated his throne."

I pull my brows together. Oz? Why would he ...?

The fae in front of me shakes his head and I remember the royals can read minds.

"No, not Oz; Finn. Did he not tell you he's High King of the Fae Realm? That's not a title one can escape, though much he tries. As soon as he claims the title again, we'll treat him with respect. But for now? No."

What? The news steals the breath from my lungs, and I resist the urge to turn my head to look behind me to confirm if this is true.

Finn?

I'm sorry, Lana. I tried to tell you.

Hurt slices through me. I'm not upset he gave up the throne—not at all—but I am upset he withheld this from me. I close my eyes against the sting of tears threatening to spill, and only open them when the feeling passes. It isn't a deal-breaker, but it's a conversation we'll need to have so we can re-establish trust. There must be a good reason he didn't tell me, and I intend to find out what it is.

The king raises an eyebrow and smirks before turning on his heel and retreating to his throne. The next fae doesn't approach me from the front. Instead, a warm presence presses against my back. A chill snakes through my body when he brushes my hair to one side and nuzzles into my neck. My eyes close of their own accord while he inhales, and goosebumps pepper my body when his breath stirs against my pulse on his exhale.

His fingers trail my back, across my shoulder, and rest on my collarbone while he circles to my front, tracing the dainty gold necklace Finn had me wear for this very king. He's the opposite of the first —still just as handsome—but where the first was all dark and brooding, this one is golden; shoulder-length sandy-colored hair swept neatly behind his pointy ears, hazel eyes with gold flecks, and a warmer tan.

I'm conscious of his fingers resting on my bare skin, and I try to keep my breathing slow and steady, to no avail. He moves his finger up my neck and along my jawline until resting just under my chin. I swallow and hold my breath when he applies pressure just under my jaw to tilt my head up.

In one moment, my head cranes high, and I keep my eyes to the chandeliers on the ceiling, and the next, his hand moves to cup behind my head and draws me flush to his body.

"I am Penn of Draconum." His whisper in my ear sends another chill through my body.

He releases my head and pivots back to his throne, somehow taking the necklace with him.

"I am Casimir of Luporia."

My view of Penn is replaced by a fae with caramel hair, lighter skin, and eyes as blue as a robin's egg. Faint freckles dot the expanse of his nose and cheeks, and while his eyelashes are long and thick, they're lighter than Grimm's. He gives me a roguish grin—his canines on proud display.

Casimir takes my hand in his and kisses it before flipping it over and inhaling the skin on my inner wrist. I resist my knee-jerk reaction to pull it back and instead allow him to continue, even when he paws at my hair. To calm me, I think of my children—their sweet faces, tiny fingers wrapped around mine, insatiable appetites, and eyelashes that fan their cheeks when they slumber on my chest.

In one swift move, I am in his arms, and he's nuzzled against my neck.

"Tell me, witch, do you taste as good as you smell?" His bedroom purr whispers in my ear just as his tongue flicks out against my pulse and I stiffen.

"Now, now. Let's not scare the poor witch," Grimm calls from the dais.

Casimir's chuckle rumbles against my temple and he releases me before retreating to his throne. My entire body trembles and I cast my eyes to the floor.

"You've come here to learn what happened to your mother, yes? And you want immortality?" The voice I recognize as Penn's greets me.

I nod.

"You ask a lot of us."

I nod again.

"You may speak. Why?"

I steal my voice before responding. "Thank you for having me here and listening to my plea. My mother disappeared somewhere in time, and I'm afraid she's in trouble, or—" I shut my eyes and will myself to speak without crying. Only once the sting retreats do I open them. "—dead. My family and I would like to know so we may have closure, or so we can help her, wherever she is."

Memories of her reading me *The Fairy Rebel* come to the surface. Tucked against her side in bed, she'd spend hours—

My half-formed thought disappears when I'm brought back to present.

"And immortality?"

"My mates are immortal. I want to spend eternity with them. And..." I glance back at Finn, regret shining in his glassy eyes, and a whisper of a smile crosses my face before I turn back towards the kings. "An alliance between fae, vampires, and witches could help unite our realms."

Whispers fill the room and I try to quiet my thoughts roaring in my head. Everything rides on this decision.

"The Queen of Vampires and her many lovers; yes ... we know all about you and your romantic relationships, *Oriflamme Queen*. It's interesting, though, you have also acknowledged your soul bond with Finn. What are your plans? Surely you don't expect your other paramours to accept him."

"My mates will accept him because he is my soul bonded mate. We may have a period of adjustment, but because I love him, they will grow to love him, too—just like any of my mates."

The chatter in the room is louder now, and Penn admonishes the court for speaking out of turn. The people are quick to quiet.

"Give us a moment to discuss. You may return to Finn's side."

I've never bolted so fast in my life. Finn embraces me and continues to hold me in his arms.

You did well. I'm sorry for not telling you.

We can discuss why you didn't tell me later because I'm afraid. What if this is all for naught?

Then we will find another way, my soul.

I rest my head on his chest and calm myself with the steady thump of his heart. His hand rubs small circles against my hip, a rhythmic pattern meant to ground me.

"Lana, you may approach the dais. We have our decision."

My pulse beats wildly, unsure if their quick verdict is good or not, and I tremble when I let go of Finn to walk to the platform.

"Queen of Vampires, we will grant you your requests ..." There's a collective gasp from the room and my knees weaken at the news. "In exchange for something in return."

"Anything." I stand stoic and keep my eyes on the floor a few steps in front of me.

"You must first agree to our terms before we tell you what we want."

My heart stumbles and I cast a quick, worried glance at Finn behind me. It's hard to miss the panic written all over his face, especially when the guards have to restrain him from approaching.

"If you accept, we grant you immediate immortality. Your second request will take some investigation, but we will tell you as soon as we have concluded our search. Do you agree?"

My chest tightens, and I squeeze my eyes shut. They might ask for anything; my children, any of my mates, or maybe even make it so the people I love hate me. I've only just found the loves of my life. And my dad? I have too many years to make up for. The risk is too big. I choose to gamble, instead.

"No. I can't agree to—"

"We vow we won't lay a hand on your family or friends. Nor will we make them hate you." Casimir cuts through the alarm spreading through the room. "Has Finn told you about fae promises?"

I shake my head.

"We can't break them."

Petrichor fills my nostrils, and I glance at the windows along the far wall where a storm beats against the glass, the crack of thunder barely sounding above the rain. It brings me back to the thrill of watching thunderstorms with my mom on the covered porch of our cabin. I'm the reason she's gone.

I owe it to her.

"I agree."

Magic snaps the air and hurls a jolt through my body, sending me sprawling to the stairs in front of me. I clench my teeth as pain radiates through every nerve, but I can't hold back a scream of agony. My hands scramble for purchase against the smooth stone, trying to gain control of the misery. The pain is unbearable, and all I can do is curl in on myself and sob. Either the screams I'm hearing are mine or Finn's.

Minutes seem like hours, wrenching and contorting my body. The pain eventually dulls, and I don't move.

"What did they do to me?" I whimper, my voice little more than a whisper.

I raise my eyes to look behind me at Finn trying to come to my aid, but the guards stop him from approaching me.

I'm okay.

He relaxes, and the guards let him go. I return my focus to the front, climb to my feet, and dust myself off. My entire body thrums with power and strength.

"Immortality looks good on you." I can tell this is Grimm speaking. Heat flushes my cheeks when he rises from his throne and stands in front of me again. He circles my body and pauses behind me. His arms snake around my middle and bring me tight against him.

I keep my eyes cast down and focus on my hands. They're noticeably silkier and creamier now, and completely blemish-free; far different from when I entered here after months in the forest.

"You have no womb. Why?"

More gasps and chatter fill the room.

"I gave birth to twins before leaving Earth, but almost died after my uterus ruptured. They had to perform a hysterectomy to save my life."

Grimm's arms tighten around me, and he whispers in my ear. "Would you like it back?"

All the air leaves my lungs and I have to hold back a sob. The chance to have more children was taken from me, and I'd give anything to have the option again. It doesn't matter if we never do, but I want to know the choice is there should I change my mind.

"Please." My voice breaks.

"Very well."

The other two kings place their hands next to Grimm's on my abdomen and an immediate, sharp pain ricochets through me for the second time in as many minutes. A blood-curdling scream rips from my throat. The agony steals the breath from my lungs and my knees buckle. If it wasn't for their hold on me, I'd fall to the floor. Tears pour down my face, and they collectively still me while I weep and writhe in torture.

As fast as the pain came on, it disappears. My chest heaves, and Penn helps me to my feet before wiping the tears off my cheeks.

"You are whole now." He searches my eyes for understanding.

"Thank you." My voice is hoarse from the screaming and crying.

He cups my face in his hand. His beautiful eyes bore into mine, and a brief sinister look passes over his face before leveling again.

"What we require from you is this." Power radiates from his voice, and it straightens my spine to attention of its own volition. Then, a haze settles in my bones.

"From this moment forward, you forget everyone you have ever known prior to our meeting."

The scream that pours from my throat nearly matches the fury at which I attack the fae in front of me, my nails sinking into his neck, blood dribbling down my wrists.

"Your womb was always intact. The only people you know are Grimm, Casimir, and myself. You were an Earth-dwelling witch we rescued from evil vampires. They hurt you, stole your memories, and brainwashed you. You have no mates. No children. No family. We just made you immortal, so you can be safe. You'll remain under our protection."

~

"Lana!" a man roars while the entire entourage of guards drag him kicking and screaming out of the room. His handsome face contorts in fury, and he nearly breaks free of the men holding him down before they capture him again. Offensive and defensive magic pours out of him, and Grimm steps in front of me to shield me from any errant attacks.

Lana, Lana, Lana, it's me. I startle from a sudden, foreign voice in my head. "I order you to unhand me!"

I furrow my eyebrows. He doesn't look familiar.

"Who is screaming my name?" I try to peek around Grimm's shoulders.

"No one, darling. Just some zealot. The guards will remove him from the palace grounds. No need to worry." Grimm embraces me in his arms.

"We won't let anyone hurt you ever again." This comes from my other rescuer, Casimir.

"Thank you." I speak softly into Grimm's chest.

"No one will discuss what transpired in this room today. Instant death awaits anyone who tries to defy my gag order." Magic sizzles in the air when Penn finishes speaking.

"Come, let's get you settled in your room so you can wash before supper. You've had a long journey." Casimir pulls me from Grimm's arms and takes my hand to follow him. The crowd of fae in the throne room part for my liberators, but still cast peculiar looks my way when we pass them.

CHAPTER 22

FINN

*T*hose *bastards*! They think to take my soul bonded mate from me just because I once said I wouldn't share a mate with them?! Lana had to have heard me in her head—I saw her startle when I yelled for her in her mind. I hope that's enough to plant a seed of doubt before I can get her out of their clutches.

It took all of their gods damned guards to haul me out of there. Because I gave up my throne, I no longer have access to the resources it will require to get her back. If I were to re-claim the throne, not only would these guards fall under my command, but they could never subdue me when I'm at full strength. I don't think they'd hurt her, not when she means so much to the realm—she's our High Queen as soon as I can crown her.

If I could, I'd take back my crown right now. But I have no army. To gain the throne again, I need to defeat the three king's armies. I know what I've got to do now; go to the Earth realm and convince her other mates that I'm her soul bonded mate and that she's in trouble.

I'll just have to figure out how to get a vampire army into Bedlam without Ebbswick keys or grimoires.

CHAPTER 23

LANA

The bedroom they give me is round. Is this a tower? A door to each of my savior's personal bedrooms connect to mine, a chaise lounge, an armoire, a picture window with a view of the mountains in the distance, and a canopied bed that can fit at least half a dozen people make up most my room. Stacks of books sit on the plush window seat, and I make a mental note to do some reading while I'm here. A large chandelier hangs from the center of the space, and below it is a plush rug I sink my bare feet into.

Just off the room is a shared bathroom with a pool-sized tub and overhead shower. I imagine they need big tubs when fae are so large; each of the kings hovers around 7 ft. I startle when I stand in front of the full-length mirror to get a good look at what greets me.

No fine lines, wrinkles, or blemishes mar my skin. I grip the vanity and lean in. Heck, I'm not even sure I have pores. My lashes are fuller, and my hair is still curly, but it's so soft now. And dare I say it — I am *stunning*. Am I taller, too? I look down and inspect my body.

Definitely, although not as tall as the kings. Maybe 6 ft 2 inches? I'm all sleek curves with hard muscle and cushion in all the right places.

My gaze catches on my pointed ears sticking through my hair. I run my fingers over the sharp tip of one before doing the same to my other ear. The kings told me they made me immortal. What they failed to mention is they made me *fae*.

I've always been beautiful ... but never like this. My appearance has taken on an ethereal quality to it, much like them, and while I was confident in my skin most days as a human, I hold my head a little higher returning to my bedroom.

I pad my way across the cool tile and open the armoire to gather a long, embroidered dress and bring it with me to the bathroom. I'm surprised when I can reach the panel on the ceiling for the tub. With a few pushes of a button, water cascades from a showerhead attached to the ceiling. After I slip out of my clothes, I stand naked in front of the mirror to admire my nude form. My hands rove over my strong curves, and I twist and turn while keeping my eyes fixed on the mirror. I hop up and down a few times.

Everything stays in place, aside from my boobs and hair.

After descending the stairs to the tub with a spring in my step, I sink below the surface before emerging to use soapberries. Just like regular soap, I get a bubbly lather and stroke my skin and hair with them. When I'm all clean, I relax my head on the lip of the tub and close my eyes, determined to relax for a bit before dressing for supper.

I don't realize I've drifted asleep while in the bath until I startle awake from someone clearing their throat. My eyes fly open, and I sit up to see three very handsome royals with devilish smirks standing at the edge of the tub. I cross my legs and cover my chest.

"You've been in here over an hour and we wanted to make sure you were okay. A shared bathroom requires expediency unless you intend for us to join you?" Casimir quirks an eyebrow at me, and my cheeks flush with heat.

"Sorry, I must've fallen asleep." Grimm hands me a soft towel and I stare expectantly at them. They're not planning on watching me get out of the tub ... are they?

Each of them undresses, never taking their eyes off me, and I scurry out of the tub — my indecent exposure be damned. Their gaze weighs heavily as I wrap the towel around me and snag my dress, all while averting my attention to their nakedness. Are they going to bathe *together*? Maybe they're lovers. I ignore the thrill the thought elicits low in my belly.

My bare feet chill on the tile while I hurry to my room and dress for supper. It's exhilarating—being here—in a different realm, but terrifying, not knowing so much of my past. Am I on the run? Will the vampires attack me as soon as I get back to Earth? Am I better off staying here and figuring out what life is like as a fae? I'm uncertain how long I can stay at the castle, and don't want to overstay my welcome.

First, I need to figure out how to make an income and then a place to live. Then, I'll work on a way to repay these kind fae for rescuing me.

I EXPECTED MORE people at the table, but the only ones here are myself and the kings. Each of them is unshy about taking measure of me; my inner vixen preens at the attention of these otherworldly, beautiful men, who, minutes ago, saw me completely naked.

"Now that you're fae, you'll need lessons to bring you up to speed on our history, your magic, and what you can expect while you're under our wings," Casimir explains while servants place dessert in front of us.

I vaguely remember thanking them for the dessert, but I can't take my eyes off of his lips. Indecent thoughts flit through my mind before I shake my head out of my stupor.

Mischief dances in his eyes, causing heat to creep into my cheeks.

I clear my throat. "On Earth, I was a travel blogger. Do you have access to Earth websites? Maybe I wrote about my life there. It'll help put together the pieces of who was in it."

Penn is quick to respond. "No."

"No, you don't have access to Earth websites, or …?"

"We have internet, but only fae sites. I'm afraid we can't access your 'blog,'" sensing my clear agitation, he continues, "… but we can send spies to Earth to research more about you?"

Hope flutters in my chest. "Please. I don't mean to sound ungrateful. I'm sorry. Thank you all again for rescuing me … and for turning me into a fae. Now I'll have the strength to fend off any attackers the next time."

"There won't be a next time, Lana. Vampires can't come to Bedlam, and we'll let no harm come to you otherwise." Penn places his hand on mine.

He glances down at the tattoos wrapping my arms and disappearing beneath my dress.

"The vampires must've given these tattoos to you. We can remove them tonight." He picks up my arm and inspects the ink.

I tense beneath his touch and try to pull back, but Penn holds me in place. His eyes flash gold before he releases me. "Sorry, I didn't mean to hurt you. I was only trying to inspect the brands. Pierce, your personal guard, said to let him know if you had any injuries from your captivity, and these are the type of wounds I'd be looking for."

I try to convince myself that his touch didn't affect me, but my mind is recalling the feel of his hands on my bare skin, the heat in his eyes when he looked at me. There is one thing I know for certain, though.

"I don't want you to remove these."

Penn looks at me in shock. "Why not?"

I tuck my arms back under the table. "I think … these are important to me." The very idea of them disappearing sends panic through my very essence.

He continues to stare at me for a few seconds, and I nervously fiddle with my napkin as his intense gaze makes my heart beat faster. He surprises me by leaning forward and regarding me seriously. "I understand why you might feel—"

"No, you don't." I blurt out.

He sits up in surprise before giving me an earnest look. "I'm sorry, go on."

"It's my past, okay? You don't know all the reasons I have these tattoos. The only way you—anyone—would understand is if they went through it themselves. What if these tattoos are the key to me gaining my memories back? I might've gotten them as a reminder of what I've gone through."

I seem to remember a lot of my past, just no one I experienced anything with. Who were my teachers? My parents? Do I have siblings? What are my friends like? Did the vampires do something so heinous to me they had to hide their tracks?

Why me?

Penn gives me a steady look. "I won't tell you what to do, but if they are memories of bad things, don't you want to forget them?"

"Bad things happen to everyone, everywhere. It's not like they're unique experiences—people suffer and die every day. There may be something good about those memories, too. It's not fair to judge them until you know what they are."

Penn smiles at me before turning his attention back to his dessert.

I turn to the other kings, who are watching me in amusement. "What?" I ask defensively when they continue to stare.

"I'm just surprised by your spunk." Grimm has a gleam in his eye. "It's refreshing, but also very endearing."

"I'm still me, inside. I just want to be the best version of myself possible now that you've given me immortality. Someday, I'll get my memories back, and when that day comes, I'll have you three to thank for my success."

I sit back in my chair confidently, but my chest aches, and my hands won't stop shaking.

CHAPTER 24

LANA

"The source of all magic comes from the moon; Luna magic blesses the land, and thus, its people." Pierce, my personal guard, leads me through the castle halls for magic lessons. "Those of the Luna order, though few, are the most powerful, as they're first in line for blessings from the moon. Without Luna fae, magic will disappear for everyone."

"Why? If they get their magic from the moon?"

He pauses in front of a tapestry and pulls the woven fabric to the side. When he pushes a smooth stone on the wall, a panel slides open to a doorway leading to stairs. "Only Luna fae get magic, but they share it with the rest of the realm. There are only a handful of them left."

Magic dances in sconces along the stairwell, illuminating our way down. "Why?"

Pierce hesitates. "I'm not at liberty to say, my lady."

I grit my teeth in frustration, but don't take it out on him. He's just doing his job. After passing a number of doors, descending flight after flight, he unlocks several before leading me to a large clearing. On one side is the castle, and the other three sides come together to form a stone wall as high as a skyscraper. Soot spoils the plush grass, and some parts are bald. This must be where spells went errant.

"Rune, meet Lana. Lana, meet Rune." Pierce gestures.

He remains near the door of the castle while I approach a handsome fae with long golden hair, matching eyes, and onyx skin. He is shirtless, and gold lines spiderweb his torso, almost like Kintsugi; the Japanese art of using gold to repair cracks in pottery. His white flowing pants dusts the tops of his feet, and next to them prowls a large cat-like creature with similar features.

The animal approaches me and I pause. Is he friendly? What do I do? I don't even know what this is.

"He won't hurt you." The deep chuckle of the fae lingers in my chest. "His name is Titan, and he's a Phelvie. He will only attack those with ill intent."

I crouch and cup my fingers for him to sniff me. His whiskers tickle my hand, and I stroke his fur, slipping the short silk through my grasp. The texture is somewhere between downy feathers and a fluffy house cat. Its huge tongue laps at my face, leaving thick slobber on my skin.

Blech. I use the sleeve of my dress to wipe it off before standing to address his owner. "Why do they call you Rune?"

Pierce chuckles before clearing his throat. "Don't answer that."

Rune grins. He stalks towards me and holds out his hand. When I take it, he pulls me in to whisper in my ear. "They'll have my head if I show you."

I step back and give him a nod. "Understood. You don't need to risk your life to slake my curiosity." Although now, I'm even more curious. I make a mental note to ask Casimir later. He tells me anything I ask.

Rune snaps his fingers, and Titan disappears. "How did you do that?"

He winks. "Magic." He tilts his head for me to follow him to the center of the clearing. We reach the middle where he tells me he's going to help me shore my mental defenses from intrusion. He says some creatures have the ability to read minds, and this can keep most of them out.

"Imagine your mind as a hallway. You, and your thoughts, stand on one end. What do you do if someone tries to come to your side of the hallway?" He taps my temple.

"I've done this before; I block them."

He nods. "Imagine a wall dividing your side from theirs. Go ahead, practice. I'll try to read your mind."

I envision the hallway and start stacking bricks in front of me. The bricks are heavy, though. I bet Rune, or any of the royals, with their thick muscles, could build this in no time at all. They can probably do a lot of things with strong bodies like theirs.

Rune raises an eyebrow. "Don't let them know you fancy me."

My mouth drops. "I thought no such thing!"

He just grins. "Don't build the wall. I heard every single thought while you tried to place the brick. This isn't the stone age. Imagine pressing a button and a wall slamming down between our thoughts."

I may not fancy Rune like he thinks, but he ... With a press of a button on the hallway's wall, an impenetrable barrier slams down in front of me, cutting off my thoughts from him. I keep the barricade in place.

"Very good." He continues speaking, but I keep catching my gaze on the gold lines adorning his body.

I point to the pattern. "Why do you have these?"

"War. It's why I have Titan, too. He formed when I was struck with a powerful spell, causing a part of me to split off from itself, thus forming a Phelvie." He quiets for a moment, as though he's choosing his words carefully. "A very good friend of mine sacrificed ... something, a large part of himself ... to intercept the spell. It's the only way to create a Phelvie." His eyes turn glossy, and he blinks away the tears.

He speaks as though this friend is no longer here, and I regret my questions. I glance at Pierce, unsure what I should say or do, before returning my attention to Rune.

"I'm sorry, I didn't mean to bring up such a sensitive subject."

"I don't mind, because he helps me. It's almost like having another set of hands, only his are paws, and his thoughts are my own ... mostly."

"Wait a minute." My eyes bulge. "*You* licked me?!"

Both he and Pierce roar with laughter while I stand there like an idiot, waiting to be let in on the joke. "Technically, Titan licked you. While we share thoughts, he acts of his own accord," he leans in conspiratorially, "... and he thinks you taste delicious."

"Here I was, starting to like you." I scowl.

He gives me a smirk. "Oh, come now. I have a feeling you and I will be great friends. As I was saying, while you were busy admiring my body, try to put your wall in place before bed. Some creatures try to catch you unaware while sleeping."

Heat flushes my cheeks, but I nod anyway. For the next several hours, he shows me defensive magic, and I spend the rest of the evening blocking both his and Pierce's attacks. I'm so worn out, my guard has to carry me to my room, and I take my supper there but don't plan to touch it.

"Oh, hello." I blink, stepping away from where Pierce just set me on my feet.

A tall, very thin fae is in my chambers. Her striking features shimmer under my perusal, giving me a peak at what lies beneath: serpent. Her slitted eyes blink to normal fae ones, and the scales fade from her skin as fast as they appeared.

"You're even prettier than they said you were." Her voice is far richer than I thought would come out and I thank her. "I'm Sarai, your lady's maid."

Her eyes dart to my guard and her cheeks flush. "Hi Pierce."

"It's good to see you." He inclines his head. "Is your family well?"

She nods. "You, too. I'm here to help Lana adjust to life as a fae." Her attention turns to me. "You'll love Bedlam."

Her long arms embrace me, and her hug is surprisingly strong for a waif of a woman. "Anything you need, anything your heart desires, we can make it happen."

I step back and gesture to the room. "This is more than enough.

Possessions mean little, although I do love to read." She follows my gaze to the stack of books already devoured on my nightstand.

"We'll get along just fine."

I return her warm smile. "I'm sure we will."

CHAPTER 25

LANA

Sarai lounges in the grass where Pierce will give me combat lessons. We sit together, watching him instruct his crew. His military unit spars with each other, swords flashing in the sunlight. He's not wearing a shirt, only a pair of black breeches, and I can't miss the way she watches his muscles ripple in the sun.

At my side, Sarai sighs with envy. "I wish I was in the Guard. He's so handsome, isn't he?"

"Yes." I pinch a blade of grass between my fingers. "He's my guard, though. I'm not allowed to look at him like that. You, however, should definitely make a move. I've seen the way he looks at you."

Sarai examines her hands wrapped around her bent knees. "I'm too shy."

"He'd be lucky to have you."

Sarai bites her lip. "I might do it."

I smile, turning back to Pierce. He shouts, "Ready!" and the sparring soldiers all straighten up. I stand and hand Sarai my shoes, eager to begin.

The kings want me to practice combat because every fae has magic, but not all fae can fight without it. This gives me an advantage should someone disable my powers. In this realm, I must be able to defend myself, especially in the public eye.

Pierce points at me. "Over here, Lana." He motions to a spot near him. "Nice and close."

I hurry, aware of his gaze on me. The soldiers give me appreciative glances and spread out around the field like a net.

I stop a bare five feet from him. Sarai moves back into the shade, propping her cell phone on the ground to no doubt catalog my embarrassment. Although, I do envy her position out of the sun. Amongst the mountains, the temperatures can fluctuate sixty degrees in the span of twenty-four hours. Right now, it's at least eighty degrees, maybe higher.

Pierce holds his sword loosely at his side. "Lana." He shakes his head, grinning. "I want to hear steel on steel. I don't want to hear you grunting and moaning."

I give him a puzzled look, but nod. "All right … "

"It'll distract the soldiers." He winks. "Bring your sword."

I yank it out of its sheath and hold it at the ready, pointing it straight ahead. My palms are already sweaty. It's one thing to learn how to fight, but to do it in front of an entire team of soldiers is another. "Like this?"

"Mm, no. You hold it too high." He steps forward and takes it from my hand, positioning the blade in front of me. "Like this."

I mimic the movement, trying not to touch his fingers with mine. "Perfect!" He lets go and addresses a group of soldiers watching our training. "Who volunteers to partner with Lana for the day?"

Every single soldier on the training field raises their hand.

Pierce laughs and walks back to me. "Since there's so many, we'll do what you Earthlings call a round robin. Just say when you're tired, okay?"

"Okay." I swallow hard.

He gets behind me and places his hands on my hips, then leans forward to whisper in my ear. I tense, but don't move. "Just relax."

Pierce walks me through simple jabs and lunges. I follow his motions, the muscles in my arms burning to keep up with him. Sweat runs down my back. He talks me through complex moves, and I follow as best as I can. The gouges in the grass have made the lawn look like someone took a battering ram to it, thanks to my constantly dropping my heavy weapon.

The first soldier up is a woman with deep-set dimples. She has no problem matching my movements, and it's obvious she's a pro.

Her silky blonde hair bobs around her shoulders as she thrusts and parries with the sword in perfect rhythm. Sweat forms on her brow, but doesn't mar her careful makeup. She spares me a quick, tight grin after she knocks my sword aside.

"You have a tell."

I raise an eyebrow. "Oh?"

"Yes." She smirks. "Your left hand twitches when you're about to attack me. I suggest you work on it."

"Thanks, I've got a lot to learn. Appreciate your help ...?"

She shakes my hand. "Captain Zara. I'm Pierce's big sister. You've got nothing to be ashamed of." Her soldiers cheer for me when she moves back into formation.

I knew he had family nearby, but not a sister. A *captain*.

"You're not bad at the sword for a beginner. Let's see how you do with hand-to-hand combat." Pierce points to a soldier towards the back.

Others part for him. His hair is longer than most of the males here, dusting to his cheekbones, his pointy ears parting sections of it. There's no room between his skin and the standard-issue workout clothes he has on—I can make out every muscle. He gives me a cocky grin and lazily snaps his fingers. Water shoots from his hand, dousing himself. His shirt is near-translucent now.

"It's hot." He shrugs and I avert my eyes. "You don't have to be so serious," he teases in a deep voice.

"Okay." I swallow. "Let's do this." I try to keep things cordial.

He jogs forward, his movement fluid. He spreads out his arms in a show of surrender as I mimic him. I don't hesitate. I leap for him, aiming a hard punch at his stomach.

In one swift move, he grabs my wrist and pulls me forward by my extended arm. I lose my balance and fall into him, knocking us both to the ground. He rolls over to pin me with the full weight of his body. The scent of coconut wafts off him, mixed with his natural pheromones.

I curl my legs, trying to kick him off. He shakes his head and doesn't budge. Heat burns in his eyes as they move from my hard stare to my mouth and back, a smile teasing his lips.

"Your attacker has you pinned to the ground. What do you do to get up?"

A vague memory tugs at me.

I know this.

I snake my arms between his to grip his head, yanking it towards me. His eyes flash at my intent and a predatory grin crosses his face.

"You don't have the balls," he whispers.

His warm breath fans my face, and instead of head butting him, I give him a long, hard kiss. He's stunned for a moment before he kisses me back, the taste of mint still on his tongue.

Both our chests heaving, I take this distraction for what it is, and still gripping his face, I raise my elbows up fast and flip him over so I'm straddling him. He may be twice my size, but even fae males get preoccupied with beautiful women.

"Can't say I've ever seen that technique before. You should help me practice." A love-struck grin curls across his face.

I whip my head to the commotion on the far side of the field. Several members of court have arrived, and the kings are peeling off their shirts and are in a dead run our way.

Shit.

When they reach us, I'm still straddling the soldier, stunned. I glance down and hurry off of him while he covers his groin with his hands.

"What in the gods' name was that?" Penn points to the soldier. His eyes are just as tumultuous, his breath panting.

My face heats. "He had nothing to do with it. It's my fault."

Penn's eyes drop to my chest, where the water from the soldier's shirt has seeped into mine, very reminiscent of Cancun at spring break. They snap back up to my face.

"A word in your room, please." He gestures to me before turning on his heel and stalking away.

The soldier's scowl turns into a grin once the royals leave. He gets up and runs his thumb along his bottom lip. "Show me some more of those skills?"

"Wait." I'm beyond confused. "I was certain you were done for, I'm really sorry."

Pierce claps the soldier on the back. "Lana, meet my little brother, Bellamy."

I do a double-take and my mouth drops. Captain Zara, Bellamy, and Pierce all have those deep-set dimples, sun-bronzed skin, blond hair, and lilac eyes. How did I miss this?

"The kings won't hurt me." Bellamy rests his elbow on his scowling brother's shoulder. "Our family mingled on Sundahlia every winter. We're distant cousins."

I shake my head and glance at Pierce. "I'd better go. Great to meet you all."

Like a fool, I curtsy and take off.

When I catch up to Penn, he's pacing in my room. The other two kings don't look very happy with me.

"What was that?" Penn clicks his tongue and points back in the direction I just came from.

"It's my fault, okay? He pinned me, and I did what I remember to get out of it. I was being stupid. I'm sorry."

The kings dart glances at each other. Why are they nervous?

"Are your memories coming back?" Casimir approaches me.

My brows furrow. "I wish." My chest aches at the life I've lost. "I know I've had combat lessons before. I must've been close with whoever taught me."

He looks hesitant. "Your witch trainer?"

I shrug. "Maybe."

"What was his name?" Grimm asks, his voice low.

"I can't remember."

Penn's hand slaps his forehead. "Right, of course you don't." He sighs. "Those vampires really did a number on your memory."

CHAPTER 26

LANA

"You and Bellamy seem close." Sarai raises a brow at me while she escorts me off the practice field. "He's been teaching you a lot of magic the last few weeks, huh?"

"Probably out of self-preservation, I'm sure." I glance behind us. Bellamy rests his arm on his sword while engaging in conversation with his sister, but doesn't keep his eyes off us as we walk back into the castle.

After I'd sent him to the infirmary for the third time because of an errant spell of mine, he talked Pierce into letting him give me private lessons, not even a week into knowing him. It's a lot more difficult to hurt someone when it's just the two of you. Especially when that someone is as good at magic as Bellamy is.

"I see the way he looks at you," Sarai says, her voice low. "He's into you."

"We're friends." I shrug, trying to downplay the way my heart speeds up at her words.

"If you say so." She gives me a knowing smile. "But I think he likes you more than just as a friend."

I'm not sure what to say to that. Outside of Sarai and Pierce, I spend most of my time with Bellamy because of the extra practices we've been putting in. He taught me his cool water trick, although for it to work, there must be water in the air, or water in the vicinity. If we ever found ourselves in the Wastelands, we'd need to bring in potable water, as the land is drier than the Atacama Desert.

He also showed me a few other things he deemed as "safe" for me to know, like how to light a fire with just a snap of my fingers. It was harder than it looked, and I nearly burned down the library while we were practicing. Thankfully, there were no books close enough to the table we were using for target practice, so nothing got damaged.

But the most impressive thing he's taught me is how to disarm a fae twice my size, all without using magic.

"Lana!" Bellamy's voice interrupts my thoughts and I look behind us to see him running down the hallway, a large grin on his face. "I was just coming to find you."

"What's up?" I ask, as he comes to a stop in front of us, barely out of breath.

"You forgot this, and I wanted to show you something." He hands me my small backpack.

I chuckle. "It's mostly just snacks in here."

Shrugging, he takes my hand and starts tugging me down the hall. "Give us a few minutes?" He gives Sarai his best dimpled smolder and she just laughs, shaking her head.

"I'll be in my room if you need me," she calls out to us as we walk in the opposite direction.

"This will only take a few moments, and then you can go back to your room to do whatever it is you do at night."

"Read, mainly."

He leads me down a few twists and turns, until we come to a door I've never seen before. He opens it and motions for me to go inside.

"Where are we?" I ask, looking around the small, dark room. It's dusty and there's a musty smell, like it hasn't been used in years.

"This is the old study." He walks over to a window and opens the shutters, letting in the last of the light. "I used to come in here all the time when I wanted to be alone."

"It's nice." I walk over to a bookshelf and run my fingers over the spines of the leather-bound books. "Do you still come in here?"

"Not as much as I want to." He comes up behind me and his chest presses against my back. "Close your eyes."

I do as he says and feel his hands come to rest on my shoulders. A warmth spreads from where he's touching me and I lean back into him, enjoying the feeling.

"Now, open them."

When I do, the room is filled with flickering candles, their light reflecting off the many surfaces in the room. "Bellamy, this is beautiful."

"I wanted to show you why this is my favorite place in the castle." He ushers me to a couch near the window. "Sit."

I do as he says and watch as he lights a few more candles until the room is aglow. He sits down next to me, and we just stare at the view in front of us. The sun is setting, and the sky is ablaze with oranges and reds. It's breathtaking.

"Thank you for showing me this," I say, turning to him. "It's really special."

"I'm glad you like it." He smiles at me, and I can't help but smile back. "This isn't the best part, though. Give it a minute."

We sit in silence and watch as the sky darkens. The stars come out, twinkling like diamonds in the night. And then, just as Bellamy said, the best part happens.

The moons rise, full and bright, as though they were hung right in this window. They coat a silver light over everything, catching the stained-glass edges and casting images on nearly every surface in the room. They depict each shifter order I can think of: from the serpent to the wolf, to the dragon and phoenix. They're all here.

"It's like being in a dream," I whisper, awestruck by the beauty.

"I come here when I want to escape reality," Bellamy says, his voice soft. "Or Zara's constant nagging about cutting my hair."

I run my hands through it. "I like it."

The loveseat we're sandwiched on is small, and with his enormous weight, I lean into him. Neither of us mind, content to just sit here and appreciate the view. "Thank you for bringing me here."

"Anytime, Lana."

"Can I ask a favor of you?"

"Of course." He shifts so he's facing me.

I take a deep inhale. "I've been here months now, and I'm no closer to finding out who I was before I came here. The facts are there; I was a travel blogger, although I have my MBA from Purdue University and graduated with the highest honors. I drive a green Jeep Liberty, and the key fob doesn't work well so I have to manually unlock it. I know that when I swim in Lake Superior, I'm likely to get tiny red leaches stuck to my body in a matter of minutes. I'm an excellent cook, though where I learned it, I don't know."

I brush the tears away from my cheeks before continuing. "Have I ever been in love? Who shaped me into the woman I am today? Am I well-liked, or did I only have a small circle of friends? Have I lived an easy life? Or did I face heartache after heartache? I don't know, but it's as though my physical body remembers, just not my mind."

"It hurts." My fist pounds my chest. "Here."

Bellamy wraps me in his arms, holding me, helping to keep me from falling to pieces. He's quiet for a long time, as though carefully considering his next words.

"I'll help you, Lana."

CHAPTER 27

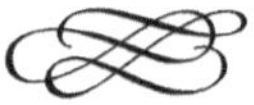

LANA

"Just like that." Bellamy's voice is like a balm to my frazzled nerves. "You're among friends now, Lana. There's no need to be afraid."

I'm not sure if it's his words or the way he says them that makes me believe him, but I relax fractionally. "Thank you," I say quietly.

"Of course." He nods and leads me down a long hallway.

For the last several weeks, he's helped me get my bearings around the castle, and now we're practicing cloaking magic. We're hiding from Pierce and Sarai. The object is to remain undetected for two hours, which is what everyone in the castle practices in case of invasion.

The scent of Bellamy's cologne fills my senses as he leans close to me, his body heat warming me. "You're doing great," he whispers. "Ninety more minutes and we win."

The rules of the game are simple. If I'm detected by either my guard or lady's maid, the timer restarts. I've lost twice already. I'm determined to win this time, taking care not to be too loud.

I concentrate hard, picturing myself as invisible. Bellamy catches my eye, amusement dancing in his lilac gaze, and I flush. It's hard to concentrate when he's looking at me like that.

"Lana." His voice is a husky whisper that sends shivers down my spine. "You're biting your lip."

I release my bottom lip and give him a sheepish smile. "I'm trying to focus."

"I know." His hand comes up to cup my cheek, his thumb tracing the line of my jaw. "But it's so cute when you do that."

Butterflies take flight in my chest, and I lean into his touch. "I'm glad you think so."

I'm so lost in his touch, my concentration falters, and what little cloak I had over us fades. Pierce and Sarai materialize in front of us, and the timer restarts.

"I'm sorry," I say, my face heating with embarrassment.

Bellamy grins at me. "If this is some way to continue spending time with me, I'm all for it."

Pierce coughs pointedly. Sarai's cheeks flush, and I cast her a knowing grin. Bellamy catches the brief exchange and narrows his eyes.

He claps his brother on the back. "Scoot. Time's ticking!"

Pierce laughs and obediently leaves, but Sarai lingers. "Good luck," she whispers before disappearing.

"What was that about?" Bellamy asks, his gaze on me.

I shrug innocently. "Just girl talk."

He studies me for a moment before shaking his head. "I'll never understand women."

But I think he likes the mystery.

We sift to another part of the castle. This time, we end up near my bedroom. Glancing at my watch, I curse. Two minutes to cloak us both before our official countdown starts.

He places his hands on my shoulders to steady me. "Breathe, Lana. You can do this."

I close my eyes and take a deep breath. When I open them again, I see the castle walls around us, but it's hazy, like looking through a thin fog.

Pierce and Sarai round the corner, and I tense, but they don't see us. I exhale the breath I was holding and relax fractionally.

"Good job," Bellamy whispers, his lips grazing my ear.

I shiver and lean into him. If I wasn't trying to win the game, I would've stayed there all day.

But the timer is ticking, and I have to focus.

I take a deep breath and concentrate on holding the cloak. It's harder than it looks, and I'm starting to get a headache. Bellamy rubs my shoulders in an attempt to ease the tension, but it's not working.

"I can't do this," I whisper, my voice shaking. "It's too hard."

"Yes, you can." His voice is firm, and I open my eyes to see the determination in his gaze. "Think of it like a blanket draping over the two of us."

My face heats at the mental image, but I do as he says. I picture a soft, plush blanket engulfing us, and slowly but surely, the haze thickens. This layer is all I can manage, but it's better than nothing.

After the two have long passed this section of the castle, I pull Bellamy into my bedroom. I collapse onto the bed, exhausted from the effort of holding the cloak, but manage to keep it up. Just two hours. I've got this.

He flops down next to me, a satisfied grin on his face. I gesture to the king's doors and tap my ear. Bellamy nods and throws a sound barrier around us, so we're free to talk with no one hearing us. It's more advanced than cloaking people, and I haven't gotten there yet.

The veil begins to wane, and I panic. Bellamy scoops me up and places me under the covers before sliding in next to me. It works better to help envision a blanket over us when there's a real one there.

A giggle bubbles up from my throat, and I burrow into him. This game is more fun than I thought it would be. Especially with Bellamy by my side. His arms are strong and comforting around me as we lie in bed, cloaked from the world.

His racing heart under my ear settles my nerves. I'm not the only one feeling this between us, it seems.

"Why did you and your siblings decide to become soldiers?" I ask, my voice muffled by his chest.

Bellamy shrugs. "It was that or work in the mines."

"Mines?"

"Yeah. On Draconum, it's backbreaking work, although the pay is decent."

"So you became a soldier to avoid that?"

He nods. "Plus, it's kinda fun."

I snort. "Fun?"

"Yeah. You get to travel, see new things, fight bad guys, and, if you're really lucky, end up under the covers with the most beautiful fae in all the realms."

My cheeks flush, and I hide my face in his chest. "I'm sure you say that to all the ladies."

"Nope."

We fall into a comfortable silence, and I close my eyes, enjoying the feeling of being safe in his arms.

"Lana?" His voice is hesitant, and I open my eyes to see him watching me.

"Yeah?"

"I know we've only known each other ... What, a month or two? But I want you to know that I ... like you."

My heart swells, and I smile. "I like you too, Bellamy."

He kisses me then, soft and sweet. And at that moment, under these covers, I know this is the beginning of something special.

I pull back slightly, resting my forehead against his. "I'm really glad I beat you on the field that day."

"You mean, you're glad you kissed me on the field that day." His beaming smile is contagious, and though I want to scowl, I can't help but return it.

"That, too."

"Forgive me if this is too forward, but would you like to spend time this winter with me in Sundahlia? My family has this really cool interconnected colony of treehouse homes I think you'd love."

My heart flutters. "That sounds amazing, actually. I'd love to."

When the timer nears the end, Bellamy gives me a chaste kiss and slips out from under the covers. He tucks me in and winks before leaving the room, sound barrier in place.

I close my eyes and let out a content sigh, feeling more at peace

than I have in a long time, and happy about what the future might
hold.

CHAPTER 28

LANA

Sarai cinches the corset tighter, and I wince as the strings dig into my skin. The dress is beautiful, but with its old-fashioned waist trainer, it's not my style. None of them are. She reads my face and lets the dress out so I can breathe.

"Would it be terrible of me to make my own?"

She cups her hand over her mouth while she considers my question. "Yes."

I frown, and she looks away. "And if I did it, anyway?"

A smile curls her lips, and she leans in conspiratorially. "Then it'd be perfect. Scandalous."

I love my new fae body, and I'll be damned if I'm going to squeeze it into a dress several sizes too small. I'll pave my own way down the catwalk here.

"I'm going to teach you a spell, but you didn't learn it from me. Pierce thinks of you as like a little sister and wants you covered up, so under no circumstances can he know I taught you. Understood?"

I nod. "Of course."

She beams, pulling out a handful of pins and vials. "I can't wait to see what you do." With swift fingers, she completely unlaces the dress, causing it to pool at my feet. "Get naked."

My eyes widen, and they meet hers in the mirror in front of me. She gives me a slight nod of encouragement. I breathe in deep and peel off my underwear and bra, my skin pebbling in the cool air. She comes to my front and places the pins in my hand before uncorking the vial and pouring it on top.

"Close your eyes and envision the dress you want to wear, down to the finest details."

I do as I'm told, picturing a black form-fitting silk number with slits up both thighs, showing off my bare legs and my strappy black heels. The neckline dips to my belly button with a halter strap, and the entire back is open except for a diamond-shaped design at the very top of my spine.

As it forms in my mind, warmth spreads across my skin, and when I open my eyes, the pins glow in my hand. "Good job." She beams again before giving me a hug and returning to the mirror.

The pins drop to the ground, and I take a step back as the dress forms over my skin, lining itself. She gasps, and I turn to the mirror.

"It's beautiful." I breathe in awe.

Her voice is barely a whisper. "Good gods."

She whirls around and steps back so she can take me in. "What did you do?"

"I don't know." The fabric falls as I turn again. "I just envisioned what I wanted."

Her eyes dart back and forth across the lines of silk adorning my body. "You have *got* to teach me this."

I chuckle. "I don't know if I can, but I'll try. When I was a little girl, I had dolls and layered the outfits to create what I wanted. I'm pretty sure this was one of them."

"Dolls?" She furrows her brows. "Oh! You mean those human toys?"

I nod. "Yup. My memories are intact, I just can't remember anyone in them but me."

She bites her lip and shakes her head while she takes me in again. "Simply ravishing." She squeals in excitement. "Let me do your hair, though. It's my specialty."

"Can I make a request?"

"Fine."

"Keep it down?" I plead.

"Of course. I'm going to work with the curls you already have."

A KNOCK SOUNDS at the door, and Pierce announces himself.

Sarai greets him. "You look very handsome." She steps back as he laughs.

His eyes twinkle as he looks down at her. "I have a guard giving me a few breaks. I'll find you when it's my turn for a dance."

"Gods in all the realms!"

My vision catches on Bellamy, his mouth agape, eyes huge. Pierce straightens his spine before whipping his head in my direction.

"Y-y-you can't wear that." My guard sputters.

"Why the hell not?" I attempt to put my hands on my hips, but only grab a handful of silk. "This was made specifically for me." I smirk and catch Sarai's glee from the corner of my eye.

"It's scandalous."

"Oh, for god's sake! It's a ball. People are going to be scandalized when I walk in with you lot. Besides, it's my party."

"I'll go change." Sarai turns back toward the closet.

"What do humans say? You look hot, Lana." Bellamy nods his head at me.

I place the back of my palm against my head. "I feel fine," I feign.

He laughs, returning to normal as he shuts the door. "You're stunning."

Pierce clears his throat and resumes a guard's stance. "The Kings request your presence in the ballroom now."

I roll my eyes. "You don't have to be so formal with me, Pierce. I'm not like that." I link my arm through Bellamy's.

Before we exit, we linger in the doorway, and I pull Bellamy down so I can whisper in his ear. "Save me a dance?"

He gives me a dimpled grin and presses a kiss to my cheek. "You can have them all. I'm off duty tonight."

"I'd really like that."

MUSIC SPILLS out of the room as we approach. The usual sound of strings and waltzing flitters to my ears. Before we step through the door, Pierce turns to me.

"Don't drink the wine."

I scowl. "It's my party?" The kings are throwing it in my honor for passing my basic magic lessons. I hadn't planned on drinking because I don't care for alcohol, but now that I'm forbidden to, I just might.

"It's for your own good."

I give him a curt nod and enter the ballroom. The music quiets, and all eyes turn to me.

The three royals stand at the forefront of the room, their mouths agape. I grin before curtseying. After a pregnant pause, Grimm is the first to recover and puts on an air of grace while moving my way. He takes my hand and bows before announcing my arrival.

A smattering of applause erupts, and the music starts back up. The kings lead me through their court to the center of the ballroom. Even their courtiers keep a wide berth from them, as though the trio are too powerful to be near to. I'm led to the center of their circle, and I turn in a slow arc, adjusting to the scent of perfume and sugary spirits. My eyes take in all the fae arrayed before me, and I blink at the sheer number of them. Everyone is here, and they're all focused on me.

"Thank you for your generosity in hosting me. I don't know what to say."

"Lana." Casimir is the first to speak. "This is your home now."

"Yes, it's all lovely." I spin around.

They decked the ballroom in what I can only describe as fae gaudy. Gold and silver lights wind through the room, held up with magic so they don't droop. Matching silk panels decorate the ceiling. They tint the lower lights purple and blue. Tiny creatures buzz about, as though they're fussing over the tiny details, but the sound is far too quiet for even my fae ears.

"I may be fae now, but I'm still very much human. Probably always will be." I bite my lip.

Grimm wraps an arm around my waist and pulls me in. "It's a lot to take in, we know. You look ... ravishing. How about we have the band play something you probably know?"

"I have a wide range of preferences. This is okay." I smile.

The kings laugh, and Grimm dips me. "Nonsense."

Grimm kisses my cheek before walking off towards the band. Penn hands me a glass of wine, and I grin at Pierce before I take it.

His face is calm and collected, but I know he's seething inside. There's something so fun about pushing his buttons. Sarai giggles before throwing her hand to her mouth. Only then does Pierce crack a smirk.

I tug Bellamy down to whisper in his ear. "Why do they call my trainer Rune? Someone said that's not his real name."

He runs his tongue along his teeth and grins. "He tattooed magic runes on his cock, so he knows when someone is sexually attracted to him."

My mouth drops.

"B-b-but ..."

Bellamy shrugs. "Why he did it, I don't know."

"So he knows when ..."

He nods. "He won't hesitate to call you out on it, either."

I glance at the band when they stop playing, and my attention flits to Grimm as he hooks up his phone to the sound system. After a few seconds of static, the telltale beat of In da Club by 50 Cent blares from the speakers.

I down the glass of wine and chase after a server walking by to hand it to him. "Thank you!"

I stride back towards Bellamy. The room looks tentatively at me, as though everyone is waiting for me to show them how to dance to this.

He meets me halfway and pulls me into his arms. I giggle as he sways us to the beat of the music before shaking my head.

"Like this."

I show him how we dance in the clubs in Minneapolis. He learns quickly before his hands drop lower on my hips. His grip is sure and strong, and I lean in to press a kiss to his jaw before we dance again.

"All humans dance like this?" he whispers. "I think you need to give me more lessons."

I grin. "Millennials do."

My head swims with the wine. It's not my drink of choice, but it's good enough. Before I know it, we've gone through some Eminem, DMX and Grimm has even played Here Comes the Hotstepper. Fae only watch me for a short time before they've figured out how to dance to the song, repeating the process with each new one playing.

Sweat plasters hair to my neck and I'm burning up. "Let's go outside to cool off."

Bellamy brings me through the crowd to a set of double doors on the far end. This leads outside to a large set of stairs. We stroll down them before I tug him to a stop near a large fountain that looks like a woman catching water in her hands. Except instead of plain water, streams of magic imbue the liquid, giving it an indigo glow.

"I've never seen anything like this." I half-drag, half-walk him to the fountain.

I sit on its edge, slipping off my heels and dipping my feet in the cool water. Bellamy does the same before sinking down next to me.

"It's beautiful here." I lean against him. "I'm glad you brought me outside."

He watches me for a moment. "You're beautiful here."

My heart stops before it beats hard. He looks nervous, unsure of himself, which is something I've never seen from him before.

Biting my lip, I look into eyes full of want and need. His gaze drops to my lips, and I grab his shoulders and pull him into a kiss. It's hot as fire, full of the desire of the last couple months of sparring with each other on the training field and our private magic lessons. My hands slip into his hair.

The kiss is bruising, possessive, and he grips my hips to pull me into his lap. He growls, a low sound against my lips that makes my core ache for him.

"Bellamy!" Penn yells. "Break it up!"

I freeze, and Bellamy growls again at the sound of his cousin's voice.

"I'm 503 years old and we can't even kiss without them interrupting." He groans, nipping at my jaw, before turning to glare at Penn.

Penn's eyes are on us, narrowed and critical before I look away. My cheeks flame as I try to scoot off Bellamy's lap, but he doesn't let me up.

"We were taking a break from the music," Bellamy says coolly. "Everything okay?"

Penn's expression tightens, and his eyes dart to me before he nods. "I need you to take Lana back inside. Sarai is looking for her."

"Fine." Bellamy stands with me before he sets me on my feet. We both slip into our shoes.

Before I can say anything, he storms towards the steps with me following him. My heart aches because I don't want to go back inside, and he looks mad as hell.

"He's just worried about me." I grab his hand. "Don't be upset."

His eyes soften. "I'm sorry."

"You don't have to apologize. He's your friend."

My heels click against the stairs, and I wobble a bit. Bellamy catches me before we ascend them, and he doesn't let go of my hand.

"You're drunk." He gives me a small smile. "I think I'm going to have to stay with you tonight to make sure no one gets any ideas about taking advantage of the new fae."

I roll my eyes. "You're worse than Grimm."

Bellamy tugs me to a stop and kisses me. "I want to stay with you." His dimples peek out at me before he frowns and shakes his head. "Sorry, the wine is talking. I mean, I do want to stay with you, but I can't."

"Okay," I whisper, as he pulls me close and presses his lips to my forehead before we walk back inside.

The music is thumping, and the lights are too bright. It makes me feel like I'm walking on air as Bellamy guides me through the crowd. People I don't know bump into us as we make our way to the dance floor.

"You're back!" Sarai says as she wraps her long arms around me.

"I had a break from dancing." I smile at her and her eyes dance with glee. There's no hiding anything from her.

Bellamy turns towards me again, leaning into my ear. "Meet me at 2 am on the bridge on the west border. There are some things you need to know. It's important."

I nod, and he turns before striding towards the doors.

"How are you enjoying the party?" Sarai asks as she grabs my hand.

My eyes follow Bellamy's back as he leaves, and my heart flutters. "It's nice. Everyone is so friendly." I speak to her but don't look her way.

"That's because they're all obsessed with you." She smirks.

"What?" I laugh and lean closer to her. "That's silly."

"It's not," she whispers. "The kings are practically in love with you. You're the first to receive any of their attention. Ever."

My brows furrow. They've hardly spent any time with me, save for meals.

"They're just being nice to me because I'm new here. That's all."

"It's more than that, and don't pretend you haven't noticed them staring at you with hearts in their eyes."

"That's just stupid. They're not in love with me."

"Fine, you don't have to believe me. I'm just glad they can finally stop pestering me about you." Her voice deepens in a mocking tone. "What's Lana's favorite color? Does she like jewels? Gold? Do you think our orders will scare her away? Has she talked about us at all?"

I register what she's getting at and cock my head before glancing towards the kings in conversation with each other. "Really?"

"Really."

I stare at them for a moment before I look back at Sarai. "Why don't I know about this? They're grown ass ... men. Males? Why don't they ask me themselves, instead of getting you to do their dirty work?"

"Aren't humans afraid of directness? And ... sex? It's supposed to stay between man and wife?" She furrows her brows.

A laugh barrels out of me. "What?!" I give her my full attention. "Have you ever met a human before?"

"Well, no. But everyone knows humans fear sexuality."

"Why would humans fear sex?" I stare at her in disbelief. "It's good. And fun."

She blinks. "Oh. Oh, dear." She appears lost in thought. "What about the Pope? Priests? And nuns? Aren't they the leaders of your world?"

Laughter steals the breath from my lungs. "Priests and nuns aren't the leaders of humans. They're holy people who believe in a higher power. The Pope oversees Catholicism, and I'm not Catholic."

I know there are some fae on Earth. Why are they telling fae back home this? I mean, it's hilarious ... but it makes little sense.

"So, they don't have sex?"

"No!" I shake my head. "Priests and nuns aren't supposed to have sex. Ever. Some do, though. But humans? I have quite a voracious appetite considering I'm a former human."

"Well, no wonder they want you so badly."

I smile through my astonishment. "Um, what?"

"They *think* you're the forbidden fruit," she says, as if it's the most obvious thing in the world. "Especially when you've caught the attention of Bellamy."

I bite my lip and stare at her, unsure of how to respond. "I'm not so sure that's any better."

"It is when you're the one they want." She kisses my cheek. "Enjoy it, Lana. It makes life very interesting when you have three kings lusting after you."

She releases me and vanishes into the crowd.

CHAPTER 29

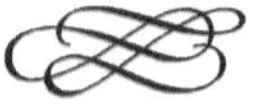

LANA

Grimm's hand on my hip sends warmth through my skin. He speaks into my ear. "May I?"

I stare up at him, his face blurred by the lights that flash around us. I'm all too aware of the other kings watching, but Grimm is the only one who matters right now. "Of course."

He leans over me and takes my hand before turning me towards him. I place my other hand on his shoulder, and he pulls me closer, his fingers firm on my hip. His scent envelops me, fresh and clean like the wind.

I'm intensely aware of his eyes on me as he leans closer. He speaks above the music. "You looked beautiful standing there, waiting for another glass of fae wine. Do you feel its effects yet?"

"Does the wine heighten feeling?" I adjust my dress. "I feel good."

He smiles, and the gesture causes warmth in my chest. "You should never be nervous around me, Lana."

I'm not sure if it's the way he says my name or what he says. The slow ballad of fae music fills my chest until my heart beats in time with it. The lights flashing around us give me a surreal feeling, like I'm caught in some dream where only Grimm and I exist.

He speaks into my ear again. "You shouldn't be nervous around *any* of us."

I glance away and watch the other kings, their stares pinned on the two of us.

Grimm turns me away from him and pulls me back, our bodies flush against each other. He murmurs into my ear. "Not when we want to be closer."

My heart races with a mixture of anticipation and desire. When the song ends and an upbeat one begins, I don't know what to say. I step away from Grimm, and he releases me.

A server comes by, and I grab another glass of fae wine. How many have I had? Three, maybe four. I'm downing the glass when Grimm looks over my shoulder. I follow his stare to see Casimir approaching.

He bows. "May I have this dance?"

I glance at Grimm before nodding my head. "Of course."

Casimir takes my hand, and I place my free one on his shoulder. He pulls me closer than Grimm did, his muscular arm pressing against mine. Affection swims in his eyes, and I find it difficult to look away from the intensity.

"How are you enjoying Bedlam?"

"It's beautiful." My eyes sweep over the ballroom that seems to go on forever, each wall lined with windows that look out over the forests and mountains. "Everything is so ... striking."

Casimir nods, his gaze still on me. His eyes look like molten silver under the lights. "We want you to feel at home."

"I do. Thank you." I don't know what else to say. They rescued me from evil vampires, made me fae, and took me in. How do I repay their kindness?

"We're happy you're here." Casimir's voice is low, like he's sharing a secret. My heart races again, but not because I'm afraid or anxious. It's excitement that causes a flutter in my chest.

The song changes again, and Casimir steps away from me, his touch lingering. He bows with a flourish. "Thank you for the dance."

I curtsy, and he walks away. Grimm steps beside me, leaning into my ear. "I have to share you."

My cheeks heat at his words, and he places a hand on my back. "Come with me." He leads me to the other kings, who stand in a semi-circle. When he stops, I move to stand before them.

Maybe I should have asked where we were going, but I'm too nervous to think of the right words. Grimm presses his hand into my back. Penn speaks first, his voice thick like honey. "You look extraordinary."

I glance between all three of them. Grimm's hand on my back is the only thing keeping me composed. "Thank you."

Casimir places a hand on my shoulder as he speaks. "We're pleased you've joined us." He tilts my chin up with his thumb. "We want you to feel as though this is your home."

I swallow, my mouth dry. "It is. Thank you for letting me stay."

Yes, I should have said something more eloquent, but I have no idea what to say. I don't notice Grimm walk away until the music switches to something from Earth. With the fog from the wine, I take a moment to recognize Pony by Ginuwine.

I grin. "Are y'all going to give me a strip tease or something?"

Penn smiles, showing a dimple. "Maybe later." He grabs something shiny from his pocket and places it around my neck. "I got this neck-lace for you."

I don't get much of a chance to look at it, but from the weight alone I know it's extraordinarily expensive. "You didn't have to." I sway on my feet.

Casimir's arms wrap around my waist from behind. "She's had too much to drink."

Penn chuckles. "She's very relaxed."

"I—"

Grimm presses a finger on my lips. "Do you like this song?" he asks, his accent strong. His fingers move up my arms to rest on my shoulders.

"I do." My insides warm with the implications of his question. He doesn't need to ask to know what I want ... how badly I need to be close to someone.

To all of them.

"Dance with us." He winks, and the foggy feeling intensifies as my heart beats faster. My body moves to the rhythm of the music, letting it seep into my bones.

I'm beautiful. Why shouldn't I rope in three sexy kings? It's the least I deserve after surviving this long.

"I want you to feel at home." I immediately forget whose lips brush against my shoulder as he speaks, but the pleasure it brings me is unforgettable.

"I do." I swallow hard. "Thank you for letting me stay. It's beautiful here, and you..." My voice trails off.

Penn cups my chin, forcing me to face him. "We want you to be comfortable with us." He stares into my eyes, and I nod as he presses his lips to mine. His kiss is hungry and demanding.

The kings drink their fill between wine and stealing kisses from me. No one speaks as they each consume as much of me as they can manage. I lose myself in the music, in the pulse of thumping hearts, in the sensation of hands on my bare skin, the slide of silk against my breasts.

Darkness shrouds us, circling like sentient smoke, blocking us from the prying eyes of the crowd. "That's Rune's gift—shadows and storms." Casimir speaks against my temple.

Song after song plays, each one taking me deeper into the promise of pleasure. When my body can't consume any more wine, I surrender to the melody, even more decadent than the drink.

In a foggy daze, a reminder tugs at my memory. I'm forgetting someone. Who am I supposed to meet?

"I ..." I stop.

Penn kisses my cheek, his lips warm and soft against my skin. "She's had enough."

Grimm's eyes meet mine. "Let's take her to her room."

I sway on my feet, and Grimm takes advantage of that, lifting me off the ground in his brawny arms. Casimir and Penn flank me, my escorts leading me out of the ballroom.

The fog lifts, and a moment of clarity penetrates my mind. "I have to meet someone." Pressing my hand to my forehead, I gasp. "I can't forget, he has something to tell …"

Penn's voice is firm, but gentle. "Who?"

I search my mind. "Bellamy."

Grimm chuckles, the sound sending ripples of pleasure to my core. "Meet you where?"

I rest my head on his chest and furrow my brows. "The bridge to the West."

"When are you supposed to meet him?" Penn's voice is softer than I expect it to be.

"Two."

They glance at each other. "We'll take you to your room to rest before it's time to meet up with him, okay?" The quiet rumble of Grimm's chest soothes me, and my eyelids flutter closed.

"Mm'kay."

It's not long before the soft press of the mattress envelops me. Grimm shushes me before tucking the blankets up to my chin and kissing my forehead, like a warm caress of silk against my skin. My eyes are already closed when I hear retreating feet and the quiet click of the door close.

CHAPTER 30

LANA

A beam of light floods my eyelids, causing me to jolt awake. A scream is on the edge of my tongue as a smooth hand clamps down over my lips, muffling the sound. I try to bite the hand, but my teeth find no purchase. The person is as fast as a viper.

"It's me," Sarai whispers.

I open my mouth to speak, but she shushes me. I nod, and she releases me. She clicks off the flashlight.

It takes a few seconds for my eyes to adjust to the darkness of the room, but finally I can make out the form of my lady's maid.

"What is it?" I whisper back.

Tears spill down her cheeks. "Bellamy . . . oh, gods."

I sit up. "What's happened?"

She wets her lips. "He's . . . he's betrayed the kings."

Shock freezes my tongue, and I can't form words. I glance towards the window. It's still pitch black, so I mustn't have been sleeping long.

"I just heard from Captain Zara." Sarai pulls off her nightgown and starts pulling on warmer clothes. She makes to grab something from my armoire before glancing at me and seeing me still in my ball gown. "He's challenging Penn for Draconum King. If he wins, Penn will lose his power and be killed."

My stomach twists into a knot of disgust. "Why would he want to be king?"

She opens her mouth to speak, but snaps it shut again.

"What is it?"

Sarai shakes her head, fear marring her face. "I can't say, but he doesn't like how they're handling things with you, and he wants to make it right." Her fae order sits just under her skin. I've never seen it so clear as now, where her pupils are slitted, taking in every small creak in the room.

Bellamy doesn't think the kings should've turned me into a fae? Rescued me from vampires? Hurt slices through my chest. "What if Bellamy loses?"

Sarai shrugs. "There's no way they'll kill him because of his bloodline. Even if it's cruel, he'll go to Bedlam Penitentiary. It won't be so bad for a powerful fae like him."

"What can we do?"

Her eyes meet mine and she stills her movements. "Nothing."

I spring from the bed, cross the floor, and fling open the door.

"No, Lana!" Sarai pleads behind me, but I don't listen. I race down the hall and skid to a stop in front of Grimm's door.

"Grimm, open up." I slam my fists against the heavy wood.

Silence greets me. I shout for him again, and I get nothing but stillness when I press my ear to the door. I put my back against the wall and slide to the floor. Tears streak down my cheeks, and I bury my face against my lap.

"He's not here." Casimir offers me his hand. He's dressed for the day, and his hair is damp as if he just took a shower.

I ignore his hand and stand on my own. "Where is he?"

He narrows his eyes, sorrow etching the corners. "Bellamy challenged Penn for King of Draconum."

"Where. Is. He?" I hiss.

Casimir doesn't flinch, but the wince that flashes across his face tells me everything I need to know. "Bellamy lost. They're taking him to prison."

"No," I whisper, feeling the world spin around me.

Casimir swallows hard. "He's being taken to Bedlam Penitentiary."

"No," I repeat, but this time it comes out like a cry. "You can't let them. He can't go there." I beat on his chest.

Clinking metal sounds from the hallway and I whip my head in its direction. "Pierce?!"

I scowl when Penn comes into view, instead. Deep slashes cut across his bare chest, and his hair is a mess. My stomach sinks when I realize what the cuts must be from. I move my sight to his eyes, but they're blank, emotionless.

"Lana," he breathes. His slumped shoulders rise slightly on his inhale, and he grimaces from the pain.

"What have you done?"

Penn flinches. "I did what I had to do."

"You can't send him there." Rage boils in my stomach, and my fists shake at my sides. "Not when he was just trying to protect me."

"I did what I had to do," he repeats, and his voice sounds far off. He's distant. Dark.

"He belongs *here*."

The moment my words leave my lips, his face changes. Anger flashes across it, and he takes a step towards me. I shrink away, morbid curiosity at how he'll act, spurring me on to see if he'll snap and go fae on me. He doesn't.

Penn swallows hard and flexes his wrists.

We stand off against each other, neither of us moving or saying a word. After a few moments, it sinks in: I have no business being here, making demands of kings of a foreign land I don't belong in.

"I'm sorry," I whisper, and rush to my room. My hands tremble as I turn the key in the lock. I slide to the floor and curl into myself as my chest tightens. I can't breathe.

How did this happen? Why did this happen? I thought Bellamy liked me and was glad the kings brought me to Bedlam.

"Lana?" Sarai calls through the thick door. "Let me in."

I don't respond.

A screech echoes from the hallway, and a bang fills the quiet.

The door shudders when Sarai slams her shoulder against it, but it doesn't give. "My lady, open the door."

"What's going on in there?" Grimm shouts.

Another bang shakes the wood, but the door remains shut.

"I need to make sure she's okay." Sarai's urgent pleas hurt my soul, but not enough to let them in. "Please."

My gut twists in agony. I don't want to hear the exchange, but it's impossible to block out.

"Leave her alone," Casimir orders, his tone strict.

"You don't understand," Sarai cries. "My lady is hurting."

"Leave her alone," Casimir repeats, and his tone is final. "She needs time to grieve."

After the sounds of them retreating die out, I pull myself to my feet and lock each of the doors to my room, including the one from the bathroom so no one can enter. I slip out of my dress and crawl back into bed, not bothering to brush my teeth or wash my face. I'll regret it in the morning, but right now, I just don't care.

Darkness greets me, and through my tears, I watch it swirl around me. Here in this sea of black, drowning feels imminent. If it comes to it, I know how to swim. It's less about swimming and more about staying afloat.

I'm not sure what time it is when I open my eyes, but it takes me a moment to adjust to the pitch black, and a knock raps against my door again.

I let it go unanswered.

"It's Casimir." His voice carries through the near-impenetrable wood. "I need to speak with you."

"Go away," I call, my voice thick with sleep. "Come back later."

"Please open the door."

I don't respond.

He knocks again, but it's gentle. "Please, Lana."

Part of me wants to answer him. He's being nice to me right now, but I can't trust any of them. Not after what they did to Bellamy. "I don't want to talk," I whisper, and a sob takes root in my chest.

Bellamy was my friend. Maybe even something more.

CHAPTER 31

CASIMIR

"Casimir!" Grimm's reprimand for my pacing stops me in my tracks.

A whine escapes me, and I shift my feet. "It's been four weeks."

"What were we supposed to do? Let him die because he opened his big mouth about Finn and what really happened that brought her here?" Penn flicks his dagger, catching it midair. "You and I both know if we had let him meet her, he would've talked and died on the spot. The magic decrees it!"

"He loved her." I scratch my nail along the groove of wood on the bar. "I'm not saying what he tried to do was okay, just that I understand."

"She's barely eating or talking to anyone," Grimm says, his voice low. "You've seen her."

"She's hurting." My voice softens. "It was a dick move."

"We had no choice!" Penn shouts and slams his glass on the bar. It shatters, pieces scattering off the counter, the sound echoing off the walls. "*I had no choice.*" His voice breaks.

My heart squeezes painfully. I know this hurts him the most. Bellamy is his cousin, and as Draconum King, Penn was the only one

Bellamy could challenge. But he did. He challenged him and lost, all because he wanted to tell Lana the truth.

"I sectioned him in the VIP area of the prison." Grimm places a hand on Penn's shoulder. "No harm will befall him."

"Keep telling yourselves that." I rub my thumb and finger over the scruff on my face. "She's not going to forgive any of us. They were close friends. More, even."

"He knew what would happen if he got caught." Grimm kicks at a shard of glass on the floor. "And he did it, anyway."

I approach the bar. "What if we change the narrative?"

"What do you mean?" Penn turns towards me.

"I don't know. Tell her he's serving community service or something?"

Grimm shakes his head. "We've already told her so many lies. They're weighing heavy on me."

He's right. "What if we don't lie?" I lean forward.

"Speak plainly, Casimir." Penn balls his fists. "Please."

"What if we tell her the truth? How he was planning to commit treason, but not the extent of it, our decision to punish him the way we did, but make him serve at Bedlam Penitentiary as a guard instead of a prisoner? It's not too late to amend his sentence."

"It's not a bad idea." Penn leans against the bar. "She might listen if it comes from you or Grimm. I can take care of the sentence change."

A weight visibly lifts from Penn's shoulders. "Thank you."

"We can try." Grimm's tone is uncertain. "What if she won't forgive us?"

I shrug. I can't say for certain. "We tell her the truth, and we figure it out from there."

Lana

I LICK my finger to turn the page of my eighth novel this week when a knock sounds on the door. It's not from the main one, but from one of the king's rooms. I set the book aside and creep out of bed, my feet chilling on the cold tile floor.

"I'm sleeping," I call through the door, but I don't open it.

"I know, but I need to speak with you."

My heart aches. It's hard to hear the pain in Grimm's voice. "Give me a minute."

I slip my robe on and secure it around my waist, then open the door.

"Lana." He takes my hands in his. His are warm, but trembling.

"Are you okay?" I ask him.

"I'm fine." He tries to smile, but fails. "It's something else, actually."

When I curl my fingers into my palm, he squeezes my hand. He holds it to his heart, and warmth floods me. "What is it?"

He clears his throat, and the muscles in his jaw tighten. "I stopped by to tell you we're releasing Bellamy from his punishment. He's not a prisoner anymore. Instead of serving here, he'll serve as a guard at the prison."

My legs weaken, and I reach for the door handle. Grimm steadies me, his grip on my elbow gentle but strong. "I don't understand."

"I don't know how to tell you this without telling you the entire story, and I can't, so I'll tell you what I can. He was planning on committing treason because he didn't agree with us on some issues. When caught, he did the only thing he could do: challenge Penn for the throne. We had no choice, and trust me when I tell you, Penn took it harder than any of us. Bellamy is his cousin. *His best friend.*"

Tears blur my vision. I knew they were related, but I hadn't realized they were so close. I wipe at them with the back of my hand. "How bad was his treason?" I usher him towards the couch.

"Bad enough we couldn't allow him to be free with the plans he was hatching. He's served his time, and now he's free."

Relief floods me. "When can I see him?" I sink into the cushions and pull a pillow to my chest.

"You won't."

"What do you mean?" My brow furrows. "Of course I will."

Grimm shakes his head but doesn't meet my eyes. "He's not your anything anymore, Lana. One condition of his release was staying away."

"What?" I lean back from him and shake my head. "Okay, I'll go to him."

"Lana." His tone softens. "He has to stay away from *you*."

I flinch. "What did I do wrong?"

"You have done nothing."

"I don't understand." The silence of the room feels like a cavern between us.

He sighs and rubs his forehead. "You did nothing. He has to stay away from you because he can't be trusted."

"He's trustworthy." I shake my head and pause on my exhale. "What about his honor?"

Grimm leans back and rests his head on the top of the couch. "I'm not explaining myself well."

"Then explain it to me with words I can understand." I cross my arms over my chest, and he looks away.

"He has details about top-secret missions he was going to spill that would've killed him instantly because of a magic decree. We believe even if it leads to his own demise, he will speak about these top-secret events with you, resulting in his immediate death. We can't let him die, so he has to stay away from you."

I furrow my brows. "Why would he tell me anything top secret?"

"He's in love with you."

I blink. "He's in love with me? Are you sure?"

Grimm nods. "Who wouldn't be?"

I laugh. "Well, he's not."

"In his eyes, you are the only one who matters. In his eyes, his duty doesn't exist. I'm not saying this to make you feel bad, but he loves you like it's the last thing he'll ever do."

I swallow the lump in my throat. "That's not love, Grimm."

"It is to him." He places his hand on my arm. "I can see your pain. I know you still care for him, but please don't go to him."

I pick at a loose string on the couch. This is fucking bullshit. "So he gets his honor, but I lose mine?"

"It's for your own protection."

"I don't understand."

Grimm sighs. "Promise me you won't speak to him."

I stare at Grimm, my gaze unwavering. "Promise me that if I agree, you'll never harm him again. There will be no more imprisonment. No punishments."

"Agreed. But you mustn't go to him."

I nod, pain echoing in my chest, but relieved he'll be okay. If Bellamy could die for me, I can buy him his freedom, even if it hurts me. "Promise me one more thing."

"You don't need to bargain for things, Lana. If it's in my power, I'll make it happen."

"I'm asking this of you because you're probably the only one who can."

He takes a deep breath and nods. "Okay. What is it?"

"Make me forget." Even as I speak these words, grief radiates through me at what's to come. "Take his memory away from me." I don't want to have the temptation of ever going to Bellamy and risking his life.

He hesitates, his face sad, but places his warm hand against my cheek. "Okay."

CHAPTER 32

FINN

The cloud cover had obscured most of my flight over the forest near the Canadian border. Early today, I emerged through a portal near the Boundary Waters, and I now fly low, using the dense forest as cover. I've been to Earth before, but the last time was centuries ago, and everything looks different. The rumble of a park ranger's truck catches my attention. In Bedlam, vehicles were outlawed years ago, so it's startling to see one in the wild. Nature is the same, but the stench of pollution taints even in this near-pristine wilderness. Through it all, remnants of her presence hang in the air like an invisible ribbon, leading me southward.

As I near my destination, her cabin comes into view, and I descend. Oak leaves cover the driveway, and the roof is mossy green. A nearby river sings to me, and I can smell the water's coolness. For a moment, I'm lost in her memories here as a child, the ones she showed me when she reminisced with me during our time in the woods.

I land on the frost-covered grass and tuck my wings away. The memories are a bittersweet comfort, but I'm here for a reason. Oz, her vampire mate, has a property nearby. As a witch, I'm hoping he has the place warded.

A teensy tiny peek inside the cabin first.

I cross the yard and enter the cottage through the front door. The old lock is no match for my magic. Inside, the smell of dust and age assails my nostrils. Cobwebs cling to the ceiling, and the windows are coated in a thin film of grime. It's obvious no one has lived here in years, yet her presence is still strong. Her core memories run deep here.

The fireplace is barren, and the ashes long cold. I brush my hand over the mantle and imagine her here as a child, happy and carefree. So different from the trauma-wounded woman I know. Sorrow briefly washes over me, but I shake it off and continue my search.

Two small beds sit in each of the far corners, and I zero in on hers. A lump catches in my throat when I lay on it. Her scent wraps around me, and I breathe her in deeply, swallowing to keep the tears at bay. Closing my eyes, I allow myself to feel her presence. It's faint, but it's there, hidden in the memories of this place.

Echoes of her laughter and happiness fill my heart, giving me the strength to continue. I swing my legs out of her bed, leave the cabin, and head to Oz's.

Stopping at the end of the driveway, I spot a handmade sign Lana must've etched in wood as a kid. It reads "No Trespassing" with inverted S's. I follow the gravel road through the woods, listening for any sign of life. A light breeze carries the faintest hint of magic on it. I follow the path until I reach a wide driveway.

The property is well maintained, and lights broadcast their beams through the trees. I approach with caution and stop in my tracks when the house comes into view. The grandeur of the place doesn't sit well with me. What drew Lana to him? She doesn't care about money or objects.

Magic vibrates the air the closer I get to the house. I try the door-knob, and it's locked. I run my hands along the perimeter, imbuing power into my fingertips. With a quick snap of my fingers, the door flies open. A pulse reverberates through the house—I've tripped the alarm—and a smile ghosts my face.

I stop in the entryway, taking it all in. My vision catches on a painting across the foyer of a woman draped in cloth and I inspect the corner signature. Why would he keep a provocative painting of a woman who isn't Lana? I lift the piece off the wall, cross to French doors on the far end of the house and chuck the painting down the ravine.

She deserves better than this, no matter how tastefully painted it was.

Ignoring the rest of the house, I come back inside and follow her scent up a stairwell, down a hallway, and into a bedroom. I'm assaulted by the smell of them—Lana and Oz. My heart constricts, and I have to remind myself I need her vampire mates.

I allow my fae vision to take over the gloomy room. The furniture is large and made of dark wood, though it's refined. The scent of her arousal lingers like a heavy blanket as I approach the bed. I snatch the pillow and bury my face in it, breathing her in. I can feel her magic sparking under my skin, and I let it consume me. The pain of her absence cuts me deep.

Slipping off my shoes, I pull the covers back and slide under them. I'm surrounded by her essence, and I allow myself to drift off into sleep. By morning, I should be face-to-face with her mates.

CHAPTER 33

LANA

I'm in bed reading when there's a knock on one door of my room. The sun went down many hours ago; it has to be past midnight by now. Who could call on me this late? I'm uncertain which door the knock came from, so I hike my duvet up to my chin to cover my sheer nightgown—devious little Sarai's doing, no doubt. She's convinced the kings sneak into my room at night to watch me sleep. "Come in!"

"Good evening." My dark fae strolls in with his hands in his pockets.

"Hey Grimm, everything ok?"

"May I?" He gestures to the foot of my bed, and I nod. When he sits, the duvet pulls down with his weight and I cover my chest with the book I borrowed from the small bookshelf near the window.

His eyes dart to the cover, and a grin spreads across his face. "I wondered why I could sense your arousal as soon as I neared your room; this is the story about the fae prince who seduced a mortal. Let me guess — you're at the part where she finally gives in to her desires and allows him to take her as a mate. Right?"

My body burns under his watchful gaze. I was just getting to the good part of the book.

"Oh, don't be embarrassed — you're one of us now. Fae are wanton creatures. Don't tell me you don't feel the desire building in you, pulling taut, desperate for release?"

My core stirs at his words.

"I ..." He raises an eyebrow at me, and I try to steal my heaving chest and pounding heart. "It's been a while. I think?" It pisses me off I can't remember a single person. If I ever get a chance to face the vampires who did this to me, I'll kill them myself.

"It would be my honor to pleasure you, Lana. I expect nothing in return, other than the victory of knowing I've given you your first orgasm in Bedlam."

"First?" I raise a brow.

He grins. "You cheeky thing."

"Okay."

It takes a moment for Grimm to realize what I said 'okay' to. I see the moment it registers as his pupils blow out, and I can hear his fast heartbeat from here—it's taken me a while to get used to heightened senses. I set the book down, and his gaze fixates on the way my nipples have tightened under my nightgown. When I toss the duvet off the rest of my body, his eyes soak in every single inch of my body, drinking me in like a man lost in the desert.

The room feels quite warm now, as though our desire has turned the space into an inferno. Grimm reaches behind him to grip his tight black t-shirt and pulls it over his head and drops it to the floor. His abs cut to a deep V that disappears below his pants, and I have to resist the urge to beg him to take the rest off. Best not to take it all the way tonight.

"Come here, so I can take off your nightgown."

I stand and fight the trepidation in my gut while I stand in front of where he's sitting on the bed. He leans forward and I feel his breath puff against the apex of my thighs while he lifts the gown up and over my head. I love the way my body looks; my curves and smooth skin make me feel comfortable in my nakedness.

With swift hands, he hoists me onto his lap so fast I let out a yelp before he spins and deposits me on the bed. Grimm spreads my knees, opening me up for his perusal.

"Look at how beautiful you are." He runs a finger along my slit, and I suck in air when he pulls his finger to his face. He rubs his glistening fingers together before putting them in his mouth—languidly licking them clean, and groans as he does so. I don't know why that's so hot to me. "You are sweeter than fae wine."

There is no time to respond before he dives between my legs and runs his flat tongue up the length of my core. He laps at it, and I let out small whimpers of pleasure before he parts me with his tongue and finds my clit, sucking in unhurried movements. A loud moan burst out of me at the pleasure of it. When he dips a finger into my warm sheath, I buck my hips towards him, and he lets a husky chuckle out before going back to devour me. He adds another finger, and it's all the encouragement I need—I slide my hands through his hair and hold his face while I grind against it.

My entire body convulses when an orgasm rips through me far faster than expected. Grimm doesn't stop until I ride wave after wave of pleasure and collapse back to the bed.

"I have to say, that was the hottest fucking thing I've ever seen."

I scramble further onto the bed and pull the duvet over me as soon as I hear the fresh voice in the room. My gaze immediately finds Penn and Casimir lounging on the couch in front of the bed—each with hooded eyes and bare chests.

"Were you guys here the whole time?!" Embarrassment creeps into my voice, and I cringe.

Grimm stands and wipes his mouth with the back of his hand. "You guys are assholes."

"We heard her yelp and thought there might've been trouble." Casimir has the decency to look guilty at the intrusion, but Penn doesn't appear to share the same sentiment.

"Don't let us stop the fun. The show was just getting started." Penn licks his lips. "Unless you want us to join. You have a rather gigantic bed ... big enough for all of us."

I scowl at him, despite the thrill his words send straight between my thighs.

"Have you reached the part in your lessons about how fae are deviant creatures with enormous sexual appetites? And how sharing mates is normal amongst royal fae?" Penn leans forward and rests his elbows on his knees.

"He's ... he's not my mate." Never mind the fact they're the only kings and none of them have mates.

"Oh, Grimm hasn't taken you as his mate; this is true. But he wants to if you let him, and he will share you with us. We'd all mark you, and you'd mark us."

I admit; learning how fae share mates to strengthen their magic intrigued me when Sarai first told me about it. Why would they want me as their mate, though? I'm nobody—they're royalty. They can have their pick of any woman. "Why?"

"You're everything we want; strong, intelligent, beautiful, kind. It's also what we need." Grimm sits down next to me on the bed.

"I've never wanted a marriage of convenience. If I marry or mate, it will be for love. Sorry."

Casimir approaches the bed and crawls onto the other side of it. "You wouldn't be without love, Lana. We're not asking for your hand right now; we only ask for an open mind to the possibility of sharing a life with all of us. In time, we hope you can see the love and devotion we have for you, and if we're lucky—you can return it."

"I don't think any woman in her right mind would turn down the opportunity to have three sexy males as her mates. I'm open to the idea, but I'll only act on it if there's love between us."

"So, you think we're sexy?" Penn has the grin of a Cheshire cat, and I toss a pillow at him with more force than I intended.

"I do. Very."

"Have you ever been pleasured by more than one person before, love?" Casimir smooths the wrinkles on the bed.

I adjust my position so I can lie back against my pillows so I'm more comfortable. "I can't recall who I've been with, let alone whether there were multiple people."

CHAPTER 34

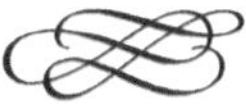

FINN

If these weren't Lana's mates, I'd have killed them already, be it by magic or by hand. Vampires are weak compared to fae. Still, I've allowed them to bind me to this chair, hoping they'll listen to me. I need their resources to get her back; I no longer have the backing of the fae realm.

Just as I thought, a reconnaissance team had captured me at Oz's cabin in Minnesota and brought me straight to them. They put me on a private jet—wasteful creatures—and brought me to Australia. All I had to do was mention Lana's name to initiate the movement.

I take a moment to size up my competition, and a smile crawls across my lips. The darker one is king. I can tell he runs the show here. The other two are hers, but I'm not sure which is Gideon and who is Auguste.

"Where's our mate?" Power radiates from Oz. Lana mentioned he was a witch before becoming a vampire.

I grin. "You must be the wizard of Oz." I can't help myself. Ever since Lana invited me to Earth, I thought about the moment I'd meet the King of Vampires and say this to him.

He just scowls at me, but the others? The small upturn of their lips lets me know they think it's as funny as I do, though they try to hide it.

"The kings have taken her and wiped her memory of *anyone* she ever met; any lovers she's had, her friends, teachers, parents, children, mates ... and me. She doesn't remember any special moment with any person."

"And who are you?" The leanest of the three paces in checked anger.

"I'm Finian Drake, former High King of the Luna court." I look each of them in the eye, one by one. "Lana is my soul bonded mate."

Fury ripples through the room and the vampires roar in anger. They dart to attack but meet the invisible shield I placed around me.

"That's impossible." The biggest one spits. "Lana would never."

"No one *chooses* their soul bonded mate. She chose to mate with you, but fate sent her to *me*."

The king strikes my shield with attack magic, but it's no use for my power.

"You assholes left her under-prepared—"

"What proof do you have?" This comes from the slimmer, more level-headed one of the three.

"Aside from the fact she brought you back to life? As my soul bonded mate, whether or not she consummated the bond, she'd have the gift of necromancy. If you need more proof, on Lana's first night in Bedlam, a berserker fae pulled her from sleep and brutally maimed her before leaving her for dead in the forest." My voice catches, and grief mutilates their faces.

The king doubles over with his hands on his knees while I tell our story.

"Witch magic doesn't work in those woods; she was defenseless, and bleeding out. I woke to her soul crying for mine. I didn't know what it was at first, but I followed the beacon of light leading me to her—*hours* away from my camp. When I got to her..."

I have to collect myself and blink away the tears. "She was cold, and so pale. There was so much blood. When I went to scoop her into my arms, her life blinked out. She *died*." I spit, so angry at how unprepared she was. "Then I gave her my blood, and I caught a flicker of life, barely hanging on by a thread. I immediately set to heal her most grievous injuries. Once I could staunch some of the blood, I carried her through the woods to a river with healing waters. All the while I used my Luna order to heal her while I ran."

The king sinks to the floor and holds his head in his hands. "He's telling the truth."

The other vampires whip their heads towards Oz.

"Every single night, ever since Lana was a small child, she dreamt of a man carrying her through the woods. She was adamant the man was not her captor but was her savior—he glowed."

The air rushes out of my lungs, and not a force in this realm or the next could stop the tears cascading down my cheeks at his admission. Lana never once mentioned this to me. Did she know I was the man in her dreams?

With a slight pull of my wrists and ankles, I ease out of the restraints. The manacles fall away with a clatter to the floor. The vampires don't make a move to stop me. I rest my head in my hands, and try to replay our every interaction.

When Lana first woke, recognition had registered on her face, but her thoughts dismissed that notion. Her reasoning? She'd only met one fae before; the monster who nearly killed her.

I raise my eyes to look at her mates. "Help me get her back."

Oz

My Dearest Sahira,

Finn is here. We've got him locked in the cellar while we try to figure out what to do. To begin with, we were outraged this fairy could claim to be anything more than an acquaintance to you. It wasn't until he told me about your first night in Bedlam that I connected the pieces.

I'll tell you this when I see you, but I need to write it down now as proof of my feelings on the issue. I don't blame you for any of this. You probably harbor a tremendous amount of guilt over something you couldn't control, knowing you. I have only one word for you: don't.

Soul bonds aren't anything you could've ignored, and not a thing would've prevented the bond from materializing. We can't be angry. If you're happy, we're happy. It'll take time, but we'll make it work. Anything for you.

Eternally yours,

Oz

CHAPTER 35

LANA

flop over and punch my pillow into submission. Why can't I get comfortable? This bed is the best money can buy, and so are my pillows. I sit up to turn on the light and glance at the clock. *Three o'clock.* I swing my legs over the edge of the mattress and kneel on the plush rug before reaching under the bed. My hands fumble around in the shadows for what I'm looking for.

I tighten my hold on the small chest and drag it towards me. My fingers tremble trying to unhook the clasp, but manage after a few tries. Inside the miniature trunk is an assortment of herbs I collected from the courtyard garden in the center of the castle. It's one of my favorite places to be when I have downtime. Once these supplies run low, I'll fill the containers with the herbs I grew myself. I'll have to—they've overtaken my room.

Placing the box on the bed, I rise and take out what I need to make a sleeping drought. It tastes terrible, but works fast. I stumble against the bed and wince at a sharp pain in my back. When the hurt recedes, I make the mixture and gulp it while squeezing my nose shut.

I don't bother putting the herbs back under the bed and instead place them on the nightstand. Within minutes of falling into bed, I'm asleep.

~

AGONY RIPS THROUGH ME, causing my back to arch at an inhuman angle. My piercing scream rattles the night. The shrieks bellowing out of me match the cadence and sting of each slice of my fingernails against my back; my attempts to claw out whatever beast is inside me proving futile.

The men nearly bust down each of their doors to get in, but I barely register the concern on their faces as sobs tear out of me. I've shredded my top from clawing at my back.

My wails barrel out of my chest and settle into my bones. Casimir falls to his knees next to me to inspect my back, and I rock on my heels as I crank my head toward the mirror on the far end of the room. Bright streaks mar my skin, and rivulets of glowing blue blood pour from the deeper slashes.

"Gods, Lana," Grimm panics. "What's going on?"

I bellow an incoherent answer and curl in on myself. Power radiates from me in such strong waves, it suffocates the room, causing the kings to clutch their chests. A shock wave blasts from my back and throws them across the room. Penn lands against the armoire, splitting one door down the middle, and knocking the breath from his lungs. He scrambles towards me, but pauses in abject horror while I lay over my thighs, gripping the bedspread beneath me from the onslaught of pain.

A final scream tears from my throat when the feeling of my back splitting in two nearly levels me. Sweat drips into my eyes, the sting no match for the utter misery ripping through me. My back strains and I raise my head, meeting the wide eyes of the kings, Pierce, and Sarai, stilling as though they've seen the gods themselves.

"What?" I croak.

Silence greets me, and my trembling hand reaches over my shoulder to feel how badly I've wounded myself. Instead of meeting gaping injuries, my fingers sink into downy silk. My breathing stills while my gaze tracks over the bedspread, across the floor, and then rises to meet my eyes in the mirror.

I blink, and shift my attention to my back. Two giant wings sprout from my shoulder blades and drape down my back like a golden down blanket. One slips and falls off the bed, and that's when I see the glowing blue tips.

Casimir rises to his feet. He approaches the bed, taking care not to startle me, and places his hand on my forearm.

"Are you okay?" Grimm meets me on my other side. The others rummage through my small medicine chest for something to take care of my wounds.

I lift my head and stare straight ahead. When I speak, my voice is hoarse. "*I have wings.*"

Gideon

HELLO BEAUTIFUL,

How attached are you to the idea of keeping Finn around? If you aren't completely smitten, I can take care of him. If you are? Well, I've prepared this list for you.

Reasons Why I'm Better Than Finn:

- *I turned your dad into a vampire when no one else would*
- *I'm charming*
- *I make you laugh*
- *I haven't stopped searching for clues about your mom's whereabouts*
- *Oz and I gave you your first DP experience*
- *I can't read your mind, but still make you happy*
- *I'm leading the initiative to figure out what happened to your mom and where she might be in time*
- *I'd storm the gates of hell for you (Bedlam, too)*
- *I bring the thunder from down under*
- *I'm the father of your children*
- *My fangs are longer than his*

- *I haven't stopped searching for Dolphina Darling*
- *We share a love for poke bowls*
- *I'm great with chopsticks*
- *You love my monster-sized cock*
- *I taught you the art of negotiation*
- *I'm not afraid to show emotion*
- *You chose me when you didn't have to*
- *I've always made my intentions clear*

Your #1 Mate,
Gideon

CHAPTER 36

LANA

While I scoot back my chair from the dining room table, Casimir calls to me from the other side. "Do you have to leave so soon?"

"Sorry." I sit again. "I have some work to do in the garden I'm building on my balcony."

"We'll get you more help," Grimm offers, scraping the last bits of food from his plate into his mouth.

"I don't want you to spend your time and energy on my project." My hands knot together. I'm already too indebted to these fae. "I'm practicing growing what I need using magic."

Grimm perks up. "Can I see what you've done?"

I smile. As Occasus King, his order and the Terra order have dominion over plant growth. The soil on Occasus is rich in minerals and organisms that fuel plants. "I'd like that."

Casimir pushes his plate away. "I want to see, too."

"You all go." I wave them forward and follow behind. "I need to clean up this mess, anyway." I stack plates and drop them in the little window leading to the kitchen, pausing to thank Clara, the chef, for the meal.

As we walk out of the dining room and into the foyer, I explain my reasoning. "The balcony garden is my way of giving back to Convectus Castle. I've used a lot of healing supplies during my time here."

The males laugh because they know it's true. More than a handful of times, I've had to patch up one of the soldiers after I screwed up during combat or magic training. Getting used to my new body hasn't been without challenges.

"It's the least I can do."

They push out through the door of the private residences. My fingers immediately tingle with my magic as we near my room. My plants are thirsty.

We cross the threshold, and I release my hold on the magic to protect the plants from their hungry gluttony. Two steps inside and I halt, stunned by all the greenery that's grown in the couple of hours I've been out. "Wow."

"You did all this?" Grimm exclaims, as if he's seeing me for the first time.

"I've had a lot of time to myself." I run my hand along a romil bush, and it reaches toward me.

The kings haven't been in my chambers since the ball because they've been busy dealing with soldier assignments—aside from their brief visit when I gained wings. I did most of the work in the first week, and have maintained or tried to hybridize some plants.

"I didn't know you were interested in healing plants." Casimir inspects a hybrid I've been working on.

With my magic, I pick a romil flower and hand it to him. "I thought I should keep some on hand, especially since I haven't felt well. My body is still adjusting to being fae."

They cast glances at each other. "What do you mean, not feeling well?" Casimir turns towards me.

"My back hurts from the strain of my wings when I practice unleashing them, and there's something wrong with my chest." My palms rub near my sternum. "The best way to describe it is it feels like the dog I raised from a puppy was tortured in front of me and I just watched it die."

Grimm places a hand on my arm to console me. "Grief?" He darts his eyes to Penn. "Over the life you lost on Earth, but can't remember?"

"Maybe," I shrug. "Some days are better than others. Sometimes, it aches so bad I spend all my time in bed, crying."

Grimm pulls me into his arms and whispers against my head. "Why haven't you said anything?"

"I didn't want to worry anyone." I inhale his scent, and it comforts me. "I've felt this way since my first night in the castle."

Casimir wraps his arms around me, too. "If you're feeling unwell every day, we need to know."

"It's fine. The herbs help on days when it gets to be too much to bear." I pat their backs.

Grimm takes my hand into his own and kisses the back of it. "We need to take care of you. If there's something wrong with your body, we'll fix it."

Penn brushes his fingers along my arm. "I agree."

I nod. "Okay."

"Maybe some time out of the castle will help," Casimir suggests. "You've been locked away in here a lot."

"I'm trying to figure out what I need to do next." I pull open my armoire and start picking out clothes.

Penn picks up a hanger and inspects the dress. "We don't want you to leave here."

"You've done too much for me as it is." I fold the dress over my arm and meet their stares. "I have to find a job, a way to support myself, a place to live?"

"You have a place to live with us." Penn gives my shoulder a playful swat with a different outfit. "We brought you to Bedlam and want you to stay."

I cross to the bathroom and pause in the doorway before turning back to look their way. "I'll think about it." The door closes with a click.

After washing up, I towel dry my hair and slip into the dress I picked out. As I'm looping my mountains of hair into a bun, a knock sounds on the door.

"Come in. The door's unlocked." I take a seat on the chaise lounge.

"Gods." Penn's eyes widen. "You look great, but I'm sure you know that already."

Casimir walks over to wrap his arm around my shoulders. "I agree with Penn."

"I'm glad you approve." I snatch up my dirty clothes and drop them in the hamper. "Lead the way."

We pass through the courtyard on our way to the front gates. A small cortège of soldiers follows us, led by Pierce. "Why are they here?" I gesture towards the GIs, and wave at the ones I recognize.

Penn's lips curl into a smile. "We're taking you out."

"I haven't had a proper outing since I came here." My steps slow. "I've got nothing to wear anywhere fancy."

"You look perfect." He throws his arm around my shoulder.

"Besides, where we're going, you won't need clothes." Grimm waggles his eyebrows.

I groan. "You're not giving me any more of that damn fae wine." Pretty sure I threw myself all over them at the ball because of it.

"Of course not." Penn holds up his hand. "Promise. If you want it, though, just say the word and we'll get it for you."

I scowl before burying my head in my hands.

"If it makes you feel any better, fae wine doesn't make you do anything you don't want to already. The drink simply lowers your inhibitions." Penn runs his fingers through my hair. "If you want us, it won't stop you from saying so."

I groan. "You're not making it any better." I stumble over a cobblestone but recover.

Just outside the gates are the stables. The horses already have saddles. I narrow my eyes and glance at Penn. "Just three?"

"I should've asked if you knew how to ride." He offers his arm to help me climb into the saddle. "Next time."

"I've ridden horses on Earth. Are they the same here?" I slip my foot into the stirrup and swing my leg over.

Penn situates himself at my back and scoops me into his arms. "Same principles here."

As he settles behind me, I can feel his body pressing against mine. He's hard as stone, and I can't help but arch against him.

Casimir grins at me over his horse's back. "You're not very good at hiding your feelings."

I scrunch up my nose. "Sure I am."

"Keep your mind closed and it won't be so obvious." He kicks his horse into a gallop, leaving us behind.

"Nah, I like her broadcasting her thoughts about my hard body." Penn adjusts his grip on me before kicking the horse to catch up. "That's not the only thing hard about me."

I giggle while we race through the woods until we reach an old, abandoned village. A stream bisects it. "Meloria was once the center of Fae trade on Convectus."

"Why is it abandoned?" I stare around at the empty roads and boarded up windows. "Seems like a waste."

"When we enacted strict pollution laws, fae moved closer to larger cities because many didn't have transportation. So a lot of small towns and villages became abandoned." Penn speaks over my shoulder.

"At least some good came from it, though." Grimm tosses a starseed apple my way.

I turn in Penn's arms to face him. "You're an environmentalist?"

"We all are." He gives me a lopsided smile that makes my heart skip. "Plus, it made sense for several reasons. We had too much pollution affecting everything—our lands, water supply, even the fae themselves. So it only made sense to clean up our act."

I nod my understanding. Before I can say anything more, Grimm pulls his horse to a stop. "We're here!" He taps the back of his horse's head, and it kneels.

"We'll walk the rest of the way." Penn dismounts, then reaches up for me.

Grimm leaps down, then undoes the saddlebags on his horse. "It's not far now." He takes a flask from the saddlebags and passes it to me. "Drink up."

"What is it?" I sniff at the flask. The liquid inside fizzles.

"It's prairie pixie juice." Grimm winks at me. "Or, as we like to call it, liquid courage."

"Is it like fae wine?"

Penn nods beside me. "Yes, and no."

"It's not naughty like fae wine, and there's no alcohol in it, just magic." Grimm shrugs. "Quite the opposite of what you had at the ball, really."

Penn grins at me over my shoulder. "It will just help you relax." He winks at me again.

"I'm not worried." I eye the drink again.

"Just a little sip," Casimir says from my other side. "It's powerful."

I tip it back slowly. The juice is sweet—like candy. I take a long pull of it before handing it to Penn, who hands it back to Grimm.

"Let's get going." Casimir swings his leg over the horse and drops next to me. "Come on, Lana. You're going to love it."

I grab his hand, and he hauls me behind him as I run after him. Penn is hot on my heels. He scoops me up before I can stop him, and Casimir laughs as he chases after us.

I cling to Penn's neck as he runs faster, Casimir on one side of us, Grimm on the other. The wind whips through my hair, and laughter barrels out of me.

We leap over a fallen tree in our path, and when we land on the other side, we stop. I stare at the nicer section of the town of Meloria. It's encircled by a waterfall and mist-filled lake.

"When people abandoned this place, we turned it into a summer village, where the fishing industry brings families for several months out of the year. No one is here now." Penn sets me down, and I step back to take it all in. There are small houses made of stone dotting the settlement. Trees hide some, while others have white picket fences surrounding them.

"They're so cute." I approach the nearest cottage and peer into the window at a small table and chairs. "Where do the families go when it's not fishing season?"

"Home to their own lands." Penn points to a large brown house in the middle of the village. "That's the main house. It used to be a lodge until we used it for ourselves and built these homes for villagers to use for free, instead of paying for a room."

I stare at the beautiful building. "It's nice." Large pillars hold up the roof, and there's a balcony off one room on the second floor.

Penn points to the waterfall near it. "That's where we're headed."

Grimm and Casimir lead the way, and we follow, with Penn guiding me by my hand. Casimir is the first to reach the top, and in a blink he's completely naked, running towards the edge.

I grip Grimm's arm. "Is the water deep enough?"

"It's why we're here." He nods. "Near where he's about to jump, it's a good fifty feet deep."

I watch as he jumps off the edge, and the males lead me up the back of it, the roar of the waterfall drowning out my gasp of alarm. I peer over the edge as Casimir surfaces, and I watch him swim to a rock beneath us.

When he reaches the boulder, his fingers curl around it, and he pulls himself up until he's sitting on top. He leans forward, resting his arms on his knees, a smirk teasing his lips while he stares up at us.

"I'm next." Grimm takes his clothes off, then steps behind me, dropping them on the ground at my feet.

Alright, then. I glance at Penn, and he's grinning at me.

"Scared?"

"Of course I'm scared!" I didn't think it'd be this high.

"You can do it, Lana." Penn's voice is low near my ear. "I've got you."

I nod, and he steps away. I strip down to my bra and panties, too self-conscious to let him see me naked in broad daylight.

Nearing the edge, my knees wobble. I cling onto Penn and peer over.

"Come on! Jump!" Grimm calls from below.

I stare at the water for a while, trying to clear my mind. Closing my eyes, I leap forward, letting myself fall.

My eyes fly open after I plunge into the cold water, and when I come up for air, Grimm swims towards me.

"You did it!" His grin is wide. "I'm impressed."

"I was always going to. I just had to convince my body."

Penn pulls me onto his back after he surfaces and swims over to the rock. "I can't believe you didn't wait for me!" He laughs.

"I had to jump as soon as I cleared my mind, otherwise it would've taken twice as long."

Grimm reaches for me and pulls me onto the rock. "Ready to go again?"

I nod. "If I sit here any longer, I'll freeze."

From the corner, Casimir watches me with a smirk. "You can stay here, and I can keep you warm."

"Uh-huh, is that all you'll do?"

He puts up his hands. "Hey, I didn't say how I'd keep you warm." He winks.

I roll my eyes. "You're all shameless."

"What do you expect?" Affection coats his words, basking me in warmth. His grin widens. "Race you to the top?"

"Sure." I drop into the water and swim to shore. By the time I make it, the others are halfway up the cliff. I take my time enjoying the view of their firm backsides.

When I reach the top, the royals give me an expectant look. Of their own volition, my eyes travel down their bodies and I throw my hands over my face.

"No! I did not mean to look at your ... at your ..."

Penn bursts out laughing. "Yes, we know. But for future reference, you can look. All of us are very proud of our bodies. We enjoy yours, too."

I drop my hand and narrow my eyes at him. "You haven't seen me naked."

"Lie," Grimm croons. "The first night you fell asleep in the tub, you had to cross the bathroom naked to reach your towel while we were undressing. We all saw you."

My face heats at the memories. "I forgot."

Grimm steps closer to me and cups my face. "We didn't forget."

"I only saw it for a moment, but I assure you, we could never forget," Penn adds. "Oh! And the time Grimm was between your thighs."

"I'm not talking about anything I've seen." My voice is barely a choked whisper. "Ever!" I shout as I leap off the cliff.

This time, I don't open my eyes.

For a while, silence reigns. When I finally come up for air, Penn swims towards me, and I climb onto his back.

"Why are you always so warm? I'm freezing."

"Compliments of my dragon order." He swims for a small cavern and sets me on a rock. "Here, dry off and get dressed while we're swimming."

I watch the three of them swim and laugh about something. Pulling my dress over my head, I pause. Did he say dragon?

"Penn!"

"Yes, love?"

I slide the dress over my hips, and it swishes around my ankles. "Did you just say you're a dragon?"

"Yes, my fire warms me." He wades over to the shore. "Why?"

Holy crap. My mouth gapes, opening and closing, but nothing comes out. Not even when he calls my name.

"I don't understand why that's such a big deal." He steps out of the water, shakes off his hair like a dog, and picks up his clothes.

"You-you have wings?" I squeak.

He runs a hand over his shoulder before he steps into his pants. "Well, yes, all dragons have wings, Lana."

"Oh." My eyes widen as I realize what he means. "You mean you're a real, proper dragon?"

He smirks. "I live most of my days as a normal fae, but my order is a dragon, so you can sometimes see me in the skies. It's why my room has the largest balcony in the castle. Earth has dragons, no? You call them dragonflies? And Komodo?"

I tuck my lips between my teeth to hold in my laugh. "Those are insects and reptiles, not fairy tale dragons." I approach him and inspect his back. It's smooth—all long planes and hard muscles. My hand trembles as I reach out to touch his skin.

"Can I ride you?"

My eyes bulge and I yank my hand back to throw it over my mouth. "I didn't mean to say that."

He licks his lips. "You can ride me anytime, baby."

"Oh, my god. You all need to get dressed." Heat creeps into my cheeks and I spin around to face away from them.

Casimir chuckles. "Can she get any more adorable?"

"She's so cute when she blushes." Grimm steps into view. "I'm glad she doesn't mind us being naked."

Penn groans, and I peek at his face. His eyes are closed, and his chest rises and falls faster. "Yes, she's not as innocent as one might believe."

I frown at him. "What are you talking about?"

"We saw your fantasies, Lana." Penn rubs his thumb over my cheek.

"I don't have fantasies," I blurt.

"Yes, you do," he insists. "The one with the three of us in your bathtub is my favorite. Well, except the shower one where we take turns with you."

"Oh." Heat creeps up my neck.

Casimir winks. "My favorite is the one where she invites us into her bed one-by-one, growing more daring as the night goes on. If I'm not mistaken, you have this one most nights, yes?" He steps closer and wraps his arms around my waist from behind.

"C-can you read my mind from your rooms?!" I squeak as I try to break from his hold.

He tightens his grip and kisses my shoulder. "Rarely. Just the loud ones. Why are your fantasies always so loud?"

"They're not." I kick out at him.

He laughs, and Penn cups my face, the two of them sandwiching me. "Don't worry, love. You can tell us the ones you want to act out. We'll make it happen."

I shake my head and avert my gaze, not wanting to see the lust in their eyes.

"Which are your favorites, Lana?" Casimir whispers into my ear. "You can tell me."

My gaze returns to Penn's in front of me, and I shrug. "I could show you."

His eyes light up, and he nods. "You can show us anything you want."

My finger trails an errant drop of water sliding down his chest. I stop it and bring it to my mouth. He watches every move, hunger flaming in his eyes.

Out of my peripheral vision, I catch the movement of soldiers in fatigues across the water. "We have an audience, boys." I point to their guards.

Casimir releases me and steps back with a sigh.

"We'll finish this later." Penn nods to his underlings across the way.

Pierce is there, as are several of the soldiers I've trained with. I guess we were loud enough for them to hear, taking bets on what we'd be doing before they arrived.

I should be embarrassed or upset, but I just shrug. "I guess we should head back."

Casimir walks by my side while we head to the horses, occasionally brushing against me. "Have you figured out my order yet?"

"By the way you constantly touch me and try to keep the peace, I'd say you're a golden retriever."

"Is that an insult?" He looks to the others, but they're red-faced and breathless, giggling like schoolboys. "I think she just insulted me."

I give him a playful shove. "Golden retrievers are my favorite."

"In that case ... thank you, but no." He stands a little taller. "I'm a wolf."

I run my fingers through his hair and smile at him. "It suits you."

We stop at the horses, and he helps me onto his. "You're going to spend time with us tonight, right?"

"Maybe." I shrug and then lean back to whisper in his ear. "Show me your wolf?"

His grin spreads. "I'll show you mine if you show me yours."

"I don't know what kind of fae I am yet." Sitting forward, I bite the inside of my cheek. I thought I'd know my order right away, but it's been months.

He takes the reins. "You'll figure it out."

194

CHAPTER 37

LANA

It's a nice evening, with hardly a cloud in the sky, and just a slight breeze to keep the heat at bay. The moons hang close in the sky, providing just enough natural light. I'm curled up with a book on my balcony, a glass of fae wine at my elbow, and a plate of cheese and crackers on the side table.

The floor beneath my feet trembles, rattling the table and my book, spilling some of my wine.

"What the hell was that?" I speak to myself before setting my book on the table and leaning over the balcony to see if anyone else noticed the tremor. A few guards mill about below, looking up at me.

"What's happening?" I call down to them.

"I'm sorry, milady. Must be King Penn."

Penn? The floor shakes again, stronger this time, and my book and wine glass topple to the ground. Miraculously, the glass doesn't shatter.

"Sorry again, milady! Maybe now would be a good time to go inside."

No sooner does he speak when an ear-splitting roar cuts the air and a large flash of light over the balcony fills my eyes. I blink, and when my vision clears, a dragon towers over me. With each flap of its giant wings, my hair whips around me and a blast of wind sends leaves scattering all over my balcony.

I stand transfixed, eyes pinned to this beautiful creature.

"This can't be real," I whisper to myself. The dragon cocks its head, then flaps its wings, stirring up a gust that nearly knocks me off my feet. I steady myself on the railing and watch it turn in circles, playfully, like a dog chasing its tail. "Penn?"

It nods.

"Oh!" My hand flies to my mouth. "You can understand me as a dragon!"

Another nod.

"Can you also speak in my mind?" I ask, making sure I'm not crazy. I'm feeling like I am.

Yes. The answer is strong and clear in my mind, no dragon lips moving.

"But—you're so ... beautiful?" Another nod. "So, you're real, you're really a dragon, and you can understand me." He nods again.

Go to my balcony. A puff of smoke accompanies his request. I turn and open my balcony door before running to my armoire for a robe. I slip it on before crossing to his bedroom door.

It's unlocked.

I open it and step out, finding myself in a room made of gold. Never in my life have I ever seen so much opulence. Gemstones, jewels, and all kinds of jewelry fill containers to the brim throughout his room, spilling onto its nearest surface. A dragon's treasure trove!

Padding my way to the balcony doors, I fling them open and find Penn's dragon form on the other side.

Hop on.

He lowers a shoulder for me to climb up. I reach for a thick scale on his back and use his leg to heave myself onto him. I throw my leg over and sit in front of his wing joints, ahead of the wings themselves.

A loud purr hums from the beast beneath me. I run my hand along his iridescent body. His scales glimmer under the moonlight like the book, The Rainbow Fish, except his pretty scales cover his entire body, and are as thick as plates of armor.

"You're so beautiful," I breathe, my voice catching in my throat.

He flutters his wings and teeters a little. I lean forward, gripping his shoulders to keep my balance, and realize he's laughing.

"I'm sorry." I chuckle. "It's just so amazing, riding a dragon."

He guffaws, and I feel the rumble of his laughter in my chest. We hover for a moment, him still flapping his wings.

I'm not heavy? I lean back so he can catch a better feel of my weight on his shoulders.

Not at all, he thinks back to me. *But hold on tight. I'll take you for a ride now.* A strong breeze rushes past me as he beats his wings, sending my hair flying this way and that.

He rises into the sky, and I twist around to see the castle of Convectus growing smaller and smaller below me. The breeze freezes my cheeks, but I can't tear my eyes away from this spectacular view. Ripples of clouds beneath us look like a silky quilt, and the moons above shine bright on all of it.

Penn tilts backward until we're flying upside down. I gasp as my stomach flips, then levels out again. I giggle at the thrill.

He dives into a canyon, and I grip his scales tighter to keep from falling off. He swoops through the valley and rises again to soar above the cloud sea.

With little effort, he swerves, his wings flapping in different directions, and I feel like we're dancing through the sky. He does a somersault and dives straight down, causing my stomach to shoot into my chest. My heart pounds, and I grip him tighter still to keep myself from falling off his back.

We whizz past mountains so fast it's a blur, and I laugh from the rush. Up ahead is a forest made of trees with golden limbs. Penn swoops low enough to touch the canopy, sending up a flurry of leaves. He swerves back and forth until we're on the other side. Layers and layers of mountains of fire and stiff peaks stretch out before us in the distance.

Penn levels his wings and hangs motionless in midair for a minute, hovering majestically.

Will you teach me to use my wings?

I'm honored you'd ask. Let them loose.

I take my arms out of their sleeves and tie the robe around my middle, so it doesn't fly away. My pajama top is still in the way of my wings, so I pull my arms in and slide the fabric to settle around my waist. With nothing impeding them, I unfurl my wings with just a thought.

The heavy plumage strains my back muscles. My wings' bones are on either side of my spine. The top of each wing connects to a cord of muscle above my shoulder blade, and from there it goes to each feather.

I extend my wing muscles, letting them rest as Penn had, and test them out. Each downstroke of my wings gives me a sense of power. I try to rotate one wing but have no control over that yet.

Penn whips his head back to get a look and does a double-take.

You're naked.

I'm not, just my top half. Without taking my shirt off, I couldn't let out my wings. I'll need to fashion wing-appropriate tops in case I ever find myself in need of flying. It's freezing this high up, and the dew point makes my skin feel damp.

Penn lowers his wings and starts flapping them, speeding us up little by little. I sit up straighter to better balance with the movement. I lift my wings out to the side for stabilization, and it works amazingly well.

We reach the outskirts of the mountain range, and Penn circles around a snow-capped peak.

It's beautiful up here, I think to him.

His grumble of agreement reverberates through me. *I could fly with you forever.* My heart swells with his words.

We swoop into a valley and rise again to meet the line of peaks. We glide along it, and my anxiety melts away from this experience. I glance behind us to see the landscape from a new perspective.

Can you stand?

Stand?!

Shift closer to my head. Lean on it as you stand so you can balance using your wings. As it's your first time flying with wings, it's best to focus on gliding to begin with.

I do as he says. It's hard to balance on his scales, but with my wings out for support, I can manage it. My hands rest on the crown of thorns jutting from his giant head while I snap my wings out. He lets gravity take hold, and instead of falling, we both glide. I keep hold of him, but my lower half dangles, and as we pick up speed, I swerve to the side. It's difficult to keep my legs under me, but I manage to get myself upright again.

Good girl. You're a natural.

I knew how to fly on Earth, but I never had wings.

We drop into a dive, and with no way to right myself, I twist around to see where we're going. We arc under the line of rust-colored mountaintops. I can't see the ground, but it has to be somewhere ahead of us.

Penn pulls himself up at the last second, and we soar over the forest.

"I never want this to stop!" I shout to him over the wind gliding over our bodies.

How tired are you?

Not at all.

Good. I have some place I want to take you.

We fly toward a lower mountain range. The peaks are more jagged and deadly looking, though the points are still a brownish red, probably marred from the fires. Penn lowers his head, and I have to lean forward to keep from slipping off. We swoop over the trees, and the beauty of Convectus unfolds before me.

A thick patch of green nestled between two crests catches my attention. Penn banks to the side, approaching the oasis in the middle of fire and ice. When we get closer, I spy a tall spire of rock and what looks like a stronghold in the middle of it.

We pass over the moat and rise to meet the rock bridge leading into a cavern. A drawbridge lifts in our direction, and we circle around the fortress again. Penn lands on the bridge, and I slide off his back. My feet hit hard stone as he folds his wings behind him.

We're here.

Where is here? It looks like a green castle in the sky. It's so different from the rest of what I've seen in Bedlam.

Penn's body shudders before transforming into his fae form. He stands in front of me, naked as the day he was born. With a single thought, I put my wings away before pulling my top back up and threading my arms through the sleeve holes.

"I'm glad you like it, but it's not a place for just any fae. It was built over a thousand years ago by dragon fae, then inhabited by dragon fae warriors. I haven't been here in a long time, but Bedlam is so vast that it's easy to forget things on the other side of it." He points to steaming vents. "Thermal activity keeps the plants growing all year round up here."

I approach a bush and pull off a purple berry. I suck the sweet fluid from its skin, then turn around to see Penn's focus on my mouth. He offers me his hand, and I take it before he leads us toward the stronghold.

The stone walls are warm to the touch, emanating with heat from beneath us. Steam billows out of cracks in the floor vents while vegetation thrives along the walls, with vines hanging down like curtains.

We pass through an archway into a large room where plants grow under skylights running up the middle of the ceiling. A large pool sits at the center of the room. Steam rises from it, and small stones line its perimeter. Penn tugs my hand again, and I follow him to a stone table on one side of the pool. He pulls out a chair for me, and I gingerly sit down before crossing one leg over the other.

Penn's fingers trail along my neck as he kisses behind my ear and down my neck. "Do you need anything? Food? Drink?"

I shake my head playfully before leaning into him with a smile.

"What do you want, then?" His voice is husky as his eyes rake up and down me like dark fire. His fingers trail along my neck, and his lips press against mine before gently kissing me.

"Just you," I whisper against his mouth. His hands cup my face while he kisses me again, more urgently this time.

He lifts me with ease to set me on the table beside him. My legs wrap around his hips while he presses his body against mine, the heat between us like sparking embers. He deepens the kiss as one of his hands slides down my side to pull my silk pajama shorts to the side just enough for him to find bare skin beneath it.

His groan rumbles through my core before he pulls away and slides a finger inside me. *So wet for me already*, he purrs in my head. I untie the robe from my waist before pulling my top off.

My back arches when he rubs the little bundle of nerves with his thumb. He catches my pert nipple in his mouth, laving with his tongue while he works his hand at my core. As soon as my breaths become shallower, he eases his fingers out of me and plants his hands under my ass and thighs to lift me.

Penn carries me across the room, down a hall, and kicks open a door with his foot. I cling to his shoulders while he transports me to a king-sized bed in the center of a lavish bedroom. He tosses me onto the bed like I weigh nothing before pouncing on me.

"Penn!" I squeal, laughing as he tickles me.

"I love flying with you." Penn's voice is a low rumble. "Just wait until we can race."

He presses his mouth to mine. I respond with equal ardor, melting into him as we touch and taste each other. The need for air forces us to break apart, and we stare at each other, breathing shallowly and listening to our wild hearts.

"I want to make love to you," Penn whispers.

I grin. "Yes, please."

No sooner do I say yes does a sound carry from down the hall.

"Penn!" It's a female voice, high and irritated.

He curses under his breath before rolling off of me. I sit up, watching as he pulls on clothes he grabbed from a drawer.

"I'm sorry, Lana." Penn winces. "Wait here."

He kisses me quickly before he turns and walks out the door, leaving me alone in the room. Hurt cuts deep. The voice echoes off the walls, and I know I have little time. I quickly dress and walk out of the room, pretending to know where I'm going.

The kings were all single ... or so I thought. I'm not about to be anyone's side piece.

I sneak down the hallway, my bare feet following the smooth stone away from their argument. It's hard to make out what they're saying, but I catch a few words.

"... not yours ... Finn will ..."

I pause, one foot in the air as I try to decide. Do I want to know who Penn is cheating on? Curiosity wins out and I suspend my movements, using preternatural hearing to eavesdrop.

There's a long pause and I can only imagine the woman is giving Penn a piece of his mind. "... bring war to Bedlam ... you love her..."

"I know the price," Penn finally snaps. "I'd pay it a million times over. You hear me?"

The other fae responds, but I can't make out the words. Penn's voice is firm, though, as he says, "Let them. She's under our protection. If they touch her, they'll answer to me."

I'm rooted to the ground as I process what I just heard. Penn is in a serious relationship, and he's protecting me? From whom? Are the vampires after me again?

The female fae interrupts my thoughts when she speaks. This time, I hear the anger and hurt in her voice. "She's not your property, Penn. You can't just claim her because you want to. It's a *soul bond*!"

Penn's voice is deadly calm when he replies. "She's mine, Ana. And I'll protect her with my life."

I wait a few moments after they've stopped speaking before I continue on my way. My heart is heavy for whoever this Ana woman is. She's obviously important to Penn, and I can't help but feel a little betrayed that he was cheating on her with me.

I'm not sure what to make of his words, but I know one thing for sure. I don't want to be anyone's mistress. On quiet feet, I rush to find another bedroom. Being in a dragon castle, each has a balcony. I find one around the corner and slip into the room before crossing to the double-doors leading outside.

Tears slide down my face while I unfurl my wings and leap off the terrace. My wings catch the air, and I'm soon soaring high above the castle. Bedlam is a beautiful realm, but it doesn't feel like home, not when I'm being lied to. I know I need to find my way back to Earth.

The pull on my muscles strains my back, especially when I soar over the peak. I grit my teeth and push through the pain, determined to find my way to a portal and back to Earth. All I need is a library to access the internet and I can figure out if I'm married, have children, parents, or anything else. My stomach churns when I think about the jagged pieces of my missing memory, leaving serrated wounds on my mind, and making me grieve for the life I had but don't know.

Flying is the only thing keeping me sane right now.

Hours later, I find a small village nestled in the foothills. It's charming, and the people seem happy. I land in a deserted part of the village to ask someone where I might find a portal. As I touch down, I tuck my wings away. The men instilled in me how important it is to keep those hidden from others. Curious about what life is like outside of my little castle bubble, I walk into the town center. Shops have closed signs in the windows, and I can tell it's late. A young couple walks by, hand in hand, and they give me curious looks.

I glance down and remember I'm wearing pajamas. Heat creeps up my cheeks and I quickly dart to a back alleyway before taking to the sky again. I circle the village a few times, but I can't find a portal. There's a feeling of familiarity tugging at my mind, but I brush it off. I'm not from this world, so how could I know it?

Sighing, I decide to land on an empty trail. As soon as I touch ground, the earth beneath my feet shakes and a rift opens up in front of me, spewing out black smoke. I stumble back, my wings automatically unfurling as I try to take flight.

That's when I see him.

Penn strides through the rift, his dragon form easily towering over the buildings. Panic races through me and I attempt to rise, but I'm rooted to the ground. He looks around, his eyes landing on me, and a wicked smile curves across his lips.

There you are, Lana. I've been looking for you.

CHAPTER 38

LANA

Fear grips my heart as I watch Penn cross the path towards me. I try to take flight, but my wings are like lead. My mind races as I try to think of a way to escape.

Lana, I won't hurt you. I just want to talk. Penn's voice in my head is soothing, but I can hear the underlying anger and desperation.

I try to take another step back, and my feet stumble over themselves. Penn shifts into his fae form before he reaches me and pulls me into his bare arms. I fight against him, but he's too strong. He wraps one arm around my waist and uses his other hand to cup my chin, tilting my head up.

"Don't be afraid, Lana. I would never hurt you." There's a possessive edge to his voice.

"Yeah? And how does Ana feel about that?" My voice is a mere whisper, my heart pounding a furious rhythm in my chest.

Penn's brows furrow, and he drops his hand from my chin. "Is *that* why you took off?" He chuckles. "Gods, I thought I'd hurt you."

"You *did* hurt me!"

He flinches. "Anastasia is my cousin, and she was scolding me for bringing you to Bedlam. She fears the vampires will come to collect you, and it'll start a war between realms. Ana has nothing against you personally, only what it might mean for our realm."

"Vampires can't get into Bedlam."

"Exactly."

TOGETHER, we sift back to the dragon castle. Ana is gone, as is the anger that had been simmering in Penn's eyes. He leads me to the bedroom we shared only hours ago, and we sit together in silence. I'm not sure what to say, and Penn seems lost in thought.

"I'm sorry for not sticking around to hear your side of things."

Penn's head snaps up, and he looks at me, his eyes searching mine. "You're too important."

"Important to whom?" The words slip out before I can stop them.

Penn's lips curve into a smile. "Important to me."

The sincerity in his voice makes my heart clench. I want to believe him, but fear has a tight grip on my chest. "Why?"

"Why what?"

I shake my head. "Why am I so important to you?"

Penn's smile fades, and he reaches out to touch my cheek. "We all care about you. Deeply."

I'm not sure what to say to that, so I remain silent. Penn pulls me into a hug, and I rest my head against his chest, letting his heartbeat soothe me. Eventually, I fall asleep in his arms.

In the morning, the steady rise and fall under my head roots me, and I trace Penn's thick abs with my fingers.

"Thank you for showing me this place."

His hand rubs a rhythmic circle against my hip. "I knew you'd like it."

"Is that why we came here?" My voice is low and raspy as he rolls onto his side to face me.

Penn nods, pressing a kiss to my forehead. "And because I wanted you to myself for a while."

I curl into him, resting my head on his chest.

His fingers trail down my neck and arm, sparking along my skin like electricity. "This used to be like home away from home for me. I spent so much time here in my early days as King when I'd convene with the others on Convectus."

"What about the rest of your family?" I ask with curiosity.

Penn sighs while he gently runs his hand through my hair, stopping when he catches on my curls. He pulls me closer and rolls onto his back, bringing me with him. We're facing each other in the middle of the bed while he explains how dragon fae procreate.

"Only a member of my order can give birth to a new dragon fae," Penn says quietly, brushing hair out of my face. "Dragons want nothing more than to reproduce. We're driven to do it—to take a King's place and continue our order."

I stroke his chest while he talks, feeling the ridges of his abs against my palm. "It sounds like a lot of pressure. Aren't there any female dragon fae, aside from Ana?" I ask softly, though a part of me doesn't want to know the answer.

"Not for over five hundred years," Penn says carefully, his eyes locking on mine. "We had a High King over every order. He provides the magic each order needs to reproduce, and when he left the throne, it threw off the balance of the entire realm. Fae already had difficulty getting pregnant, and it's near impossible now."

"What can we do?" I brush my mouth against his neck while I kiss his collarbone.

"If we don't get the magic back into balance, our realm will eventually die. You, me—all of us will be extinct." He kisses the top of my head while I fight the tears burning in my eyes.

I pull back to look at him, and my tears spill onto his chest. "How can we balance the magic?"

"Either the High King needs to reclaim the throne by defeating the army of each continent, or we need a High Queen to take his place. Only a High King or Queen can supply magic to the realm." Penn says. He exhales and unclenches his fists before brushing my tears away, cupping my face and kissing me gently. "We've been searching for someone to be our High Queen since Bedlam went off balance."

"How do you know when you've found your High Queen?" My voice shakes as I ask the question.

Penn kisses me again before pulling back, his eyes clouded with worry. "We can create one."

I lean away. "Then why haven't you? Everyone is at risk!"

"The High Queen can either be the High King's soul bonded mate, or the shared mate of the three remaining kings. She'll become a Luna fae." Penn kisses the tip of my nose.

My heart pounds in a furious rhythm. "Who will you make High Queen?" I scramble off him. Like hell I want to dalliance with Penn when he needs to busy himself with finding a High Queen to save us all.

"Come now, Lana." Penn grabs my shoulders and pulls me close, "we have you." He rests his chin on the top of my head.

Fear strangles me. "You don't know what you're asking." I barely choke out the words. The thought of three kings sharing me is frightening. "I only just became fae. I don't even know how to fly properly with these new wings, and I barely know a thing about Bedlam, save for what I've learned in history books."

Penn chuckles at my words. "You can fly just fine." He kisses down my neck until his lips are on mine. "You just have to feel the air beneath your wings." He presses harder, pulling away only when I'm gasping for breath. "And as for the other concern, we can teach you all about your new kingdom."

"I'm not your High Queen, Penn." With a frown, I sit up and look at his face. "I don't know how to handle three males ... you're asking too much." He rolls onto his back and looks at me as I push him away. I'm poised on my knees above him. "Your High Queen is out there somewhere, but it's not me."

He reaches for my hand while I lean forward to press my lips to his cheek.

"We're not asking for much." He looks up at me with a mix of sadness and frustration. "You were chosen because of who you are, Lana." He takes hold of my waist and rolls so I'm beneath him. "I knew it the moment I saw you." He buries his face in my neck, breathing in softly. "And I will fight for you until my last breath." He whispers in my ear.

The words create a fire in my belly, spurring pleasure between my thighs. Penn feels so good on top of me. He lifts his head and looks down at me, his eyes locked on mine. "Never doubt I'm yours." He captures my lips with his.

His mouth moves against mine almost reverently while I feel him hardening against my belly. The kiss is angry and hungry and desperate all at once, and it makes me ache in ways that scare me. Penn's hands slide up my sides until they're beneath my arms and he pulls me even closer, so we're chest to chest, hip to hip. He rocks slowly against me as if trying to get inside of me without actually penetrating me because of the thin piece of fabric separating us.

"Be ours, please." Penn groans the words into my neck while his hips move between my thighs.

"Penn," I moan when he drives harder against me. My back arches off the bed, seeking to get closer to him. I place my hand against his chest, and he pauses his movement. "I'm flattered, really, but I need time to think about it, okay?"

He nods. "Of course. I'm sorry."

I pull him back in for a kiss. "Any female would be lucky to have the three of you. Ruling a realm is what's holding me back, not you. Alright?"

"Okay." His fingers trace idle movements along my tattoos. "I got carried away."

I shake my head. "No, it's okay. Really." I glance to the window to gauge time. "Should we let the others know where we are?"

"Yeah," he sighs. "We should head back before they get worried. I don't have my phone on me.

CHAPTER 39

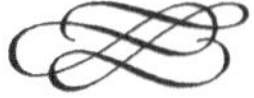

OZ

"We can't just leave him in the dungeon." Auguste paces the room.

"I know ... we just need to talk this out first." Gideon unscrews the bottle of whiskey and takes a swig before passing the amber container my way. The kids are with Dad at the beach so we could interrogate our captive without the children hearing, and now we're in the den drowning our sorrows.

"This is so fucked."

I raise an eyebrow at Auguste, because he rarely swears. Maybe he's finally cracked like the rest of us have. He's been trying to put on a brave face while Lana is gone, but he's not eating like he normally does, and I catch him thumbing through her pictures when he thinks no one is looking. He was the last to win her affection, but their bond is just as strong as Gideon's or mine. She never loves in half-measure.

Why he's trying to appear unaffected, I'll never understand. We're *all* devastated. And now? The rawness in my chest has multiplied tenfold. Lana has the purest heart, and she deserves none of what she's gone through.

"Did any of you feel her die?" My voice croaks, heavy with tension and fear of the unknown. I tilt my head back and rest it on the back of the couch.

"No. I still feel the pull of our mating bond, but I can't feel her emotions anymore. Not since she stepped through the portal." Sentiment lays thick in Auguste's voice.

"Same here. I miss her, and I miss how giddy she got laughing at her own jokes. She had a hard time telling them."

I cast a glance at Gideon and smirk. "She's the master of lame jokes. How about any time she bought someone a present, she'd spoil the surprise and give the gift right away? Then she'd feel bad we didn't have a present to open on the occasion, so she'd go buy, or make, another one."

Our reminiscing lightens the mood only for a moment before grief hangs heavy like a velvet curtain.

"I don't blame her." I cut through the melancholy quiet. "For her soul bond with the fairy. I heard legends millennia ago about how rare those types of mating bonds are, and there's nothing you can do to stop them. We're lucky the new bond didn't override ours."

Gideon runs a hand over his face. "Those only happen with fae? Why does Lana have one? She's a witch."

"The bond doesn't care if she isn't fae. Only one of them has to be." Auguste looks up from his phone.

I sit up. "So, the King of the Luna Court left his position because he knew Lana was out there somewhere. Would he, being mated to someone else, have severed that?"

Between the time we left Finn in the basement and now, we've poured through everything we know about the fae realm, its royalty, and how this impacts Lana. Auguste has more details coming in every few minutes from all our contacts across the globe.

"Like with vampires, fae only take one mate. Only, they never take another if theirs dies. If he found someone else to mate with who wasn't his soul bond, the connection to whoever their soul chose would've been destroyed. They say in these instances, the fae go on with something missing inside of them, despite there being a different mating bond in place. The soul always yearns for what could've been."

"That's ... tragic. And terrible for whoever they ended up mated with." I absentmindedly scroll through my phone. I keep a folder of all the things I want to show Lana when she comes home; pictures of us cuddling the kids, videos of the guys doing stupid shit, and improvements we've made around the properties.

"When we bring Lana back, are we really going to share her with that ... overgrown, silver-haired wanker?" Gideon clenches his jaw and flexes his fist.

"I don't think we have a choice." I tap my finger along the drink in my hand. "Their bond trumps ours, and I think we would only push her away if we tried to alienate him. We'd lose her all over again."

We sit in silence for several minutes, passing the bottle around. The alcohol burns out of our systems quickly, but if we drink fast enough, it numbs the pain for a moment or two.

How did things go so wrong? I've only just found her, and just like my first wife, she's been taken from me.

Gideon tosses a blood bag to Oz. "Can you do a communication spell and reach her in Bedlam?"

"I can tr—"

"Won't work."

We jump to our feet and glare at Finn standing in the entryway. I knew the dungeon wouldn't keep him long. He's *fae*. The strongest, fastest, most cunning species in any realm. This one isn't just any fae, though. He's the High King, no matter if he abdicated his throne. There's no stronger *thing* in this world or the next.

"Why not?" I'm the first to talk. The other two are so wound up, looking ready to attack should Finn say the wrong thing. While I still stand, I know I'm no match for him. Not even the three of us combined would be. Better to be on his good side.

He strolls to the coffee table and sniffs the bottle of whiskey. "Why do Earth-dwellers drink this swill?"

"Many drink to numb their pain." I nod my head for him to try a sip.

The High King slugs the amber liquid and makes a face. "I wouldn't even give this to the Caspari."

"... treasure guard?" My Italian is weak compared to the other languages I know. I glance at Gideon, but the fae answers before I can ask.

Finn shakes his head. "The Caspari are violent creatures who eat our waste. They'll eat just about anything. Earth could use a horde or two to take care of your polluted oceans and landfills."

Interesting. "Hmph. And why won't my spell work?" I grab another bottle—this time, bourbon—and pour everyone a glass.

Finn leans against the wall, crossing his arms and his legs at the ankles. "The first thing the other kings would've taught her is how to guard her mind."

"I already taught her that." I shake my glass so the ice swirls around. "I've always been able to get inside her head. Because we're mated, she can't keep me out."

The fae clenches his teeth and shakes his head. "No. That was when she was a witch. Your power?" He laughs. "It's but a crumb to the amount she holds now. You think her necromancy was powerful magic? She got that from me, and we hadn't even recognized our soul bond or met at that point."

"I'm not following. Does Bedlam amplify her powers?" Gideon takes a seat on the couch, and we each take our own.

"They could've just made her immortal, but they didn't." Finn's gaze flicks between the three of us. "She's fae now."

I spit out my drink and the room thrums with tension. Lana ... fae? I feel the eyes of the others on me, watching me carefully for any reaction. I don't know what to feel.

Gideon sits there, mouth agape for a moment, before furrowing his brows. "The fae created witches. She can't be entirely different, right?"

Finn shrugs. "Appearance-wise? She's taller, maybe a little leaner. More muscle and sleek curves, silky curls, flawless skin." He looks wistful. "Pointed ears. Lengthened canines, but dainty. It took the three of them to change her. I could've made her immortal by myself if my powers were strong enough. I have a damper on my magic after leaving the throne. The only way to get it back is to reclaim it."

None of this changes things. "And ... personality?" Not that it matters. She's still our mate.

"Hard to say. I didn't get to talk to her after they changed her. With her not remembering any person she ever met, combined with their brainwashing—"

"What do you mean?" Auguste inclines his head to the side.

"When they made her forget everyone, the assholes told her they rescued her from evil vampires on Earth who stole her memories. They planted the seed that you are not to be trusted. Even called me a zealot when I tried to reach her. It took the entire guard to drag me out of there. I spent months trying to sneak my way back in, but they've got the entire place warded. Most parts of the castle are impenetrable."

I flip the coffee table over, spilling our drinks, before throwing it against the wall. The wood splinters and falls to the floor. My muscles bunch and bulge in fury, and my fangs slide to their full length.

I never knew it could feel like this. It's as though a piece of my soul is missing, and a deep ache in my gut gnaws at my insides. The pain has nothing to do with the bagged blood we're drinking, either. Lana is my *mate*. The other half of me. With her absence, I want to crawl out of my skin.

I glance at Gideon. His eyes are shut, his face scrunched in agony. He's hurting, too. We all are. We're but shells of our former selves. Lana tore through here like a woman caught in a hurricane.

"Wait." Gideon places a tentative hand on my shoulder. "Her dreams. You've infiltrated them before. Can you do it from here?" His features soften and hope flashes across his face.

"I'll try every opportunity I can."

Finn

I'M SORTING through a closet full of clothes to find something to fit my large stature when a knock sounds at the door to the bedroom I've been given.

Wrapping the towel around my waist, I make my way to the door and open it to find Gideon on the other side. He puffs his chest while he takes a measure of me. His eyes immediately find my oldest tattoo.

"You got a tattoo of Lana's stork bite?"

"Her what?"

He gestures to my lower abs. "The birth mark on her forearm."

I follow his gaze. "This is on her arm?"

"It's barely visible anymore, but she has those circles and then a blurry one on her right forearm, near the crook of her elbow. It was darker when she was a kid, but now it's just a faint mark." He digs his phone out of his pocket and scrolls through several folders. He stops on one titled, "Little Lana," and swipes until he finds one showing a faint spot on her arm.

"It's a lot more subtle than I realized ..." I cross to the bed and sink down onto the edge, resting my elbows on my knees. I'm lost in thought when Gideon clears his throat. "My entire life, for millennia, I've dreamt of this symbol. I'd scribble it in the margins of notebooks, sketch it out in the sand when I was on a beach, tattoo it onto my skin." My voice breaks and I look away. "She saw the symbol in my journal, and later on my body. I had her in the clouds one night when she spotted the symbol in the sky: it was the moons."

"Why would she have a birthmark of the moons from a fae realm?"

I shake my head. "Probably the same reason I'm her soul bonded mate. It's fate."

His jaw clenches and his nostrils flare.

All I can do is smirk. "How do you think it felt learning my *soul bonded mate* has not one, but three other lesser mates?"

"Lesser?!" he explodes.

I shrug. "That's what the fae call anyone who isn't a soul bonded mate."

"So, you think of us as lesser beings?"

"I didn't say that."

"You might as well have." He steps back, his features pinched in anger.

"Gideon, I didn't mean it like that." I reach out to him, but he steps back again. "It's just a term."

"A term you use to belittle us." He turns on his heel and stalks out of the room.

CHAPTER 40

OZ

"It's bad enough the fucker has a whole ass soul bonded tattoo he shares with Lana, but he also has her birthmark etched on him? That's just too much."

I follow him as he storms to his room to grab a sketch pad before pounding on the door to Auguste's bedroom.

"What's up?" he answers, bleary-eyed and shirtless. He glances at me over Gideon's shoulder and raises a brow.

"I know you're busy, but this is important." He slaps the notepad against Auguste's chest. "Look at this and tell me what you see."

He takes the pad and his brow furrows as he looks down at the sketches. After a minute, he looks up at Gideon. "You're learning how to draw?"

"No. Help me decide which of these to get a tattoo of."

"Why would you want a tattoo of a clown?"

"It's not a clown, it's Lana." He points to the sketch of her with her wedding dress. "This is her on our wedding day, and this is her with her stork bite."

He looks at Gideon like he's crazy, and I'm inclined to agree with him. "Don't do this."

"Why not? If the stupid fairy can get tattoos representing her, I can, too."

"I'm not saying don't get a tattoo ... just not any of these. Let me work on a drawing for you. I'll show you what I come up with." He takes the pad back from Gideon and shoos us out of his room.

CHAPTER 41

FINN

The warm water soothes my aching muscles, and the sun bakes my skin. The waves soothe me as I float on my back. Noise from the beach takes me out of my reverie. I sit up and scan the shore, and my eye catches on an older man with two children. They stand in the sand, watching me. A faint recognition of their features has me swimming towards the shore.

A small gust of wind propels me towards them, and I get out of the water. The man holds his hand out to me. "Finn, I presume?"

"Yes." I take his hand and shake it.

"I'm Alphie, Lana's father." He holds out his other hand to the children. "These are my grandchildren, Rose and Bennett."

"Bennett ... Rose." A pang of grief grips my chest. I clear the emotion out of my voice. "Your mother told me so much about you two; mostly her hopes and dreams for you." I run a hand through my wet hair. "She never would've left if she had any other choice—her only goal was to get back to you two as soon as she could."

"What have you done with our mother?" Bennett asks. Rose looks near tears, and I soften my features. I see so much of Lana in them.

I crouch so I'm at their level. "She's in the fae realm, waiting for us to bring her home."

"Why can't we just go get her?" Rose sniffles.

"It's not that simple. The fae realm is a dangerous place, and we're not the only ones who want her. Even if it's the last thing I do, I'll bring her home to you. I swear it. Do you know what happens when a fae makes a promise?"

She shakes her head.

"We have to keep it."

Rose wipes her tears with the back of her hand. "Do you love my mom?"

"More than anything." I place my hand over my chest, right where it aches like a festering wound.

"I'm not calling you dad." Bennett scowls.

I ruffle his hair. "Maybe someday you'll call me friend."

"I guess that's better than nothing." Bennett shrugs.

Alphie clears his throat and I stand. He takes in the tattoos snaking up my arms and the one sitting low on my abs, and he smirks. "So you're the reason Gideon's been such a grump."

"I have no idea what you're talking about." I brush the sand off my hands and legs.

He grins, his eyes twinkling. "He's having Oz enchant a tattoo on him right now of Lana."

"What?" I laugh. "Why would he do that?"

"I think he's trying to prove something." Alphie shrugs. "I'm going to get these two inside for supper. You should clean up."

He leaves, and I gather my things before I walk back to the house. I'm not sure what to make of Gideon's actions, but I know I need to talk to him. He's had a chip on his shoulder since I arrived. I enter the house and find him in the kitchen, a sandwich in one hand and a beer in the other.

"Hey," I say, leaning against the counter. "Alphie told me you were getting a tattoo."

"Yeah, so? It's done." He takes a bite of his sandwich and washes it down with a swig of beer.

"Why?" I raise an eyebrow.

"Why not?" He shrugs and rises to his full height, though he's still not as tall as me. "Lana likes them, so I thought I should get one, too."

I shake my head. "It's just ... you need to understand I'm not your competition. I would never try to take Lana away from you. I love her, too. We're bonded, remember?"

"I know." He shoves the rest of the sandwich in his mouth and swallows. He tosses his bottle in the recycling and leaves me standing in the kitchen alone.

CHAPTER 42

CASIMIR

I wake with an ache in my chest. Over the coming days, the pain will grow until I'm incapacitated. First, I'll have difficulty waking. When I do rise, it'll feel like I never slept a wink, and exhaustion will take over. Without warning, I'll liquify on the inside, never breathing again. I won't ascend to the spirit realm. Instead, I'll descend to Aggonid's realm of fire and ash to spend the rest of eternity tortured and maimed.

I know the others feel the dread building inside them, too—foreboding a gruesome death and an even worse afterlife.

I thought we had more time.

Swallowing a pain tonic on my way to round up the others, I clench my teeth at the onslaught of another stab of pain.

I stumble into Penn's room, where he lays against his bed, gripping the sheets that have half-fallen off the mattress. Grimm sits in an armchair, clutching his hair. I cross to Penn's medicine chest with clumsy fingers.

This is the price you pay when you don't fulfill your end of a fae bargain.

"Penn. We will all die, and this will all be for naught if you don't

have someone fetch her mother. Lana needs to know what happened to Annabelle." I collapse onto his bed.

"I know," he breathes. "I'm too weak to sift. *Pierce!*"

Our most trusted guard materializes instantly. He was a handsome fae before he took a blade to the face, leaving a thick scar splitting his brow down to the middle of his cheek. The sword just missed his actual eyeball. Pierce takes in the situation and draws his weapon, darting his gaze around for trouble.

"We need you to go to Penn Island and bring Annabelle Chapman to us immediately. This is life or death."

With a quick nod of his head, he sifts out.

Lana

"LANA, we have our royal storyteller here to visit." Casimir pops his head through my door. "Feel like a story?"

I set down the book I'm reading and shrug. "Sure." I've spent most of the afternoon studying the history of Bedlam. If I'm going to continue living in this realm, I need to know more about it.

He opens the door all the way and steps in. Behind him is a human woman, perhaps in her late fifties, with long, silky brown hair and big doe eyes with creases in their corners. She bows low, causing her dress to skirt the floor. I invite her to sit next to me on the couch and introduce myself.

"It's a pleasure to meet you. My name is Anna."

The rest of the men file in and perch themselves all over my room. Why do they look sick? As soon as the woman leaves, I'll have to ask them. A moment later, Sarai drops off refreshments for us.

"This is the true story of a witch from Earth named Annabelle Chapman," she begins. "She was a time traveler who came through the portal twenty-six years ago. The woman infiltrated the castle by befriending some servants and eventually got an audience with the three kings."

"What did she request?"

"It wasn't what she requested, but what she tried to do. She tried to trick the royals. Her mistake was not knowing they could read minds."

I whip my head to the smug fae propped around my room. My eyes catch on Grimm's gaze, and he gives me a wink. I straighten my spine and turn back to Anna. My breath catches and I wince. My morning combat session with Pierce kicked my ass, and I still have my evening one with Casimir tonight.

"What happened to her?" I nibble on something resembling a petit four before placing it on a napkin in my lap.

"They banished her to a remote island near Bedlam Penitentiary. As a witch, she can't go to the fae prison; she didn't get a death sentence, and she'd never survive an hour there."

"Where is she now?"

"She's a servant."

I glance at Casimir. He usually answers anything I ask. "Is your servant treated well?"

"Of course she is." He raises a brow. "What kind of rulers do you take us for?"

I shrug.

"I must take my leave now, my lady. Thank you for allowing me to share a story with you." Anna stands and excuses herself from the room. Interesting story, I guess, although I'm not sure why it's so important to know. Are they worried I'm trying to betray them, or trick them?

I furrow my brow and shake my head; the boys have more color to them now. Perhaps the lighting had made them look sick.

CHAPTER 43

OZ

"Why didn't you send your spy to Bedlam before Lana went?" Finn's lips set in a thin line. "She never would've needed to go!"

I clench my teeth. "We didn't have this contact before. She never would've met you if she hadn't."

Finn's stiff shoulders loosen a smidge because he knows I'm right. We're all strung out right now. With a sigh, I school my features and lean back in my chair. We're at the dining room table in Gideon's house in Sydney. As the head of security for our family, we've been using his ocean front residence as mission operations ever since we heard that the royal fae had wiped Lana's memories.

Gideon excuses himself from the room while he answers the front door. While we wait, Auguste helps me unroll the giant map Finn made of Bedlam. The fae realm is far larger than we expected. There are six populated continents, as well as several islands. Within each continent are capital cities. Four cities seat fae royals. One is vacant after Finn's abdication of the throne, and the last capital city is where the royals regularly convene. The latter, Convectus, is where we believe they're holding Lana.

I stand when Killian and Gideon enter the room and shake our spy's hand. "Is she okay?" I gesture to the seat next to me, and we gather around the table. Each of the males have their own tells when they're anxious; Finn paces, Gideon taps his heel against the wood floor, Auguste grips the arms of his chair. And me? I try to control everything. On more than one occasion, I've butted heads with Lana's soul bonded mate.

Killian keeps darting his eyes to Finn, so I clear my throat. "*Lana*. Is she okay?"

He wrings his hands, but doesn't take his eyes off the pacing fae. "My contacts at the castle tell me she is still on Convectus, although she doesn't make any appearances outside the walls, aside from a brief visit to some abandoned villages. They keep her closely guarded. We suspect they might move her to Sundahlia or the Tristique Islands." Killian's hands tremble. "There is another thing ..."

Finn slams his fists on the table, and Killian nearly tips his seat over. We've spent months trying to gather intel, and my attempts at infiltrating her dreams have failed.

"Do you need to excuse yourself from the room, fairy?" I shoot him a glare for scaring our only connection to Lana. We need this witch. The exorbitant amount I pay the man won't matter if he's too scared to disappoint Finn.

Finn grits his teeth. "Carry on."

With a quick glance at me, Killian continues, but allows his greasy red hair to fall into his eyes to shield himself from Finn. "It's the mother, Your Majesty."

All heads whip to the soft-spoken man.

"Annabelle Chapman? What have you heard?" Auguste leans in.

"Sh-sh-she's there."

Goosebumps pepper my skin. "With Lana?" I keep my voice even to tamp down the hope building in my chest. If her mom is there, we can bring them both home as soon as the next Bedlam Moon ... unless we can figure a way in before then.

Killian's gaze flits around the room before landing on mine. "Yes."

I don't have to breathe, but at this moment, all the air escapes from my lungs. Not for long, though.

"What condition is she in?" Finn's eyes narrow.

The witch shakes his head. "Not good, I'm afraid."

I tilt my head, and Finn growls.

"They've wiped her memory, too. The royals have forced her into servitude in the palace. I never would've known this was the Annabelle Chapman you were looking for if it weren't for the story they make her tell the court as its royal storyteller and servant."

"Story?" Gideon takes out his tablet to scribble notes.

"They compel her to tell a story of a witch named Annabelle Chapman, who thought she could trick the fae royals into eliminating an entire species. Neither her nor Lana know who each other are. It appears they bound her mother's magic."

Killian flinches when Finn picks up his own chair and smashes it against the table, sending splinters flying. Gideon scowls at him and mutters under his breath, "beast."

Finn flicks his wrist and all the pieces mend together, as though the chair were never damaged.

"She's been there for *twenty-six years?* Assuming Bedlam is where she went after vanishing from near the pond when Lana was eight." Alphie, Lana's dad, speaks for the first time.

Once upon a time, Annabelle was his sun, moon, and stars. I'm not sure any love for her has waned after all these years. Tears threaten to spill, and he blinks them back when I place a hand on his arm to comfort him.

Gideon taps his fingers on the table in a nervous rhythm. "What species could Annabelle possibly want to wipe out?"

"Vampires."

CHAPTER 44

LANA

$\mathcal{I}$ retire to my room after supper, eager to fly again. I've missed the sound of the wind rushing past my ears as I glide on currents near the castle, but there are more challenges to be had out in the forest. The kings have a late night dealing with our plans to head to Sundahlia, the warm continent many fae travel to for winter.

To prepare for my lengthy flight, I fashion a pouch around my waist with herbs and potions, just in case I run into any trouble and get injured. Power surges through my veins and I want to take advantage of its energy. After an hour of drawing, wrapping, and searching for materials in my room, I pull on my leather pants and a stretchy shirt made to accommodate my wings. I tug on my boots, lace them up, and grab the bag.

Wind whips my hair as I slip out the door and onto my balcony. Cool air fills my lungs as I take a deep breath and open my wings. I step off the edge and let gravity pull me toward the ground before I flap hard and soar into the sky. Guards mill about, but don't notice me. Not that I think they'd care—I'm not a prisoner here—but they might insist I take someone with me.

It takes hours to reach the forest's edge. My stomach flips as I near the top of a tree, and my wings make a whooshing sound as I glide just inches from the canopy. I sail over the treetops before I find a stream and land on the bank. I lean forward and let my legs drop out from under me, landing with a gentle splash.

The cool water gives me goosebumps, and I let it cascade over me as my eyes adjust to the moonlight. An owl hoots, and I look up to see specks of light fluttering over the moon. Moths. Something brushes my arm and I jerk back.

A mutant-looking frog plops into the water and I laugh, then spy something else in the distance. A rustling sound makes me turn my head and I spot a white bunny hopping through the trees. She sees me and pauses, then hops toward where I wade in the water.

I nudge forward on my knees and hold out a hand. She hops closer, sizing me up with her little pink nose. I reach my hand out again and slowly; she nudges it with her wet nose. "You sure are cute." I pick her up and she snuggles into the crook of my arm.

We walk along the bank, and I let her wiggle down to eat some clover. "You're pretty sweet, aren't you?" I cock my head to the side. A swishing sound comes from behind and I turn around, half expecting to see one of the kings.

I'm met with a grotesque, hideous creature. It's furry and has two eyes that blink at me. Its mouth opens and closes as it pins me with its gaze. I gasp and take a step back, almost slipping on the wet grass, but right myself by flinging out my wings for balance. The bunny darts into the trees, not even looking back.

"What are you?" I ask it. The creature lets out a high-pitched shriek and limbers closer, its giant maw still snapping.

I step back, and my foot falls into a hole, causing me to lose balance. I scramble on my hands and knees around the outside of the hole, trying to find some purchase on the wet dirt. The scent of earth fills my nostrils. The creature scuttles toward me and I reach for the short knife strapped to my leg.

The knife slips from my hand and lands on the creature's paw, causing it to turn and swipe at me with sharp claws. I scream and jump back, narrowly missing its razor-like nails, and that's when I notice it: a small, shaggy black mass of fur clinging to its side. "What the hell is that?" I ask no one in particular. The creature's eyes flash and it hisses at me, then pounces.

I jump back and flap my wings hard as the creature's body slams into me. The air whips out of my lungs and the furry creature, once attached to the beast, falls to the ground just within my reach. My eyes dart to the limp critter lying in a heap on the forest floor just as the monster shrieks and scrambles for it.

Blood dribbles from the small bundle when the creature lifts it into its arms. The animal clutches it to its chest and turns to the sky, howling in agony.

I scurry to my feet, approaching the beast with a placating gesture. "Is this your baby? Let me help."

The beast's head whips around, and I freeze, my heart thudding hard in my chest. My eyes lock with the creature's and everything around me disappears. With slow and measured movements, I reach my hands towards the infant. The animal doesn't fight me when I take the small furry body from its arms. It regards me with sadness, its dark eyes welling with tears.

I lower myself to the ground and inspect the wound. The creature doesn't move, but its eyes burn into me with silent gratitude. I study the small kit in my arms and notice three holes near its neck. "It's been shot," I choke.

The beast lets out a series of deep, guttural sounds, and my eyes dart up to meet it. "You're talking?" I ask. The creature nods and lets out a soft whimper, as if asking for permission to come closer.

"I don't think it's safe for you to be out here, but I'm going to help your baby." Whoever shot its baby could still be out here. The creature lets out a high-pitched whimper, and I smile. "You understand me?"

The beast nods again, this time letting out a soft grunt.

I stand up, taking the small bundle in my arms, and step toward the being. "I'm going to use magic to heal your little one. Is this okay?"

Its eyes widen and it lets out a distressed cry.

"I won't hurt him, I promise."

The beast lets out a soft yelp and I nod.

"Okay." I take a deep breath and focus on the magic inside of me. The fae magic is drawing on the essence of nature to help me heal, but I need more. I glance at the canopy of trees around us, and an idea comes to me.

"We need to move to a clearing. Do you know of one?"

The creature nods, then takes a few steps into the forest. I stand still for a moment, scanning the trees until my eyes fall on an open spot a few hundred yards away.

"Lead the way," I say, pointing toward the clearing.

The creature emits a soft howl and strides into the forest. I follow close behind, leading with my chin as the infant's small head bobs gently against my shoulder.

We reach the clearing after a few minutes of weaving around tree trunks. The creature scampers toward a rock at the center and lets out a series of yelps, which forces me to blink several times.

"Oh, you want me to stand here?"

It nods.

I hug the infant close to my chest and glance around the open space. There's something about it that makes me nervous, like I'm being watched, but I dismiss the thought.

"Okay, here goes nothing." I take a deep breath and focus on my magic. My chin lifts to the night sky, soaking up moonbeams and drawing from nature around me. I channel the energy around us and let it flow into the baby. The beast watches with fascination, its eyes widening as its child's body glows.

I release the overflowing energy inside of me and into the baby. The creature lets out a high-pitched yelp as the furry body begins to heal. The infant's fur changes from damaged to healthy in an instant, but there are still three holes near his neck. I study the injury and glance at the creature, who is watching me with a mix of concern and curiosity.

"How long has he been like this?"

The animal lets out a series of choppy sounds, then glares at me with its head cocked to the side.

"You don't know?"

It shakes its head and lets out another whimper, this one more agitated than the last.

The beast moves closer to me, its head still tilted to the side.

I let out a gasp and jump to my feet, baby still in my arms, and approach the creature.

"My gods, who did this to you?!" Tears spill down my cheeks.

It inclines its head forward and I can see a deep wound near its neck. The smell of burnt flesh fills the air, and I gag as I reach out to touch the injury.

"I'm so sorry." I reach for my fae magic and draw from the moonbeams surrounding us. The woods are silent as I let the energy flow through me and into the beast's neck. It lets out a soft moan, and I let go of the energy, watching in awe as the creature's wound heals.

Its head jolts up and it whimpers, its bright green eyes meeting mine.

"W-w-w," it attempts to speak.

I place my hand on its shoulder.

"I can't understand you."

It lets out a small howl that sounds like thunder in my ears.

My skin rises into goosebumps, and I take a step back. "What are you?"

The creature rolls its head to the sky, then lets out a loud howl, almost like it's clearing its throat. "W-werewolves d-did this. Not shot."

I furrow my brows. "What?" I didn't know werewolves were real.

"C-c-can you save him?"

I look down at the baby in my arms. "I think so."

Its shoulders relax, and it lets out a sigh of relief.

"We need firewood. Can you find some?" My fingers probe the area around the infant's wound.

The creature nods and heads into the forest. I sit on a rock and wait.

"Don't worry." I stroke the infant's forehead with my fingers. "I'm going to save you." Gently, I place my hand against its side. My magic pulses through me and into the creature's body before seeping out.

My eyes pass over the body, and I focus on the three holes near its neck, specifically the one closest to the head. The two deep gashes begin to close before my eyes, and I let out a gasp.

The mother runs back with a bundle of firewood in its arms. I gently place the infant down and arrange the wood into a proper fire. The mother lets out a soft whine as I kneel by the baby.

"He'll be okay."

A flame creeps up from my hand and the fire hums to life. It's like it came out of nowhere, but I know that's not true. My fae magic is taking over my body, and I can't control it yet.

The sound of growling brings me back to the moment. I whip my head up and see a pack of what must be werewolves standing behind the mother. Their sharp teeth glint in the moonlight, and I dart in front of the beast, protecting the mother and child.

"Back off." I form a ball of fire in my hand and throw it at the werewolves. It ignites when it lands in the center of the pack, and they all howl, running off into the forest.

I turn back to the mother and my heart aches.

She looks at me with wide eyes, tears streaming down her cheeks. "Only werewolves can hurt the Tolden."

"Tolden?" I ask.

"Child of the woods." She gestures to the infant, who is looking up at me with wide silver eyes. "I protect them."

"Wait ... so you risk your life for a baby who isn't yours?"

The surrounding forest is silent. "Of course," it says finally.

"Why?" I'm in awe. Most creatures, especially fae, are selfish.

"Why not? I am like you, new fae, risking her life for a child who isn't hers."

My heart swells and I give her a sheepish smile. "I suppose you're right." I pull the baby into my arms while I warm a vial on a hot stone from the fire. "And who ... or what are you?"

"They call me The Crucey."

"Oh." I blink at her. "And what do you prefer I call you?"

She stares blankly at me. "Crucey is fine." She smiles, revealing sharp, dagger-like fangs.

I nod. Testing the contents of the potion bottle on my wrist, it's just warm enough. I cradle the infant in one arm while I pour the liquid over the gaping wound.

The infant glows under the light of the full moon, and I watch as it heals. A warm tingle spreads through my body where I'm in contact with its fur. Slowly but surely, the wound closes. When I'm done, the baby sleeps peacefully in my arms.

"Thank you." The Crucey bows. "I must take the Tolden to a safe place before he wakes up, but ... you are welcome to join me."

"I'm sorry." Glancing towards the woods, I sigh. "I have to get back to the castle. But please, visit me if you ever need help again. Do you know where to find the Convectus castle?"

She nods. "I owe you, new fae. I am not bound by the magic that seals these lands. Seek me, and I will give you any answers you need."

"Thank you." I give her a warm smile. "I'm Lana."

"The pleasure is mine, Lana, New Fae, Uniter of Realms."

Before I can ask her about the last bit, she takes off into the woods with the Tolden tucked into her side.

I turn towards the path back to the castle and let out a groan. I left in such a hurry that I wasn't paying attention to where I was going. Now, I'm lost and don't know how to get back to the castle. I could sift, but I want to get a lay of the land first.

"Shoot," I curse.

I spread my wings and take flight. Maybe I can get a better view of where I'm going from up in the sky. I fly until my wing muscles burn, and when I take one look at the land below me, I know why Penn never wanted me to fly without him.

The forest is vast, and most of it so thick, you can't see the sky when amongst its roots. I've only been in one section of it, and I have no idea where to go. Giving up, I let my wings take me back down to the ground. I land roughly and find myself face to face with a group of tiny creatures. Their bodies are covered in red fur, and their long noses twitch to the side when they sniff me.

"What are y'all?" I ask, looking around at their tiny bodies. They're only ankle height.

They chitter in unison.

"Come here, little bird," a husky voice calls from the bushes.

They scream, turning to run away. In a flash, the bird-like critters disappear, and I'm left inching backwards, frightened.

A fae steps out from the shadows of the thickets. He is tall, broad shouldered and built for fighting. His eyes are yellow and in the shape of a cat's pupil. He holds two swords and smirks. "Little far from the castle, your majesty."

"I'm no queen." I let out a shaky breath, stepping back. "Who are you?"

"I am Aed." His deep voice rumbles in my ears. "And you are a fool." He lunges, his swords aimed at me. I roll to the side and spring up, only to face him again.

He smirks. "Maybe not as big a fool as one might expect." He eyes the magic brewing at my fingertips. His swords drop from his hands, clattering in the dirt in front of him.

"Wh-what are you doing?"

A smile crawls across his lips. "Finally." He unbuttons his shirt and pants, leaving them in the mud beside him. He fishes in his pockets for something before pulling out a wallet and tossing it to me. "Be sure my family gets this."

"What are you talking about?" I furrow my brows.

He steps several paces away from his clothes before pulling off his jewelry and chucking them into the heap. "The three kings?" He chuckles. "Never thought they had it in 'em. Ask them about the day you lost your memories."

I flinch. "I don't understand."

"They took your mem-" He drops to his knees. His face turns purple, and veins pop up like worms across his skin. He slumps to the ground with a thud, and I move back, frightened by what just happened.

I take several tentative steps towards him and crouch next to his body, feeling for a pulse.

No, no, no, no, no, no.

Nothing. My fingers walk along his ribcage to the center of his chest, and I place the heel of my hand against his sternum before interlacing my fingers. *Shoot.* How many compressions am I supposed to do? Twenty or thirty?

I opt for thirty and push hard and fast, all while trying to bring him back to life with magic. I place my mouth over his and breath into his lungs. Once. Twice.

I repeat CPR until my lips tingle, my fingers cramp, and my head swims with dizziness. Thirty minutes? Or have I been doing this for an hour? Tears pour down my cheeks at my defeat, and I bury my head in my hands.

Without thinking, I snatch up his wallet and pull out his identification. Aedon Shineseer, age 9,326, Lion Order, of Serapi City, Rexuna.

After gathering his clothes and accessories, I tuck them under my arm with the wallet. I catch sight of a fae in the distance as they dart behind a tree.

"Hello?" I ask, unsure of what to do next. The fae makes no attempt to show themselves once more.

I take a step, and my foot sinks in the mud. "Ah." I pull back my leg just as a silver light sweeps across the forest like a wave coming to shore. I shiver and crouch down.

The bright light fades, and I look up to find a female crouched in front of me at eye level. Her short hair is white as snow, but her skin is dark as night. She wears clothes more appropriate for the beach, with sandals on her feet and green leaves for a patchwork dress.

"Unite the realms." The tiny girl with dainty features demands before standing up.

I crane my neck back to see this new fae's face. "Do what?" I scuffle backwards and catch sight of Aed once more. His eyes are still open and staring into nothingness like his soul has left this realm.

When I turn back around, the small woman is gone. A terrible sense of foreboding washes over me. I stumble over to Aed's body and fall to my knees. I choke back a sob and cradle his head in my lap.

"I'm so sorry." I reach for his hand and hold it as more tears fall down my face. "What ... what am I supposed to do now?" Maybe I should sift back to the castle instead of flying so I can get help.

He said to be sure his family gets this. What did he mean, "the day you lost your memories"? The kings took my what?

Before I know what's happening, darkness glides over me like a shadow at dusk and lightning cracks through the trees. My body feels light as air, and my sight dims until everything is black. The last thing I hear is Rune whispering, "You'll be alright." Then nothing but silence.

~

Casimir

"How much did she learn?" Penn growls.

Rune shakes his head. "I don't know. I reached her when Aed was already dead. Enough, maybe." His nostrils flare, but he doesn't elaborate.

A whine escapes from me. "If she knows we were the ones to wipe her memory ... she'll never forgive us."

It's bad enough she had to hear it from Aed. We've just learned that he'd taken out a large life insurance policy to take care of gambling debts if he passed away, which explains why he committed suicide. What I don't understand is why he'd do it by giving away our secret.

Grimm paces across the room. "I took her memory of Bellamy. We can explain this is what Aed meant."

He looks at each of us and we give a firm nod of our head.

"We'd better wake her and find out what she knows." Grimm places a hand on her rosy cheek. He leans down to press his lips to her forehead, stirring her from sleep.

She blinks her eyes open and wiggles against the soft blankets. "What are you doing here?"

Penn stands from his seat by her bedside and walks towards Rune with a grave expression.

"I ran into a fae called Aed in the woods." Her brows knit together as she stares at each of us in turn. "He said something, I don't know what..." She gasps and sits up so fast it knocks my breath out of me. "*You* took my memories? Why?"

"How much did you hear?" Penn asks calmly as he takes a step towards her.

"Enough to know you haven't been honest with me." She glares at him before looking around the room like an animal caged. "Why did you take my memories?"

Grimm approaches the bed. "They didn't. I did, because you asked me to."

She flinches. "Why would I do that?" She swings her legs out of bed and buries her face in her hands.

Grimm crouches in front of her. "Penn has a cousin named Bellamy who is in love with you. He's Pierce's brother. You two grew close, and on the night of the ball, he planned on telling you some top-secret things that are protected by a magical decree preventing our realm's secrets from being divulged. You witnessed what happened to Aed—that's what happens to a fae who tries to get around a magical decree: instant death. That's what was going to happen to Bellamy, and we couldn't allow it. When I explained this to you, you begged me to take his memory from you so you wouldn't go to him where he's stationed now."

She's quiet for several minutes before raising her head to look at Grimm. Tears rim her eyes. "Is Bellamy okay?" She shakes her head. "I don't remember him."

Grimm nods. "He's fine." He glances back at the rest of us, and I nod to show that she believes him.

"What about Aed?" She wipes her eyes. "Where's his family? We need to tell them what happened."

Penn takes her hand in his and squeezes. "I took care of everything. We retrieved his body and paid for a proper burial."

Lana adjusts her billowy top. "Thank you." She turns towards me. "Did I love him?"

"Bellamy?" I furrow my brows. "You two trained together for a while and were affectionate with each other over the months. Other than that, I don't think your feelings matched his for you."

She seems to consider this for a moment before giving a curt nod. "Thank you for telling me."

Penn clears his throat. "Do you remember anything else?"

"Not really. Although, there was a small fae with short white hair who warned me to unite the realms. Before that, I met The Crucey and her Tolden before some werewolves in their wolf's form intimidated us."

Everyone freezes. "Did you say The Crucey?"

She nods her head and stands. "I healed a wound on its throat before saving the Tolden." She looks down at her hands before running them over her arms. "I don't know what's wrong with me, but it seems like I'm constantly on the verge of crying."

Penn folds his arms over his chest. "Maybe you're just upset about what happened to Aed and need time. But The Crucey? Are you certain that's what you saw?"

She furrows her brows. "She told me who she was. Why?"

"Lana, The Crucey alone could've, and would've, shredded you to pieces." I cast a worried glance at the others. "The Crucey with a Tolden? You never would've survived her wrath. She's the deadliest creature in all the realms, kills indiscriminately, and enjoys every second of it. She rules the Wastelands. No magic can control her."

Penn squeezes her shoulder. "You said she talked to you?"

The Crucey in the woods? If she's away from the Wastelands, the Tolden must've been a newborn. It's probably why there's been more sightings of werewolves lately. Tolden hearts can cure their curse.

"She tried to kill me at first until the baby fell and I noticed the blood. A werewolf had attacked them, and the little one was dying, so I offered to help." Her eyes water. "It took little to scare the werewolves away when they came back to the clearing. Just some fire."

I run my hand through my hair. "Gods, Lana, you're really lucky she didn't kill you."

She meets my eyes. "The Crucey said she owes me, but I'm just glad to have saved a life."

"I can't believe you had a full conversation with her." Rune rubs his chin. "You might be the first to ever get through to her."

Lana shrugs. "She's definitely sentient and intelligent. Maybe she's just misunderstood?"

Penn laughs and pulls a picture up on his phone and hands it to Lana. "This is what she does."

Lana's eyes widen before handing the phone back. "Maybe if we find a way to keep the Tolden safe, she'll be less on edge?"

We nod. "We'll put together a team to come up with ideas. Are you okay with leading it, Lana?" I place my hand on her arm.

"Absolutely, thank you."

CHAPTER 45

FINN

"Why did you abdicate?" Oz passes me the platter of steaks.

I slide a T-bone onto my plate. "The other kings wanted to share a mate together. None of them felt a soul bond, but I did. Since reaching maturity, I knew fate intended on me having one. Thousands of years it took before I felt Lana—the moment her mother first knit her in her womb."

"So, you left to find her, or what?" Lana's dad asks.

"One day, five hundred years ago, I had the urge to leave, so I did. They vilified me for it."

Gideon scowls. "Do you think they're retaliating against you leaving by stealing your soul bonded mate?"

I puff my cheeks and expel my breath before averting my gaze. How will her vampire mates handle the truth? "There's no doubt in my mind."

"What do you think they plan on doing with her?" Alphie takes the platter from me.

"They'll do what they planned all along—they'll mate her." The very thought causes my chest to squeeze like a vise.

"How can they do that if she's already soul bonded?" Oz stills.

"Only fae royals can share mates. Their bond is secondary to mine, as I'm High King and soul bonded. If they mate her, the bond between them will never break; she'll be tied to them forever. We'll all be tied to them. We have to get her before they do. High Kings and Queens can create other High Kings and Queens. If three of the lower caste royals mate the same High Queen, they can produce High Kings and Queens."

Auguste pauses the fork to his mouth. "Lana had a hysterectomy when the twins were born. She can't get pregnant."

I avert my gaze, focusing instead on my food. "Before telling her their price, they gave her womb back. She's no longer barren."

Gideon tries to blink away a tear, but it cascades down his face instead. Vampires are creepy as fuck. Bloody tears?

CHAPTER 46

LANA

Harsh light floods the room beyond my eyelids, and I groan. "It can't be time to get up already."

"I'm sorry, My Lady," Sarai coos from my bedside, "but it is."

I bury my face in the pillow. "Is it really?"

"The kings requested you ramp up your combat training," she reminds me.

"I thought we were friends," I complain into my sheets. "You're supposed to take my side."

"I am your lady's maid. Though they pay me handsomely, we *are* friends." Her rich voice thunders as she ushers me from bed. "My loyalty is to you and not to the kings."

Peeking at her through a gap in the covers draped over my head, I perk up. "Does this mean you're going to let me sleep in?"

Sarai scoffs. "Only if you want Pierce to lop off my head."

I sit up, wide-eyed, but scowl when I see her grinning.

"You're mean."

She nods. "And you need to get dressed before your breakfast gets cold."

I glance across the room, where she's hung technical clothes for me to wear. As I pull my nightgown over my head, my gaze catches on the space where the dark bruises used to dot my chest. I swallow as the memories of yesterday flash through my mind: As if I hadn't already been through enough this week with watching Aed die and learning about my wiped memories of Bellamy, the events of last night keep playing over and over in my head.

Lord Farran's cruel hands, his hot breath against my skin, and the disgusted expression plastered across Pierce's face when he discovered us. I'd been so startled to find him in my room after returning from supper; I didn't even think to scream. He slipped a hand around my mouth, and everything after that became a blur. Though Pierce interrupted us before he could get very far, the parts of my body where his hands had been still feel so dirty. I want the memory of Lord Farran touching me gone from my mind forever.

The urge to flee overcomes me for a moment. I want to disappear into the snow-capped mountains and forget all about yesterday.

The girl in the mirror looking back at me is a face I'm still getting used to. It's me, but not. Flawless skin, dark, curly hair tangled across my shoulders, eyes wide with fear. I've yet to tell the kings about the lord's intrusion to my room. He scaled the castle wall and climbed over the railing to my balcony while the royals went to court after we dined together.

"Sarai," I say too harshly, the disgust still on my tongue. "I want to tell the kings about Lord Farran today." After Pierce made Lord Farran leave, I had him get Sarai for me, and I told her everything. My gut turns at what Pierce thinks of me.

Her head cocks, and she smiles like I've made her day. "Pierce will be pleased."

"What do you mean?"

She tosses my clothes to me. "Let's go eat, and I'll explain it over breakfast."

As she escorts me to the dining hall, I ask. "What about Pierce? He should be told as well."

"Tell me what?" Pierce asks.

I jump at the sound of his voice.

Sarai gives me a knowing smile. "The news would spoil your appetite." And then she turns to leave.

I take in Pierce's beauty, despite the thick scar marring his face. It gives him a rugged appearance his otherwise perfect features would lack without it. His tanned skin is a sharp contrast to the black jeans and t-shirt hugging his body. I can tell why Sarai is so taken with him —they're a good match.

He strides toward me, and I back away. "I need to tell you something, but you can't freak out."

"Is this about you and Lord Farran?"

I wince. "How did you ..."

"Do you honestly think I thought you gave your consent to the creep?" His gaze drops to where I have a death grip on my bag, then back to my eyes. He steps closer, and I step back again.

"Pierce," I say as calmly as possible. "I'm serious."

"You didn't answer me," he murmurs.

I blink. "What?"

"Should I end him now, or later?"

I swat him and whisper. "You'll do no such thing! He deserves consequences, but not death."

"He touched you."

I close my eyes briefly, trying to hold back the tears. "I know, but I'm okay. And he won't be able to again—I know what he's capable of now. There will be no hesitation next time."

He stares at me, and I'm not sure if he'll listen to reason. I take a deep breath and try again, speaking slower this time.

"Listen, I appreciate your protection. If it makes you feel any better, I'll double my training, and we'll make sure I'm better prepared in case he comes after me again. I just really don't want you to kill him."

Pierce's eyes soften, and he nods. "Very well, I won't kill him."

"Thank you." I exhale a sigh of relief.

"You've got to tell them now, though."

I chew on my bottom lip. "I need to eat first."

His eyebrow rises in question, but he doesn't ask me anything else.

I fill a plate full of eggs and bacon, then find a seat at the table with Pierce. It's silent as we eat, but it's not an uncomfortable silence. When we finish eating, he stands and offers his hand to me.

"Time to face the music, Lana."

I swallow hard and take his hand.

We walk in silence to the throne room, where the kings are waiting. I'm grateful for the small amount of time to brace myself before I'm in front of them. I take a deep breath and square my shoulders, then step into the room.

Pierce gives me a small squeeze on my hand before taking his place on the wall behind me.

My eyes find Casimir first and he perks up before beaming me a smile. Penn looks stoic as ever, but he inclines his head slightly. My face splits with a grin, relieved he doesn't seem angry I'm in here.

Last, I meet Grimm's gaze. There's a fondness in his eyes I haven't seen before. He's the first to speak.

"Lana, you know you don't have to have an audience with us if you need something addressed. Are you alright?"

I stiffen when my vision catches Lord Farran amongst the nobles.

It's probably obvious I'm nervous, with my wringing hands, and Pierce's firm grip on the hilt of his sword. My eyes dart again to the cruel fae across the room before coming back to the kings. They miss nothing, and whip their heads in Farran's direction.

"I'm fine," I murmur, and all three of them turn back to me, their expressions sharp.

"It's good of you to come before us, Lana." Grimm speaks up. "We don't want you to feel you have to wait to speak with us."

I nod my head, grateful for his understanding.

"What issues have you come to address?" Casimir asks, concern thick in his voice.

"After supper last night, I returned to my room to find Lord Farran ..."

"How did he get in?" Penn sits up, cutting me off. His eyes are blazing and steam billows from his nose. This is the first I've seen him anywhere close to revealing his order—I've never seen him so angry. He looks murderous. Nervous murmurs ripple through the room.

"I found the balcony door open." I gesture with my hands in the air. "But he cornered me, and ..."

"Start from the beginning," Penn instructs me.

I nod my head and take a deep breath. "Pierce dropped me off at my room before standing guard outside my door. When I shut it, the first thing I noticed was my door ajar. I know I'd closed it because Sarai reminded me before leaving for supper." I clasp my hands together to steady their tremble.

"When I went to close it, that's when I saw him sprawled on my bed in his underwear. I thought maybe he was drunk and wandered into the wrong room. H-h-he moved so fast ..." Tears swell in my eyes. "Before I knew what was happening, he had me pinned to the bed, forcing his tongue into my mouth and his hands under my dress. Our scuffle alerted Pierce, who barged into the room and made Lord Farran leave."

The fae in question shouts. "Liar. You invited me to your room, begging me to fuck!"

Pierce draws his sword. "Watch how you speak about my Lady." His voice is low and deadly.

Farran sidles up to him, his mouth set in a thin line. "You know she's nothing more than a whore. You're probably fucking her, too. She'll spread her legs for any ..."

"You dare touch who isn't yours?" Penn roars. "Lady Lana is under our personal protection. Never will I tolerate someone insulting her!"

Grimm shouts. "Guards!" The line of armor-clad men and women draws weapons and approaches the Lord, who has the nerve to look shocked.

"But I'm of the Serpent Line! You can't do this!"

A guard brings Farran to his knees, and another draws his sword. With a nod from Penn, he brings the sword down towards the lord's neck.

"No!" I throw my hand out and the weapon clatters to the ground. Oh, *shit.*

"I'm sorry, I'm sorry. Please. Don't kill him. His cruel words and assault don't warrant the taking of his life."

Shocked gasps echo through the room. I wince. This is bad, so very bad. I've just insulted and challenged the very kings who not only saved my life from vampires, but are defending my honor. *In front of their people.*

I sink to my knees in supplication. "Please, mete your judgment on me for my insubordination, but don't kill him." My head hangs low, my eyes focusing on the tile in my field of vision. Gods, they're going to kill me.

Bare feet enter my line of sight, and the fae they're attached to crouch in front of me. He grasps my chin and tilts it up so I look him in the eyes. *Grimm.* His eyes are soft when he takes my trembling hands in his and helps me to stand.

He wraps me in his arms and whispers in my ear. "You are very brave, and give compassion where none is due. It is not the fae way to allow anyone to bring harm to one of our own without punishment."

Tears stream down my cheeks while I cling to his chest like he's a lifeline and I'm adrift at sea.

"Lord Farran, we strip you of your Lordship, your land, your accounts, real estate, and titles. You are an enemy of this realm and will spend the rest of your days in Bedlam Penitentiary. Your crimes make you ineligible for parole. You've brought dishonor to the Serpent name, and we strip you of your lineage. Your sentence is *vita damnationem.*" Penn's eyes flash gold, and he looks at the guard holding the criminal down. "Sift him to the penitentiary immediately."

A shout chokes off when the two disappear from the throne room. The chamber is silent for a pause, before murmurs drown out the pounding of my racing heart. Grimm gives me a squeeze again.

He casts a glance to Pierce. "See to it she makes it safely to her room? Please check for intruders before leaving her. We'll work on assigning an additional guard to keep watch."

Grimm hands me off to Pierce, and I keep my eyes down. He offers me his arm and leads me from the throne room. When we're beyond the doors, he places a hand on my forearm and grins.

"The kinder thing would've been to let him die."

Killian

Using a silencing spell, I run through the empty castle halls undetected. Oz is my boss, but he's nothing compared to the High King, Finian Drake. If I fail my recon mission, he'll crush me. He's known as a benevolent ruler, but as the most powerful fae in all the realms, you don't cross him. Ever. I failed him once, and can't do it again. How was I supposed to know the kings had swiped her memories more than once, offering a clever coverup for Aed's confession of their treachery?

I stop at the end of a hall lit by wall sconces. It's the way into Lana's room, where I believe she's being kept. I'm not sure how good the protection spell is on her door, but I've practiced my best spells for the occasion.

Voices come from around the corner, and I duck into a dark alcove. Two guards wearing black leather armor and holding swords pause in front of the door. Fae have guns, but prefer close combat, and you're a weak fae if you need a mortal weapon. Only the best trained warriors carry swords. I guess these guards are elite in the Bedlam realm.

They're talking about Lana and a man named Farran who attacked her a few days ago. He's not in the castle anymore, but I get the impression his punishment is far worse than death, if the rumors about Bedlam Penitentiary are true. She petitioned to have him sent there instead of getting killed.

The guards walk away, and I slip into the hall. I don't have the information I need yet, so I'll keep trying. Maybe Lana's door isn't guarded every night.

I open her door and go inside, shutting it carefully behind me. Her bedroom is huge, bigger than my entire house, and filled with books and plants. I touch nothing, just in case anything is spelled for detection.

My eyes closed, I cast a spell to check for magical signatures. Faint outlines of energy appear. The strongest curls in an oval around the bed, with three lines branching off like rays of starlight. A fainter, oval of black energy appears on top of the bright one, almost like it's only ever been here for a short period. Could this be Farran's imprint?

Lana hasn't been in the room since he was here. I crouch low to the ground, not taking my eyes off the imprint. I form a small ball of energy in front of me and direct it at the imprint, sending another wave of energy through it. The black magic reacts, undulating on the surface.

The power is putrid, full of poison and decay. It's not the kind of magic Lana has ever used, and it doesn't belong in her room, either. This is dark and comes with ill intent. It *has* to be Farran.

Where are you staying, Lana? I cast another spell to point me in the general direction. Slowly, the magic guides me to an ornate door on the far end of her room. It has a symbol of a heart on it.

My breathing comes faster. Is Lana in danger? I ease the door open and find a new energy on the other side, this one neither evil nor good, like most fae's signatures. I step inside and watch my steps on the dark grey stones. There are no lights, which means I'm either in an unlit hallway or a closet.

I conjure a small ball of light and point it in front of me. Another *bedroom*? Connecting to hers? This must be one of the king's rooms; expensive tapestries line the walls, a gigantic bed sits on a high platform, and the furnishings are rich mahogany. I force myself to ignore my curiosity. Lana's room is the only one that matters right now.

Before turning back around, I pause. Is she staying in this room? I check for magical signatures and find Lana's on the bed. It's strong, so she's been here recently. A murky imprint is on the leather couch near the far wall. It doesn't belong to anyone I recognize, but is the same energy from her door. This energy is also on the bed, but faint.

She must sleep on the bed, and the king takes the couch. I was certain they were mistreating her here, but if they've got her in their room after an attack, they must want her alive. She's valuable to them.

CHAPTER 47

CASIMIR

*L*ana lies in Grimm's bed, her hair fanning over his silk pillow. The only noise coming from her is the sound of her deep breath as she sleeps. In the stillness of the room, a clock ticks loudly as it slowly makes its way to midnight. She spent most of her day and night training. I know Lord Farran's attack spooked her.

I nod at the others, and they follow me to her room. This afternoon, we had staff remove her bed and burn anything he might've touched. It's another reason she isn't in her own rooms. Tomorrow morning, we'll have an entirely new bed for her.

We stand with our daggers drawn, preparing to make our sacrifice. Penn begins the ritual.

"With the slice of each blade,
a blood sacrifice is made.
We give our blood,
our wounds we flood.
Line this room,
to keep her safe from doom.
For this spell, we kneel,
Our blood oath we seal.

No villain will she meet,
Lest death, they'll greet."

With that, we slice our palms open and stream the blood across the threshold of her room. Gritting my teeth against the pain, I hold my hand over the doorway and let my essence drip all the way across.

Blood seeps from under the door, pooling on Lana's side of the doorway. I run my hand along it, flinging drops to coat the room. The blood seeps into the ground and evaporates.

No one enters these chambers but us, Sarai, and Pierce. The King's Guard, the fae knights, and the High King himself will die if they try to cross this threshold.

Finn

"You look like crap, Killian. What happened to you?"

His wounds have healed, but there are slashes in his clothes and dried blood soaked through. Looks like he might've barely escaped Bedlam.

"Leaving the castle, I ran into some kind of panther prowling the grounds."

I chuckle. "Must've been Titan. Rune see you, did he?"

"If you're talking about the man with gold tattoos and hair, no. I was about to cast a diversion spell when the beast attacked me."

"Phelvie only hurt those with ill intent, so I'm certain Rune saw you."

Killian swallows. "Damn lucky I scrounged for healing potions in the castle after I left Lana's room. I would've been dead."

"You were in Lana's room? Did you talk to her?" Oz sits up. "How is she?"

"Someone named Farran attacked her. Was waiting in her bed, completely naked, save for his skivvies. I know the fae are protecting her." Killian moves for his bag and hands a parchment to Oz. "She's staying in the king's bedrooms now."

I grip the arm of the chair. "*Lord Farran?* I'll kill him." He was always such a creep.

Killian chuckles.

"The fuck are you laughing for?" I slam my fists on the table, causing the spy to tremble.

He clears his throat. "It's just ... the guards. They said Lana petitioned for the kings not to kill him."

"Why the hell would she do that?" Gideon cocks a brow.

Glee dances in Killian's eyes. "They stripped him of his land and titles before they sentenced him *vita damnationem* at Bedlam Penitentiary."

Amusement bubbles up my throat and turns into a raucous laugh. The spy joins me, while the vampires look on as though we've gone mad.

"What's vita damnationem?" Oz runs a hand through his dark hair.

I grin. "A life sentence to the worst prison in all the realms. It makes Aggonid's hell look like a theme park for babies."

The vampires share in the joy. "Think Lana knew she was giving him a worse fate than death?" Auguste leans in.

"Not a chance."

Auguste

My love,

I hope this letter finds you well, given the circumstances. We've just learned of Lord Farran's attack on you. At first, I was upset to hear you didn't want him killed. I would've been far less lenient. Although, learning you sentenced him to a worse fate brings me joy I cannot begin to describe.

Gideon's obsession with besting Finn has kept us entertained in your absence. I think Finn secretly loves it. So far, the only thing Gideon has on him is his fangs—Gideons are longer.

Speaking of competition, please know we're not upset. I know Gideon doesn't hold it against you either, he just wants to prove he's the better male.

It's gotten so bad, he even challenged Finn to see who could capture the most koalas in Featherdale Sydney Wildlife Park. Harmless, right?

No. It's illegal to hold koalas, so the two of them spent six hours in jail before we figured out where they were and could bail them out. Did that stop them? No. They moved on to crocodiles next.

Please come home soon. Their lives depend on it.

I love you.

Always,

Auguste

CHAPTER 48

OZ

Killian barges into the room, out of breath. "They used a blood sacrifice spell to ward her room. No one but the kings, her personal guard, and lady's maid can get in." He looks to the window. "I don't think they're going to let her leave without a fight."

"We need a plan." Gideon stands. "A fail-proof one."

"Why don't we just knock on the front door?" Auguste asks, his arms crossed over his chest.

Finn leans forward in his seat, dismissing the notion. "They'd be waiting for us."

I down the bagged blood and toss it into the garbage. "Nah, I think Auguste is onto something. We figure out how to get into Bedlam, find out where they're at, and declare war."

Any of us would level countless realms, take on endless armies, whatever it takes to get her back. Who knows what the kings are doing to her while we sit around trying to be heroes? I watch Finn, wondering if he's good enough for Lana. Fate paired them together, but does that mean he's the better choice? Gideon catches my scowl.

The fairy smirks at me. I've tried to keep him out of my head, but his powers are too strong.

Gideon leans into me to whisper in my ear. "At least I know we're probably more well-endowed than the beast."

Finn whips his head towards us, mirth dancing in his eyes. "I believe her exact words were, 'this isn't going to fit,' while she couldn't even wrap her hands around my girth."

Killian spits out his water and clears his throat. "Pardon?"

The thought of Lana with the fairy makes my stomach turn. I can't blame her, but it still frustrates me. We were happy, just the four of us, perfectly in tandem with each other. At least I can take comfort in knowing I make her deliriously happy ... and satisfied.

I smirk. "And your point?" I ask the fairy, trying to get him back on track.

He glares at me. "I'm here to help, not argue about who satisfies Lana more. It's really not even a competition, and it's unfair of me to point out my body was literally made for her exact preferences." He stands and paces the room.

I ignore the ache in my chest, and I'm grateful for Auguste getting us back on track.

"We have a few obstacles. The first one being the portal, because vampires can't get in. Witches can, but only on a Bedlam Moon, and we just had another one pass. I don't want to wait any longer than necessary."

Something we can agree on. I direct my question at Finn because, as High King, he should know how the portal works. "Is there any way around the portal's restrictions?"

Finn runs his hand through his hair. Gideon's thoughts project so loud, they break through, even though I wasn't listening for them: *At least mine is better than his. He practically looks geriatric with his almost-white hair. Or is it silver?*

"My ancestors created the portal with Luna magic when they made witches as a means for them to seek safety from persecution. To minimize risk, they only made the door available during the Bedlam Moon, when magic is at its strongest."

Gideon stands, another indignant thought of his shouting into my mind. *No way am I going to let this beast make me look smaller than he is.*

"Can we just blow the fucking door off?" Gideon growls in frustration.

Finn pauses his pacing. "You got a throng of people you can sacrifice in a blood spell? That's what it'd take to undo this kind of magic."

I still my hand. "As a matter of fact, we do."

Auguste whips his head to me. "The Lapis Templar."

Finn looks between us. "Aren't they the cult who kept trying to kill Lana?"

I grit my teeth. "Yeah, since she left, we've been rounding them up for sentencing. We've got a few hundred right now, and tabs on at least another three, four hundred. How many you need?"

"That should work. We need to kill a powerful witch, too." Finn glances at me. "I don't think Lana would appreciate me sacrificing you."

A smile curls across my lips, and I quirk an eyebrow. "The leader of the cult is Dolphina Darling, a vampire witch who is responsible for atrocities all over the world in the name of her cause. When Lana went to Bedlam, she slaughtered entire families of vampires sympathetic to Lana. She also is liable for the death of my son and wife before I became a vampire."

I pull up a digital map marked with all the sightings we have of Dolphina. Most occur near our place in Patagonia, where we had our last public gathering. Nothing in Australia at all.

"She only goes where you've been seen in public, Oz." Gideon points to several locations in the Midwest United States, Québec, Chile, and Massachusetts. "You're who she wants. The one she always wanted. You're going to be our bait."

"So, we lure her in, capture her, and then what? Bring everyone to the portal? How will we do that?" I ask.

"We won't need Oz as bait. I'll cast a spell to connect the remaining Lapis Templar on Earth to the portal and call them home. No one can resist the pull." Finn grins.

Auguste's eyes widen. "Won't they know what's happening?"

"They'll go through their day like any other, and have the sudden, inexplicable urge to go to the location where the portal is. As soon as they come within miles of the portal, they're trapped, even if they somehow become aware things aren't right."

Chills race up my spine. "And you're sure she'll show, too?"

"If she's the leader of the Lapis Templar, absolutely."

This is a good plan. Blow the lid off the portal, and we can get the vampires in. "Good. I'll work on drafting orders to round up our troops to come through the portal. We'll help you fight for the throne, but what about Lana's memories? She won't come with us willingly, even if we bring an army to their door."

"All I need is to get her alone and I can override their magic, but first, I have to be High King again. Otherwise, my magic isn't powerful enough." Finn looks at each of us in turn, and we all nod.

"If you have to take the throne, we'll need to figure out how to make this work between all of us. We have our court here, and I don't think any of us will let go of Lana. Ever." I cross my arms.

The very thought of Lana being gone forever? I can't even conceive of it.

Dad speaks up. "We have enough of a plan to get started with."

WE MEET with the others in our group to relay what we know about Lana's abduction, and everyone works on preparing for the siege on Bedlam. Finn looks distracted, and when he makes for the door, I stop him.

"I'm all in on your plan, but is this how it's going to be? You taking off to do your own thing without saying a word? You don't know enough about Earth to wander alone. It's dangerous." I shift my weight, staring at the floor.

Finn sighs. "I'm adding another person to the sacrifice."

"Who?"

"Lana's ex-fiancé."

Pain grips my chest. Fiancé? Judging by the look of the others, they didn't know either. "What are you talking about?"

Finn furrows his brows. "The one who hurt her."

"Get Hannah on the phone, now." My tone brooks no argument.

Maeve calls her using FaceTime, and we crowd around the screen. She has a huge smile on her face until she sees how upset everyone is.

"Guys? Maeve? Is Lana okay?"

"I need his name and location, Hannah, and I swear if you keep this from us, we're going to have a problem," I bark.

Maeve scowls at me before turning back to the phone.

"Hey, babe, the boys want to know about Lana's ex-fiancé?"

The color drains from Hannah's face. "He's a jerk. I knew he was bad news, but she wouldn't listen to me."

"Hannah?" I run my hand through my hair. "Tell me what you know."

"His family is old money in New York City. They have a house right on the water. One day, he asked Lana to go out there to look at it with him." Hannah flinches. "He didn't even have a formal proposal for her. He just wanted to show off his wealth and tell Lana he wanted her in his life. They dated for several years, but no matter how much time we spent together, I hated him. He has a cruel streak."

"What's his name?" Finn looks serious.

"Ross Van'Astor." Hannah exhales sharply. "His family are just awful people, and he's got some pretty terrible friends, too."

Finn nods. "We'll pay him a visit. Thanks."

"I don't understand what's going on." Hannah frowns.

We don't wait to hear Maeve explain. Instead, we follow Gideon towards the jet. We need to get to New York City. Now.

CHAPTER 49

OZ

We land somewhere in northern New Jersey, and Auguste rents a car while we're at the airport. Finn, Gideon, Auguste and I travel through the city to find this Ross Van'Astor character. The closer we get to the financial district the more expensive things get. Eventually, we reach a small enclave of houses right on the water. One in particular stands out. It's impressive, and it's technically in the middle of the city.

There are no guards, though. "Finn?"

The fairy looks around at the other houses along the street.

"This is it." Gideon steps in front of us, and Finn nods.

"What's he doing?" Auguste cocks an eyebrow in Finn's direction, but no one answers him.

Finn chants and manipulates magic around him. Before long, a red glow surrounds the entire building. "He's here."

I look at Finn with newfound respect. Maybe this fae can teach me a thing or two. I can't wait to see what he brings to the table when we get back to Bedlam, and everything he taught Lana.

Auguste unlocks the front door. "Is that necessary?"

"Yes." Finn casts another spell to lock it behind us, and I follow him inside.

The putrid scent of wet dog overwhelms my senses, and I cover my nose with the sleeve of my shirt. "Gross."

"It's coming from the room down here." Gideon points to a set of stairs leading downwards.

We head to an underground level, and Finn reaches out a hand to touch the wall. "There's a bedroom around here, and something else."

Gideon opens a door on the right, and we all come face to face with a cowering human. Running from shoulder to hip are three thick scars. Ross Van'Astor is in the corner, and he has nothing on but a pair of boxer briefs. He's corded with muscles, but compared to us, he's small.

"What's going on?" His voice shakes as he tries to make himself look bigger than he is.

"Van'Astor?" I sneer at him. "You're the one who hurt Lana."

He flinches, and his bravado almost disappears, but he pulls his shoulders back. "I don't know what you're talking about. I haven't seen that heifer in years."

Finn steps forward and presses a finger into Ross's chest. "You need to be more careful what you say, beast."

We move in, but Finn stops us. "Don't let him bite you."

"Why not?" Gideon keeps moving towards the ex-fiancé.

With a wave of his hand, Finn has the little weasel manacled to the wall. "Watch." He places his hand on Ross's chest, and Finn glows a bright blue. The captive contorts his body as it reacts to whatever the fairy is doing to him.

Then, one by one, his bones break, causing Ross to howl in pain.

"I should have done this from the beginning." Finn smirks, and his skin continues to glow that otherworldly blue.

Thick fur coats the manacled man, his features lengthen, and a snarl rips from him. He's a werewolf? How the hell did he keep this from Lana?

Finn spares me a glance over his shoulder as he approaches the werewolf. "Now, I can kill him."

"No." I grab Finn's shoulder and pull him back. "We're using him in the ritual, remember?"

He steps back, but looks disappointed.

I sigh. "Maybe we could ..." I look over at Auguste and Gideon.

"We'll take him on the jet." Auguste steps forward and stands in front of the rapidly shifting wolf who was Ross Van'Astor just a few seconds ago. "We'll treat him nice. Finn, can you keep him from shifting while we transfer him?"

"Of course. After all, Luna fae gave werewolves their curse." Finn's face hardens.

∼

Oz

WE HAD to sit with this werewolf's stench stinking up the plane the entire way to Gideon's place in Sydney. We've brought him here for questioning and then we'll transfer him to a holding facility. He's too important to let loose before the ritual.

I set the small briefcase on the kitchen counter and extract the silver knives from inside.

"What's that?" Finn asks as he enters the room, followed by Gideon and Auguste.

"I'm going to get answers," I say as I walk towards the basement door.

Understanding flashes in his eyes, and he steps back, giving me room.

I descend the stairs, and the stink intensifies. I find Ross Van'Astor huddled in a corner, naked and trembling where he's chained to the wall.

"What's going on?" He looks from me to Gideon, who towers over him.

"We're going to ask you some questions," I say as I step closer. He sniffs and shrinks back, but doesn't try to shift. "Good boy."

I set the silver down on the floor in front of him and take a step back. Finn stands behind me, ready to assist if needed.

"You're going to answer our questions, or this will get very painful," Auguste says.

Ross swallows hard, and his eyes go wide when he takes in the silver. "I'll talk."

"Why Lana?"

He shakes his head. "She meant nothing to me. Just a hot piece of …"

I don't give him a chance to finish his sentence. I grab the blade and shove it into his thigh. He screams, and the sound echoes through the basement.

"Wrong answer." Gideon's voice is calm, but there's an edge to it. "Try again."

"I was hired!" Ross yells as he writhes in pain. "They paid me to get close to her and find out everything I could."

"Who?" I demand as I twist the silver.

"I don't know!" He cries out. "Please, they'll kill me if they find out I talked!"

"What the hell do you think will happen if you don't?" Gideon chuckles.

Ross Van'Astor sobs, and I ease up on the silver. "I don't know, I don't know! This was over a decade ago!"

"Who hired you?" I demand again.

"I swear, I don't know." He gasps for air. "They just called me and told me what to do. I'd get an easy five mil for marrying her."

"Do you have a name?" Finn asks.

"No, no, I swear." Tears stream down his face. "Please, just let me go. I won't tell anyone, I promise."

I step back, and Finn takes my place. He leans in close and grabs Van'Astor's neck. "One more wrong answer, and I'll snap your weak little spine."

Ross's eyes go wide, and he nods frantically. "I'll tell you, I'll tell you!"

Why is he afraid of the fairy and not me?

"Who hired you?" Finn asks again.

"It was a group. I don't know their names. They just paid me through an offshore account. I got half after the first year together, and then I'd get the rest after the wedding." He shudders as Finn tightens his grip.

Gideon spits. "You cheated on her, and I want to know why."

"I was promised more money if I got her pregnant." Ross gags as Finn increases the pressure. "They wanted an heir."

"None of this explains why you cheated on Lana." Gideon's voice is like ice.

"I was supposed to make her think I loved her," Ross whimpers. "A couple nights after our engagement, I was at the bar and took home a blonde co-ed who'd been hitting on me all night. Normally, I don't fuck other supernatural creatures, but her rack, man ... Lana walked in just as I was finishing inside this chick. I was so screwed. She dumped me, and I didn't get the rest of my money."

"You disgust me," Finn growls as he steps back.

The ache in my chest grows, knowing how badly this must've hurt Lana. No wonder she never talked about this guy. Was her trauma so deep, I didn't see these memories when we mated? I knew she'd been cheated on, but none of the details.

Auguste stills, and tilts his head to the side, inspecting this vile man with a predatory stare. "Dolphina."

"You know her?" Ross lifts his head. "She ghosted me after Lana split."

CHAPTER 50

CASIMIR

There's nothing quite like shifting under the moon. Sure, in the beginning, it was excruciating. Now, I shift so fast it feels like coming home. Fog settles over the grounds like a shroud, and I can hear the faintest whimper.

Taking tentative steps, I tilt my ear towards where I hear the sound. It's coming from Lana's chambers. Is someone in her room hurting her? As fast as my paws will carry me, I race to her room, shifting into my fae form as I reach her door. Pierce says something, but the blood rushing in my ears drowns him out.

I have to get to Lana. Using magic, I place my hand over her lock and open it. In the center of the room, Lana thrashes on top of her covers, screaming in terror. Pierce doesn't stop me as I cross to her bed.

I wrap my arms around her, trying to calm her. She's soaked in sweat, her body trembling. "Casimir." She gasps, clinging to me.

"I'm here, love." I nuzzle into the crook of her neck, trying to soothe her. "I'm here."

Slowly, she relaxes in my arms, her breathing evening out. I keep holding her until she falls asleep again. I shift her off me before slipping out of the room to talk to Pierce.

I keep my voice low. "How often does she have nightmares? We never hear them."

"Nearly every night." He's hesitant to speak. "I think it's her subconscious, missing them."

Missing them. Finn and the vampires, I presume. Maybe even Bellamy. I nod my head before shifting back into a wolf. Pierce opens her door for me, my nails clicking on the floor while I make my way towards her bed.

I leap onto it, curling up next to her. Her natural scent is much stronger when I'm in my wolf order—it's sweet, like fruit, with a hint of spice. I place my head on her stomach, taking comfort from her cool skin. My body runs hot, especially with all this fur. I'll be here when she wakes up, ready to protect her from whatever demons haunt her dreams.

❧

Lana

SUNLIGHT GREETS me before I even open my eyes. For a moment, I'm disoriented, not sure where I am. An enormous weight holds me down, and I'm afraid I'm having sleep paralysis again. I try to move, but I can't.

Then I hear a deep, calming voice in my head, just before I scramble to the other side of the bed.

Wolf!

I'm about to scream when the wolf transforms into a very naked Casimir. I gulp, averting my gaze. "Casimir!" I clutch my chest. "You scared the crap out of me."

"Sorry." he nuzzles into the crook of my neck, his body heat lingering against mine. "I heard you scream, and I couldn't stand not being there for you."

"It's okay," I whisper, still trying to calm my pounding heart. "Do you want to get dressed?" Against my free will, my eyes linger on his exposed skin. Arms and legs like tree trunks on this one.

He smirks. "No, but if you want me to, I will." He plops onto the bed, belly-up, and I don't know how I never recognized what his order was before he told me.

"I like your wolf." I bat his arm with a pillow, and he chuckles.

Casimir yanks me close to him and nuzzles into my neck. "He likes you, too." I clutch onto his arm, basking in his heat when his skin turns to fur right under me.

He licks me from my collarbone, up my neck, and across my face. "Blech!" I scowl. "Not the face!"

His enormous paws pin me to the bed, showing me just how much bigger than me he is. A grin crosses his maw before transforming into the handsome fae grin I've come to know and love.

His eyes dart to my mouth and back to my face. "You taste so good." He sounds so wistful.

"Casimir!" I giggle, slapping his chest. "You're not going to eat me."

"I could." He kisses me, long and deep, before pulling back to look at me. "You're so tiny I could do it in one bite. I don't think I will, though. Then I'd miss doing this." He presses his lips to mine again, softer. He nods. "Yes, I think I'll keep you."

My hand comes up to rest on his face. "Do I get no say?"

He groans. "Of course you do, but I hope it's along the lines of, 'Keep me forever, Casimir, and I'll give you endless belly rubs and scratches behind the ears.' Seriously, it feels so good, even when not in my wolf form."

I laugh and shove him. "You're ridiculous."

"But you love me, anyway." A statement, not a question.

"I cross the line at belly rubs and scratches. I'm not doing anything else with your wolf." My hands rest on his bunched shoulders. "Actually, the idea kind of freaks me out."

He chuckles before he claims my mouth with his. The press of his lips is softer, more possessive. I wrap my arms around his neck and deepen the kiss, melting into him.

When we finally break apart, both of us are breathless. "Keep me, then," he whispers.

"Okay." I nod.

CHAPTER 51

LANA

Since my arrival at the castle, I've yet to leave the grounds, save for Meloria. That all changes today. We're going to Sundahlia for winter. We're taking a *ship*. Apparently, they ward the entire border from teleporting, or sifting, as the fae call it. I know Penn can fly as a dragon, and I think the others have wings in their fae forms if they want to bring them out, but I haven't seen any.

Most of Bedlam is millennia ahead of Earth when it comes to technology, and in other parts, it's like we're back in the 1600s. They're not averse to technology. Instead, they recognize how damaging some of it can be. Strict laws exist realm-wide to prevent pollution, waste, and corruption.

Sail powers ships, and if necessary during calm winds, giant oars. This one has three masts. We stalk up the steep gangway, and the ship's captain removes his hat and bows when we board.

"Captain Shallowind, do we expect fair seas?"

"Aye, your majesty. The avia's are another story."

"What of them?" Penn presses.

"We'll have to skirt North around the Cerulean Isles; the avia's are nesting early this moon cycle." The captain scowls. "Must be the imbalance; it's affecting everything."

"What are avia's? Birds?"

The captain gives me a gap-toothed grin. "None you've ever seen, my lady. These are the size of the ship and can crush a fae with its weight alone. They have talons as long as a spear, a beak even longer, and teeth as sharp as the tip of a sword."

I shudder.

Grimm tucks my arm in his and whispers in my ear. "I'll protect you. No need to worry." He leads me to the bow, where I grip onto the railing and watch the activity on the dock below. My personal guard and his unit are here, but none of the females. Males direct heavy crates and chests up the gangway using their magic, and food supplies follow. I crack a smile at their wildly inappropriate sea shanty about bedding mermaids.

A cool wind whips a curl from my braid, and Grimm tucks it behind my ear. I turn towards him. "Have you ever 'bedded' a mermaid?"

Everyone within earshot roars in laughter and heat burns my ears. "What?"

"My lady, there's no such thing as mermaids." A handsome fae with waist-length braided hair grins and drops from a rope next to us. He bows, and runs to the stern, dodging crates dancing mid-air to the hold.

"I've never 'bedded' a mermaid." Grimm's eyes dance with mirth. "Though, if you're into role playing, I'm not opposed." He nips at my neck, sending pleasure straight between my thighs.

Before I can comment, Penn whisks me away, leading me into a dance to the sailors' shanty about a queen and her kings.

The fae on the deck clap when we finish. Despite the cool air, I have to wipe the sweat from my brow from dancing. These sailors sure are a wicked lot. Penn gives a bow to me before turning me around to find Casimir holding out a hand. I take it, and instead of leading me into a dance, he leads me below deck.

"I couldn't let them have all the fun." He glances over at me before stopping in front of a large, ornate door with a carving of a woman on the front. She has wind-blown hair and glassy eyes. "These are our chambers." He turns the brass handle and shoves the door open with a creak.

They've bolted a massive, canopied bed to the floor, with white drapes tied at each poster and pooling to the feet of the bed. Along the sides and far wall are rows of windows, decked with cream-colored curtains and black pull-down shades to keep the room dark if necessary. I spin around.

"Where are the other beds?"

Casimir raises a brow. "This is it."

"We're ... sharing a bed?"

"This is a ship, not a castle. We might be able to take one of these drapes and tie you a hammock in the crew's quarters, if you prefer? Although, that's likely to result in the end of a lot of lives the longer we're at sea."

"No, no. This is fine." Fire swirls low in my belly at the idea. Will this trip change things? I pivot and walk to the window and look at the water below. Things are calm right now.

"If you want to come back on deck, we're about to take off." Penn startles me and I jump.

"Gods! Don't sneak up on me." I place my hand over my chest.

He and Casimir chuckle before bringing me up the steps.

Lana

I'm the first to crawl into bed tonight. I spent the evening eyeing the water, trying to spot any new creatures. Pierce kept a close watch so I didn't go overboard. Most were fish, but I did spy what the crew call spearsnakes; they look like regular snakes, save for their razor-sharp tails.

The mattress depresses next to me, and I roll over. My eyes meet Grimm's, and his are brimming with mirth.

"Sorry, didn't mean to wake you."

"I wasn't asleep yet. Where are the others?"

"Meeting with Captain Shallowind about the forecast next week. We might have to pass through a storm."

I sit up on my elbow. "Are we safe?"

"In his capable hands, you have nothing to worry about." He winks at me. "I'll keep you safe." I give him a playful shove and he chuckles.

He tucks his pillow under his head and grins when he catches me staring at his bare chest. With a flick of his hand, a tiny orb of swirling light hovers right above us, casting thick shadows and accentuating the deep indents of his abs.

"I'll never tire of magic."

"I thought you'd want a better look."

Scowling, I bury my head under the covers. Grimm is laughing when I hear the creak of the door and shuffling feet.

"This *fucker.* He's gone for a few minutes and Lana loves him. Is loving him. No. His *cock.*" Is Penn ... drunk?

I yank the covers down when I realize what he just implied. My glower gives him pause, and he raises his hands in a placating gesture.

"Sorry drunk, I think I'm love."

Casimir slaps a hand onto Penn's shoulder and steers him to the head before he lumbers back in. A grin plasters his face when he spots Grimm and me in bed. He pins me with his stare while peeling his shirt off. My eyes dip to the deep V where his low-slung pants sit, taking in the thin trail of hair resting between his abs. He stalks towards the bed and crawls in next to me.

He plops down and slings an arm behind his head. "You keep looking at me like that, we won't be getting much sleep tonight." I slap him with a pillow.

"Are all fae this arrogant?"

He shrugs. "You're fae, too."

Our playful banter stops when Penn returns from the bathroom. "I wanted to lay next to Lana." He pouts.

Oh, is Penn a *sappy drunk?* Of the three, he's the one who is a little rough around the edges. Dominant. A smile curls across my lips.

"Next time." I give him a wink before turning over and closing my eyes.

It's not long before snores echo through the night. I yank the pillow out from under me and bury my head, trying to block the noise. When it persists, I briefly think of shoving something in their mouths to shut them up. A sock?

The bed shakes, and I lift the pillow to see Grimm chuckling. I mouth *it's not funny*. He cups my ears with his hands, and immediately the snoring stops.

You must be a light sleeper. I'll teach you this spell in the morning. Grimm's voice in my head startles me.

I make to respond out loud, but he places his finger against my lips to silence me, so I nip at it.

Naughty.

Narrowing my eyes, I give him my middle finger.

We can do that, too.

He grins, and I catch sight of his dainty canines. While I have my own now, it still catches me off guard any time I see fae smile with them. And now I'm staring again. Grimm's gaze darts between my eyes and mouth, and I have to school my breathing.

I'm not sure who moves in first, but before I know what's happening, his lips press against mine. He pulls me flush to his body, the evidence of his desire firm against my stomach. There's no rush in his languid kiss. Gods, it's like he's making love with his mouth.

He grins against my lips before pulling back to look at me. My eyes are hooded, drunk on lust. His hand finds its way to the nape of my hair, pulling my face to him, his other hand sliding under my hip to hold me close.

Grimm lets go of my tresses, his fingers trailing down my ribcage. When he reaches my lower abdomen, I buck my hips in invitation, grinding against his erection. I slide his hand down the front of my silk pajama shorts, urging him on. He groans against my mouth when he finds nothing between my pajamas and my skin.

No panties? What did you want to happen tonight? He pulls back and smirks.

Before I can give him a piece of my mind, he rubs my clit and I let out a whimper. His lips crash to mine. *Shh, I don't want to share tonight.* When satisfied I'll stay quiet, he leans back to watch my face. Adoration swims in his eyes.

I hook onto Grimm's shoulders, burying my head against his neck to stifle my moans. His fingers spear me while he continues to rub with his thumb, sending me higher, higher.

That's it, come for me, baby.

My thighs clench, abs contract, and I fall apart under his touch. I lay against his chest, but flinch when warm liquid falls on my face. Pulling back, I swipe my face and startle at the sight before darting my eyes to Grimm's shoulder.

You're bleeding!

I know. Guess you've discovered your claws.

Holding my hands in front of my face, I find delicate claws replacing my nails. My panic causes them to retract, settling back into my fingers. I immediately reach my hand to staunch Grimm's wounds, but he pushes my hand away.

Don't heal it. I want your mark on me.

CHAPTER 52

LANA

"Aww, fuck. I missed it again!"

I startle awake when Penn rests his head on my stomach. "What did you miss?"

He groans. "It smells like sex in here!"

I throw a pillow at him, and Grimm is busy getting dressed across the room. He has a meeting with the crew about battening down the ship for the storm. I bury my head under the covers, but this just puts Penn and me under there together. He has the puppy dog look in his eyes again, which is normally what I see on Casimir's face.

"We didn't have sex," I whisper.

"I could bathe in your pheromones there's so much of it." The bedspread lifts and I find Casimir on my other side, waggling his eyebrows. His laser-focused gaze heats the longer he stares. He glances over my shoulder and gives a slight nod of his head. They sandwich me together, and I become lost in the scent of their cologne.

"Gentlemen," I purr. "What can I do for you?"

They don't answer with words, but their actions speak volumes. Casimir dives in for a kiss, his hand cupping the back of my head to deepen the connection. While his tongue probes my mouth, I feel Penn's hand ghost over my stomach and up to my breast. He teases my hard nipple through the thin fabric of my shirt, and I arch my back to give him better access.

I moan as their hands continue their exploration, Casimir sliding down to tug my pajama bottoms off while Penn moves his mouth to my neck and sucks gently on my skin. I writhe beneath them, wanting more and not wanting it to end. Finally, they stop and pull away, both of them looking a little dazed.

"We want you," Penn says gruffly. "All of you."

I can see the want in their eyes and it's all I need.

"Then take me," I say, opening myself up to them.

The boat lurches and my hands fly out. I'm suddenly on my back with Penn hovering over me, his eyes dark with a preternatural hunger brewing in them.

"Are you sure?" he murmurs.

I nod. His lips crash down on mine until the ship tilts so badly we roll off the bed. I giggle and wrap my legs around his waist as he carries me to the balcony.

"Penn, put her down," Casimir orders.

"Nah, I got her."

Penn pushes open the door to the balcony and steps out into the cool night air. He sets me down on the railing and I shiver. I watch as he pulls his shirt off, revealing his chiseled chest and abs. My fingers go to my lips.

"Touch me," he begs, "Please."

I comply eagerly, running my hands over his chest and down his stomach. He shudders under my touch before taking me in his arms and setting me down. Casimir stands behind me, his hands on my hips, as he watches over my shoulder.

Penn steps closer, pushing me back against Casimir. I can feel his hard length pressing into my back. Penn kisses me deeply as Casimir teases my nipples with his fingers. I moan into Penn's mouth while rain pummels us, drenching my tank top. When lightning strikes nearby, we scurry inside, laughing.

"I think we're going to have to get creative," Casimir says, his voice a low rumble.

"Very creative," I agree.

I scramble out of my clothes. He pushes me back onto the bed and covers my body with his. The storm rages outside, but all I can feel is the heat of his skin.

Casimir kisses his way down my stomach until he reaches my core. I arch up off the bed, gasping as his tongue swirls around my clit. Penn kneels on the bed beside me, kissing and licking my nipples while Casimir devours me.

"I'm going to come," I moan, throwing my head back.

Thunder cracks, shaking the entire ship right as I'm falling apart between them. At this moment, Grimm bursts through the door with some of the crew. I'm too far gone to call it back—the orgasm rips through me like a wildfire, burning through everything in its path— and I arch off the bed.

The crew backpedal out of the room while Grimm approaches the bed with predatory intent. I bite my lip, leaning into Penn, who's busy sucking my neck. Casimir crawls onto the bed, taking my other side.

Grimm hovers over us, thrumming with power, his eyes swirling with something dark. He licks his lips. "We're entering the heart of the storm, and need to secure everything to the ship. This isn't over. Not even close."

I don't have to ask him whether he means the storm or what he walked in on us doing.

CHAPTER 53

FINN

I'm getting impatient waiting to make a move on Bedlam, but I know we can't botch the job. Most nights, I spend pacing in the bedroom Gideon gave me, or walking along the beach. I run through scenarios in my head, working out every angle, and coming up with alternative plans if things go awry.

I've been here months already, but the passing of time stretches on the longer I'm away from her. Does she feel the ache, even though she doesn't know me anymore? Nausea roils in my stomach at the thought she might forget me forever.

I'm her soul bonded mate. It has to count for something.

Earlier this afternoon, Oz and the gang texted me a ton of pictures and videos of her with the new phone they got me. My cell doesn't work on Earth. Lana is all smiles and laughs wrapped in the arms of her vampire mates. She looks like she's having a blast with them, but damn if it doesn't make my chest hurt.

I'm not just separated from her, but she's become the thing that's defined me. Without her, I feel like a shell of myself. The thought of never seeing her again ... just thinking about it crushes me.

The texts keep coming and I can't look at them anymore. I toss the phone across the room and flop back on the bed, staring at the ceiling, wondering how to get Lana back.

I'm startled when the door flies open and Oz appears in the doorway. After I look at his face, I notice Gideon and Auguste fill the hallway behind him. Panic is etched into their features, and I rise to my feet.

"Is Lana okay?"

"Th-the twins." Gideon can hardly utter two words, he's trembling so badly. "They're gone."

"What?" I rush past Oz and race down the stairs, headed for the garage. The threesome follows me.

"Dolphina," Oz growls and slams his hands on the wall, punching it with tremendous force. Gideon follows suit, pounding his fist so hard the concrete shatters.

"She must have come in through the window while we were sleeping," Auguste says, his face grief stricken and his eyes haunted. "There was a note."

"What did it say?" I ask, trying to hold on to my composure. I have to be strong for them.

Gideon unfolds the paper and reads it, quivering so badly he has a hard time keeping the note in his hand. "She said she stole the twins and won't give them back unless Oz agrees to be with her. He's to send word by nightfall three days from now. This must've been her end game; why she cursed Lana and sent her to Bedlam."

"She's been stalking me for millennia," Oz says, his voice echoing in the silence. He shoves a hand through his hair and paces. "I should have killed her the first time she caused Lana trouble."

"We'll get them back," Auguste assures him, but the words sound hollow to my ears.

No one speaks until Gideon finally says, "She's going to kill them."

Oz whips his head up and glares at his best friend with resolve in his eyes. "We're going to save them." He turns to me. "You know we can't let her hurt our kids, right?"

His sharp tone isn't what knocks me off guard. It's 'our kids', and I nod. No matter what the cost to me, Lana or her mates, the twins cannot be harmed. Even though they're not mine by blood, they're every part of me that matters.

"Then we fight," Oz finishes with a hard edge to his voice. He clenches his fists at his sides and starts toward the door. "Auguste and Gideon, get your ass in gear and let's go plan this thing out."

Gideon trails after him as he leaves the room. I stare blankly ahead for several seconds until Auguste shakes my arm and brings me back to life. They need me more than ever now that the twins are gone.

"What do you need me to do?"

He looks relieved. "I don't know how we can get out of this mess without you. Can you do a locator spell?"

"I have to do it on each twin, so I can tell their energy apart."

"Do what you have to do. We'll make sure we guard the house."

With a deep breath, I nod and follow Auguste out the door. The others are waiting for us in the foyer, and I stand before them, taking one of Rose's tiny shoes into my hands.

I hold the slipper in between my palms and close my eyes, feeling the energy rise around me. I chant in a language first spoken by fae tens of thousands of years ago. The words are unfamiliar to my tongue after years of disuse, but I feel the magic leave me and enter the slipper.

"Rose is in a dark place where there is a river," I say, before Auguste asks. He's been watching me intently, and I know he wants to make sure she's okay. "It's cold, and she's frightened."

"Is there any way to find out where the river is?" Gideon asks.

I open my mind for Oz to see what I see. "I can only pinpoint a general area, so we have to go from there."

Rose watches Bennett, who sits near a window with a view of the snow-covered landscape. He's not happy, but he doesn't cry. She crosses to where her brother is and crawls into the chair with him.

The flow of time rips near us, causing Oz to curse. "She's leaving them alone. We have to go."

"Let me see where they are now," I say, hoping it'll give me a better starting point.

I reach out to grab Oz's shoulder. "Watch."

As soon as Dolphina leaves the cabin, Bennett and Rose rummage through cupboards. They have little time before she returns, and they know it. Their dark heads move as one as they search for anything they can use to escape.

Rose finds a knife and hands it to her brother before taking a second one for herself. The weapon is small, but it'll have to do. Their large eyes dart to the door, and Rose tugs Bennett outside.

They're in the mountains. The scene blurs, and I pull out of Oz's head long enough to tell him. "We'll find them."

I project the image into Gideon's head. As soon as he sees the view, he stands. "I know where they're at!"

"How could you possibly know?" Auguste asks.

"I'd recognize those peaks anywhere. It's near to where I grew up in the Dolomites."

How'd she get them to another continent so fast? The only way to find out is to follow.

"Wait, wait." Oz holds his hands up in front of him. "Are you sure you know the place?"

"Yeah, the flight alone is twenty-two hours." Gideon nods. "Call Wren and tell him we'll meet him at the airfield in ten minutes."

I stare at Gideon, puzzled. "Who is Wren?"

"One of our closest family members who is our pilot. His boyfriend, Sebastian, is usually co-pilot. They flew here as soon as we arrived."

"Okay, ten minutes is all I need." Oz readies to leave the room and I stop him.

"We don't need a plane. I'll sift us there."

Hope blooms on his face. "Thank the gods."

WE SIFT to Venice before taking a helicopter on the other side of the ridge from where Gideon thinks the twins are. Auguste called in part of the family's security team, who've secured the location and verified Dolphina isn't in the vicinity at present. With the twins not in any present danger, they didn't want to scare them further by moving in without us.

The helicopter lands in a clearing, and we set out on foot. We're close to the cabin now, and we stop at the edge of the tree line.

"From what I can see, there aren't any guards," Auguste says quietly. "I think we're ready. If the twins are here, they're in the cabin. I don't see any sign of them outside."

"I'm going int ..." Oz starts.

"No." Gideon holds up his hand and turns to face each of us in turn. "We're going together as a group. I'm not splitting up this time."

"I agree," Auguste says. "We come in, get the kids, and get out. We're not going to risk their safety."

We nod and follow Gideon into the cabin.

The interior is dark, but I take only seconds to scan the shadows for Rose and Bennett. "They're in a back room."

Gideon leads us through the living area and down a short hallway to the only other door. He pushes it open, and we freeze as a loud blast echoes through the small space.

Rose and Bennett jump up from their hiding spot, ready to face whoever had entered. She grips her knife tightly in one hand, while he holds a smaller one in the other.

"Rose, Bennett," Oz says softly.

They drop the weapons at the sound of Oz's voice, tears filling their eyes as they run to him. He lifts them in his arms, shielding their small bodies. "I've got you. I'm taking you home."

"You came for us." Rose's lip warbles.

"Of course we did." Gideon crushes them all in a tight embrace.

"Our hearts broke when we found you missing. We never stopped looking."

Gideon's eyes meet mine over the top of Rose and Bennett's heads. "Let's get them home."

Oz kisses the top of Rose's head before they follow Gideon out. No sooner do they step over the threshold do the twins let out a scream.

"Get her!" Oz shouts, and I stop in my tracks.

Dolphina stands in front of her car, arms outstretched to Oz. Her eyes burn an even brighter red as her smile widens. "Oz, Oz, Oz! I've missed you so much." Her gaze lands on the twins. "I told you daddy would come for us! I'm your new mommy! Isn't that wonderful!?"

"No!" Rose screams, tears streaming down her face.

"Never!" Bennett adds, his tiny hands balling into fists.

Oz sets them down and they both run to Gideon. They latch on tightly, fear and anger radiates off of them in waves. Rose's knife is back in her hand, ready to strike if necessary.

"It's okay." Gideon cups their faces and wipes the tears away with his thumbs. "She's not your mommy. I promise. She can't hurt you anymore."

I step in front of Dolphina, blocking her view of the others. "Months I've dreamt of doling out the exact punishment you deserve. Did you really think I'd let you have them? After what you did to my mate?"

"Think you can stop me? You're just a pathetic fae." A wicked gleam enters her eyes. "You can't even save her. You've no idea what I have in store for the little bitch."

I freeze, my hand in mid-air. My anger flares again when I remember everything Lana went through because of this woman. *Lana. Lana. Lana.*

"You don't know me." I lower my hand and let the magic build in my palm.

She grins. "I know all about you, what you are, what you can do. And I've been waiting for this moment."

"There's no place to run, Dolphina." I let the magic loose, and she's thrown back into the car with a loud crash.

The door pops open, and she knocks her head on the edge. She spits blood on the ground, eyeing me with hatred. "You're weak, fae. You wouldn't be alive if it wasn't for Oz."

She raises her hand to cast magic at me before her eyes go wild with alarm. I raise a fist while she claws at her chest.

"Your first mistake was messing with my mate. Your last mistake was not knowing the origins of a witches' magic: Luna fae. And you've just met their High King."

My power gives witches their magic and I can take it away. I'm about to deal the killing blow when a hand rests on my shoulder.

"She doesn't deserve a swift death."

I turn to meet Oz's hard stare. The sadness in his eyes forces my hand to drop. He nods in approval, and I step out of the way.

My magic keeps Dolphina pinned against the passenger door. "As High King of the fae, Giver of Magic, Uniter of Realms, I hereby revoke your magic, Dolphina Darling."

A blood-curdling scream erupts from Dolphina as her magic is stripped from her body. Her skin turns pallid, eyes black as onyx, and her hair crumbles to ash before floating away on a breeze. She used magic to make herself beautiful, but now her outside matches what's within: a hideous monster.

I'm not one of those Luna who nurtures the planet and everything on it. I'm a warrior, and that means dealing out punishment when necessary. "You'll spend eternity as a living corpse in the Finlandian dungeons until we come up with something more useful for you."

Dolphina's eyes flicker with panic. "You can't do this to me."

"I just did." I turn and walk back to the cabin.

CHAPTER 54

FINN

Since abdicating the throne, I've lived a relatively solitary existence in Noble Wilds or in Rift Pass. For all intents and purposes, I've only had the company of my own mind. But since Lana's soul called to mine, I've learned that despite my preference to have her all to myself, having more than just servants and advisors around has its benefits.

I was already aware of the family dynamics between Lana's mates. During our journey through the forest, we talked at length about what life was like for her on Earth. I'm most nervous about meeting Hannah, Lana's best friend. She already knows and loves the vampires, but how will she feel about me? I didn't get to speak with her much when we FaceTimed her to get information on Lana's ex-fiancé. How much does she know about me?

She's the first to arrive for the weekend. I meet her on the front steps as she makes her approach. Surprising me, Hannah envelopes me in a tight hug instead of giving me an extended hand for a formal greeting.

"Oh, Finn!" she squeals. "You are here! You're really here."

I glance at Oz and Gideon behind her before releasing the hug.

"You told her about me already?" I ask in disbelief.

"She's Lana's best friend, and Maeve's girlfriend. Maeve was the first to break the news." Oz shrugs.

"I've heard a lot about you, Hannah. I'm glad to meet you, although I wish it were under better circumstances."

"You." She points a finger at me. "Don't talk like that until we've had wine and cheese with you and my friends. I need to hear all about what happened in Bedlam. You owe me that much, and I will get the full story out of you!"

I know she will. So far, Hannah has not failed to be anything less than a whirlwind. "Come on in."

She loops her arm through mine as we walk inside the house. The moment I close the door, she is on me with rapid-fire questions.

"I already know that you are fae—awesome! But how did you meet Lana? When are we busting her out?"

"Can we go one question at a time?" I laugh. "The story of our meeting may be difficult for you to hear. Let's get you settled in before I tell you. May I take your travel bag?"

She hands it over readily. "Are you still staying here, too? Don't run away from me yet, okay?"

Oz and Gideon step through the front door as we make our way to Hannah's room. I set the bag down and gesture across the hall. "I'm right here."

"Good."

The clomping of sandal-clad feet alerts us to the twins' approach. I turn around as they slow to a stop, Rose clutching Auguste's hand and Bennett tugging on Gideon's.

"Auntie Hannah!" Rose runs to her.

"Hi, babies." Hannah coos at the top of the girl's head when she reaches them. Rose presses a kiss on Hannah's cheek.

Bennett scowls. "I'm not a baby!"

Hannah winces. "You're right, I'm sorry. You two grow so fast. Are you still my favorite nephew?"

Bennett's glower lessens, and his face breaks out into a huge grin. "Yes!"

He shoves at Rose and throws his arms around Hannah's neck in a bear hug.

Hannah chuckles and rubs her cheek on the top of Rose's head. "You two are my joy. I've missed you so much, and CJ says he can't wait to see you soon."

I study the three of them. It's clear she loves them very much. I can't help but envy her, and wonder where CJ, her son, is.

"I've missed you too, Auntie Hannah." Rose twirls in her dress.

"Are you staying for a long time?" Bennett asks with an adorable, hopeful look on his face.

Hannah shoots me a quick glance before answering. "Only for a few days, and then I have to head back."

"Oh." Disappointment is clear in his voice, and Rose whines.

"I won't be gone forever, just a little while because CJ is at his dad's house for the week. He will miss me if I'm gone too long." She kisses the top of each head and then sets them on the ground.

"Here." I crouch to the twins' level and extend a hand. "I want to show you the cool shells I found on the beach while Hannah unpacks."

Rose takes my hand, and Bennett follows suit. "Can we see them now? How many did you find?"

"Yes, and I don't know yet, but we can count them together. Come on."

I lead the two to the back door and point out the shells littering the bamboo floor of the porch. Their eyes widen as they stare at my offerings from the sea.

"Wow, there are a lot," Rose breathes.

"Were you looking for shells, too?" I ask them.

Bennett nods, and Rose responds to my question. "We were looking for crabs and fish, but we couldn't find any."

"Well, maybe if you go out early tomorrow morning, the tide will have brought you what you want." I wink.

Since I've been here, they've grown rapidly. More than humans and vampires. I see so much of Lana in them, and I hope to see more of her in them as they age.

"Can I have this one?" Rose lifts a small pink shell.

"You two can have as many as you want."

Rose tackles me with a hug and kisses my cheek. "I'm going to go show it to Daddy." She takes off towards the house.

"Do you want any?" I kneel in the sand next to Bennett.

"Yes." He quickly picks out three. "I'm going to go show them to Grandpa."

He runs back to the house. I chuckle and stand up, brushing the sand from my knees.

"Thank you for that." An unfamiliar voice startles me from behind.

I immediately recognize her as a vampire. She offers me a hand. "I'm Pippa Imperialus, and this is my mate, Elliot." She points to the vampire standing next to her, holding hands.

"I'm Finian Drake. It's nice to meet you." I take her hand.

"So, you're the one who saved Lana." She squeezes. "Thank you. She's very special to us."

"I've heard." I study her face. "Aren't you the one who saved her, too?"

She shrugs. "Even if I weren't a doctor, I still would've done all I can to help her. She's the best thing that's ever happened to this family." She winces before casting a glance at her mate. "I mean, she's really brought everyone together."

"I agree." Elliot grins. "We're very lucky."

What I've learned about vampires is at odds with everything I thought I knew. They're not always dangerous, blood-thirsty creatures. I never dreamed I'd be friends with them, but now I can't imagine not having them as family.

"I want to thank you, too, for taking care of Lana. We all appreciate it." Elliot offers me their hand.

I shake it. "She's everything to me." My voice breaks, and I clear my throat.

The three of us are silent for a couple of minutes, watching the waves crash against the shore, before Pippa speaks up, breaking the trance I'm under. "I know you probably have questions."

"I do ... Please tell me everything about her. Even the most inconsequential facts would make me happy."

"Are you sure? I don't want to overwhelm you." She folds her hands in front of her.

"Positive." The bones-deep ache of her being away gnaws at me.

We walk to the house, and I revel in the stories the two tell of their time with Lana. Their stories paint a picture of a woman I haven't yet met, but want desperately to know better. Our time together was so short—most of it spent denying what we knew in our souls.

"That's just a small sample of what we have. We have a lot more pictures and videos to show you, too." Elliot nudges me with an elbow.

"Thank you for taking the time to do this. I appreciate it."

"It's our pleasure." Pippa smiles, her eyes shining with adoration when she looks at her mate.

"We're so happy to have you in the family." Elliot kisses Pippa's cheek. "I'm going to see if the others have arrived yet."

"Okay." Pippa waves them off.

We watch Elliot walk back toward the house. "Excuse me for a moment," she says. "I need to go get my things."

"Oh, of course. I didn't mean to keep you."

She chuckles. "It's not a problem. I'll be back in a few minutes." She waves goodbye before walking to the house at an inhuman pace.

I stare at the door after she closes it behind her. It's not long before Hannah makes it outside. She hands me a bottle of beer, and I take it. I don't have the heart to tell her Earth alcohol is terrible.

"So, Finn, let's hear it. How does my best friend measure up to the guys' versions?" She cocks an eyebrow.

"We were only together a few months before the kings wiped her memory. Hearing what they have to say about her and what I know only makes me yearn for more. I hardly know her. There's so much to learn."

I take a drink of my beer.

"I understand." She sighs. "I'm still trying to get used to all this supernatural stuff. Witches, vampires, and fae?"

"You know there are a lot more supernatural creatures than that, don't you?"

She shrugs. "I guess I never thought about it." She looks around at us. "Are all the stories they tell true? Dragons, mermaids, sea monsters?"

I laugh. "I guess you could say they are."

"What do you mean by that?" She frowns.

"Most supernatural creatures are fae of some sort who can shift into other 'animals' or 'beasts.' Mermaids aren't real, but sirens are."

Her eyes widen. "On Earth?!"

I chuckle. "Earth is dangerous for many supernatural creatures because humans don't like what they can't understand. They tend to stay in Bedlam."

"Maybe we can change that." She takes a drink of her beer. "Move to a harmonious co-existence?"

We'll have to figure something out if I have to share Lana with vampire royalty and maintain my own throne.

CHAPTER 55

LANA

The crew enters our chambers to clean up dishes from supper and remove the table. Space is a premium on the ship, and we stow the table to give us more room in our bedroom. The five of us lie on the enormous bed, telling jokes, and letting our stomachs settle. Thanks to magic, everyone on the ship eats well. There's no risk of running out of food or water.

I pull a curl taught into the air and wind it around my finger. "What do three royal fae do for fun?"

Casimir sits up. "Normally we're on our respective continents and only get together every few months. This is the longest amount of time we've spent together as adults, save for university."

The creaking of the ship fills the silence between us. "Did you attend together?"

Penn shakes his head. "I attended Draconor, Casimir went to Moonfire, and Grimm went to Bedlam Academy."

I furrow my brows. "When did you spend time together at university then?"

"I spent a lot of time stealing their girlfriends," Grimm grins and my mouth falls open.

"You didn't!"

Grimm shrugs. "It got so bad, I had to make a pact to share. I didn't know how to control my order back then."

Before I can ask what he meant, he continues. "I'm up for continuing this tradition." Grimm nuzzles into my neck and pleasure coats me like a silk blanket.

My head swirls with lust, lining my body with goosebumps. *What's happening?*

"Yeah, I think I can get on board with this." Penn plants a kiss on the inside of my wrist.

I hold in my sounds of pleasure. "Grimm, what are you doing to me?"

Penn kneels over me so I look at him upside-down. "You haven't figured it out yet?"

I scowl at him.

My frustration disappears when desire burns through it. I feel like I'm crawling out of my skin with need. My hands rove over my curves, capturing the attention of the three fae surrounding me. As soon as eagerness came on, it disappears. I try to catch my breath as the echoes of pleasure still pull taut at my core.

"What the hell was that?!"

Grimm runs his tongue the length of my neck, stopping right behind my ear. "I'm of the Incubus order." He releases more of his power, causing me to squeeze my thighs for friction. "From the moment we met, I could see your sexual attraction to me, even without using my powers on you."

I roll onto my side facing him. "Is this the first time you've used your powers on me?"

"No." he gives me a rogue grin. "I gave you a tiny taste for just a moment, not long after we met, to see if you could resist me. You couldn't, so I withdrew. My intention is not to coerce you into anything."

"I see. What's changed?"

He smiles. "Nothing, except your thoughts. It seems you've grown fond of us."

I bury my head in my hands and groan. How mortifying. Who

wouldn't be attracted to them? They're fae, so they're obviously beautiful ... but they're wicked smart and funny, too.

Casimir lowers my hands. "We made our intentions clear from the start, Lana. Please don't be embarrassed. If you'll have us, you'll make us the happiest fae in all the realm. We promise to be worthy of your affection."

"What are you asking me?"

"Be ours, Lana." Grimm cups my cheek. "We aren't asking you to take the mating bond right now. You don't have to decide about being our mate any time soon. Consider this our official courting, if you'll allow us?"

"No mating bond?"

"Don't get me wrong, if you want the mating bond we'll do it right now, because we're ready." Grimm caresses my face. "We don't want to push you into something *you're* not ready for. *We're* all in. Say yes to being ours, and we can cross that bridge when we get to it."

"Okay."

"Okay?" Casimir looks like a hopeful puppy dog.

I roll my eyes and grin. "Yes, I'm yours. You should know I'm not willing to share you. If we're doing this, there can be no other women —fae or otherwise."

They let out a collective breath. "There can be no one but you." Penn trails a finger along the stitching of a decorative pillow.

How the heck am I going to handle three fae? Penn chuckles at my thoughts. An idea comes to me, so I sit up and scoot off the bed. The kings eye me with curiosity while I stalk to the armoire. I slip my pajamas off their hanger before entering the head to change.

When I return to the room, the males sit with their backs against the headboard, but make to stand when they catch sight of what I have on. I shake my head "no," and they pause.

"Gods, would you look at her?" Penn says it like a curse and a benediction.

I don a saucy grin before giving a slow spin so they can view the rest of the black lace negligée that's more string than actual clothing. With a finger, I slide one bra strap down my arm, and then the other.

The fae look ready to pounce when I reach behind me to unhook the tight band around my chest, and allow my top to fall to the floor, exposing my breasts.

"Fuck." This is the first time I've heard Casimir swear. He's more polite than the others.

They groan when I turn around, but cut short when I bend over to remove the strappy heels on my feet. One by one, I slip them off. I continue to unsnap the garter belt, taking my time to roll the stockings down one at a time. After kicking them off, I shimmy out of the barely-there panties. Completely bare, I spin back around to face them.

My hand caresses my breasts while the other trails the length of my stomach and between my legs. They jump off the bed and approach me, but I use my new fae speed to take their places on the bed.

"Your turn."

They race to take their clothes off, but I tsk. "Slower. Give me a show."

"You're a wicked one, aren't you?" Fire burns in Grimm's eyes.

I grin and bite my lip while they give me a strip tease. Their speed picks up when I spread my legs and run my fingers through my folds, finding the little nub of pleasure. I moan. Casimir is the first to make it to me. He takes my hand and runs his tongue against my fingers before sticking my digits in his mouth, one at a time, never breaking eye contact.

Casimir presses his lips to the inside of my ankle, trailing his fingers up my thighs. His expert hands massage and knead me before settling himself right at my apex. He glances towards Penn, who appears at my side.

"You ready for this, little bird?" He coos in my ear.

I grin and capture his lip between my teeth. He growls and I release it. "I may have smaller wings, but I sure look cute with them, yeah?"

"More like sexy as fuck."

My eyes catch on Grimm, cock in hand, giving his rapt attention to me spread between the others. "Does the lust in the room fuel your magic?"

"Since you've come into our lives, it's been the only way I've fed my power. The myth of my order preying on sleeping women isn't true, but I can't help the lust drifting to my room when you dream of fucking one of us. Or, when you read your dirty books."

"Show me what your magic can do?"

A feral grin crosses his face. Like a spark to gasoline, my entire body erupts with a burning need for him. I whimper and claw my way off the bed with a preternatural speed and fling myself at Grimm. Tackling him to the ground, I grab his hands and place them on my breasts while I line up his cock and impale myself with it.

A moan crawls its way out of my throat while I rock against him, and I throw my head back, my curls brushing against my bare back with every thrust. Grimm sits up, and I wrap my legs around his waist and dig my claws into his shoulders.

"That's it, good girl." He growls against my neck, his lips resting against my pulse.

Each move causes pleasure to radiate through me, rushing through every nerve ending. Grimm lowers me to my back, but I swing my leg to get back on top instead. I'm near feral, all sharp nails and desperate desire to chase my bliss.

My wings open of their own accord, my magic reaching for his. His hands come to rest on my lower hip, holding me close as we move together. I can feel the ridges of his abs under my palms and the sweat has turned his hair into dark ringlets that cling to his forehead. He kisses me then, deeply, claiming my mouth. Our tongues tangle until I'm breathless and panting against him.

"You want more," he growls against my lips. "Don't you?"

"Take what you want," I whisper back.

And he does. He flips me over so fast I yelp, and he sinks in deep, both of us crying out in pleasure. In a blink, we sift to the bed, scattering the others for a brief moment before they, too, descend on me. Penn moves me so my back is to his front, sliding inside with one smooth thrust, all while Grimm pounds me. His hands glide down the arch of my feathers, each touch igniting a flurry of pleasure at my core. We move together, our bodies slick with sweat, until I reach my peak.

I fall apart between them, my orgasm ripping through me without mercy. Grimm follows the tail end of my release, the press of my nails firm against his shoulders as he stills against me. His mouth presses to mine like a kiss, a gift, a blessing, lingering until Penn pulls him away from me.

My body is on fire, alive with need and want. I arch my back, pressing myself closer to Penn as he rocks into me. His mouth moves to my neck, licking and sucking while his hand comes around to rub circles on my clit. I'm so close, but he pulls away before I can fall over the edge, cleaning himself off before coming around to my front. He moves slowly at first, giving me time to adjust to him. When I'm ready, he picks up the pace, until we are moaning and gasping for air.

A low chuckle in my ear trails the soft moan I let out. "We're just getting started, little bird. Are you tapping out on us?"

I roll my head back and forth and tuck my wings back in. "Never. I'm just too hot with my feathers."

Casimir opens the balcony doors, letting the evening breeze in. I heave a sigh.

Penn's hot body turns cold on top of mine, and my eyes widen. "My dragon order lets me breathe fire and ice." He chuckles when I pull his chilly frame close to my overheated skin.

I cry out as he starts to move harder, the intensity of his thrusts quickly driving me towards another orgasm. Penn lifts me, carrying me across the room until I'm slammed against the bedroom door. He kisses me passionately, his hand tangling in my hair. "Mine," he growls against my lips. I moan in response and wrap my legs around his waist. He carries me out onto the balcony, rain soaking us both. The swirling sea rages below us, angry and tumultuous, like our fevered movements.

"Yours," I agree, before claiming his mouth in a searing kiss.

"I want to be inside you when I come," he says gruffly. "So deep you can't tell where I end, and you begin." His words send a shiver down my spine, and I moan in anticipation.

"Big talk, but little follow through," I tease. He growls, his eyes alight with desire, and his need presses against my core. I arch up to meet him as he sinks into me. We both gasp at the contact. He begins to move, each thrust harder and faster than the last. I unfurl my wings, wrapping around us both, letting my magic flow into him.

Penn cries out and I feel him swelling inside me, pushing me closer and closer to the edge. With one final thrust, he sends me over, calling out my name as he follows me into bliss.

He holds me here, the drizzle cooling our skin, allowing our heaving breaths to settle. My head rests on his shoulder, and my heart keeps time with his.

A warm body presses against the back of my wings, so I tuck them back in and lean into Casimir's touch.

"Mine," he growls, pulling me out of Penn's grip.

I giggle and wrap my arms around his neck. "You all get to keep me."

He carries me into the bedroom, and the others have taken seats around the table, sharing a bottle of fae wine between themselves.

Casimir lays me on the bed, his gaze never leaving mine. He presses reverent kisses to my skin. Each one ignites a new fire within me. I arch my back, offering myself to him. He growls and accepts my invitation eagerly. He pushes inside me in one smooth thrust, and I cry out. Our bodies move together in a perfect rhythm, my wings spreading to give him better access. The sounds we make are feral, our movements desperate. I claw at his back, clinging to him as he brings me to the edge of sanity and back. I shatter around him, my body shaking with pleasure. He follows soon after with a deep guttural sound.

"Mine," he growls again, just before he comes. I collapse bonelessly against him, and he cradles me close. We lay there afterward, panting and sweaty, our bodies trembling with aftermath of our orgasm. I'm about to drift off, happy and sated, when a warm washcloth presses to my skin. I open my eyes to find the men cleaning me up. A glutted smile crosses my face, and I make to sit up, but they insist I rest instead. The grin stays while sleep greets me.

Lana

I BRACE my hands against the walls and will the ship to stop throwing me around. I've never been on seas like this before. We're passing through the Parallel Abyss—some of the most dangerous waters we'll journey through—in the middle of a storm.

Penn wraps his arms around me from behind and helps me to our chambers. All the water has spilled out of the giant tub in our room, so he calls for a crew member to take care of it while he ushers me to the bed. I fall onto the mattress and roll into a ball.

"Cursed sea," I groan. My stomach roils and though I close my eyes, everything still spins.

"Is she still sick?"

I'm too busy trying to heave my empty stomach to hear what Penn says next. I left the contents on the poop deck, where I was trying to get some air. The kings work around me. After a few minutes, Grimm scoops me into his arms and lifts me above his head to place me in a makeshift hammock tied fore-to-aft between two posters. As soon as I settle into the fabric, I let out a sigh.

I barely feel the ship rolling anymore, just the up-and-down of the swells. Casimir hands me a warm cloth to place over my eyes, and Penn gives me sodroot to place between my teeth. My tongue burns from the heat of the root, but I'll do anything to soothe my stomach. Someone cracks a window to let in some air.

CHAPTER 56

LANA

For days, the rain drenches us. We pass so many islands; I don't want to go below deck, for fear I'd miss out on anything. The raging seas meant I couldn't take a bath to warm my bones, but now things have calmed.

"Lana," Penn calls, his voice stopping me in my tracks. I turn around to face the three fae kings gathered together.

"Come with us," Penn says, soon followed by Casimir and Grimm. They're all dressed in light, water-resistant pants. They're shirtless, enjoying the warmer weather, while I enjoy their view.

Casimir is the first to reach me. He takes my hand and brings it to his lips, kissing the back of my hand. "We'd like you to join us tonight, but let's get you warm first." His voice is gentle.

"Where?"

"We're dropping anchor by a small channel of islands where we have a beach house. We can stay as long as you'd like."

I lick my lips and notice the others watching me. I nod. "That sounds nice."

The three of them smile and we continue below deck towards our chambers. Everything smells fresh. Never-ending rain washes away weeks of scum that build up on the crew and the deck.

Penn opens the door to our room, and I gasp, taking it all in. Candles line nearly every surface and a steaming bath with flower petals scatter throughout the water.

"We knew you'd be cold, so we had one of the crew bring in hot water." Grimm speaks from behind me.

Casimir takes a handful of soapberries and crushes them into the tub. After agitating the water, thick bubbles form. I waste no time stripping out of my clothes and slipping under. Finally. I can get warm.

I lean my head against the edge of the tub and let out a content sigh. The men are chatting amongst themselves, taking no regard for their nakedness as they, too, undress. Grimm is the first to join me, sitting on the edge of the tub. He reaches a hand out and traces it up my calf, over the curve of my thigh, then around to cup a breast. The others join and take their places around me. Each one of them taking turns caressing my body, washing away the cold and stress from our journey.

There's nothing innately sexual about our bath time. Sure, their hands linger, but this is more about being in each other's presence and helping massage the aches from our muscles.

I stand and let the water drip off my body. Heat crawls up my cheeks at their hungry gazes that stay locked on me. "Enough teasing." My own voice is husky with need. "I'm starving."

They chuckle and reach for towels. Soon, all three get dressed as I slip into a gown that hugs my hips and flows to the floor.

At dinner, I'm the only one in the room that's fully dressed. The men are shirtless once more and in light pants. Casual. Relaxed.

"Lana, are you okay?" Penn asks me, concern clouding his eyes at how I'm not eating.

"I'm fine," I whisper, pushing the food around my plate.

Casimir scoots his chair closer to me and wraps an arm around my waist. Grimm and Penn do the same from each side, sandwiching me in between them. "What's wrong?" Penn asks. I can feel his breath on my neck, his lips pressed against the skin.

I turn to look at them, and Grimm leans forward to place his mouth on mine. Teeth scrape my lip and I'm soon pulled onto his lap, his tongue in my mouth. When I come up for air, I chastise him for making a scene in front of the crew. No other females are on the ship. At first, I thought it was superstition, but Casimir explained it gives the crew incentive to make it home to their families. Those who prefer the same sex are lucky, I suppose.

Grimm smiles and pulls me close so my chest is pressed against his. "I don't think they mind one bit," he whispers in my ear, his arms wrapped around my waist. "Go on. Finish eating."

I return to my seat and pick at my food. The royals tease me for my lack of appetite.

"I can't help it," I sigh, resting my head on Casimir's shoulder.

"We can get you something else." Penn's brow furrows with concern.

"No, it's fine." The bones-deep ache in my chest makes me uncomfortable, and I don't want to complain and have them see me as weak. "I'll keep eating." They share a look among one another, but don't push the issue further.

"Might I have a word alone with you?" Penn asks after dinner. The others agree and head off to our chambers while I follow him to their board room.

"We know something is bothering you," he explains, taking a seat on the table, pulling me between his thighs.

"It's nothing." I can't tell them I'm in pain, that my chest feels hollow and is making me miserable. Being on my period makes it worse, too. Sarai always made me a tonic back at the castle. A part of me wishes she were here, but with her father sick, I couldn't ask her to come along.

"We know you well enough to figure out when something is wrong." He continues to press me.

I've kept an iron gate on my mind; I don't want anyone worrying.

"Fine." I put my hands up in surrender. "I'm on my period and my chest aches."

He nods, as if this makes sense. "That's normal for a female of any species, I think. I don't understand why telling us would bother you."

"It's just the pain." I sigh, leaning into the arms I throw around his shoulder. "I used to have Sarai give me a tonic with my birth control tea back at the castle, but I'll be fine." With all the magic in the realm, you'd think menstrual pain is non-existent. Apparently, the fae pissed off the gods, too. This is far worse than what I went through as a human.

"Nonsense. You're in pain, and we want to help you get better. We'll ask the cook for some yalsome root and make you a tea."

"Yalsome root? For cramps?" I'm sure he'll tell me it works. It should, considering how quickly it numbs injuries.

"Yes." He stands and kisses my forehead. "Or we could get you some fae wine." He waggles his brows.

I groan. A few nights ago, I drank the stuff like it was juice. I made a fool out of myself in front of the entire ship. "Not that." I shake my head, wishing away the memories.

"Then tea it shall be. As soon as it kicks in, we can take the dinghy to the islands." He squeezes my hand. "Are you sure there isn't anything else bothering you?"

"I'm fine, Penn. Really." I smile and cup his cheek in my hand.

"Let's go find that root before the others get impatient." He kisses my knuckles before leading me out.

Grimm walks down the hall, a wide grin on his face. "Did I just hear you want to root?"

"Shh." Penn holds a finger to his lips. "It's her time of the month."

"Oh." Grimm's eyes widen before he furrows his brows in confusion. "Alright. Are you okay?"

"We're going to make her a tea, so she doesn't have to suffer the pain." Penn wraps his arm around my waist and kisses my cheek.

"I'll come help." Grimm rubs my arm before going in the opposite direction with us.

In the kitchen, we explain what's needed to the cook, who is more than happy to help. He pulls out a jar of yalsome root and goes about boiling water for the tea.

"Are you feeling any better?" Casimir asks when enter the room.

"I should be able to stand in a few minutes," I answer, wincing as the pain continues its cycle.

Grimm returns with an entire basket of yalsome root and hands it to Penn. "Can you make sure we load this for our stay on the islands?"

"Of course."

By the time we make it back to our room, the pain subsides, and I can pack. We bring blankets and pillows to the dinghy, along with a stash of food for ourselves.

Penn starts the boat, and we're off to explore. When we round the ship, my mouth drops open at the sight. Small islands covered in lush green plants suspends itself high above the water—just floating there, as if powered by magic.

"They're called the Tristique Islands." Penn wraps his arm around my waist and kisses the top of my head.

Grimm nods. "These are uninhabited, unless we come to visit. We'll explore as much as possible on our trip."

"How do you set them down? I mean, don't they just float away?"

"We'll take them down and then put them back up when we leave." Penn walks along the edge of the boat as we sway with the waves.

"I'll show you how to set them down once we land. It's easy." Penn helps me to stand in the boat and gestures to the others. "Everyone, gather in a circle."

Once we're all around him, he holds his hands up towards the sky. The nearest island drops like a slow elevator. One by one, we step onto the island until it's flush with the water again. He lowers his hand, causing the island to rise.

"That was super cool." I breathe in the fresh air and let it fill my lungs.

"It's amazing what you can do with magic." Penn takes my hand and leads me to a patch of bright orange flowers. "These are called bracky blooms, and they're edible. If you get the sap on your skin, it will cause euphoria."

I crouch and pull one out of the ground. "What do you mean?"

He kneels beside me and plucks one of the smaller yellow blooms. He breaks off a stem before rubbing it on his hands. "It feels like a drug, but it's perfectly harmless." He pops it in his mouth and chews, demonstrating that I can, too.

I draw my brows together.

"Want to try it?" He hands me the stem.

I chew on the tip, letting it dissolve onto my tongue. The taste is sweet, like honey or sugarcane. I wipe my hands on the ground and scrub until I'm sure it's all off before standing up.

"How long does it take to work?" I watch the others pick various plants.

"About thirty seconds." Penn studies me carefully. "How do you feel?"

My eyes catch on the flutter of wings as a butterfly lazily flits from one bloom to the next. I wonder if it's affected by the sap like Penn said. "I feel... really good."

A smile curls across his face. Everything feels better than good, actually. It feels perfect. The pain in my chest disappears. The worry in my mind fades away. I'm left with nothing but the warmth of the sun on my skin and the happiness that comes with finally being free.

"See?" Penn squeezes my hand. "I told you it was harmless." I take a deep breath and let it out slowly.

"This place is amazing." And it really is. The colors are so bright, the air so fresh. I can't imagine anywhere else I'd rather be.

"I'm glad you like it." Penn smiles at me, and I can't help but smile back.

"I love it." I look around at the others. They all seem to be enjoying themselves, too.

"Do you have any idea how beautiful you are?" His voice drops to a husky whisper.

I feel my face heat. "I didn't know euphoria would make me so open to flattery."

He wraps his arms around my waist and pulls me close. "I'm serious."

"I feel light and free, like I could take on the world. And I don't think it's the euphoria working on me. I feel amazing about myself when you look at me like that."

"You're always beautiful, no matter what." He kisses me softly. "So, you're going to be our queen?"

I twist a strand of his hair around my fingers. "Oh, I don't know ..." I dart out of his embrace and run towards Grimm. I jump onto his back, shrieking with mirth about saving me from Penn.

"I'll get you back for that." Penn grabs my waist and pulls me off Grimm, tossing me over his shoulder. He slaps my ass and keeps his hand there.

My chest rumbles with laughter. "Put me down."

"After you say yes." He carries me over to the others.

I wrap my arms around his neck. "Yes." I nuzzle into his neck before pulling back and pressing my forehead to his. "I love you."

His eyes widen in surprise before a slow smile spreads across his lips. "I love you too."

He sets me down and pulls me close. "And you'll be our queen?"

"I don't know if I'm ready to rule. The crown isn't what I care about. You all could be beggars on the streets, and I'd still love you."

"Did she just say she loves us?" Grimm glances at Penn and Casimir before turning back to me.

"You heard right." I pick a flower hanging from the tree above us and twirl it between my fingers.

"Are you really in love with us?" Grimm joins me under the tree.

I look into his deep blue eyes and nod. "I am."

He kisses me softly and wraps his arms around my waist. "That's all we need to know."

Penn steps in front of me and pulls me away and into his arms. He kisses my cheek, then the corner of my mouth, before capturing my lips in a long, drawn-out kiss.

I giggle against his lips when he pulls away. "Who's next?"

He grins and shakes his head. "You're insatiable."

I beam up at him. "Only with you three."

I take Casimir's hand and lead him into the jungle.

"What are you doing?" Penn has to jog to keep up with us.

"You know these plants, right?" I motion to the tall trees and thick foliage.

He nods. "We need them for spells we can't do on our own."

"Do you know any aphrodisiacs?" I glance up at him.

He swallows thickly and nods again. "Yes."

Casimir's eyes widen as I guide him over to a tree.

"Are you sure about this?" He caresses my cheek with his hand. "Grimm is basically a walking aphrodisiac if he turns his powers on."

I nod and smile to reassure him. "Yes, I'm sure." I know what it feels like under Grimm's power, but I want to know what it's like with nature and his combined.

He gestures towards a nearby tree with a large, bulbous trunk. "Pull up some of this root."

I kneel and dig around the roots until I find the ones he means. I yank them out of the ground and hand them to him. He takes out a dagger from his belt and slices them open. He chops the white insides into tiny pieces and slides them off the knife before handing it to me.

"Can you cut these?" He gestures to a row of red fruit.

"Sure." I grab the knife and cut all the fruit in half before removing the pink insides. He digs in his pack for a small steel mug with a handle.

He adds the fruit to the root and hands me a small, stoppered bottle with a blue liquid inside. "Add a couple drops to the mix."

I uncork it and pour a small amount into the mug. He stirs it with his finger to mix it together, then slides the mug toward me.

"Let's get to the house before you drink that, unless you don't care about all sorts of creepy crawlies joining in." He stands and offers me his hand.

"For the record, I don't really care." I take his hand and let him lift me up.

He wraps his arm around my shoulders and leads me to a well-kept stone house. In between natural pavers is a thick moss that hugs the ground. I follow him inside. Crimson, green, and blue pillows are everywhere. Grimm is setting up candles on the mantle above a fireplace made of stone.

Penn strides towards me and presses a kiss to the top of my head. "Go get comfortable, love."

I sit down on the green upholstered love seat and wrap my arms around myself. Casimir joins me and rests his hand on my leg, the warmth of his skin seeping into mine. I smile at him before taking a sip of the drink in the mug. The flavor explodes against my tongue, a sweet surprise, with just a hint of tart.

Penn sits beside me and takes the mug from my hands, then sets it aside. He pulls me into his lap so I'm straddling him, grinding against where he's hardening beneath me.

I moan softly when Grimm joins us on the other side of Penn, kissing up my spine while unzipping the back of my dress so it falls off one shoulder. He continues kissing until he reaches my ear, then nips my lobe with his teeth.

The aphrodisiac thrums through my body, causing a whimper to pull from my throat.

Casimir slips his thumb under the strap of my dress and peels it down my arm, exposing one breast to his warm mouth. He laves it before taking my nipple between his teeth and giving a gentle tug.

I shift in Penn's lap so he can unzip me from behind and slip out of my dress. I arch against Grimm when I feel him bend down and kiss each cheek of my ass through the sheer lace fabric of my panties.

My hand flies out to stop him. "Wait, I forgot, I'm on my period."

The men pause their attentions.

"Yes, this means you're a fertile female ... is this ... is this a problem?" Casimir studies my expression.

Heat creeps into my cheeks. "Well, no, but I'm sure for most men it is. Aren't they grossed out by blood? The smell, the look, the mess?"

Penn rolls his eyes. "Human men are so weak. They see blood and cringe. We see a woman on her cycle as a sign of fertility. Fertilization is so rare, I think it's fae's way of trying to ensure a positive outcome."

I raise a brow. "Is that why you all have been so touchy-feely lately?"

"We always want you, but right now? It's like placing a wounded animal in a river full of harpis sirens. We're ravenous." Grimm's lust-filled eyes scan my lacy undergarments.

I throw my hair behind my shoulders and stare at my manicured toes. "I didn't bring my birth control tea—it's still on the ship."

"Good."

My head whips to Penn. "Good?"

"You're going to be our queen. Of course we want to put a baby in you." He presses his lips to my stomach before pulling back.

I look around to each of the kings, meeting their eyes one-by-one. "And you're sure you all want me as your mate? I need to remind you, I refuse to share you three with anyone else."

Casimir lets out a deep chuckle. "Oh, yes. We love you, Lana, and want you to be our queen. There is no one but you."

I narrow my eyes. "Where will we live? You each have continents to run."

Penn shakes his head. "We'll take a united front on Convectus."

"Will you help me get my memories back?"

The room quiets for a moment. They cast glances at each other before turning back to me.

"Yes, we will." Casimir grabs my hands and brings them to his lips.

My heart soars. "Okay. We're doing this." A smile curls my lips.

I may not remember anyone in my life before Bedlam, but who I have now? I can't imagine a life without them in it. They encourage my hobbies, lend a hand when I need help, and give me the strength to face my fears.

"We ask one thing of you in return, but it's okay if you say no." Penn's eyes flash gold, and it takes me a moment to remember he asked me something.

"What is it?"

"To take the mating bond, you need to do a blood bond with us. Say you'll always be ours?"

I laugh. "Of course."

He pulls a knife from his belt, running the blade over his thumb. I watch, transfixed, as blood wells up and then slides down his skin. He extends his hand to me, and I don't hesitate to take it. A sharp pain accompanies the cut he makes on my finger, and he passes the blade to the others. Our blood mixes together, and he presses our joined hands to my heart.

"With this, we are bound for all eternity. You are ours and we are yours."

Energy thrums in my hand before ricocheting through my body, knocking me back into Penn beneath me. I moan as the energy floods my veins and I can feel each of the kings inside of me, their claiming mark branding me.

My moon tattoo burns, the heat intensifying until it's unbearable. I cry out as my skin shimmers and then splits, new skin forming over the top.

When the pain finally fades, I raise my hand to examine the new tattoo. A crown is inked over my moon, with three smaller ones surrounding it.

"What is this?"

"A symbol of our unity." Grimm's voice is rough with emotion.

I trace the lines of the tattoo, my heart swelling with happiness. I'm finally theirs. Completely and utterly theirs. And they are mine. Forever.

Penn kisses me again while Grimm undoes the ties around his waist that hold up his loose pants. I'm sandwiched between the two of them on the couch, while Casimir moves behind to plants kisses up the column of my neck.

Eyes closed, I arch my back, giving into the sensation of their hands on my bare skin. My body thrums with magic, a power so deep, it radiates from me.

"Lana?" Concern lines Penn's voice.

My eyes pop open and I scramble backwards off the couch, falling into Casimir's lap.

"What's wrong with me?!" I shriek.

I barrel across the floor and to the bathroom. My gaze catches on the bright blue glow coming from every surface of my skin. The longer I stand here, the more the luminosity wanes. I whip my head, meeting my eyes in the mirror.

The kings crowd around the doorway. I cast a tentative glance their way before returning to my reflection. Casimir clears his throat. "This is a Luna fae glow." His voice is gentle. "When you're healing, hurting someone, under the moon, or aroused, you're going to glow."

I press two fingers to my cheek and lean in. "Is this why I bleed blue now? And have some blue feathers on my wings?"

"It appears so." Penn pushes through the others to stand behind me. "You're beautiful." His gaze meets mine in the mirror and his hands land on my shoulders.

I give him a small smile before turning to Casimir. "What about my magic? Is it different?"

He nods. "Yes, your magic is lunar."

Penn steps closer, and I tense. "What does that mean?" My voice is barely a whisper.

"It means your magic is linked to the moon. When the moon is full, your power will be at its strongest. Your order supplies magic to the rest of the orders." As he continues to explain, they usher me to the living room, and I tune him out.

All I can focus on is the fact that I'm glowing. I'm a freak. A walking, talking nightlight. And not just any nightlight, but one with some serious magic behind it. Magic that could easily kill someone if I'm not careful.

"Lana." Penn's voice breaks through my thoughts, and I jerk my head up. When did I sit down?

"Sorry." I shake my head and give him a small smile. "I'm just a little overwhelmed."

He nods and tugs me closer until I'm sitting in his lap. "We'll take care of you." His hands twine through my hair, and he leans in to brush his lips against mine. The kiss is gentle and reassuring, and I sink into it.

"Am I always going to glow? Why haven't I seen others of my order?" Questions leap out of me, but I focus on the most important ones.

"No, you won't always glow. Only during arousal, under the moon, while healing, and hurting others." He pulls back slightly and meets my eyes. "As for others of your order, there aren't many left. There are a few living on Rexuna, but that's it."

"How come?" I whisper.

"They were hunted down and killed." Casimir's voice is hard, and I flinch.

"Who did this?" My voice is a little higher than usual.

"The werewolves." Casimir's voice is cold, and I shiver. I've never heard him speak with such disdain.

"Why?" The word is barely audible.

"Millennia ago, the leader of the Luna order gave a group of fae from my order this curse," Casimir's voice is tight, and I can feel the anger radiating off him. "At first, the new werewolves were thrilled with their new powers, until they tried making more werewolves. This only created humans who turn on the full moon, rather than at-will."

I peer intently at Casimir. "I don't understand. If Luna fae supply magic to everyone, why would the werewolves want to kill them off? And how can they, when Luna are the most powerful order?"

"Werewolf fae discovered if they can get Luna blood, they can inject it into a werewolf human to get them into Bedlam, provided they come in during a Bedlam Moon. They're trying to create an army of werewolves here to take over." The disgust in Casimir's voice is evident.

"But they're still stuck with diminishing power, since only Luna fae gets it from the moon?" I frown. "It'll kill off the entire realm."

"Yes, but they're desperate. They've been looking for a way to increase their influence for millennia." Casimir sighs. "What they can't get as magic, they can get from mass numbers. They want to control the fae so they can have an army that can't be stopped."

"What can we do to stop them?" My voice is small.

"We need to find the leader of the werewolf fae and kill him." There's no hesitation in Casimir's voice.

I curl into myself. This is too much. I'm a freak with some serious magic. My order was hunted down and killed. And now, we need to find the leader of the werewolf fae and kill him.

I take a deep breath and try to calm myself. This is something I can do. I'm not alone. I have my mates. We'll figure this out together.

CHAPTER 57

OZ

"*D*o you think the reason the twins are aging so rapidly is because of the change that happened in their cells when they got sick?" I set the paper down.

Pippa and I sit at Gideon's dining room table while we pore over the twin's labs. We're coming upon their first birthday, and they look and act as though they're fifteen. It's not a steady climb, either. The more that time passes, the more the cell multiplication intensifies. When Finn arrived, they were toddlers, and that was only four months ago. How soon before they're physically and mentally eighteen? Do we intervene medically or magically?

"I think it's safe to rule out them being vampires or witches." Pippa sets her pen down. "We've seen no magic and they don't need blood, although they can drink it with no ill effects."

We're silent for a moment before she asks, "What would you say if I suggested fae?"

I chuckle. "I'd tell you that without magic or supernatural elements, it's impossible. We tested their DNA before they were even born."

She looks up, a worried expression on her face. "Maybe the blood-work wasn't enough."

"What do you propose?" I ask.

"We find a fae volunteer and test their DNA against the twins'. We should know for sure whether they're fae. They're the only supernatural species I know of who grow as rapidly as the twins are, and stop growing at a physiological age of twenty-five. Fae usually complete the entire cycle within eighteen months of birth—it's why seeing a fae child is so rare."

Lana never went to the fae realm before this, and the twins are biologically mine and Gideon's ... this makes little sense.

Pippa puts a hand on my shoulder and stands. "I'm going to ask Finn to speak with us if that's alright?"

I nod, barely registering what she asked. My mind is still absent when Finn sits next to me. He slides a folder of papers in front of Gideon, and I watch dispassionately as he flips through the documents.

I see a picture of Finn and Lana's mating tattoo and my eyes widen. I've seen the symbols before; they're fae script. When he came to Earth, he brought with him as many pictures as he could. As High King, he can bring anything through the portal, even if he isn't actively seated.

"What did you need to speak to me about?"

I'm speechless, and Pippa takes her cue. "Would you be willing to give us some of your blood to test against the twins? We suspect they might be fae, however improbable this is."

He blinks. "Why would you suspect that?"

"When they were born, their growth followed a curve that would be expected for babies between a witch and vampire. About six months ago, they became so ill we feared their death. It was only then that their cells multiplied exponentially, and their growth along with it."

Pippa's voice catches when she continues. "There's no other explanation I can think of. I've never seen these cells before, and their physical development is too accelerated for human, witch, or vampire children—even after consuming copious amounts of supernatural blood."

Finn nods. "I'm happy to do so."

"Thank you." She pulls out a vial and needle. Finn rolls up his sleeve while I watch from across the table.

My senses pick up the sound of his blood dripping into the vial; I can smell the iron in it. It's brimming with magic. What would it do to a vampire to drink fae blood?

"That's all we need." Pippa stands and places the vial in her bag. "Thank you. We'll let you know as soon as we have answers."

Finn nods and Pippa leaves the room.

I watch the rise and fall of his chest, the tension in his shoulders.

"Fae rarely have children, if ever. While they're cherished because it's so rare, they're targets for kidnapping. Over time, babies evolved to grow fast, rendering kidnappings virtually non-existent."

"Finn, what does fae blood do to vampires?"

"You're not drinking from me."

I raise my hands and take a step back. "I'm not asking, just wondering what it would do."

He sighs. "Most fae blood is a drug for vampires. It makes them high, unable to control their baser instincts, and ... they're insatiable. It's a way to weaken the fae—a drug and feeding ground for them."

My eyes fix on his throat. I can hear the blood rushing under his skin, and it takes all I have to keep my fangs in check.

"I'm sorry." I clear my parched throat, catching his gaze. "I didn't ask for this."

He takes a step back. I turn away from him, walking towards the door. My thoughts are spiraling. I can't think straight, and without drinking my mate's blood, I am never satiated.

Finn

"Dad!" Rose bursts through the door, out of breath with fear carved into her features.

My nose finds the blood before my eyes do.

"They all went to check on the troops." I grab her shoulders. "Whose blood is this? It's not yours or Bennett's. Are you two okay?"

I look behind her for her brother, but don't see him. She shakes her head, pulling me out the door towards the water. My heart stops at the sight along a sand dune: Bennett, on his knees over a teenager bleeding out.

Using my preternatural speed, I rush to their side and cast camouflage over us. With gentle movements, I place my glowing hands next to the jagged edges of her side and push healing magic into the limp girl.

"I know you're scared, but you did the right thing. What did this?"

Bennett can't speak. He just stares down at where his hands glow against the girl's wounds, clearly in shock.

"I don't know." Rose's voice comes out as a choked whisper. "We found her like this. Is sh-she going to make it?" By the time she's finished, she's sobbing.

"Come here and apply pressure to the wound."

I watch as she retracts her hands from the contact as soon as she starts glowing like her brother, but puts them back on my encouragement. My fangs elongate and I slice a cut open on my wrist before placing it over the girl's mouth.

"We've got you, c'mon."

The girl swallows. Her eyes flutter open, wide with shock, but she's silent.

"Don't move, you're hurt." My voice is gentle, and I watch as she absorbs the words, nods her head, and drifts back to unconsciousness.

Bennett's hands remain on the injury next to his sister's, his eyes now looking at the girl in wonder. Rose scoots away and I slide my arm around her shoulders and pull her against me.

"It's going to be okay," I say over and over again until the words are only echoing in my mind.

"Do you know her name? Her parents must be worried sick." Alphie paces the hallway just outside Rose's room.

She shakes her head. "We've never seen her before."

He nods and leans into the doorframe. It's been two days since Bennett found a semi-conscious teen on the beach, and no one knows who she is.

I turn to look at Rose and Bennett near the bed. The girl's eyes are still closed, though she's on the mend. She's sleeping most of the time, and when she wakes, she's lucid for only moments.

Both Oz and I have tried to catch glimpses of who she might be in her thoughts and dreams, but they only consist of a large-barreled gun. Gideon and Auguste have run her description across international missing human registries, but nothing matches her description.

For now, we wait. In the meantime, the bloodwork confirmed what we already know: the twins are fae.

Not only that, but they're Luna fae.

I knew our soul bond was powerful, but I didn't realize that our mating would change the offspring she'd birthed before we ever met.

Oz

In my peripheral vision, a bright flare of magic summons my attention, and I pause in the foyer to admire the glowing twins. Rose sits on the floor next to Bennett, with the injured girl in the middle.

Their hands rest on the girl's side, making the final repairs to her injuries. I knock on their door.

"Hey kids, how are things going?"

They gesture towards the girl. "This is Teresa McKenna. She just aged out of the foster care system in America before coming to Australia. You couldn't find anything because she's not missing; she has no parents."

I nod and squat down beside them. "That's what we thought. We're going to ask her a few questions now, okay?"

They both smile and move their hands away from Teresa's body and help her sit up. She blinks and looks around, fear contorting her features.

Bennett goes to his knees in front of her. "Hey, it's okay. We're here to help you." He reaches out and touches her hand, then looks back at me. "See?"

She clutches onto him, her knuckles white. "Who are you guys?"

"My name is Oz, and I'm one of Rose and Bennett's dads. You're very lucky those two found you when they did. They saved your life."

She stares down at her body and places a hand where the bite used to be. "I was dying." Her gaze slowly rises to meet mine. "They ... healed me."

Rose nods, then asks her, "Do you know who hurt you?"

"No." She shakes her heads. "He had a gun."

Auguste and Gideon walk into the room, and she jerks her head to look at them. "Who are they?"

I motion for Gideon and Auguste to come closer. "This is Gideon and Auguste. They're Rose and Bennett's dads, too."

She looks at me like I'm crazy, then slowly drags her gaze back to Gideon and Auguste. "You're Rose's dad? And Bennett's?"

Gideon kneels down next to her, a look of concern marring his features. "This must be a lot to take in."

She looks at him, her eyes widening as if she thinks he might attack her. "I don't understand."

"How much can we tell her?" Bennett looks to me. "She's not like us."

I kneel down in front of her. "You're right, she's not." I motion to Rose and Bennett. "They're fae, Teresa. I know it might be a lot for you to take, but they could save you because of what they are."

She looks at Rose and Bennett, who both nod in encouragement. "Fairies?" She closes her eyes for a moment before she bows her head. Teresa considers her words before she speaks. "My parents died in a climbing accident." Tears fall down her cheeks. "I lived with my aunt and uncle for a while, but I just got in the way. When I was sixteen, they put me in the system, but no one wants teenagers."

"Where are you staying now?" I hand her a bottle of water.

"On the beach. I spent all I had to get a plane ticket." She lifts her head and studies me. "I've seen you all walking along the shore."

I glance at Gideon, and he gives me a nod. "You're welcome to stay here as long as you'd like. We can set you up with a room, get you some clothes, and whatever else you need. You've been through a lot, and it doesn't sound like you have family to take care of you."

She takes a deep breath and wipes her eyes. "Thank you, but what about your kids? I'll probably end up messing everything up."

"No way. We got this." Rose gives her a bright smile, and she gets one in return.

Bennett takes Teresa's hand. "Come on, the guest room is this way."

I smile at them as they lead her out of the room. She's too thin, and her clothes are dirty. No one, especially as young as she is, should know what it's like to go hungry or without a roof over their head.

Gideon turns to face me. "What do you think?"

I rub my chin, lost in thought. "She's telling the truth—all her thoughts matched what she told us."

"I don't think she's human, though." Gideon straighten the bedsheets. "Those eyes? They're more yellow than green."

"It's because she's not. She—" Finn gestures behind him. "Is a werewolf."

That's probably why she didn't so much as flinch at the news the twins are fae. It's because she's a supernatural creature, too.

CHAPTER 58

OZ

It's after midnight, and the kids' giggles echo down the hallway as they run to the guest room. I shake my head; Teresa spent the night teaching the twins how to play Uno, and they've burned through Gideon's stash of junk food in the pantry. They're going to be up all night now. How do we parent one-year-old teenagers?

I glance at Auguste, who's sitting on the edge of the bed and staring at his hands. He doesn't hear me until I call his name the second time.

"You okay?"

He runs a hand through his hair and nods. "Just thinking about what Teresa went through. It's not right what happened to her."

"No, it's not. I wish we could've gotten to her sooner ... before someone hurt her. Do you think it was a hunter?"

"Maybe. We should put together a team to track down who shot her, and in the meantime, confront Teresa—gently—about being a werewolf." He stands.

I give him a nod before collecting Gideon and Finn for a much-needed discussion with our part-time furry.

As we enter the guest room, Teresa sits on the bed, and Bennett and Rose perch around the room while playing floor is lava. They grin when we have to explain to Finn what's going on.

"Do you want real lava? I can make real lava." Finn raises his hands.

"No!" Rose shouts, and Finn grins at her.

He jumps onto the dresser. "What kind of fae do you take me for?"

Bennett cackles, and I just shake my head. Seeing Finn interact with the twins is bittersweet; I'm glad they have him because he's good with them, but I'm also not thrilled I have to share. The twins or Lana.

"Hate to put you on the spot, Teresa, but you probably saw this coming." I cross my arms and she freezes. "When did you first shift?"

She looks down at her feet dangling just above the floor. "On my eighteenth birthday. I'm sorry I didn't tell you."

Finn hops off the dresser and crouches down so he's at her level. "We're strangers. It's understandable, and we don't hold it against you."

She nods before darting her eyes to the twins. "I didn't know I was a werewolf until I shifted, and there's only been a single moon cycle since. I understand if you want me to leave."

"Nonsense, you'll stay here with us. You say it's only been a month since you turned?" I raise an eyebrow and turn to Auguste. "Check our database for any werewolves friendly to our family. She's going to need all the help she can get."

IN THE DAYS leading up to the full moon, the guys and I build a reinforced dungeon of sorts in the basement where we originally had Finn chained. We've brought in the Luppin's, werewolves related to our extended family, and they gave advice on retrofitting the bars to minimize damage to Teresa in case she gets out of hand.

They give everyone a crash course in werewolf culture, like how to deal with the anger and violence that comes with the full moon. I take Bennett out of the room with me during the conversation about Teresa's first heat cycle. Haven't quite figured out how to broach puberty and sex when my twins turn into full-grown adults by the time they're toddlers.

We decided Teresa will come with us to Bedlam, because we could use her help. As High King of the fae, Finn can help her shift on command. The trick is to get her through these first moons before she can shift on the move under any sky.

Tonight, Pippa and Elliot take the twins to a hotel. This is simply a precaution, just in case Teresa doesn't handle things well.

The full moon sits high in the sky, its glow reflecting on the water. We're all in the dungeon, Teresa behind bars, and we stand on the other side of them. I'm not looking forward to the poor girl shifting, but it has already started. The smell of blood and fur fills the room, and Teresa's screams echo off the walls.

"Please," she cries, "kill me. It hurts!" Her words end on a whimper.

Auguste tries to soothe her, but it's no use. She snaps her teeth, snarling, while racing towards the bars and yanking on them. The change is too strong, and her anger—too great. We can only watch as Teresa morphs into the wolf, her body writhing in pain.

Eventually, the change calms, and Teresa is left panting on all fours. We step closer towards the cage, but she growls at us, baring her teeth.

"It's okay." Finn keeps his voice gentle. "We're here to help you."

Teresa's yellow eyes meet his, and she seems to calm at his words. The way to help the sentient part of her stay to the forefront is through communication. We'll have to be patient and help her through this, but I'm confident that Teresa can make it through.

We sit here all night. The vampires taking chairs, and Teresa behind the bars until she shifts back into a human. Maeve unlocks the cell door to help her while the rest of us head upstairs.

"The Luppins said Teresa comes from the Van'Astor line of were-wolves." I glance at Finn, and he pauses on his way to the kitchen.

Murder swims in his eyes. "Lana's ex-fiancé?"

I nod. He's about to march back into the basement, but I put a hand out to stop him. His eyes trail from my shoulder down to the hand I have on his arm, and I yank it back. "Don't get any ideas, Finn.

We've already corroborated her story against several sources. She's really an orphan, and this is just a coincidence."

"It's too easy."

"Stranger things have happened. How is it Lana ends up going through a portal no one ever uses, only for her soul bonded mate to rescue her at the last minute?"

"Touché." He nods, but his face still looks unconvinced. "Fine, we'll give her the benefit of the doubt for now, but she's on probation."

We continue to the kitchen, where Gideon is already working on breakfast. It's a somber mood, and I'm not sure whether it's because of Teresa or the fact we have to leave for Bedlam in a few hours. So much can go wrong.

CHAPTER 59

FINN

Oz leads us up a snow-capped mountain they call Cerro Capilla to the portal Lana took into Bedlam. Our army of vampires and witches trail behind us, camouflaged with my magic. Excitement tingles inside me as I imagine seeing Lana again soon. My whole life is in Bedlam, being held hostage by fae I used to consider my friends.

The mountain gets steeper, and I shout to Oz. "How much farther?"

He steps deftly over the snow. "It's only about an hour more of hiking to the portal, if that."

I nod and reach into my inner pocket to check on the bloodstone. We crafted this last night to help blow the portal. My magic has kept it warm and snug inside the protective barrier I built around it so it doesn't break or shatter. Earth fabric is far more fragile than what we craft in Bedlam, and Auguste's clothes are too small and tight on me for much movement. I'd rather not break the stone.

I tuck it back into my coat and quicken my pace until I'm walking beside Oz. If I were alone, I'd break out my wings. It's how I got to Australia to find Lana's mates. Why fly on a plane when I can get there faster on my own?

"Still have the blade?"

"Of course." Oz glances at me. "Dolphina, Ross, and the cult still contained?"

I don't bother giving a response. Oz knows we've got them locked up and magically contained.

We hike in silence, the only noise being the crunching of snow and heavy breathing from behind me. Lana's mates and I climb onto a ledge overlooking a small valley. It's filled with members of the Lapis Templar, unable to move from their spot, unable to make a sound.

I spy Dolphina Darling towards the edge, trying to break the hold I have on them. Without my throne, I can't beat three lesser fae kings, but I can hold a horde of cult members, no matter their species.

Oz reaches into his pocket and pulls out the blade. "Don't we need to get closer?"

"No, we need to keep back from the blast. Can you put your army in a protective sphere in case there's an avalanche?"

Oz nods. "I've got it." He takes a few steps back and I drop the camouflage.

My heart soars, seeing the enormous amount of people who fight for my mate. I'm a naturally quiet, reserved fae. I don't like crowds and I cherish my alone time, but seeing these people come to our aid is humbling.

Oz stands beside me and faces the crowd. "High King Finian Drake of the Luna order is Lana's soul bonded mate. He's going to blast the portal to the fae realm off so we can bring everyone into Bedlam." He gestures towards me. "I'm going to place everyone in a protective sphere in case of an avalanche or ricochet from the blast."

He turns and kneels, thrusting the blade into the snow. "We must offer our blood to the portal, so it knows we mean no harm, and we're not trying to destroy the realm. It will know our intent to get Lana home safely."

Punctuating his words, Oz slices his palm before handing the blade to me. I mimic his actions, relishing the sweet bite of pain before passing the blade on. It makes its way around the group until everyone has made their sacrifice.

The Vampire King gestures and the sphere encasing our army glows, slowly shrinking in size until it's a glimmering blue, impenetrable by outside forces.

"Something's wrong," Teresa barely whispers, her eyes wide as she stares at the portal. Now that she's had her first shift, with my hand on her, she shifts in mere minutes. Her hackles raise and she bares her teeth. I keep a separate protective sphere around her. This one protects the others in case she gets out of control.

I follow her gaze and see what has her so alarmed. The portal is darkening, turning a deep, inky black.

"What's happening?" Gideon murmurs.

Oz and Gideon step closer to me. I have no answers for them. I'm as confused as they are.

"I don't know," I tell them honestly. "But whatever it is, it's not good."

The darkness churns and pulses like a living thing, and I take a step back. There's something wrong here, very wrong.

Without warning, the ground trembles and Maeve loses her footing. She flails her arms, grasping for anything to keep from falling, but she's going too fast. I lunge for her, but I'm not fast enough.

She disappears over the edge with a scream.

"Maeve!" I cry out, horror washing over me.

I don't have to think about it. I spread my wings and leap off the edge, flying as fast as I can. Wind rushes past me as I search for any sign of her.

There's a splash of color above the snow below and I zero in on it. I drop like a stone, scooping Maeve up in my arms before she can hit the ground.

We land, my wings fanning out around us to cushion our fall. I pull Maeve into my lap, and she wraps her arms around me, burying her face in my chest.

"It's okay," I murmur, stroking her hair. "I've got you."

We sit like that for a moment; me rocking Maeve gently as she trembles. Finally, she pulls away and looks up at me.

"Finn," she breathes. "You … have wings."

I give her a small smile. "Surprise."

Maeve reaches up and traces the edge of one wing. "These are freaking *badass*. Wait 'til Hannah and CJ hear this."

"They're Lana's favorite."

I help Maeve to her feet, and I fly her back up the mountain. We're both shaken, but unharmed.

When we reach the top, the vampire court greets us, relief clear on their faces. Oz claps a hand on my shoulder.

"Thank you, brother."

I nod, still shaken by how close Maeve came to meeting her death. It's a reminder of how dangerous this mission is, and how much is at stake.

We can't fail. Lana needs us.

I stand at his side, preparing to burn the bloodstone so I can blow up the portal. Since Dolphina has already tried to kill everyone involved in this fight, I will not hesitate. I place the bloodstone on my palm, and it flares with heat until my skin scalds.

Hurling it at the portal, the stone shatters into a thousand pieces. As soon as I chant, shrieks erupt from our prisoners and the portal spins faster and faster, tearing through space and time. It sucks up all the cult members into its swirling abyss before shrinking to a pinprick of light. I wait, knowing it will explode.

The earth rumbles and the sky shudders above us. The mountain rocks back and forth but stays in place, despite the ominous hissing sound, like it's struggling to stay in one piece.

The portal shudders and I throw up my own protective barrier. Oz does the same for the rest of Lana's mates and we wait. A shock wave ripples out and the earth beneath us erupts. The mountain we're on crumbles and rolls, each rock bigger than my head as it rockets towards the portal.

Protection spheres deflect the rubble as it flips and tumbles, preventing our army from getting injured. The portal explodes with such force my orb nearly gives. When the dust settles, the entry to Bedlam is no longer obscured by magic.

Before we can celebrate, a piercing scream cuts through the noise. The mates and I go ramrod straight, dread a crushing vise against our chests.

What the fuck are the twins doing here?!

Our army of vampires spin towards the sound at the bottom of the narrow mountain pass. Half a mile down lies a small boulder, and under it—Bennett.

Rose shrieks, attempting to push it off her brother.

I'm uncertain whose bellows echo through the canyon; mine, our army, or the vampire courts'.

Everyone rushes down the mountain at breakneck speed. I take my wings out again and fly over their heads, reaching them first, trying to assess the situation. Bennett lies motionless, blue blood dribbling from his mouth.

No.

The vampire mates reach us next, and together we roll the boulder off his little body. As he's fae now, he has the body of a teen human, but he's still no match for a thousand-pound rock.

"He pushed me out of the way!" Rose's shrieking sobs burrow into my soul.

We fall to our knees, the stench of blood-soaked mud filling my nose. Teresa's whimpers behind me turn into sorrow-filled howls.

Bennett's aura is gone, his chest doesn't rise, and I don't have to put my head to his heart to know it no longer beats. This feels like falling without wings, with no safety net. You try to scramble for purchase, knowing the end result is dire, though you still try.

Oz grips my shirt, red tears marring his face and spittle flies from his gritted teeth. *"Please."*

I blink rapidly and wetness rolls down my cheeks. "I don't—I don't know if it'll work. He's not a mature fae."

Gideon cradles Bennett, haunting sobs wrenching from his very soul.

"I'll pay whatever price is asked of me." He bares his fangs. "Fix him!"

I shake my head, grief eating me alive. "You don't understand. Fae have so few offspring not only because fertilization is rare, but because you can't bring children back from the dead."

Oz hangs his head, wails shaking his body, a vision of a father breaking.

CHAPTER 60

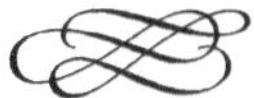

OZ

A section of my soul shatters, echoes of its remains splintering like stars in the sky. The pieces scatter, skittering across time and space, never to be whole again.

Bennett.

I'm so sorry for failing you.

My eyes catch as Finn reaches into his pocket, pulling out the dagger we used in the ritual. He cranes his head to the sky before slicing a line across his wrist. Horror ripples through the crowd as his cerulean blood pours from his wound.

He lets out a roar, chanting in archaic fae. I stare at the bloody steel when he places it in my palm. It takes a moment before understanding dons on me. I wrap my hand around the blade and slice my wrist open, joining him in the repeated chant before passing the weapon to the others, our combined blood spilling to the soil.

The clouds gather in an angry mob, and lightning strikes in rapid succession. Between one blink and the next, an ethereal form descends from the storm. Power emanates from this creature so fierce, and her skin glows such a bright blue, I have to squint.

"Finian." Deep affection coats her words.

"Mother." A sad smile paints Finn's face.

Her eyes take in the situation around us, and grief crumples her beauty. "Oh, Finian." A tear tracks down her cheek. "You can't."

"I must."

The blade is in his hands again, and he positions it at his heart. He glances back at me, determination strong in his features before whispering. "Tell Lana I'll see her again; when the land has claimed my body, Luna calls me home, and my beams kiss her skin. I'll never be far."

Shock freezes me.

"I, Finian Drake, High King of the fae, Giver of Magic, Uniter of Realms, Son of Luna, Soul Bond of Lana Finlandian, give my life in exchange for Bennett Finlandian's."

He doesn't hesitate. Plunging the dagger into his chest, the air escapes his lungs before he stills, and keels over.

"NO!"

CHAPTER 61

FINN

The first face I see is hers. She presses a hand to my cheek, my sad smile echoing hers. I make to sit up, but she shakes her head.

"I don't accept the exchange, my sweet son. You're too important. The realms need you."

The scent of blood permeates the air, and I lift my head and look down at my prone body. Her hand wraps around the dagger and yanks it out before her other staunches the blood. Healing magic pours out of her and blankets my body, racing to every surface, seeping into my bones.

"No," I push her hand away. "*Bennett.*"

"Shh. Your life is too great a price—"

"No!" I roar.

Never once have I raised my voice at my mother. Not when I was a small child, nor when she was killed and became the Luna goddess.

Mother tsks. "My sweet. Oz settled the bargain."

Panic races through me and I sit up, head whipping around for any sign of him. "No."

I jump to my feet.

No. No. No. No.

Lana will never get over this. Neither will the children.

Mother places a hand on my shoulder, stilling me. I meet her eyes. "My brave son, I am so proud of you." Tears spill down her cheeks.

A haze settles over me, and I catch sight of Bennett walking our way. Dried blood soaks his clothes, and his hair is a mess, but otherwise, he's whole.

"I'm sorry," I croak.

He pulls me in for a hug. I still for a moment before returning it, squeezing tight, breathing through the pain radiating from my chest where sweet relief meets crushing grief. My legs crumple beneath me, the crushed rock and mud marring my knees. I tilt my head to the sky, tears waging war on my cheeks before splashing against the top of Bennett's head. The moisture smudges my vision.

It was supposed to be me.

My shoulders shake as I stand, bringing him with me. "Bennett, I'll fix this, I'll make this right—"

More arms wrap around my back, and it takes me a second to register the aura.

We part, and I whip around. "Oz?" My breath catches.

"What was the price?" I study him, trying to discern what's different about him, but I can't place it.

"My magic."

Relief lifts a weight from my shoulders. "I can give you—"

"No," my mother's sad voice calls from behind me.

"But—"

"It's the price we bargained, and he can't acquire magic through other means."

I blink back the tears. Losing your magic? Cutting you off from source? I can't fathom the lifelong grief that would cause, but it's less than that of losing a child. A price I'd pay a million times over.

Oz claps me on the shoulder. "I'll be okay now."

I nod before turning back to my mother.

She gives me a sad smile. "I must go now, my sweet. You make me so proud."

I puff my cheeks and breathe through clenched teeth, trying to blink back the tears before they inevitably fall. It's been millennia since I've heard her voice, felt her touch, cried in her embrace.

She crouches in front of the twins, cupping their cheeks. Magic pours off her palms, brightening the twin's skin for a moment before returning to its normal color. After whispering in their ears, she stands, and crosses to me.

"Must you go?"

The skin around her eyes crinkles when she beams at me. "You have everything," she glances around at the crowd of vampires, "and everyone you need."

She presses a kiss to my cheek before vanishing.

As soon as we've passed through the portal, I add a temporary door only we can get in and out of, and restore the portal to its original state, hidden inside a mountain. Most don't use this one, anyway, because it leads to Noble Wilds. I'll decide later if I'll ever make this accessible again, considering it leads to my land.

I collapse to my knees on the other side. The ground is smooth, but still unstable because of the earthquake. I glance back at Oz, who's already on his knees at the portal entrance. We stare at each other, relief washing over us now that we've completed the second part of our mission.

Gideon reaches for the goo dripping off the trees.

"I wouldn't touch any of that excrement if I were you." I warn.

He recoils in disgust. "Beasts."

Alphie caught up not long before the last of us passed through the portal. He was supposed to stay behind with the twins, who had tricked him into thinking they were asleep in their beds when they followed us to the portal.

So now, all of us are in Bedlam, determined to get Lana back.

CHAPTER 62

LANA

The kings are on deck, helping the crew navigate craggy rocks while we near our final destination, and I keep my eyes on the water. Our situation is precarious because the channel is narrow, surrounded by towering cliffs, and deadheads large enough to pierce our hull. This would be dangerous during the light, and it's even worse at night.

We can't come during the day because of the basilisk nesting grounds on top of the cliffs. They're a breed of basilisk who can swim in the water, and they stand upright on their hind legs. They have no wings to speak of, but they can mimic human speech.

The closest we can get is nightfall because the creatures sleep all day, and they don't like the dark. Their natural predators, whale-like creatures called belu, prowl under the water at night, waiting for unsuspecting basilisk to fall in. So, we brave the darkness. The only advantage for us is that fae can see just as well at night as we can during the day.

The battering rain and thunder drown out the movement of our ship over the water and the periodic scrape of the hull on a boulder. The waves are rough, tossing us around like a toy. I hang tight to the rail and try to ignore my stomach.

"We'll have to take our chances and move fast so we can get past this," Penn yells, trying to be heard over the storm. Water sprays up around us, drenching us with endless sheets of icy rain. I'm soaked through to my skin and the wind whips my hair back.

"Aye!" a sailor on deck replies, and Penn turns to me with a grin that's both excited and mischievous. I can't help but smile back, though it's forced because I'm miserable in the elements.

"Come on, love," he shouts over the rain as he holds an arm out to me.

I shake my head. "I'm not going in!" Like hell, I'll be the only one warm and dry. We're a team.

The crew rushes to the bow and spans the starboard and port sides, trying to use magic to decimate obstacles before the ship nears them. When the lightning flashes, I spot something in the skies, flying right for me. My heart leaps, a sick feeling souring in my stomach. It's coming fast, right at us, its slitted eyes glowing in the darkness, shining an eerie red against the blackness.

Thunder cracks as I let out a scream, and no one hears me. My freezing hands don't work right. My body doesn't move. *What's happening to me?*

The fae cloaks us and puts us in a sound bubble. With preternatural speed, she presses a blade to my throat. I swallow, nicking my skin. Her face gets close to mine and she snarls.

"You should've died the first time I killed you at the portal!"

I draw on the elements, pulling enough magic to me to break her cloak. Shouts from the crew draw the attention of my mates.

The fae shrieks, "For Dolphina!"

Before they can reach her, she draws the blade across my throat, cutting my carotid artery. My blood spurts in her face and she just laughs before shoving me overboard.

I go in hard and let in a panicked breath as I sink down deep, too deep to see the ship above me. I'm tangled in the skirts of my dress. Panic floods my body and I kick hard for the surface, but I don't know which way is up. I reach out with my arms in a panic, trying to swim in any direction.

My chest is on fire, and I feel the approach of unconsciousness. I'm going to drown, if I don't bleed out first.

I can't breathe.

My self-preservation kicks in, and I take an involuntary gulp of water in a desperate attempt to pull air into my lungs.

Penn

THE KINGS and I are the first to jump in after Lana. Captain dropped anchor as soon as she fell in. Half the crew fights the berserker shifter, and the other half is in the water searching for her. The pure panic on her face and the surge of dread through our mating bond will haunt me forever.

I went in after her thinking it would be like any other rescue, but she's gone, disappeared under the water.

How long has she been under? How long can she hold her breath?

We scream her name, but the crash of the sea on the cliffs and the storm drown it out.

I dive deeper into the water, further than the rest of them. A tug of alarm through our bond sends a fresh wave of fear through us. I dive deeper, scanning, searching for any sign of her.

Far below me I spot her pale skin glowing a faint blue, but she's still sinking deeper. I push myself down after her, my arms and legs sending me through the water. My magic flares and I can tell she's unconscious and losing oxygen.

I race through the water, praying to the gods I will make it in time. My lungs burn, but I will them to fight, just a little longer. I propel myself towards her limp body.

Lana! I scream into her mind, hoping she can hear me. *I can't lose you. You have to fight! I'm coming for you, love, just hold on!* Fae can survive drowning if we get to them in time.

I struggle through the dark, cold water. The most gut-wrenching, soul-tearing pain rips through my chest. I cry out, the force of it knocking me back. My lungs sputter from the intake of water.

NO!

Casimir

OUR MATE IS GONE. Penn's scream of agony pierces my heart, but none more than the wail coming from me. She's not coming back. The mating bond severed only moments ago, burns bright before snapping completely. Sharp pain levels me as the best part of me tears from my body.

CHAPTER 63

CASIMIR

*I*t took nearly an hour to recover her body. Pierce made the kill shot to the berserker. Lana's face is bruised and battered, the wound on her neck still angry, but her eyes are closed and she's still. She doesn't respond to our touch or commands. Her skin is so translucent, her veins map the way to the heart no longer beating in her chest. Even in death, her beauty is unmatched.

Penn is inconsolable when I find him. Pain sears through me and I don't know how to ease it. Grimm trails behind me, a haunted expression on his face. We're all broken.

I don't let go of her when Captain lowers the ladder for us. Hoisting her over my shoulder, I climb up and fall to my knees once on deck. My arms cradle her, and I sob, not giving a shit the crew can see me. Every single one of them adores her. She's irreplaceable. Not only because she's our mate, but because of what she means to our realm. What her loss means for the fate of everyone in it.

How long do we keep watch over her? I lose all sense of time, far past the numbing of my extremities and the sting of the cold. Every minute feels like a lifetime. Is there a timeline for mourning the death of your mate? Between the three of us, we must've used dozens of our feathers, trying to resurrect her, with no luck.

Why didn't it work?

Everything is bleak compared to the gaping wound inside me. What's the purpose of this miserable existence without her bright light, filling our lives with joy and laughter?

Night turns to day and day to night again. Not once have I left her body, but the crew made a makeshift shelter on the deck to protect us from the elements. After we brought her body aboard, Captain maneuvered us out of the channel, and we're now moored next to a small island. When he did this, I don't know. I didn't see or feel anything; I'm lost in my own world of grief and despair.

Grimm and Penn tear me from my sorrows to pry me away from Lana. Reluctantly, I let them take her while I go below deck to grieve. We all need time alone with our mate before giving her a proper burial.

My feet carry me to the armoire where she keeps her clothes. I won't have her wearing the tattered outfit she died in. When my hand wraps around her favorite blue dress, the soft material soothes me. There's a part of her close to me. I press the material against my cheek and inhale her scent, wishing she were here.

I turn around when the door opens. Grimm holds Lana in his arms and places her on the bed so we can change her into her burial dress. My hands shake as I hand the dress to him. With small, measured movements, the three of us remove our mate's clothing and put her in the last outfit she'll ever wear.

We say nothing. Not even when we brush out her tangled hair, or when we slip heels onto her feet. We work together in silence, grim expressions on our faces. Coming to terms with losing her is slowly destroying me.

The sins we committed added an immeasurable toll to our souls. If not for the fate of our people, we never would've taken the risk. If only we had known the price we were paying in the end.

When she's dressed, Grimm places a pink flower in her hands. I take one from the vase on the dresser and give it Penn. I want her to have every bit of the beauty only Fae possess when she goes over the veil and joins our ancestors.

Fae don't decompose like humans, nor do they get rigor mortis. Traditional royal burials have a four-day mourning period before a funeral pyre closes the door on Bedlam. This gives the soul time to find its way. I take comfort knowing her pure heart will take her to Luna's veil, and not Aggonid's realm of pain and suffering.

Crew brings in chairs for us to sit around the bed and mourn her, but we sit on the bed instead. I don't think any of us expected to fall in love with her. She was a means to helping secure the realm, but her tenacious spirit drew us all in. Yes, in the end we were mates, but our hearts connected long before she took the mating bond.

Day turns to night, and I'm the last to pass out by her side, having shed so many tears I'm a hollowed-out shell.

CHAPTER 64

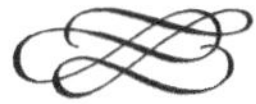

FINN

Our army marches through the thick woods of the Noble Wilds. We used this portal because it's on my land, and no one can intercept us while our army acclimates to the fae realm. Lana's vampire mates and I lead the front, while the rest of our family takes second row. We keep a grueling pace because it won't be long until fae realizes the portal is breached.

A powerful magic stirs in the air, bringing with it fresh memories of Lana. I push them away as I pick up the pace. A foreboding sense of her magic niggles at our bond. She doesn't seem close, so why do I feel she's in danger?

My heart races and adrenaline courses through me. Wild panic surges through the bond like a tsunami, bringing with it a sense of dread so thick it nearly chokes me. My hand flies out to stop everyone while I try to make sense of what's going on. When I dart my gaze to her vampire mates, their eyes are wide with fear.

A searing hot fist cleaves my soul in two, ripping our soul bond right from my chest. I fall to my knees, screaming in agony. After the onslaught of pain, I claw at the ground and grapple at my chest where she used to reside. The bond is severed, and her magic is gone.

My head falls, and the sun against my back warms me as I lose myself to darkness. The torture of losing her is too much. I pray for death, because living without her ... it will be a never-ending torment.

"I can't live without her." Oz weeps. "I can't live without my mate."

Our army hovers frantically above me, all of them waiting for me to make a decision. Hope stirs in my chest when I remember. My feather.

"We run." I give a command, still broken with pain. "We travel until we find her."

CHAPTER 65

LANA

"Why are you crying, my love?" I reach for Casimir's grief-riddled face. "Are you alright?" He ignores me, and crosses to our armoire.

"Love?"

His hand wraps around my favorite blue dress and presses the material to his cheek before breathing in deep. I whip towards the door when it creaks. Penn enters, his face haunted, too.

"What's going on?" When they ignore me, a nervous chuckle bubbles out of me. "Who died?"

Grimm crosses the threshold cradling a woman in his arms and carries her to our bed before laying her down. I rush to their side, wondering who is hurt. There aren't supposed to be any other women aboard.

I make to rest my hand on Penn's shoulder and instead, fall right through him.

"What the …"

I touch my own cheek, half expecting my hand to go right through, but it doesn't. I'm solid.

"What's happening?"

When I look back up, Grimm is weeping over the woman's body and Penn is on his knees, head in his hands.

And then it hits me.

I'm dead.

They're grieving me.

The weight of their sadness is a physical blow, and I stagger back. This can't be happening. I can't be dead. There has to be some mistake.

"Guys! I'm right here!" I scream. My fists attempt to beat at their hunched forms but fall right through them.

That's when my eyes land on my body, and the giant gash across my neck.

No. No, no, no. This can't be happening.

I'm not dead. I can't be dead. There's too much to do and see. I don't even remember who I am. We're supposed to have babies, spend our winters on Sundahlia, and help the Tolden and Crucey defeat the werewolves.

But as I watch my mates grieve me, I know what I want to deny.

I'm dead.

I sink to my knees, the full weight of my sadness crashing down on me, and I let out a keening wail. The tears come hard and fast, like drops of rain, and I mourn my own death.

I cry for the life I could have had, the family I could have raised, and the future I'll never see.

I cry for the mates who have lost me, and the pain they must be feeling.

For hours, they mourn me. For hours, they weep and wail and tear at their hair. They hold each other tight, and try to find comfort in one another.

But eventually, they sleep.

And I watch over them, as I will for the rest of eternity.

I cry until I have nothing left, and then I curl up on the bed next to my mates, and I let myself fade away.

When the ship quiets, my body rises from the mattress, and I'm pulled towards the light.

No.

"*No!*" I scream, clawing my way back towards the bed. "I'm not ready! I'm not ready to go!"

An ethereal woman hovers outside the window, and she smiles at me. Her features tug at a memory, and try as I might, I can't place her.

"It's time, my love." Her words act like a siren, its harmonious tone like a balm to my soul.

"No," I sob. "Please, no."

But she only smiles and extends her hand to me.

And so I go. I pause, turning to where my mates sleep restlessly next to my body.

"I love you," I whisper, tears blurring my vision. "I'll always love you."

The woman calls to me, and I turn. Her sad smile is the last thing I see before I'm pulled into the light.

And then I'm gone.

CHAPTER 66

LANA

Blinding blue light flares to life, and I'm momentarily disoriented. When my vision clears, I stand frozen, overlooking Bedlam. I'm hovering over the top of an enormous mountain. Below us is a mountain pass with a home nestled between the peaks. In the distance are the twinkling of city lights, a raging sea, towering spires pressed through the clouds, an entire world I never got to explore.

Pain in my ribcage has me doubling over. I shriek, and the woman's alarmingly familiar laugh tinkles through the air.

"What did you do?" I rasp, clutching my side. When I pull my hand away, there's blood on my fingers. What's happening?

Her hand rests on my face, the familiar warmth seeping into my skin. "Oh, my sweet." Tears stain her cheeks. "It's you."

"Me?" What is this mad woman talking about?

She pulls me into her arms and hugs me close. "You don't remember, do you?"

Her words are like a key turning in a lock, and memories try to come flooding back, but they get stuck halfway. I can see flashes of a life lived, but nothing concrete.

"Who are you?" I croak.

She presses something into my hand before her lips land on my cheek. "Find them," she whispers. "Find your mates."

And then she's gone.

I'm left clutching a feather, staring at the empty spot where she was just standing.

What the hell just happened?

CHAPTER 67

LANA

*A*ir fills my lungs, and I gasp before sitting up. My gaze darts around the room before landing on my mates scattered around me on the bed. I run my hands over myself before settling on my neck, checking for injuries. Relief washes over me. I'm … alive?

I turn to Grimm, watching his pinched brow. I've never seen them so troubled in sleep. My eyes roam over Casimir before landing on Penn. I lay a soft press of my lips against his cheek.

He sits up, blinking at me. "My love."

I lean down to embrace him. He clings to me, like a sailor hanging onto a buoy at sea.

"I don't want you to go," he cries into the crook of my neck. My eyes water with unshed tears.

Grimm startles awake, causing the others to rise, too. They all stare at me, a mixture of emotions flitting across their faces. Even the bond surges with activity; confusion, elation, and disbelief all flow through.

"I did go." I furrow my brows. "I watched you prepare my body for burial, and I kept screaming, but no one could see or hear me. You all mourned for me. How am I back?"

Penn blinks and darts his eyes to the others. He shoves away from the bed and stalks to the other side of the room. Casimir crawls closer to me and kneels at my feet. He sets his hand on my knee, and Grimm moves to sit by my head.

Penn topples over the armoire in a fit of rage. "This isn't real." He slams his fists against the wall. "She died, and she isn't coming back."

Tears choke my throat. "Penn," I call out.

He displays anger, but we all know what this really is. The depths of our shared pain over my death has splintered reality. We're all teetering on the edge of reason, trying to decipher what is and what isn't.

"I died, but I came back." I get up and approach Penn.

The others follow.

"This isn't real," he growls, curls of smoke streaming from his nose while his fangs and claws descend in warning.

"It is." I move behind Penn and wrap my arms around him. "I felt it when my body died, and now I'm back." My eyes fill with tears. "Don't you feel me? Feel our bond?"

He spins around and crushes me to his chest. The rest of them tense, ready to intervene if necessary. When Penn takes a step back to cup my cheeks, they exhale, and I hold my breath.

"Are you in there?" he asks, his voice raw with emotion.

The air expels from my lungs, relief a sweet balm to my soul. I nod and smile through my tears. "I'm in here." I press my palm to his chest.

CHAPTER 68

FINN

We wait under the cover of night, the inky sky providing the perfect camouflage, and the moon refueling my magic, however temporary. My heart is pounding in my chest, adrenaline coursing through my veins. Bringing Teresa and the twins is risky, but I know they can handle themselves. Teresa, with her uncanny werewolf intuition, and the twins, being children. The four of us huddle close, waiting for the signal. My magic is crackling around us, a low hum in my ears. I can feel the others' magic as well, swirling around us like invisible ribbons.

Petrichor fills my senses as the rain starts to fall, tapping a staccato beat on the leaves around us. A bolt of lightning pierces the sky, briefly illuminating our surroundings in an eerie blue light.

I take a deep breath, bracing myself for what's to come.

Crouching to their level, I ask the twins if they're ready. When they nod, I pull them into my arms, giving them both tight hugs. When the storm surges, Rose and Bennett have their cue to head towards the castle.

I hop from rooftop to rooftop, keeping a careful eye on them, lest they run into trouble before I can join them. Teresa prowls below me, her senses on high alert. We're getting close now, and the guards are becoming more numerous.

The guards turn their attention to the two small figures racing towards the castle. Rose and Bennett stop in front of the castle doors, and I cloak Teresa and I close behind them.

"Sir, do you have any work for us?" Rose's voice trembles, but she stands tall.

"We're here to help with the storm, if you need us," Bennett adds.

The guard hesitates. "Where are your parents?"

"Dead, sir. It's just us." Bennett lays it on thick.

The guard looks uncertain, but he nods. "You two don't have to earn your keep. Let's get you inside." He nods to the others, who heave the doors open.

We're in.

Rose pauses briefly in the entryway, her eyes growing wide at the grandeur of the castle, concealing what she's really doing. She drops a tiny vial of blood magic on the stoop, while I use the sound barrier to recite an incantation that'll allow us through undetected.

I tug on her shoelace when I finish, her cue to notice and buy us some time. She kneels, slowly tying the laces into bows. Bennett drops to help her, and the guards shift uncomfortably.

"Hurry up, will you?" One of them mutters.

When the blood disappears from the threshold, signaling the success of the spell, I tap her heel. "Sorry," she says, and crosses the threshold with Bennett right behind her.

The rest of us slip in unnoticed, the door swinging shut behind us.

We round the corner and come face-to-face with Titan and Rune. The guard leading us stands at attention, saluting the shadow and storm fae.

"What's going on?" Rune growls.

"I'm leading these two orphans to the East wing, where Mara might be able to make up some rooms for them." The guard answers.

Rune's hand rests on Titan's head, stroking the obsidian fur. "I'll handle it from here," he says, his eyes locked on Bennett and Rose. "I'll take them to Mara."

Titan bares his teeth, and the guard backs away.

Rune ushers us down the hall towards the East wing, his hand still on Titan's head. As we walk, I can feel the tension in the group. We're all on edge, waiting for something to happen.

When we reach the East wing, Rune stops in front of a bedroom and unlocks the door. He glances down the hallway before ushering everyone inside.

When the door shuts, I enlarge the silencing bubble to encase the room and drop the cloak.

Rune whips around when Titan tackles me to the ground. His enormous claws press into my chest as he leans down to lick my face, the smell of a fresh kill still on his tongue.

I laugh and ruffle his fur. "Good to see you, too, boy."

Rose and Bennett both look relieved when they realize that the giant black Phelvie isn't going to eat me. When he lets me up, I rise to my feet and brush the dirt off my jeans.

My eyes meet Rune's, and he stalks over to me before grabbing me in a crushing hug.

"I didn't think I'd ever see you again," he whispers, his voice tight.

"I'm sorry," I murmur. "I didn't mean to get you involved in all this."

He pulls away and shakes his head. "I owe you for saving my life. Even without that, it isn't right what they're doing."

He glances towards the twins and Teresa, who's shifted back into her human form. I introduce them.

"Gods, you look just like her." Rune's voice is soft as he looks at the twins.

"How is she?"

Hesitation crosses his features, and I know it isn't good news. He runs a hand through his silky hair, and Titan's tail twitches.

"Happy."

I nod, despite the war waging inside of me. I'm relieved she's being treated well, and as her soul bonded mate, devastated she's thriving without me.

"And Annabelle?"

"Come," he says, grabbing my hand and leading me into the room.

We reach a desk with a computer stuck on a lock screen. Rune steps up and unlocks it with a few quick clicks. A video feed pops up, and I see Annabelle Chapman scrubbing the walls in a tiny room.

She looks pale and frail, her hair spread around her like a halo of silver. Dark circles mar the skin under her eyes, and her shoulders are stooped. She looks like she's given up.

But she's alive. And that's all that matters.

I turn to Rune, my heart pounding in my chest. "When can we get her out of there?"

He sighs and rubs a hand over his face. "It won't be easy," he says. "The kings have guards posted all around the castle, and they're always on the lookout for anything suspicious."

"We'll just have to be careful," I say. "We can't leave her in there any longer."

He nods and turns off the computer. "I'll see what I can do."

ROSE AND BENNETT trail behind me through the halls of Convectus Castle. Rune has created a diversion by calling an all-guards magic training in the courtyard, so there's a skeleton crew on watch.

Teresa is a hundred yards ahead to pick up on Annabelle's trail. Because we have such a narrow window, we wouldn't have time for me to use my magic to find her.

As a servant, she should be in the servant's quarters, but I suspect they've got her under lock and key. We pass soldier after soldier, completely unaware of our presence. I'm grateful for my glamour.

Eventually we make it to the servant's quarters and find Teresa waiting for us in a separate hallway with a single door at the end. She nods at me, and I step into the room, my glamour dissipating.

Annabelle sits on the floor with her back to me, hunched over her tray of food. She jumps to her feet and backs into the corner when she hears me clear my throat. Her eyes immediately dart to my ears before going to the moon emblem on my tunic, furrowing her brows before meeting my gaze. I grit my teeth at the cloaked binds she has on her magic, circling around her wrists, and she's none the wiser.

"I'm High King Finian Drake …"

She interrupts. "There is no High King. He left us." Her eyes widen and she bites her lip while her thoughts run wild. She's kicking herself for speaking out of turn to a fae.

I take in her huge doe eyes, tangled hair, and dirt-smudged face. There's a startling resemblance to Lana in her features, but there's also a fragility about her. I can tell she's broken.

"There is a High King, and I am he." I take a step closer to her, and she takes a step back. "Your daughter is my soul bonded mate."

She shakes her head. "I'm sorry, you must be mistaken. There is no family for me. I'm a servant."

"Your name is Annabelle Chapman, and you were born in Minnesota. Twenty-six years ago, you disappeared, leaving your eight-year-old daughter, Lana, alone." I keep my tone calm, despite my anger at the position she put my mate in. "She grew up in foster care, and after her adoptive parents died, she went to figure out what happened to you."

Annabelle laughs before turning hysterical. She wipes the tears from her eyes. "Thank you for giving me a new story to tell." Crossing to the door, she opens it to let me out.

I drop the glamour from Rose, Bennett, and Teresa. Annabelle startles before glancing at me. "What's the meaning of this?"

"What he says is true, Grandma." Rose's eyes water, so I wrap her in my arms.

"Your daughter is my mate." I say it again because I need her to understand.

She gasps and covers her mouth. "I don't know why you'd play such a cruel trick on an old woman, especially a lonely one. Be gone, the lot of you!"

"You're a time-traveling witch, and the kings removed your memories when you tried to trick them into eliminating vampires." I take a tentative step towards her and gesture towards the twins. "These are your grandchildren, and you're Lana's mother. I can prove it."

Annabelle's face crumples as fresh tears fall. "You've gone far enough, fae."

"Please," Bennett begs, and Annabelle's eyes meet mine right as I freeze her where she stands.

Though I don't need to touch her to give her memories back, because she's weak compared to me, I place my hand on her shoulder as a gesture of goodwill. It's scary to have zero control over your actions. My magic races through her body, seeking memories and burning through the binds around her mind and magic.

I witness the moment both return, and she drops to her knees, sobbing. "Lana! Where is she?!"

We help her to her feet, and she clings to us as if we'll disappear if she lets go. "Please, take me to her."

I glance towards the twins, concern heavy on their conscience, and speak into their minds. The last thing I want is them thinking their grandma doesn't care about them.

She's in shock right now. We'll have to give her some time.

They give me minuscule nods of understanding. I meet Teresa's eyes and let her know it's time to leave, so she darts out the door and we follow behind. As soon as we leave the castle, we can sift.

It takes us half a day to make it out of the castle and sift to the small island we have everyone hidden on. During the journey, we fill Annabelle in on everything that's happened, including how her daughter ended up in the clutches of three kings.

Hannah helps Annabelle get set up in a tent near the center of our army. She's exhausted, both mentally and physically. We give her some space, but Rose and Bennett remain to help her acclimate.

She emerges from her tent for supper, waiting in line with the rest of us.

"I thought I'd never see you again."

Annabelle freezes before turning around, and it's like I'm witnessing this unfold in slow motion. As soon as their eyes connect, she falls to her knees, sending her empty plate hurtling to the muddy ground.

"Alphie," she chokes through her tears. "I'm so sorry."

He runs to her, and she clings to him as if he's the only thing anchoring her to the realm. They exchange no other words for several minutes, just tears that say so much after all these years. Regret. Guilt. Fear. Sweet relief. And love.

Alphie whispers in her ear before scooping her into his arms.

I stand back and give them their moment, feeling like an intruder, and place a silencing bubble around them. We don't need to be privy to their first contact in three and a half decades.

I gather plates for the two of them before gesturing to seats at a table far from everyone else so they can have a chance to connect.

Their reunion is one I dream of every night between Lana and me.

CHAPTER 69

LANA

The sound of metal tearing earth cuts through the quiet. I shoot out of bed and cover my ears against the incessant blaring throughout the house. I can't think; my brain is on fire with the noise.

Our houselights flash in rhythm to the alarm. The buzz cuts off just as Pierce and his guards burst through the room, shouting, and find the kings and me stark naked.

"What's going on?" My groggy voice cuts through the cacophony of movement.

Pierce rushes to my armoire, grabs a dress, and tosses it at me. "My Lady, the portal's been breached. Get dressed and gather your belongings. We must get you to the bunker."

"What?" I say with a whisper, my voice lost in the frenzy.

Casimir crouches at my level and grabs my face. "It's the vampires, Lana. They've found us. We have to move you."

Terror surges through me. I nod robotically and he kisses my forehead.

"Pierce," Casimir says while releasing me. "I want you and the guards to make sure she's safe."

I shake my head and clutch onto Casimir's arm. "Don't leave me, please."

He kisses my cheek. "I'll be back, never far away." He turns to the guards and Pierce. "We can't let them take her. She's our last hope."

They all nod and my legs turn to jelly, and Grimm slips his arm around my waist and guides me to the bed.

"We have to put on shoes." He places a pair in front of each of us.

I barely register as I slip them on. My eyes dart to each of their faces and all I see is fear. I fumble with the shoes and whimper. "I thought the portal has never been breached before?"

Grimm tips my chin up to him. "It hasn't until now."

I can't keep up. "How did they find us?"

Grimm grabs the back of my head and kisses me while his other hand goes around my waist. "We don't know, but if they breach the bunker, you're to go straight into the portal. Make your way to the waterfall in Meloria and we'll collect you from there."

I break from his kiss. "I can fight, Grimm. Let me do this."

He shakes his head. "You're too important, Lana. We can't risk it."

"Don't you know how important you are to me?" I wipe my tears with the back of my hand.

Penn presses his lips to my forehead, and I breathe in his scent. I lean into him, letting his warmth embrace me. "We'll protect you to the end."

In a blink, we sift to the shelter. I've been here once before, during a tour of the castle my first few weeks here. It's less a bunker and more of an enormous one-room house made to house several thousand people for months.

Captain Zara pauses in front of me. "Pierce will keep you safe here. Do not open this door for anyone but myself or the kings, understood?"

I nod and she slips me some weapons from their holsters on the wall. "Just in case. Stay here until we come for you, or if they breach the bunker, sift to the falls."

I clutch the weapons, feeling their weight in my hands. "Okay."

The kings take turns hugging me and whispering sweet words about how they'll come back as soon as they can. They flash me smiles as they sift away.

The door closes with a snick and I'm alone, surrounded by concrete walls. A moment later, Pierce appears in front of me with a plate of food.

"The kings ordered this for you," he says with a small smile, his dimples falling into place.

I laugh. "I couldn't eat a thing even if I were starving. You go on and have it."

"Nah." He shakes his head. "We were just finishing breakfast when the alarm sounded. You doing okay, Lana?"

I glance at the plate and scowl. "Not really. My entire world is about to fight evil vampires who held me captive and have traveled literal realms to get me back."

"They're probably going to have a conversation first. Maybe get a little worked up, enough for the audience at least." He runs his hand through his blond hair.

My eyes narrow and I study his face. "You think?"

He nods as he pours a cup of coffee. "All will be fine."

"Sorry you have to babysit." I wince.

Before he can respond, Sarai and several other staff sift in with a handful of guards. Sarai throws her arms around me.

"I was so scared they got you!" she cries, and I return her hug.

"I'm alright." I pull away to look at her. "Everything will be fine. Speaking of, you should be with your family."

She shakes her head. "Mom is spreading Dad's ashes on Rexuna now, where they first met."

Pierce pulls her into his arms. "We're glad you're safe."

I turn to the guards. "Where are Rune and Titan?"

Lawson, a member of Zara's unit, answers me. "They've joined the fight. Not to worry, they can hold their own." He winks.

Sarai holds out a jar of tonic. "I brought you your chest medication."

"Actually, for the first time in Bedlam, my chest feels great." Every day and night, I've dealt with a terrible ache in my chest, but ever since I died, it's gone. Maybe I'm not tethered to Earth anymore?

Sarai smiles. "Glad you're feeling better."

We play card games for hours while waiting for news. It's almost suppertime when my kings sift in.

Grimm grabs my hand and pulls me into his arms. "We're getting you out of here."

I blink up at him. "What happened?"

"We know the vampires have an army with them on Convectus. There's a terrible thunderstorm preventing us from moving in to get them. The entire place is warded, so we can't sift to them," Casimir answers, and I turn around to face him. "I don't think we should wait for your coronation."

I lower myself to the couch. "When?"

"Now. We'll call in the army and a few of the members of court. This is strictly a precautionary measure." Penn offers me his hand. "Once we have the location of this brigade, we'll be able to plan an attack. As soon as you are High Queen, we as your mates, will have our powers increased. This way, we have a better chance of fighting the vampires."

I take his hand and we cross to the trunk Sarai brought full of our clothes. She hands me a purple floor-length gown and shoes with bows on the side. I strip and dress quickly while the other staff sift in and out of the shelter. Pure adrenaline fuels me, and I have little time to think about how much danger I'm in.

"Where will we do this?" I ask as I brush my hair.

"Right here. We have staff fetching banners and chairs, so it looks like the throne room." Grimm snakes his arms around my waist and kisses where my neck meets my shoulder. I lean back into him.

"I'm scared." It's the first time I've ever said it, and my voice cracks.

"We'll be at your side. I'm not planning on letting you out of my sight again." He squeezes me tight.

Penn turns me around and smooths my hair over my shoulders,

then leans down and kisses the top of my head. "You're going to make a great High Queen."

Grimm and Casimir usher me to the front of the room where they've set up a makeshift throne. As hundreds of soldiers sift in, my nerves grow.

Pierce, Captain Zara, and several other soldiers move to the dais to brief me on what will take place. One in particular keeps his eyes pinned on me. Judging by his striking resemblance to Zara and Pierce, I'm going to bet this is Bellamy.

He makes to speak to me, but I raise my hand and lean in. "Whatever'll kill you for telling me, please, don't say a word. I've asked my mates to take my memory of you to prevent this. Please don't let it be in vain."

Bellamy flinches before turning his head towards my ear. "What we had was real, Lana. If the coming war means anything, someday you'll know the truth. I won't break the magic gag order if you don't want me to." He turns to look me in the eye. "I'm sorry."

I nod. "If it's any consolation, I'm sorry, too. I did what I had to do to keep you safe."

He presses a kiss to my cheek before returning to formation behind me. I swallow hard, but my emotions remain in check.

My kings join me on the dais, and the room falls silent. Casimir smiles at me, pushes my hair behind my shoulders, and plants a kiss to my temple before stepping to my side.

Penn takes my hand and kisses it. "Ready?"

I nod. "As I'll ever be."

Bellamy steps forward to take the crown from Sarai, meeting my gaze as he does. He hands it to Pierce, who passes it to Casimir.

Casimir nods and lifts his chin, commanding the room as he speaks. "Stand before us, soldiers of Bedlam. The time has come to crown our High Queen!"

My shout of "For Bedlam!" echoes through the room, and the soldiers all roar back. I'm touched by their willingness to fight for me.

Penn steps forward. "As your King, I vow to serve you with all that

I have." He bends down and kisses my cheek, then returns to his place by my side.

Grimm takes a knee, kissing my hand. "I humbly bow before you, my High Queen, and I vow to protect you with all that I am."

Casimir bows next, taking both my hands in his and placing them on his chest. "As long as I live, my High Queen, you'll be safe. I vow to protect and serve you for all my days."

Pierce falls to both knees. "I pledge to be your right arm, High Queen Lana, and I vow to serve you with all that I am."

After swearing their fealty, the kings and my personal guard slice their palms open, swiping their blood across my face. I carve my hand, and the crowd gasps as glowing blue blood drips onto the floor.

I make my way around the crowded room, marking each forehead as the soldiers swear fealty to me, and I in return. When I finish with the soldiers, I vow my allegiance to my kings.

My mates kneel before me, each with a hand on the silver, jewel-encrusted crown. "I swear to serve you, my loves, and pledge to protect and provide for our people as High Queen of Bedlam."

I bow, allowing them to place the crown on my head. Magic sizzles in the air, marking the moment I officially become High Queen.

The sound of crunching metal bursts through the quiet. Bunker doors, believed impenetrable, blow open, spewing dirt and debris everywhere. Soldiers draw their weapons and turn towards the intrusion, but magic causes them to freeze mid-stride.

Like the parting of the Red Sea, the uniformed room of men and women split down the center, revealing the small retinue of infiltrators. They pause before stepping into the room, and I come face-to-face with who I presume to be my abductors.

I bare my teeth. The only inkling I have of something amiss is the surge of strength I feel coursing through my veins when my eyes land on the group, and an easing in my chest that startles me. Is it from the final culmination of something I feared for so long, or the relief of finally getting answers to why they stole something so vital to me: my memories?

I take in their faces, studying them, trying to discern whether I remember any. The most beautiful creature I've ever seen stands frozen at the front, eyes boring into me, as though I hung the moons. I immediately recognize him as fae, but that's as far as it goes. My gaze sweeps over the first row of vampires, their handsome features just as foreign to me as the first.

It's time to pay for your crimes, boys.

CHAPTER 70

FINN

The ache eases in my chest at the sight of her. Lana wears royal blood on her face like war paint, giving a wild edge to her beauty. She bares her teeth at the sight of us before raising her hand to draw power from those around her.

A grin splits my face. *Remarkable.*

I siphon the magic from the room, leaving nothing for her to draw from before putting my hand in the air. With a slight pull, I snap the magic gag order in place over the realm preventing anyone from talking about what happened in the throne room all those moons ago. The king's eyes flare with fury, but they're in the same frozen immovable state as their army.

"Lana, I'm High King Finian Drake, but you call me Finn, or sometimes 'babe.' We're soul bonded mates, and you've been lied to." I motion towards the vampires. "Oz, Auguste, and Gideon are also your mates. They didn't take your memories." I gesture towards the kings. "*They did.*"

OH, what a cliffhanger! Does Lana believe her mates? And what ever will she do about her other mates she's bonded to? Read Wicked Bedlam to find out.

Wondering which supernatural order you'd be in Bedlam? **Take the quiz at kathyhaan.com/quiz** and see if you're a vampire, witch, or shifter. Share your result in our brand new Facebook group, The Bedlam Fae Society.

GUIDE TO BEDLAM & THE
CHARACTERS

*P*lease note, these may contain spoilers. **Read with caution.**

XOXO

Aedon Shineseer: A lion shifter fae with a gambling addiction.

Aggonid's Realm: Where bad fae go when they die, they'll spend eternity tortured and maimed.

Bedlam Penitentiary: The fae prison located far North of Bedlam. There's no crueler fate.

Bellamy: A soldier at Convectus. He's Pierce and Captain Zara's brother, and is of the dragon order. Deep-set dimples, sun-bronzed skin, blond hair, and lilac eyes. He grew up with Penn on Sundahlia; they're cousins.

Berserker: A loyal fae order with uncontrollable rage and a predilection for casting curses. Feasting on internal organs helps keep the anger at bay, especially if it's a womb.

Belu: This whale-like creature is a natural predator to basilisks.

Bloodstone: A stone used in blood sacrifice rituals.

Bracky Blooms: Edible yellow blooms found on the Tristique Islands, and if the sap gets on your skin, it'll cause euphoria. It's sweet, like honey or sugarcane. When ingested, its effects are multiplied.

Casimir: Molten silver eyes, wolf order, King of Luporia

Caspari: Violent creatures who eat fae waste. They usually travel in hordes.

Captain Shallowind: Captain of the ship that takes Lana and crew to the islands.

Cerulean Isles: Where the avias nest. Located between Sundahlia and Convectus, and South of the Tristique Islands.

Clara: Chef at Convectus Castle.

Convectus: The main continent where each king convenes for important realm matters.

Cruah Bush: Provides nuts with healing properties. They don't taste good, though.

The Crucey: Deadliest creature in all the realms, kills indiscriminately, and enjoys every second of it. She rules the wastelands, and no magic can control her. She cares for the Tolden and keeps them safe from the werewolves. Tolden hearts can cure their curse.

Dragonbolt: Built by dragons, it's a small castle of fire and ice on Convectus.

Finn: High King of the fae, and of the Luna order. Lives on Rexuna most of the time. Ashy blond hair, icy blue eyes, he glows blue at times. Lives on a mountain in Noble Wilds during moon season. Can clean and dry clothes by patting and rubbing vigorously. Smooth, tanned chest, washboard abs. Tattoo just under his belt line that's of four moons, one shooting through the sky.

Gala: A small village on the outskirts of Noble Wilds and Loier Mountain. It has cobbled stones and mostly deserted streets at night. Has a small town hall and a five-bedroom inn with an old-world boutique hotel feel to it where Finn and Lana stay the night. Around the corner is a clothing store.

Grimm: A fresh and clean scent like the wind. King of Occasus, he's of the Incubus order. Has dark hair and Tahitian-blue eyes.

Ground Gnomes: Bury your tattered clothes, and the ground gnomes will mend them with their magic. Don't forget to toss in a few coins when they're done, or they'll hunt you down. They don't talk, but they do chitter.

Harpis Siren: The size of a small mountain lion, this beast has sharp fangs, razor-like claws, bioluminescent hair, and a tail. A distant relative to a siren, it's more animal than sentient being.

Ilab: These are bear-like creatures who love witches' blood, and most live in Noble Wilds.

Loier Mountain: The mountain just before reaching the first town on the edge of Noble Wilds, located on Convectus. Just on the other side of this is the town of Gala.

Mara: A servant at Convectus Castle.

Meloria: Was once the center of Fae trade on Convectus. It's encircled by a waterfall and a mist-filled lake.

Moon Season: Occurs every six months and lasts for thirty days. This is known as the Bedlam Moon. The Luna order is strongest then.

Noble Wilds (on Convectus): The most remote woodlands. There's a portal here, but no one really goes to it. There are lots of wild animals and dangerous fugitives. No witch magic works here and it's warded from sifting in and out. The portal is three hours from the top of the mountain where Finn keeps his camp during moon season. A healing river, the Sanaquam, runs through these woods. It takes four months to walk out of the woods from the portal. High mountain climate.

Parallel Abyss: Some of the most dangerous waters between Convectus and Sundahlia.

Penn: King of Draconus, who can shift into a dragon.

Penn Island: An island located next to Bedlam Penitentiary, where mortals, witches, and other creatures serve time for lesser crimes.

Phelvie: Cat-like creatures who attack those with ill intent. They're sentient-like animals who come from their owners. The only way to create one is for a killing spell to be intercepted by someone else, and the interceptor to sacrifice something great to spare a life.

Prairie Pixie Juice: Liquid courage, a type of drink resembling fae wine. No alcohol, just magic, and it helps you relax. It's sweet like candy.

Rexuna: The continent West of Convectus where Finn is from. It contains Rift Pass.

Rift Pass: Mountainous region where Finn lives most of the time. This is on Rexuna.

Ross Van'Astor: Former fiancé of Lana's, treated her like crap, cheated on her. Werewolf.

Rune: Trainer with long golden hair, matching eyes, and onyx skin. Gold lines spiderweb his torso like Kintsugi. He owns Titan, and is a fae of shadows and storms.

Sanaquam River: Located in Noble Wilds on Rexuna, this river has healing properties. Careful, Harpis Sirens swim rampant here.

Sarai: Lana's ladies' maid. Fancies Pierce. Can shift into a serpent.

Sea of Triune: A sea on the South side of Rexuna.

Serapi City: Where Aedon Shineseer is from on Rexuna.

Sifting: Like teleporting. Not all fae have this ability, and if a powerful enough fae wards a location against sifting, you have to walk. You must be a shifter or royal to sift.

Soapberries: Small, blue berries with cleaning properties. Just squeeze them between your hands to clean skin and hair. Don't eat them.

Sodroot: A root that helps quell nausea when placed between the teeth.

Spearsnakes: Like regular snakes, but have razor sharp tails and live in the water.

Spirit Fish: Large silver fish with wings. No one has ever caught one because they're magic-resistant.

Starseed Apples: A turquoise fruit that's crisp to bite into. The taste is bright and watery like a sweet cucumber.

Sustai Birds: Birds that nest near portals, and leave a slimy excrement.

Terra Order: Can move Earth and grow plants.

Titan: A Phelvie belonging to Rune; formed when struck with a powerful spell, causing a part of Rune to split off from himself, thus forming a Phelvie.

Tolden: Children of the Woods, these creatures are guarded closely by The Crucey. Their hearts cure the werewolf curse.

Tristique Islands: A group of magic-powered islands that float above the sea. It's uninhabited, except when one of the royals uses a house on one of the islands.

Yalsome Root: A root for cramps and numbing injuries.

ACKNOWLEDGMENTS

Dearest Readers,

I don't write for money, fame, or any other accolades. I do it because like you, I love to get lost in a story. Stories of faraway lands keep the demons of my past and present at bay, giving me a reprieve, however brief, from the echoes of its presence.

Tales of Bedlam is my favorite of the series so far, and I promise you'll get your happily ever after in the series conclusion, *Wicked Bedlam*. I have many more books planned in this fae realm, taking place before, adjacent, and after the Bedlam Moon series. You'll hear more from some of your favorite side characters, and may even get a cameo or two from some of the main cast.

In the about section of my blog, I keep a catalog of everything I'm working on. I also list events taking place around the globe—I hope to see you at some of them.

None of this would've been possible if not for the outpouring of support from readers, family, and friends who devoured Bedlam Moon and begged for ***more***.

I have so many of them to thank, namely:

- **Theresa**, thanks for talking me out of having your favorite character get eaten by a shark. Love you, even though I tried to kill your fave off. I'm sure my readers thank you immensely.
- **Jess**, once again, your edits and support mean the world to me. Reading your comments on my favorite lines breathe

life into me when I'm in the trenches, editing my little heart away with your feedback and suggestions.

- **Leo**, does your talent know no bounds? The cover, the map, *everything*. I'm so proud to be your mama. Someday, when you're well past eighteen, I'll let you read these stories.
- **To my other children**, your enthusiasm for what I do fuels me. How did I get so lucky to have such amazing kids?
- **Lori**, can you believe I wrote another 'whole ass' book? Thanks for being my ride or die. Can't wait to celebrate the release of your champagne brand.
- **Readers**, you're why I do what I do. Seeing you gush over my stories literally gives me—and my work—life. If not for your words of encouragement and love of my characters, I would've folded after my first negative review. Thanks for giving my book a chance, even those of you who hated my writing. Tiny authors like myself rely on your constructive feedback to better hone our craft.

XOXO
Kathy

WICKED BEDLAM CHAPTER ONE

ROSE

There's something inherently cathartic about staring down the barrel of a proverbial loaded gun. I'm finally facing my captors after spending so many moons terrified of our inevitable encounter. All the tension, the fear, the anxiety of not knowing who I am, what the vampires want with me, and what the fae are planning to do about their infiltration, come rushing to the surface. It's terrifying, but it gives me a sense of clarity, like I'm outside looking in.

It's empowering, this moment, and I take a step forward. The makeshift throne room is large and dank, the air thick with the smell of dirt and machine oil. The distinct scent of urine wafts from where some of the soldiers stand frozen, their fear palpable even in their immovable state.

My gaze cuts to the procession of intruders. The obscenely gorgeous creature in front of me is a liar, his words laughable at best, because my kings would never do what he accuses them of. Kidnap me and steal my memories? They love me. I know it with the same certainty that I know the Earth's sun will rise in the east and set in the west.

But as I take in his features, there's a tugging in my chest. A ghost of a memory, just out of reach.

I open my mouth to refute his claims, but he continues speaking.

"I didn't tell you I was high king because I wanted to spare you the pain of having to make a decision between your vampire court and the fae court until I could figure out a way to give you both, but the time for secrets is over." His voice is laced with emotion and shock blasts through me before anger floods my veins.

So he already admits he's a liar. I take another step forward, despite my hesitation, because I'm drawn to him in a way I can't explain. My magic pulses in violent waves; my leash on it slipping, but not before I release Finn's hold on my kings. They stumble forward, shouting as they stand in front of me, protecting me from the trespassers.

"Don't listen to him, Lana." Grimm slides a possessive arm around my waist. His incubus power pours off him like sheets of molten lava, and my chest rises and falls in dramatic fashion, my breath coming quick.

Finn's honeyed words continue to spill from his lips, but their ruse is up when a tall vampire with sun-kissed skin, deep blue eyes, and dimples so pronounced they could cut glass steps out from the line, and in preternatural speed, surges towards the dais.

He's a blur of motion as he vaults over the twisted metal and the ruined entrance to our bunker, and I gasp as I realize he's coming for us. Instinctively, I step in front of my kings, shielding them as the vampire they call Gideon barrels towards us with ferocious intent in his eyes.

Fear like I've never known spikes through me, and without thinking, I raise my hand, pulling power towards me as I prepare to defend my kings; a surge of protective fury fueling me. I tap into a well of magic I didn't know existed. It's in the air, the ground, the very fabric of the realm, and it rushes to me eagerly as though greeting an old friend. A bolt of blue lightning laced with black flames flies from my fingertips. The heat emanating from the blaze is intense enough to singe the fine hair on my arms, but I don't falter.

It's too late for him to correct course, and he's barreled into by the sheer force of my magic. Gideon's fear-laced face cries out as he's struck by the magical bolt slamming into him. It throws him across the room where he falls to the ground with a thud; his body engulfed in flames.

Agony like I've never known lances through me at the sight of him lying there so still, and my chest expels all the air from my lungs as I crash to my knees. Deep, keening wails echo through the room as my kings rush to my side, but I can't tear my gaze away from Gideon's prone form.

Why is it so loud?

The shrieking shreds my eardrums, and it's only now I realize the sound is coming from me.

Oh, no. Not Gideon. Doesn't Rose know we love him? That *she* loves him? Better check out Wicked Bedlam for your happily ever after.

ABOUT THE AUTHOR

A blood descendant of Wild Bill Hickok and a long line of artists and creators, like Jane Austen and Emily Dickinson, **Kathy Haan believes the secret to telling a great story is living one.** The second youngest, in a massive horde of children between her parents, she did her best to gain attention and kept everyone entertained with jokes and wild stories.

She lives a life of adventure with her hunky husband, three children, and Great Pyrenees in the Midwest United States. While this is her debut novel, you might've seen her work in Forbes or Fortune, where she's a regular contributor.

ALSO BY KATHY HAAN

Bedlam Moon Trilogy (Complete)

Lana sets out to find the truth about her past, and when a hot vampire begins to unravel it for her, she's caught up in the web of an evil cult, prophecies, and curses. All while falling for the King of Vampires and his royal court. This is a why choose romance.

Bedlam Moon (Bedlam Moon Trilogy Book 1)

Tales of Bedlam (Bedlam Moon Trilogy Book 2)

Wicked Bedlam (Bedlam Moon Trilogy Book 3)

Fae Academia Series (Incomplete, 9 planned)

A spin-off of the Bedlam Moon Trilogy, we follow Lana's daughter, Rose, while she attends a magical university. The summer before college is perfect until the family begins to receive threats, and Rose ends up getting into a different college from her twin brother and her boyfriend. A male roommate, his hot friends, and a sexy professor all find themselves eager to win her affection. This is a why choose romance. Books 1-3 are Rose's story, books 4-6 are Nova's, and 7-9 will be Bee's story.

Bedlam Academy (Fae Academia, Book 1)

Arcane Scholar (Fae Academia, Book 2)

Forbidden Rose (Fae Academia, Book 3)

Moonfire Academy (Fae Academia, Book 4)

~

Aggonid's Realm Series (Incomplete)

A Realm of Fire and Ash (Aggonid's Realm, Book 1)

A Realm of Dreams and Shadows (Aggonid's Realm, Book 2)

A Realm of Grief and Sorrow (Aggonid's Realm, Book 3)

When the commander of an elite group of phoenixes ends up dead for real, she tries to convince the fae devil there's been a huge mistake. Can she convince him to let her go before he snags her heart? This is an enemies to lovers why choose romance.

<u>Fae Gods (Incomplete)</u>

Fae Gods (April 2023)

Fae Guardians (TBA)

They watched their charge her entire life, completely invisible to her and only intervening when necessary. When they get fed up with her miserable marriage, Jocelyn's fae god watchers decide to help. After all, no fae of royal lineage deserves to be left to wilt away on Earth. They devise a plan to reveal their true selves to her, calling themselves the Marriage Doctors. But what happens when, during the course of their live-in lessons, the infallible gods fall for their off-limits charge? This is a why choose romance.

~

<u>Bedlam Penitentiary (Incomplete)</u>

Bedlam Penitentiary (TBA)

At the most ruthless prison in the fae realm, you're either at the top of the magical food chain, or you've got to form alliances with those with the most power. Because at a prison where you must expend your magic or you'll die, it's a no man's land full of dangerous criminals. This is a why choose romance.